FOREVER RESTORED
WHERE GRACE BEGINS

CURTIS L McKENZIE

Written Inspirations, LLC
Publishing

RICHMOND HILL, GA

Written Inspirations, LLC
9390 Ford Avenue, Ste 7
Richmond Hill, GA 31324
www.writteninspirations.com

Publisher's Note: This is a work of fiction. Names, characters, places, and incidents are a product of the author's imagination. Locales and public names are sometimes used for atmospheric purposes. Any resemblance to actual people, living or dead, or to businesses, companies, events, institutions, or locales is completely coincidental.

Book Layout © 2025 BookDesignTemplates.com

Forever Restored: Where Grace Begins / Curtis L. McKenzie -- 1st ed.
ISBN 979-8-9999733-0-6 (Hard Cover)
ISBN 979-8-9999733-1-3 (Paper Back)

Dedication

To every young girl and woman who has endured domestic violence, sexual assault, abortion, abduction, the horrors of human trafficking, or been made to feel you have no voice—

You are not invisible.
You are not forgotten.
You are deeply seen, fiercely loved, and immeasurably valued.

This book was written primarily with you in mind.
Because your story matters.
Because your voice matters.
Because *you* matter.

May these pages carry hope into the shadows, lift your countenance, and remind you that healing and empowerment are not only possible but also your birthright.

From the Author

No matter who you are or where you find yourself in life, it is my earnest prayer that this story reaches beyond the pages and into your spirit. May it be a vessel through which God whispers to your heart, reminding you that you are seen by Him, known by Him, and deeply loved by Him. You are not an accident, not a background character in this world. You matter—profoundly, undeniably, beautifully. May every chapter affirm this truth: that even in your brokenness, God is working a beautiful restoration— because some of the strongest bridges are built from brokenness.

— CURTIS L. MCKENZIE, AUTHOR

Contents

CHAPTER 1

The Night Everything Changed

Thunder cracked like a war drum over the bruised-red sky of Frampton, Illinois—like the heavens were ripping apart. It was enough to shake loose windows in their frames and make the old streetlamps shudder. It was the kind of mid-September evening that made the air feel tight, electric, as if the city itself was holding its breath. Ominous clouds churned above, swollen with menace, casting an eerie crimson hue over the buildings and broken pavement below. The air felt thick enough to choke on—humming with something that didn't belong just to the weather.

The storm wasn't just in the sky. It was also in the streets. Every lane clogged with traffic, bumper to bumper, a herd of metal inching forward beneath flickering streetlights—cars locked in an endless crawl down Main and Cedar, exhaust fumes swirling into the heavy air like foul breath. Engines idled in frustration. Horns blared like warnings, long and sharp. Exasperation mounted as wipers squealed across windshields slick with the first sprinkle of rain. Somewhere in that tangle of taillights, a siren wailed, slicing through the restless hum like a blade cutting cloth. Someone was running out of time somewhere.

Then came the wind, sweeping through the city like a phantom—tearing through alleyways and underpasses, sending leaves spinning in frantic circles. Old newspapers, discarded wrappers, and dust lifted off the ground and carried away like ghosts. Storefront awnings flapped violently in turbulence like ragged flags. A street sign clanged against its post, sounding hollow and foreboding. On every corner, people looked up—some mesmerized, others petrified. A storm was coming. And it wasn't just the weather.

At the far edge of Southside Frampton, a small, tired bungalow slumped under the weight of the gathering storm. The house, its paint peeling and gutters swaying, appeared to have secrets tucked behind its thin walls—secrets that didn't need thunder to shake them loose. A single porch light flickered—an old bulb trying to hide a darkness too big to contain.

Rain tapped a cold, relentless rhythm against the windowpane of the smallest bedroom, like fingers drumming out a warning. Inside, thirteen-year-old Frieda Winslow sat on the worn carpet, knees hugged so tight to her chest that the fabric of her nightgown stretched thin under her arms. The damp cotton clung to her skin where sweat met the cold breeze of the coming storm. Her back pressed painfully against the wall as if trying to fuse herself to it and disappear inside the plaster. Her breath came shallow. Her eyes were glazed but dry—too exhausted to form tears.

The soft tapping of rain against the window intensified into an urgent, relentless beating that matched the wild thud of her heartbeat. Lifting her eyes to the cracked ceiling, she gazed straight through it, far beyond the roof that couldn't keep the real storm out.

Thunder rumbled in the distance like a beast waking up, but Frieda hardly flinched. It wasn't the storm outside that troubled her. It was the one inside the house.

Muffled shouting leaked through the walls—sharp, venomous words slicing through silence. Then came the crash. Something heavy. Glass, perhaps. Or a chair. A door slammed forcefully enough to rattle the picture frames in her room.

Frieda buried her face between her knees. *Not again*, she thought. Each breath she took felt like borrowed time. And at that moment, huddled on the floor of that weary little house, she wasn't a child waiting out the rain. She was a girl trying not to come undone.

From the living room came voices—sharp, rising, jagged like broken glass. Her father's words were thick, wet with liquor and something hostile that never stayed buried long. Her mother's voice rose back, brittle but still sharp enough to cut.

"You never listen, Dana!" The words tumbled out, slurred and sticky with anger. *"I told you. It's not what you think!"*

"Then what is it, John? You say this all the time!" her mother shot back, voice trembling with exhaustion that had nowhere else to go. *"But you never stop!"*

Another loud crash split the air—something glass, maybe the coffee table. The sound stabbed through Frieda's ribcage. She flinched hard, hands flying to her ears too late to block the noise. The tremor ran through her body and sank deep in her belly, where fear had lived for too long. She drew her knees closer; her forehead pressed to them now. Her breath caught in shallow gasps.

Her father's temper had worsened over the past few months. The drinking started first—at night, then during the day. Then came the infidelity, the accusations, the yelling, the shoves. Her mother had tried to stand tall, to keep things together. But Frieda heard it now: the cracks in her resolve, the fear underneath the fire raging ever so fiercely.

Frieda rocked slightly, whispering the only prayer she knew.

"God… please. Please make it stop."

She had said it before—dozens of times. But nothing seemed to change.

A door slammed hard enough to rattle the thin walls. The lamp on her nightstand shivered, its pull chain clinking softly. Then— silence. Not the hush of peace, but a silence that vibrated. A quiet so sharp she could feel it pricking at the base of her spine.

She lifted her head just enough to hear. One breath. Two. And then—a sound that would echo in her bones for the rest of her life.

The crack. One single, deafening crack that didn't belong to thunder. Louder. Closer. Final.

A gunshot.

Frieda jerked upright so fast her neck popped. For a moment, the world dropped away—no rain, no wind, no thunder rolling overhead. Just the boom echoing in her bones and the rush of her pulse drowning out everything else.

She rose slowly, legs shaking beneath her. Her palm scraped the wall as she stood, fingers splayed against peeling paint. She pulled her bedroom door open. It swung wide on silent hinges that should have screamed. The hallway stretched like a tunnel—long, dim, the overhead bulb flickering like a dying star. Her bare feet made no sound on the floor but padded softly down the hallway. She moved slowly—one step, then another—each one sinking her deeper into something she didn't want to see. But she *had* to see.

The living room was dim, a light coming from a flickering lamp in the corner. The TV droned on, black-and-white shadows flickering across the walls. An old movie—some romantic scene playing out in whispers, oblivious to the ruin that lived under its soft glow.

The smell hit her first—a harsh, hot bite of gunpowder wrapped in something coppery and wrong that twisted her gut.

Her mother was on the hardwood floor. Dana Winslow. Strong-jawed and bright-eyed once, hair always brushed back neatly even on the worst days. She was Frieda's lioness. Frieda's shield. Now—her mother's body curled awkwardly on the floor near the couch, one arm outstretched reaching toward the hallway as if trying to protect something—or someone. Her eyes were wide open, unblinking, staring at something Frieda couldn't see—blood pooled beneath her—dark, spreading slowly, like a living thing. The front door swung open an inch at a time, letting in gusts of storm air that made the curtains flutter like something alive.

Frieda's father was gone. She took a single step forward, then another—knees buckling so badly she almost fell. She lowered herself beside her mother, her knees resting on the hardwood floor. Her hand hovered inches above Dana's open palm, trembling so violently she couldn't close the gap.

Then she let out a scream that ripped from the depths of her soul. It tore through the house like a siren—raw, guttural, full of agony. It pierced the silence, spilling past the porch and into the streets beyond. She pressed her forehead to the edge of her mother's shoulder, shaking so hard the world blurred around her. She wanted to hold her mother. To shake her awake. But she couldn't move. Finally, she collapsed beside her mother, arms shaking violently, mouth open in a silent sob.

Outside, a neighbor's voice rose—urgent, panicked. A screen door slammed. Lights flipped on in nearby homes. Tires squealed on wet asphalt.

Then the sirens came—fast, wailing, filling the block with pulsing red and blue light. The walls caught the colors, throwing them back in jittery patterns that danced over the family photos still clinging to the hallway.

Flashlights sliced through the darkness. Doors burst open. Boots pounded through the house. Police radios hissed and crackled. Officers swept room by room, weapons drawn, voices commanding.

"Clear! Bedroom's clear! Suspect fled!"

A female officer stepped carefully into the living room, eyes scanning the scene. She knelt beside Frieda, the metallic tang of her badge mixing with the iron scent that coated the floor. Her eyes softened at the sight of the trembling girl.

Frieda's eyes stayed locked on her mother's face—those open eyes that didn't see her anymore. Her lips moved, but no sound came.

"Sweetheart," the officer said gently, placing her fingers lightly on Frieda's shaking shoulder, "… look at me. Are you hurt? Can you hear me?"

Frieda didn't move. Her tear-filled eyes were wide, staring through the officer like glass.

The only sound she heard was her very own heartbeat, thudding like war drums in her chest.

The woman tried again. "Can you hear me? What's your name?"

Still no response. Just the steady rise and fall of Frieda's chest and the numb emptiness on her face.

The officer turned to her partner. "We need paramedics! She's in shock—Hey, honey. Stay with me, okay? Stay here."

But Frieda was already slipping—something inside her curling away, folding in on itself like a dying star.

The night everything changed wasn't just when thunder split the sky and the gun cracked the air. It was the night Frieda Winslow's world ended—and the girl who sat sobbing on the blood-soaked floor would never fully come back.

Not the same. It seemed not ever.

House of Faith
Heart of Fury

The funeral unfolded like a dream dipped in ash—slow, muffled, and hard to breathe in. The sanctuary was heavy with the perfume of lilies and roses, their sweetness cloying in the still air. Every breath Frieda took felt like swallowing fog.

She sat in the front pew, rigid and unmoving, her black dress too tight at the collar, her stockings itching against her knees. Her shoulders drawn high; her hands folded in her lap with fingers pressed so tightly together the knuckles turned white. Her face—pale, expressionless—might as well have been carved from stone.

Around her sat people she didn't know. Strangers dressed in somber black and navy, dabbing at their eyes with tissues and murmuring words that vanished into the silence. Aunts, she barely remembered. Neighbors who had smiled politely over fences but never knocked on their door. Church members who now wept but had never asked how her mother was when she still had breath in her body.

They sang *"It Is Well With My Soul"*—a slow, aching rendition led by a small choir at the pulpit. But Frieda knew: nothing was well. Not in her soul. Not in her body. Not in the hollow that had opened inside her since the moment they told her the truth—that her mother would never wake up. That the shot fired that night had taken more than just her mother's life. That her father had been the one who fired it.

The casket sat closed at the front of the church, flanked by two towering wreaths that looked too beautiful to belong in a place so soaked with grief. A framed photo rested on a velvet-draped stand. Her mother—smiling, radiant, alive—forever frozen in a moment that now mocked the room.

The preacher's voice droned in the background—some well-rehearsed meditation on eternity, storms calmed by faith, and the peace of heaven. But Frieda didn't hear him. She heard static. A low, buzzing hum in her skull that drowned out everything else. She couldn't cry. Couldn't speak. The scream lodged in her throat was a living thing, sharp and burning, but it refused to rise. Her mother was dead. Her father was in prison. And Frieda? Frieda was a ghost in a girl's body. Floating through the motions. Swallowed by silence. And no one—not even God—felt close enough to touch.

AFTER THE LAST SHOVELFUL of earth had fallen over the casket and the mourners drifted away like smoke, the cemetery settled into a deep, aching quiet. Gray clouds churned low in the sky, pregnant with rain, and the wind picked up, stirring petals from the wreaths into soft spirals across the damp grass.

Frieda stood alone, her small frame hunched beside the fresh grave. The weight of her grief pressed her downward, deeper than the soil that now covered her mother. She didn't move. Couldn't. The world felt like it was ending in slow motion.

Then came the sound of footsteps—measured, careful—approaching from behind. A gentle hand, warm and steady, settled on her narrow shoulder.

"I'm taking you home, baby," came a voice—low, calm, and firm like a hymn that refused to falter.

Frieda turned, blinking against the sting in her eyes.

The woman before her wore a simple navy dress, pressed and modest, with a silver cross resting just above her heart. Her hair, once black, had softened to gray at the temples and was pulled back in a careful bun. Her face was lined with time and grace, and her eyes, though tired, held the kind of quiet strength that didn't ask permission to endure.

"Grandma Lois?" Frieda's voice came out raw, barely more than breath.

Lois Winston gave a soft nod. "Yes, child. It's been too long."

THE RIDE BACK was silent except for the rhythm of rain tapping against the roof and windshield. The sky had opened, and water streamed in silver sheets down the windows, distorting the world into a blurry watercolor of streetlights and sagging rooftops.

Frieda sat in the back seat of Lois's old sedan, her arms tightly crossed over her chest, chin tucked low, face turned toward the window. Her black dress was wrinkled from the long day, and her shoes were caked with cemetery mud. She said nothing.

The air in the car was thick with the scent of peppermint oil and worn leather—familiar, almost maternal. It reminded her of peppermint tea on winter nights, of Sunday dresses ironed to perfection. But it also reminded her that this was not her mother's car. Not her life. It smelled like someone else's story.

Lois drove slowly, hands at ten and two, her eyes flicking occasionally to the rearview mirror. She didn't press for words, didn't offer platitudes. But at a red light, she reached one hand back, her fingers searching until they found Frieda's cold ones. She squeezed them.

"You're safe now, baby," she said softly, with a conviction that made the words feel like a promise.

Frieda didn't respond. Her fingers remained limp. Her forehead touched the window, the cool glass soothing her fevered thoughts. The rain blurred everything beyond the glass—trees, signs, houses. It made the world look as shattered as she felt.

"No," she whispered, her breath fogging a tiny circle on the glass. "I'm not."

LOIS'S HOUSE SAT LIKE A HYMN on the corner of a quiet street—small, composed, and steeped in something sacred. Inside, everything smelled of lemon polish and the passage of time. The air was thick with the scent of old paper, warmed wood, and lavender soap. Floral curtains fluttered slightly in the breeze from an open window. Crosses adorned nearly every wall—oak, brass, ceramic— each one polished and intentional, like Lois had hung them with prayers.

The coffee table was a shrine of routine: an open Bible with dog-eared pages and underlined verses sat beside a pair of reading glasses and a tea mug with faded roses on the rim. The pages of Scripture curled slightly from years of use, corners soft as worn fabric. A crocheted doily rested on the armrest of a floral loveseat, and a cut-glass bowl of butterscotch candies shimmered beneath a lamp that cast a warm amber glow.

Frieda stood in the doorway like she didn't belong in her own body. Her arms hung at her sides, fists clenched inside her sleeves. Her eyes roamed the room, taking it in with suspicion, like the house itself might lunge at her. It was too quiet. Too clean. Too full of things that hadn't broken.

Lois stepped beside her and gave a gentle nod down the hallway. "Your room's at the end, baby. Fresh sheets, drawer space, closet's empty if you need it."

Frieda didn't answer. She just stared—at the framed verses in gold-trimmed edges, the faded photo of a young Lois and an unknown man on the mantel, the glossy surface of the piano she would not dare touch.

Lois spoke again, softer this time. "You can come in, child. There's nothing to fear here. No one lives here but me."

Frieda took a single step. Her sneakers squeaked faintly on the hardwood floor. The air shifted around her like it was watching.

Dong. Dong. Dong.

The grandfather clock in the corner let out three hollow chimes.

Frieda flinched like it had shouted at her. She clenched her jaw. "I hate that sound."

Lois turned her head slightly. "What's that, baby?"

"Nothing," Frieda said too quickly, the word cutting off like a slammed door.

THAT NIGHT, the hallway glowed softly with the dim light of a single lamp. The floral carpet muffled every footstep. A light knock on the bedroom door barely broke the silence. Lois stepped in, holding a ceramic mug between her hands.

"Just something warm to help you sleep," she said gently, setting the cup of milk on the nightstand. The steam curled up like ghost-breath in the cold room. "I'll let you rest. I'm down the hall if you need anything." She paused, her gaze resting softly on Frieda's face, then quietly closed the door behind her.

Frieda sat on the edge of the bed, stiff as a statue, the blanket untouched, the cup of milk untouched. The room was plain but lovingly prepared. A handmade quilt. A vase of plastic daisies. A tiny wooden cross above the headboard. The quiet was so deep it had shape. It pressed against her skin like something alive.

Frieda didn't move. She didn't cry. Her arms curled around herself as the walls inched closer. The silence turned loud. And in the dark, beneath her breath, she whispered into the ceiling—into the shadows, the past, the ache that stretched from her gut to her bones:

"I hate you."

The words trembled out like a curse. Frieda didn't know who they were for—her father, her absent mother, the God her mother used to pray to in the kitchen, weeping into dishwater. Maybe all of them. Maybe herself.

House Rules and Holy War

THE RULES WERE WRITTEN NOWHERE, but they were etched in every corner of Lois Winslow's house — stitched into the lemon-polished floors, the walls that smelled faintly of peppermint oil and something older, like memory that refused to fade—no sneaking out. No swearing. No skipping school. Pray before meals.

Sit straight in church every Sunday, like your soul might slip through the cracks if you didn't hold it tight. To Frieda, those rules weren't guardrails — they were a leash. A velvet chain that smelled like old hymnals and lemon Pledge, tying her to a life she didn't ask for, couldn't breathe inside.

Every morning, Lois sat at the kitchen table in her faded lavender housecoat. The fabric was soft, having withstood years of washing, and the hem frayed where it brushed her slippers. She held her teacup like a ritual — porcelain, hairline crack down one side — and her Bible lay open beside her, its onion-skin pages bruised with underlines and notes in tiny, looping handwriting.

She hummed softly as she read — old hymns, broken pieces of "Blessed Assurance," bits of "Precious Lord" drifting between sips of black tea. It filled the kitchen, that ghost-hum — a soft fog Frieda felt clinging to her hair, her sleeves, the inside of her skull.

Frieda hated mornings more than she hated rules. She stumbled in late most days with her hoodie pulled low like a battle flag. Her sneakers dragged on the linoleum, scuff marks trailing behind her like proof she hadn't floated in on holy thoughts.

She'd drop into the chair across from Lois with all the grace of a falling brick, grab the cereal box, and stab at the soggy flakes with her spoon like they might fight back if she didn't keep them in line.

"Good morning, Frieda," Lois would say, soft but clear — like someone ringing a church bell just once.

Sometimes Frieda grunted. Sometimes she didn't bother. Sometimes she shoved the spoon in her mouth, clinked it against her teeth, and stared at the clock on the wall like she could glare the hands into skipping straight to tomorrow.

Then came the prayer. Always the prayer.

Lois would bow her head, eyelids soft, lashes trembling like moth wings. Her hands, weathered but sure, folded together so gently you'd think they'd break if they squeezed too tight.

"Lord, thank You for another day," she'd begin, her voice a hush that somehow filled every corner of the small kitchen. "Bless this food. Touch Frieda's heart. Remind her she is Yours. Even now. Especially now."

Frieda would roll her eyes so far back she half-hoped they'd stick — just so she wouldn't have to see Lois, wouldn't have to see that stubborn calm. One morning, she let her spoon clatter to the table and snapped loud enough to shatter the hush.

"Here we go again," she muttered, voice dripping poison she wasn't sure she even meant.

Lois didn't blink. Didn't flinch. Just finished the *Amen* and lifted her head, eyes meeting Frieda's like the girl's glare was the last thing in the world that could scare her.

But then came the morning Frieda snapped for real. The spoon slammed into the side of the chipped cereal bowl, milk sloshing onto her hoodie sleeve. She leaned forward across the table — close enough for Lois to see the tiny scar above her eyebrow from the night she'd run too fast through the alley behind the old liquor store.

"I'm not your little church girl," Frieda hissed, voice sharp enough to cut the quiet in two. "Stop acting like I am. I don't need your prayers. I don't need your old songs choking me while I eat my breakfast."

Lois didn't recoil. She just set her teacup down — gently, like even the porcelain deserved a soft landing — and folded her hands again, resting them on the open page of her Bible.

"No," Lois said, and her voice was softer than Frieda expected, which made it hurt worse. "You're not my church girl. But you're still God's child. And you'll stay in this house as long as you need — even if you hate every breath I pray over you."

Frieda let out a dry, humorless laugh that cracked at the edges. She shoved back her chair so hard it screeched against the floor — loud enough that a picture frame on the hallway wall tilted sideways.

"Stop wasting your breath, Lois. I'm not listening. I'm not yours to fix."

Lois looked up at her granddaughter then — not with pity. Not with fear. Just that same quiet certainty that wrapped around Frieda's anger like a net.

"Maybe not," she said, the words floating out like steam from her tea. "But you're mine to love. And His to find. And I won't stop fighting for either."

Frieda's fists balled at her sides. Her shoulders twitched, wanting to swing at something — anything. But there was nothing to hit in that kitchen except a woman whose calm felt like an iron gate she couldn't shove open.

So, she stormed out — the hallway swallowing her boots in three angry strides. The door to her room slammed hard enough to rattle the clock off the wall. The house shivered. The old picture frame fell. But Lois didn't.

She sat there in the hush that fell after Frieda's rage. She lifted her teacup again with steady hands and turned another page in her Bible, her lips moving soundlessly as she recited the next Psalm.

Outside Frieda's door, the smell of peppermint oil and old lemon polish curled under the crack — a quiet reminder that sometimes war doesn't roar. Sometimes it hums. Sometimes it kneels. Sometimes it just waits — patient as stained glass — for the prodigal to come stumbling home.

The Blue Cards and the Walls Between

LATER THAT EVENING, Frieda pushed open her bedroom door with her foot, shoulders sagging under the weight of another day she mostly spent trying to disappear. She flicked on the lamp — the cheap yellow light pooling across her unmade bed, the crumpled hoodie at the foot, the tangled sheets that smelled like old laundry soap and stale peppermint from the hallway.

At first, she almost missed it — a slip of pale blue perched right at the center of her pillow like a secret waiting to breathe. She stepped closer. Hesitated. Picked it up between two fingers like it might bite.

A note card — small, the corners sharp. Lois's cursive — that perfect, slanted script Frieda had seen scribbled on grocery lists, birthday cards for church ladies, donation envelopes.

"The Lord is close to the brokenhearted and saves those who are crushed in spirit." —Psalm 34:18

She read it twice. The words dug under her ribs, unwelcome. Then, before her chest could tighten more, Frieda snapped the card in half. Then in quarters. Then, in smaller scraps until the words were nothing but confetti, she let fall through her fingers into the wastebasket by the door.

The next day, she found another one. This time tucked under the edge of her mirror — so she'd see it while brushing her hair into that high ponytail she thought made her look untouchable.

"Fear not, for I am with you..." —Isaiah 41:10

She ripped it fast. Shoved the shreds into her backpack to toss at school.

By the end of the week, they kept coming. Propped under her alarm clock. Slipped into her shoes. Pinned to the inside pocket of her worn denim jacket. Each one was neatly written. Soft ink on cool blue. Tiny lifelines she wanted no part of. She tore every single one to pieces. Stuffed them under her mattress, down the drain, into the trash behind the old shed out back.

But they kept coming. And every night, so did the prayers. Sometimes Frieda lay in the dark, eyes fixed on the ceiling she wished she could peel away. Through the thin drywall, Lois's voice slipped in — soft but strong, like a hum stitched into words.

"Father, cover Frieda. Heal what's broken. Remind her she's not alone. Don't let her forget You're near, even now..."

Frieda would yank her blanket up, press her headphones deeper into her ears. The bass line pounded — angry, defiant — but her name still floated through the drumbeat like smoke she couldn't blow away.

"Amen," she'd spit under her breath, mocking the old woman's hush. Sometimes she'd laugh loudly on purpose when Lois passed her door, so that she'd know the prayers were pointless.

One afternoon, she found Lois folding towels at the kitchen table. The scent of lemon oil lingered on her housecoat. Another blue card peeked from under the edge of the laundry basket. Frieda snatched it up, snapped it between her fingers. "Stop it. Just—stop it."

Lois didn't look startled. Didn't even pause in her folding. She just lifted her eyes, those calm wells of soft brown that Frieda hated because they looked like hope made flesh.

"I will not stop loving you," Lois said, voice quiet but carved from granite. "I will not stop reminding you Whose you are."

"Whose? Frieda barked. "I don't belong to anyone, Lois. Least of all your invisible God."

She expected Lois to argue — to scold her, threaten to take her phone, lock the door, lay down new rules with a snap like the slap of a ruler on a desk.

But Lois only smoothed the corner of a folded towel. Sat there like a rooted oak.

"You don't have to believe it yet," she said. "Doesn't make it less true. Doesn't make Him less close."

Frieda's throat tightened. Her hands itched to slam the folded basket onto the floor just to see something break — something *visible* that shattered when she wanted it to.

"You think you see me?" she whispered, the rage leaking out raw. "You think you know what I am? What I've done?"

Lois stood — slow, every joint stiff but steady. She crossed the tiny stretch of linoleum until she stood inches from Frieda's clenched fists.

"I see you," she said, voice trembling just once at the edges. "I see the fight in you. I see the hurt too. I see the girl the Lord is holding onto when she thinks she's too far gone to be found."

Frieda turned away, shoulders rigid. She scraped her palm across her cheek before Lois could see the shine there.

"Save your prayers for someone who cares," she spat.

"I am," Lois said. The faintest hint of a smile touched her lips — not triumphant, not mocking. Just sure. "You just don't know it yet."

THAT NIGHT, Frieda lay curled against the far wall of her bed, knees drawn up. She tried to drown the prayers out with the tinny snare of her music. But under it, the hum of Lois's whisper slipped through — softer than the bass, stronger than the snare.

"Father, cover her. Keep her. Remind her she's still Yours."

Frieda squeezed her eyes shut. Being hated would've been easier. Being punished would've been simpler. But being *seen* — that was a battle she didn't know how to win. And a war she wasn't ready to lose.

So, she pulled the blanket over her head and lay still as the old house settled around her — lemon oil, peppermint, hymns humming low through the walls like an unspoken vow. And somewhere, buried under the blanket's weight, a single torn scrap of pale blue hid beneath her pillow — one she hadn't shredded. Not yet.

The Crossroads

Three years passed — each one pressing down on Frieda's shoulders heavier than the last. The small house that had once smelled like safety and Sunday dinners had shrunk into a cage of lemon polish, stiff floral curtains, and scripture verses that watched her like guards posted on the walls.

By sixteen, every squeak of the floorboards under her shoes sounded like judgment. Every corner smelled too clean. Every doorknob turned too softly, as if the house itself was afraid to wake the ghost of the girl Frieda refused to be.

Lois meant well — Frieda knew that deep down, even if she'd never admit it. But good intentions felt suffocating when you were drowning, and the only thing offered was more rules, more prayers, more verses taped to your mirror like they could hold back the night.

It started small—the sighs. The eye rolls that lingered until Lois would clear her throat in that soft, sharp way that made Frieda's jaw tighten. Dishes left in the sink. Towels left on the floor. Detentions for skipped classes, forged signatures on crumpled permission slips.

And then — the boys. Late nights. The smell of menthols and cheap cologne clung to her hoodie when she crawled back through her window before dawn.

She wore the rebellion like a badge. Like armor. And worst of all — it worked. The sting of Lois's disappointment didn't feel like a wound anymore. It felt like proof that Frieda could still hurt something when she couldn't feel anything herself.

THE THURSDAY IT BROKE WAS WET. Rain slicked the cracked sidewalks and filled the Frampton gutters with oily rivers. By the time Frieda crept up the porch steps just after eleven, her hoodie clung to her shoulders, shoes squelching softly as she wiped them on the welcome mat that mocked her with its stitched *God Bless This Home.*

She eased the door open, trying to slip in with the hush of a ghost. But the lamp in the living room glowed soft and steady — waiting. Lois sat in her recliner, legs wrapped in a worn quilt. A small embroidery hoop rested on her lap, needle dancing in and out of fabric with the calm precision of a heartbeat. Her glasses perched on the end of her nose, silver hair pinned tight in a low knot. The only sound was the soft pull of thread and the whisper of her humming — half-hymn, half-warning. Frieda tried to angle toward the hallway.

"Mm-mm."

Lois didn't even look up — just cleared her throat with that low hum of finality that felt heavier than any locked door.

Frieda froze mid-step, shoulders stiff. She exhaled, turned around slowly — the posture a mix of defiance and dread. She crossed her arms tight across her chest like they could shield her from Lois's gaze.

Lois pushed her glasses up, still not meeting Frieda's eyes. She set her embroidery needle down on the side table with care, every movement deliberate.

"Curfew ended two hours ago," Lois said, her voice calm as cool water. "It's after eleven. Where you been, Frieda?"

Frieda shrugged, lips curling into a smile that didn't reach her eyes. "Out."

Lois lifted her gaze then — steady, warm, but firm as an iron gate.

"Out where?"

"Nowhere special." Frieda's tone turned sharp. "You wouldn't approve anyway, so why ask?"

Lois's jaw shifted just enough to catch the lamp's glow along the soft lines near her temple. She folded her hands in her lap.

"Don't stand there and tell half-truths, child. Not in this house."

Frieda's breath caught in her throat. Her fingers drummed on her elbows. "This ain't my house. I'm just stuck here."

That stung — a small flicker across Lois's eyes — but she didn't rise to it. She only nodded once, as if confirming something old and inevitable.

"You got anything to say for yourself?" Lois asked, softer now — but her softness always felt heavier than any shout.

Frieda's eyes flicked to the floor, then back to the door behind Lois — measuring the steps it'd take to flee again. She shrugged. "No, ma'am."

Lois's lips tightened — not in anger, but in resolve. "You're grounded, Frieda. Two weeks. School and back. No friends. No wandering around like you got no name and no home."

Frieda's laugh came sharp, small, bitter. "I don't have any friends worth losing, so good job, I guess." She lifted her chin. "What else?"

Lois's breath hitched — just once — then steadied. "Go to your room. And lock the window tonight, Frieda Winslow. I'm not so old I don't know your ways."

"Keep your prayers for yourself, Lois," Frieda shot back, voice rising. "They don't stick to me anymore."

Lois rose slowly, the old recliner creaking. She stepped closer — so close Frieda caught the faint smell of peppermint oil and the talcum powder Lois used on her hands.

"You think they don't stick because you're running," Lois said, voice calm but fierce enough to hush the rain on the window for a heartbeat. "But you can't outrun the kind of love that kneels for you in the dark, Frieda. You can hate me all you want. You can hate Him all you want. I will not stop covering you with these prayers — whether you want them or not."

For a moment, Frieda's mouth opened — a retort poised on her tongue, something ugly and final — but it caught in her throat. Her eyes burned hot. She turned on her heel instead. Her sneakers thudded down the hallway — each step a promise that she'd break the house rules again just to remind herself she still could.

The door slammed behind her, rattling the frame. She ripped off her hoodie, flinging it to the floor as if it might catch fire on the carpet. Through the crack under her door, Lois's hallway lamp spilled a thin line of warm yellow. A sentinel. A warning. Or maybe just a reminder that someone was still there, whether Frieda liked it or not.

She sat on her bed's edge, heartbeat still loud. She waited. The lamp clicked off. The old floor creaked. Lois's door whispered shut. And like clockwork, Frieda moved. Socks swapped for shoes. Hoodie back over her curls. Window eased open — the screen already pried loose from last month's storm.

Her feet hit the damp grass. The night pressed cool and reckless against her cheeks. Somewhere behind her, the house kept its small lamp glow buried behind a locked door, and a prayer whispered in the dark.

She didn't know where she was going. She didn't care. Only that every step away felt like proof that love couldn't catch her — not tonight. And yet, in the echo of the window frame closing behind her, Frieda heard it anyway: a hush she hated more than any lock.

"God, bring her back safe. Bring her home." And under that hush, the storm waited.

THE CITY WASN'T ASLEEP — not really, not at this hour, not in this part of Frampton. It breathed differently after dark — slower, heavier, a pulse that drummed under the cracked sidewalks and flickered neon signs. Streetlights buzzed overhead, throwing pale circles onto puddles that reflected nothing back. Somewhere blocks away, a siren rose and fell like a warning sung too late.

Frieda walked steadily under that noise. Her hands were buried deep in her hoodie pocket, her thumb brushing the dead phone she hadn't bothered to charge. Her breath rose in soft clouds. She pulled her shoulders up, eyes tracing the pools of light ahead. The corner store glowed like a crooked lighthouse at the end of the block — flickering fluorescent lights and a neon *OPEN* sign that buzzed louder than the street behind her.

She leaned her back against the brick wall outside — its surface cool and rough beneath the thin fabric of her hoodie. Fresh tags covered the bricks — sloppy names, jagged threats, half-finished crowns. She traced them with her eyes, pretending she could read a story in the paint.

Behind her, the city muttered and cackled: teens huddled near the dumpster, passing a bottle wrapped in a brown bag, laughter too loud. Smoke from a joint curled lazily in the air, mixing with the tang of old oil and something sweeter she couldn't name. A pair of glass doors squeaked every time someone pushed through. The flickering lights above spat insects in and out of the glow. Frieda watched it all, trying to look invisible.

Then she saw it. Across the street — just beyond the puddles catching the streetlight — a black SUV rolled in slowly, its tires whispering on the wet asphalt. The windows were dark, too dark. Not the kind of tint that keeps out sun — the kind that keeps secrets inside.

The passenger door cracked open. A man — hood pulled low, hands buried in his sweatshirt pocket — leaned out and murmured to a girl standing alone by the curb. Frieda's heart stuttered. The girl couldn't have been older than fifteen — thin arms wrapped around her chest, eyes darting like a cornered rabbit. They spoke in sharp whispers. The girl slipped something small from her pocket — a folded square, maybe pills, maybe cash. The man took it quickly, then nodded toward the backseat—a silent command.

Frieda's nails dug into her palms inside her pockets. She held her breath as the girl stepped back and shook her head. Her shoes squeaked as she turned fast — vanishing into the side street without looking back. The SUV lingered — headlights humming, engine low. Watching. Frieda forced her eyes away.

A spark snapped to her right — the click of a cheap lighter. She turned. A girl — older than the one at the curb, but not by much — leaned against the wall a few feet away. A lit cigarette glowed between her fingers, the smoke curling around her face like a veil. Tattoos covered both forearms — vines, barbed wire, and tiny letters she couldn't read. The girl's eyes cut across Frieda's hoodie, her damp shoes, the scuffed knuckles poking out of her sleeves.

"Hey." Her voice was husky, edged with something too old for her age.

Frieda swallowed. "Hey."

The girl flicked ash to the ground and tilted her head with a sly grin. "I ain't seen you 'round here before." She dragged on the cigarette, slow and measured, then exhaled in a ribbon toward the gutter. "Name's Keisha. You?"

Frieda hesitated. Her instinct flared — that warning heat in her ribs that Lois's rules used to press down. But here, there were no rules. No windows watching. No prayers humming through thin walls. Just streetlight and smoke.

"...Frieda," she said finally.

Keisha laughed low — a sound rougher than the siren still echoing blocks away. She flicked her cigarette toward the gutter but didn't drop it yet.

"You a runaway?" Keisha asked, tone casual but sharp enough to slide under skin.

Frieda shifted her weight. "No. Maybe. I don't know."

Keisha huffed a short chuckle, teeth catching on the filter. "Sounds like a yes to me. Let me guess — strict house? Churchy guardian? Rules for breathin'?"

Frieda's jaw twitched. "Grandma. House full of Bibles. Rules for everything. Even how to say 'Amen.'"

Keisha's grin twitched wider — not kind, but not cruel either. Like they'd just cracked open the same wound and peeked at the scar.

"Mine had me readin' Psalms every night like it'd scrub the sin outta me. Guess what? Didn't stick." She shrugged. "I left. Been three years. Got people now. Real ones. Look out for me. Not like them fake saints."

Frieda's eyes narrowed — the corner store's neon flickered behind Keisha's head like a crooked halo. "How'd you survive?"

Keisha's shoulders lifted under her denim jacket. She opened her hands like a magician, showing empty palms. "Street smarts. Hustle. Some help when it counted. It ain't easy. But you know what it is? Free."

She paused. Flicked the half-burned cigarette into the puddle at Frieda's feet. "You wanna meet 'em? The Crew?"

Frieda's pulse stuttered — instinct roared no in her ears, but something lonelier than sense answered for her. "...Okay."

Keisha's grin softened, just for a breath. Then it sharpened again — business now. "Good. But first — street rules." She lifted three fingers, ticking them off like a list of commandments.

"One — don't trust anyone with clean shoes. Means they ain't had to run yet. Means they ain't real."

"Two — never sleep in the same place twice. Corners remember faces. Cops too."

"Three — if a boy helps you, he wants somethin'. Always say no. Loud. You got that?"

Frieda nodded. Her mouth was dry. "Got it."

Keisha leaned in — close enough Frieda smelled the stale smoke and something sweet, maybe bubblegum under the smoke. "You carryin'?"

Frieda blinked. "What?"

Keisha cracked open her jacket — not wide, just enough to flash the steel grip of a pistol tucked under her waistband. "Heat. Blade. Somethin' to make boys think twice."

Frieda's breath stilled in her chest. "No."

Keisha's smile flickered again — sharp and knowing. "Then stick close. Some folks don't care if you're a kid."

She jerked her chin toward the mouth of a narrow alley — shadows pooling there like a secret that had teeth. "C'mon. Let's meet the crew."

Frieda's feet moved before her heart could protest. The corner store's glow faded away behind her shoulders. She felt it — the last good piece of her standing under that streetlight, staring at the SUV that had already swallowed one girl's courage. But her steps kept going — soft on wet pavement, breath caught between hope and something she didn't dare name yet. A line crossed—a prayer silenced. A door cracked open to the dark. And the night — the night just watched, waiting to see if she'd ever find her way back.

The Initiation

THE ALLEY BEHIND THE CORNER STORE smelled like engine oil, stale beer, and the ghost of last night's cigarette smoke. Overhead, a flickering streetlight cast jagged shadows on the brick walls where faded murals bled into fresh graffiti—bright tags overlapping each other like warnings, names of the dead spray-painted in shaky white letters that dripped like tears.

Keisha walked ahead, shoulders squared, her sneakers crunching over broken glass. Frieda followed, hands jammed into the pockets of her thrifted jacket, every step echoing in her ears louder than the muted beat pulsing from somewhere up ahead.

They slipped through a sagging chain-link gate into the back lot of a rundown auto shop. The air inside hit Frieda like a fist—thick with grease, sweat, burned rubber. Somewhere near the shop doors, an old boom box coughed out distorted bass lines—low, growling hip-hop, the lyrics buried under the hum of voices and the clink of bottles.

A cluster of teens sprawled across busted car seats and threadbare couches—older boys in hoodies with frayed cuffs, a few girls perched in pairs, knees pulled tight under their chins as they passed around cheap beer and cigarettes. Frieda's eyes watered when a cloud of smoke drifted her way—sharp, chemical, heavy enough to make her throat tighten.

Keisha stopped just inside the open garage door and clapped her hands once, sharp enough to slice through the chatter.

"Yo!" she called out. "Got somebody new tonight."

Heads turned. Laughter died down. All eyes found Frieda— narrow, curious, some bored, some hungry.

A wiry boy with gold caps on his teeth and a scar that traced from his hairline down to the edge of his jaw pushed himself up from a car hood, arms crossed as he drifted closer. He smelled like cheap malt liquor and sweat. His eyes flicked over Frieda like he was deciding what she was worth.

"This a church girl?" His voice scraped like gravel. He tilted his chin at Keisha but kept his eyes locked on Frieda.

Keisha's grin was all teeth and defiance. "Used to be." She hooked an arm around Frieda's neck, pulled her in closer. "She got fire, though. I see it. Y'all will too."

Frieda's heart battered her ribs so hard she was sure he could hear it.

"What's your name, sweetheart?" the boy asked, leaning close enough that Frieda caught the sting of stale beer on his breath.

Frieda swallowed. Her tongue felt too big for her mouth. "Frieda."

The boy chuckled, but it sounded like a dare. "Frieda," he echoed, drawing it out. He cocked his head. "You runnin' from somethin'? Or runnin' to somethin'?"

The truth slipped out before she could catch it. "I don't know."

He barked a laugh—dry, mean, amused. "Honest, huh? That's the realest thing I heard all damn night." He turned, nodding at Keisha. "Keep her close. She gonna need it."

Keisha squeezed her shoulder, voice dropping softer. "Don't sweat him. You ain't gotta prove nothin' tonight. Just watch. Listen. Learn the pulse."

Frieda's knees wobbled as Keisha guided her toward a torn sofa near the wall. She perched on the armrest, spine straight as a ruler, trying to look like she belonged. Someone wordlessly shoved a warm soda into her hand. She held it tight but didn't crack the tab.

Laughter rose and fell around her—stories traded like poker chips. Near misses with patrol cars. Beefs settled with bats and cheap blades. Small boasts that sounded like hymns in this concrete sanctuary. She caught snippets—*Lex said*—*Keisha said*—like prayers repeated under breath.

She watched Keisha drift from group to group. When Keisha spoke, the others leaned in. She had weight here—respect that bent heads and silenced arguments.

And then there was **Lex**. He leaned against the dented door of a battered sedan in the center of the garage—hood propped open like a dead thing. He didn't talk much. Just watched, arms folded, phone glinting in his hand like a secret. When he did speak, voices dropped. Laughter stilled. He didn't notice Frieda at first—until he did.

He pushed off the car, boots scuffing oil-dark concrete, and crossed to her in three easy steps. Up close, he smelled of cheap cologne and asphalt, his gaze sharp enough to peel back her ribs.

"You loyal?" Lex asked. Just that. His tone was flat, his eyes unreadable.

Frieda's mouth went dry. She glanced at Keisha, who just raised her brows, waiting.

"Yeah," Frieda said finally, the word small but steady.

Lex studied her for a heartbeat longer, then let a slow grin bend one corner of his mouth.

"Loyalty'll get you far," he said. "Disrespect'll get you gone."

His eyes skimmed her again, from her scuffed sneakers to her trembling hands gripping the soda.

"Frieda, huh? That ain't no street name. You stay with us, your new name is Dove."

"Dove?" Frieda repeated, tasting it, trying to understand if this was praise or a curse.

Lex's grin sharpened, a flash of teeth in the haze. "Yeah. Dove. 'Cause you too sweet for the block."

The others laughed—snorts, sneers, someone flicking an empty can against the wall so it clanged like a cheap bell.

Lex lifted a finger to his lips. The garage fell quiet as if someone had hit pause on the noise.

"Y'all got a problem with that name?" he asked. His tone was playful, but the edge beneath it could cut steel. Heads shook in silence.

He stared into Frieda's eyes—cold and calculating. "And you? You got a problem with that name?

Frieda felt her stomach twist, but her head shook before she could second guess herself. "No, sir."

"Good," said Lex.

Message received—a line drawn in the grime.

LATER, WHEN THE CLOCK TICKED DEEP into the hollow hours, they cut her thumb—just a nick at the base where the skin met her palm. Lex did it himself with a boxcutter, the blade cold against her pulse. The sting made her flinch, but she held still.

Keisha pressed her thumb to Frieda's, blood mixing in the flickering glow of a single bare bulb.

"That's it, Dove," Keisha murmured near her ear. "You in now. Don't forget it."

The buzz in her veins felt like adrenaline—or poison. She couldn't tell which.

Outside, Keisha walked her back through the alley, the city beyond humming low and hungry. The back gate clanged shut behind them. Frieda could feel the cut on her hand throb with every heartbeat.

Keisha lit a cigarette, the flame sharp in the shadows, and passed Frieda a scrap of folded paper.

"What's this?" Frieda asked, voice rough.

"Address. Spot, we crash sometimes. You get locked out? Run outta excuses? Go there. Ask for Smoke."

Frieda tucked it deep into her pocket, fingers brushing the tiny cut bandaged in her sleeve.

They reached the corner store's blinking neon sign. Keisha blew out smoke, eyes narrowed.

"You got potential, church girl," she said, voice softer now but still carrying steel. "Just don't forget the rules. And don't cross Lex."

"You ever cross him?" Frieda asked. She regretted it the second it left her mouth.

Keisha's mouth twitched—almost a smile, but something colder, older.

"Once," she said. "Never again."

BY THE TIME FRIEDA CRAWLED through her bedroom window, dawn pressed gray and thin at the edges of the sky. Lois's house smelled like warm toast, coffee brewing, maybe a hymn humming low through an old radio in the kitchen.

Frieda lay flat on her bed, staring at the cracks in the ceiling. Her thumb throbbed beneath its bandage—a pulse that reminded her she'd chosen this. She didn't feel safe. But for the first time in forever, the fear didn't swallow her whole. She belonged—

somewhere—to someone. And for a girl who'd spent so long on the outside, that was enough—for now.

CHAPTER 4

Cracks in the Crew

The auto shop was louder this time—louder, hotter, and meaner. The big overhead doors were cracked open just enough for the night air to leak in, carrying the sound of tires on wet pavement and the pulse of bass that made the walls tremble.

Inside, music blared from a battered speaker duct-taped to a rusty shelf. The smell of oil and burnt rubber tangled with the sharper bite of something acrid—smoke, sweat, chemicals. Sparks popped now and then from an old welding torch at the far end of the garage.

There were new faces in the corners—boys with raw eyes and twitchy hands, girls perched on dented fenders, passing around cheap liquor in plastic cups. They laughed too hard. Or didn't laugh at all. Their edges were sharper than the ones Frieda remembered when she first slipped through the shop's back door weeks ago, hungry for rebellion and blind to its teeth.

She'd thought this place would taste like freedom. Instead, it pressed against her ribs like a dull blade, a tightness that wouldn't let her breathe right. She sat near the back now, half-hidden behind a dusty red tool cabinet. From here, she watched it all—watched a boy no older than fifteen lean over a flattened soda can, his skinny shoulders hitching as he snorted up whatever lines he'd cooked onto its surface. His eyes watered when he looked up, but no one paid him any mind.

A few feet away, Shonda—barely eighteen, maybe—sat cross-legged on an old car hood with three other girls. They giggled between themselves, voices high and cracked. One of them tapped the inside of her arm, veins blooming blue under the garage's flickering light. The snap of the syringe cap made Frieda's stomach flip.

Closer to the center of the floor, Keisha perched on an overturned milk crate, counting a roll of cash—quick, practiced flicks of her thumb, the green bills snapping together like a heartbeat gone wrong. Lex prowled the floor nearby, flip phone pressed tight to his ear. His voice cut through the music in sharp barks: *"Product. Shipment. Late money."* Every word dropped like a stone in Frieda's chest.

She leaned back, pulled her knees up under her chin, and tried to look unfazed. Invisible. She wanted to disappear so badly her bones ached with it. Keisha caught her staring. She tucked the cash into her bra and wandered over, steps slow and easy like a cat stalking prey.

"Dove," Keisha said, her voice pitched low so only Frieda could hear. "You good?"

Frieda forced a small smile, one she knew didn't touch her eyes. She could taste the lie before she said it.

"Yeah. Just tired."

Keisha cracked open a warm can of soda and held it out. Frieda took it, the fizz gone flat against her palm. Keisha sank beside her on the concrete floor, back against the tool cabinet, legs stretched out. She bumped Frieda's knee lightly with hers.

"First few weeks always feel weird," Keisha said, eyes drifting to where Lex was still pacing. "You'll get used to it."

Frieda turned the can in her hands, staring at her reflection warped in the dull aluminum. She tried to swallow the question, but it clawed its way out anyway.

"What do you guys actually do, Keisha?"

Keisha's eyes flicked to hers—sharp, assessing. She shrugged once, like she was tossing a stone into a pond to watch it sink.

"Whatever pays. Move stuff, deliver stuff, watch doors. Lex pulls the strings. We hold it down. We eat."

"And if… someone wants out?" Frieda asked. The words felt heavy on her tongue.

Keisha stilled. The smile she'd worn—sharp-edged, half-warm—slipped just a fraction.

"Why you askin', Dove?"

Frieda looked away, eyes snagging on Shonda's giggle as another needle vanished into skin.

"Just wondering."

Keisha sighed—long, low, like a mother tired of scolding a child who kept asking why the sky was blue.

"You don't just walk away from the people who protect you. That ain't how loyalty works out here."

A sudden shout cracked the stale air like a slap. Near the back entrance, a scrawny kid stumbled through the doorway—hood half off, a smear of blood at the corner of his mouth, eyes too wide for his face.

"They jumped Jamal!" the boy yelled, breathless. "By the bridge off State! Said he owed!"

Lex snapped his phone shut so hard it cracked. He stalked forward, boots echoing on oil-stained concrete.

"Who?"

"Some dudes from 9th Street. Warlord crew."

The words hit the shop like a thrown match. Laughter died. Music still thumped, but it sounded distant now—like it belonged to another world.

Lex's jaw twitched once. He pointed a finger so close to the boy's nose the kid flinched. "He with anyone?"

The boy shook his head. Sweat beaded his upper lip.

Lex snorted, low and mean. "Then he's on his own." He spun on his heel, already redialing his phone, muttering curses into the receiver.

Frieda pushed herself upright, voice cracking through the sudden hush. "You're not gonna help him?"

Lex didn't even look back. "He ran his mouth, made his mess. We don't clean up for cowards, Dove."

She felt something in her chest cinch tight, like a wire pulled too hard. She turned to Keisha—searching her face for something human. For the girl who taught her how to duck a punch and sleep under bridges without freezing.

Keisha's mouth was a thin line now. She held Frieda's gaze, but her eyes were dark, tired, guarded.

"Sometimes people gotta learn the hard way," Keisha said quietly. "It's just how it is."

Frieda didn't remember standing. Didn't remember slipping the soda can onto the crate behind her. She drifted through the shop like a ghost, past Shonda's hollow laugh, past Lex's barked threats, past the cold metal door that slammed shut behind her with a hollow echo.

The streets swallowed her footsteps. The city felt wrong—too bright in places, too dark in others. Every brake light made her flinch. Every laugh around a corner felt sharp as glass. She wasn't bold anymore. She wasn't free. She was just a girl in a borrowed hoodie with someone else's name echoing in her ears like a dare.

WHEN SHE REACHED LOIS'S STREET, the porch light was on. Warm, golden. Ordinary. She stopped on the sidewalk, heart banging so loud she swore the whole block could hear it. The house—once a cage she'd rattled her fists against—looked like shelter now. A soft place to land if she could just bring herself to enter. She reached into her pocket and pulled out the scrap of paper—Keisha's list of places to hide out, folded so many times the edges were soft. She stared at it under the streetlight's flicker. Then, slowly, she tore it in half. Then again. And again. Tiny pieces floated from her palm, caught by the night wind, carried down the empty street like dead leaves. She didn't go inside right away. But she didn't turn back, either. And for the first time, the night didn't feel like freedom. It felt like a door she'd just stepped out of—and left wide open behind her.

The Confrontation

THE CORNER STORE HADN'T CHANGED. Same faded sign buzzing overhead, stuttering like a dying insect. Same cracked sidewalk glistening from the day's leftover rain. But tonight, the air carried an edge—sharp, metallic, mean. The kind of cold that didn't just sting skin—it cut deep if you breathed too much of it in.

Frieda stepped off the curb, the soles of her sneakers whispering across damp pavement. Her hoodie was pulled tight, hands buried in her pockets, thumb brushing the lifeless screen of her dead phone. The city muttered around her—somewhere, bass thumped from a passing car, and a dog barked in the distance—but none of it touched her. Everything felt too still, like the block itself was holding its breath. Waiting.

She spotted them before she reached the alley: Keisha, leaning against the crumbling brick wall like she belonged to the night itself, arms crossed. Her face half-shadowed. Her posture unreadable. On either side of her stood two unfamiliar boys—wide-shouldered, blank-faced, wearing black puffer jackets zipped to the neck. They didn't speak. Didn't move. Just stared as Frieda approached, their eyes narrow and cold. Her steps slowed as she neared, the gravel beneath her feet loud in the quiet.

"Hey," Frieda said, voice light but unsteady. She swallowed hard. Tried again. "Keisha."

Keisha didn't move at first. Then her chin lifted slightly, eyes sweeping over Frieda with practiced disdain.

"You've been ghostin'," she said flatly, the words slicing through the cold like a razor. "Since that night."

Frieda shifted her weight, the chill threading up her spine. "I've been thinking."

Keisha raised an eyebrow, unimpressed.

"About that girl," Frieda continued. "The SUV. Something was off. You saw it too."

A slow tension tightened Keisha's jaw. But her expression didn't change. "Street's always off, Dove. You know that. What's your point?"

"This wasn't turf beef," Frieda pressed, her voice firmer now. "She was scared. She ran. She didn't want to go with them. You felt it—I saw it in your face."

Keisha gave a bitter chuckle, but there was no humor in it. "Girls run all the time. Doesn't mean they don't go back."

"This is bigger than that. This is trafficking," Frieda said, stepping forward despite the way the boys' shoulders squared at her approach. "Lex knows more than he's saying. And you—Keisha, you were there. You *felt* that girl's fear."

Silence. Then, slowly, Keisha peeled herself off the wall and took a step closer. The scent of menthol and hair grease drifted between them. Her eyes didn't blink. Her lips parted in a tight line, voice dropping low.

"Watch what you're stirring up, Dove," she said. The nickname landed hard—like a slap instead of a whisper.

"I'm not stirring," Frieda said, jaw clenched. "I'm waking up. You should too."

Another step. Closer now. Face-to-face. Eye-to-eye. A stare-down. Their breath hung between them like frost.

"You really think you can fix all this?" Keisha hissed. "Run back to your grandma and her prayers? You think that's gonna save you out here?"

"I'm not trying to be saved," Frieda snapped. "I'm trying to save *her.* And every other girl being dragged into this mess while we stand by and pretend it's just the game."

Keisha's eyes darkened. Her hand moved fast.

Click—a flash of silver. A switchblade glinted under the streetlight. She pressed the tip just below Frieda's jaw—light enough not to cut, but heavy enough to promise it could.

Frieda's breath stilled. Her spine locked in place.

Keisha leaned in, voice like ice in the dark. "You remember what Lex said about loyalty?" she whispered. "Disloyal girls disappear."

Frieda's pulse thundered in her ears. Her hands stayed in her pockets, fists clenched so tight her nails dug into her palms. But she didn't move. She didn't blink.

Click. The blade disappeared as fast as it came. Keisha's hand dropped. "You're on your own now," she said, softer than before, but sharper somehow. Her voice held no heat. No remorse. Just the cold finality of a door closing.

She nodded at the boys. "Let's bounce."

Without another word, they turned—boots crunching grit and gravel—and disappeared into the alley's throat. The flickering overhead light sputtered one last time, then held.

Frieda stood alone, the silence swallowing everything. But she didn't move. Not yet. Because something in her had cracked open. Not with fear. With clarity. This wasn't just a warning. It was war.

Hours Later

BY THE TIME SHE HEADED HOME, Southside Frampton felt like it was holding its breath. The night was cold enough to make her nose sting; her hands were shoved deep in her pockets. Her hoodie hood pulled low. She kept to the shadows, but the shadows felt thinner tonight.

Trash rustled in the alleyways — the wind pushing scraps of old flyers and plastic like ghosts. Somewhere blocks away, a dog barked once, then stopped. Frieda's steps were quick, her sneakers slapping damp concrete in a syncopated rhythm with her heartbeat. She turned a corner too fast — shoes slipping through a shallow puddle that caught the yellow shine of a dying streetlight overhead. She felt the water soak through to her socks, sharp and cold. That's when she heard it — footsteps. Just behind her. Not fast. Not frantic. Just steady. Careful. *Choosing* to match hers. She didn't turn. Not yet. She kept moving, steps faster, breath catching at the back of her throat.

"Hey, hey girl..." The voice slithered out of the dark like oil spilled on wet asphalt. Slick. Mean.

She spun. A man stepped out from the shadow between a rusted fence and a busted dumpster. He was tall but too thin under a cracked leather jacket. The brim of his cap threw his grin into half-shadow, but the teeth caught the streetlight — yellowed, too wide. He smelled like liquor and cheap cologne that couldn't hide the rot underneath.

"Where you off to in such a hurry, huh?" His voice was too sweet, too slow.

Frieda took a step back, shoes sliding. "I'm just going home." Her voice felt too small, a ghost of itself.

He stepped closer, the grin bending. "This late? Ain't nothing out here but trouble. You scared, baby girl?"

He lunged. Too quick. A blur of leather and teeth.

Frieda's scream ripped from her chest raw and jagged. She staggered back, her shoulder slamming the brick wall. Her palm scraped old paint and cold concrete. Her heart battered her ribs so hard she thought it might break out.

He grabbed at her sleeve again. But another shape split the night.

"Back off!"

A voice, sharp and electric as a snapped wire. Keisha. She hit the man square in the chest, palms flat and furious. He stumbled back a step, shock flickering through his greasy grin.

"This one's with me," Keisha hissed. Her jacket flared just wide enough to catch the glint of steel tucked against her hip. "You wanna try it? Huh? You wanna test me tonight?"

The man's lip curled — an ugly sound slurred through his teeth — but his eyes flicked from Keisha's hand to her mouth, then back to the alley behind him. He spat at the gutter. "Heffer, ain't worth it anyway." He turned, shoulders hunched, boots splashing through the same puddle Frieda had slipped through minutes ago. The silence he left behind felt bigger than his threat.

Frieda collapsed back against the brick, the chill seeping through her hoodie. Her breath scraped in and out of her throat like it might fail her any second.

Keisha didn't touch her. She just stood there, arms crossed, eyes glittering mean and tired.

"You good?" she asked finally.

Frieda nodded — barely. The lie tasted like salt.

Keisha shook her head. "Don't just wander these streets like some lost church lamb. This ain't your grandma's pews. You walk these corners; you keep your eyes up. And your blade closer."

"Blade?" Frieda echoed, her voice smaller than she meant.

Keisha sighed—her breath fogged in the dark. She reached inside her jacket, pulled something small from an inner pocket — a slim folding knife, black handle, silver edge dull but real.

She pressed it into Frieda's palm, curling the girl's fingers around it until they made a fist.

"Till you get your own fire," Keisha said. Her voice held no warmth but no cruelty either. "Don't say I never gave you nothin', Dove."

Frieda stared at the knife. At Keisha. At the dripping puddle where the man's footsteps vanished. For a moment, the city felt huge around her — all flickering lights and broken promises. And she knew. This life she thought she could dip a toe into? It had teeth. And it almost bit through her.

She squeezed the knife tight enough to dig half-moons into her palm. And this time when she looked up, she didn't flinch. Not from the dark. Not from Keisha. Not from herself.

Cracks in the Dawn

THE HOUR BEFORE DAWN in Lois's house was always the quietest — that thin slice of night when even the wind outside seemed to hold its breath, when the pipes behind the old walls ticked like a tired clock winding down. But for Frieda, there was no quiet tonight. She lay curled tight on her side, knees pulled up high under the heavy quilt Lois had washed and folded so many times it smelled like lemon soap and starch. The fabric scratched at her chin, where she burrowed deeper, as if she could bury herself away from the echoes rattling around her skull. But the covers couldn't muffle them.

That grin — yellow teeth split wide under the streetlight. The slick hiss of the man's laugh still lingered in her ear, like oil she couldn't scrub off. And that girl by the SUV — fifteen, maybe. Too thin, shoulders hunched like a question she hadn't found an answer for. And Keisha — standing there like stone, pistol tucked in her waistband as easy as a wallet, fingers steady when she'd pushed that man back into the dark.

Frieda squeezed her eyes shut. The inside of her skull bloomed with the same scenes, sharper in the dark. Her stomach rolled. She pressed a fist to her mouth to keep the bitter taste down. She wanted this, didn't she? Wanted out. Wanted *free*. No Lois hovering with prayers folded neat as napkins beside the dinner plate. No scriptures taped to the mirror like sticky reminders she couldn't breathe around. No curfews. No house rules.

The street was her rule now. Freedom. But why did it feel like a trap with no walls? Why did the dark feel thicker *outside* than it ever did behind Lois's old floral curtains?

A tear slipped warm across the bridge of her nose, wetting the edge of her pillow. Frieda jerked her hand up, scrubbed it away rough — annoyed at the softness of it, at the weakness. She forced a breath through clenched teeth.

"This is what you wanted," she hissed into the half-dark, voice trembling so soft she could pretend no one — not even God — could hear it. "Freedom, right? This is it."

But the word felt like a lie when it hit her tongue. Bitter. Empty. It tasted like the stale smell that clung to her hoodie — smoke, wet asphalt, the ghost of Keisha's menthol breath. It didn't feel like freedom. It felt like falling — tumbling backward through the dark, arms pinwheeling for something solid to catch, but finding nothing but air and echoes.

She turned her face into the pillow, the edge scratchy against her cheek. She squeezed her eyes shut so hard her head throbbed. If Lois's door creaked open right now, Frieda would've buried herself deeper. Would've pretended to be asleep. Would've lied through her teeth if asked. Because the truth was rawer than any punishment Lois could hand down: She didn't feel grown. She didn't feel strong. She felt cracked—hairline fractures splintering wide behind her ribs where even the prayers she claimed she hated used to live.

Somewhere down the hall, a floorboard sighed — the house settling into the slow hush that always came before Lois rose to make tea and hum those hymns that wrapped around the walls like incense. Frieda hated how badly a part of her wanted to hear that hum right now — like it could stitch the pieces of her back together, even if just for a breath.

She pulled the covers tighter over her head, letting her breath fog the inside of her little cotton cave. Another tear. Another swipe of her sleeve across her eyes. Another whisper so soft the walls barely caught it:

"Don't come looking for me," she lied to the dark.
But under that, deep as marrow: *Please — someone catch me before I hit the ground.*

When it Felt Like Love

The next night, the city air felt damp — sticky with drizzle that hadn't quite made up its mind whether it wanted to be rain or just mist. Frieda's hoodie clung to her arms as she walked, sleeves tugged low over her hands. She didn't know if she was looking for Keisha's crew tonight or running in the opposite direction — maybe both.

Streetlight after streetlight stretched ahead, their glow fractured by wet pavement and cracked concrete. One flickered overhead as she stepped beneath it, buzzing like an old neon sign about to burn out. She wrapped her arms tighter across her chest, the knot in her stomach twisting tighter with every echo of her own footsteps.

Behind her — another set. Her heart stuttered. She glanced over her shoulder. Nothing but shadows dancing behind a broken fence. She walked faster. The footsteps did too. She spun so fast her hood slipped back from her head. Her breath caught sharp in her throat.

A man was jogging toward her — mid-twenties maybe, lean frame wrapped in a gray hoodie, black jeans, shoes scuffed like he'd run a mile just to find her. His breath puffed white in the cold as he lifted both hands, palms open.

"Hey! You okay?" His voice was pitched low, careful like he could hear her pulse thundering through her chest.

Frieda stepped back, shoulder brushing the cold metal of a chain-link fence. "Who are you?" Her voice cracked — it annoyed her more than the fear.

He slowed a few feet away, boots skidding to a wet stop on the sidewalk. Hands still up, like a promise.

"Sorry — didn't mean to spook you. I just... I saw that dude following you. Tall, leather jacket. Been tailing you since the liquor store on 82nd."

Frieda's throat tightened. "What guy?" She hadn't seen anyone. Her pulse kicked harder.

He jerked his thumb over his shoulder, eyes scanning the street behind them like he expected to see a shadow slip from the alley. "He dipped when I called you. But he was clocking you, for real. You gotta keep your head up around here."

His voice wasn't fake pleasant. It was steady — calm but with a rough edge. She could smell faint cologne under the sweat. He didn't look away from her eyes once.

"Name's Dante," he said, lowering his hands. He tucked them into the pocket of his hoodie, shoulders hunching slightly to show he meant no threat. "I live off 84th, near the old laundromat. Ain't a creep, I promise. Just didn't sit right, seeing him tail you like that."

Frieda studied him — the curve of his jaw, the faint scar near his eyebrow, the little smile tugging at the corner of his mouth that wasn't really a smile at all. He seemed to know how to talk people down—like he'd done it before.

"I'm Frieda," she mumbled.

Dante tipped his chin, a slow acknowledgment. "You live close by?"

She hesitated, shifting her feet. "Sort of." It wasn't a lie — it wasn't the truth either.

He looked her over once, but not in that greasy way she'd grown used to dodging. "This part of Frampton ain't what it used to be," he said. His voice dipped softer. "If you're walkin' here this late, you gotta keep sharp. Head up. Ears open."

Frieda crossed her arms tighter over her chest. "I can handle myself."

A smile twitched across Dante's lips. "I don't doubt that, Frieda. But even soldiers roll with backup." His eyes stayed locked on hers — calm, warm, like they might hold the streetlight back for a second.

"Why'd you help me?" she asked. Her voice was sharp to hide the ache behind it.

Dante leaned back a bit, shrugging like it wasn't complicated. "'Cause I saw you. And you looked like somebody who's had enough people walk past."

The words hit her ribs so hard she almost flinched. She swallowed the sting before it could show on her face.

"Thanks," she muttered, glancing down at her shoes, one toe kicking at a cracked bit of pavement.

"You got somewhere you're heading?"

She paused, lips pressing together. "Not really."

Dante nodded — slow, patient, like he could read every word she didn't say. "I get that. Listen — how 'bout you walk with me? Just 'til we hit the main drag. I won't talk your ear off. Won't ask for your number. Just don't want you alone till you hit the lights."

Part of her bristled. The other part — the cracked, quiet part — gave in. She nodded.

They started walking. His pace matched hers — no rush, no lagging behind. The streets muttered around them: a car backfiring somewhere far off, wind tugging at old flyers at the bus stop, a neon sign buzzing half-dead over a closed pawn shop. He didn't push. But when he spoke again, his voice was gentle, a soft scrape in the dark.

"You runnin' from something?"

Frieda's eyes flicked up at him, then away. "Maybe."

He didn't laugh. Didn't tease. Just nodded once like that was all he needed.

By the time they reached the next intersection — a corner splashed with harsh white light from a busted bus shelter — Frieda slowed to a stop. She could hear her pulse in her ears again, but it didn't feel like fear this time.

Dante leaned against the shelter's metal pole, arms folded, watching her with that same steady stare. "You don't owe me nothing," he said, voice low, nearly drowned out by a passing car. "Girl like you — you got fire in you. I can see it."

Frieda scoffed, but it came out soft. "You don't know anything about me."

Dante's grin curved at one edge, a flicker of warmth in a city that hadn't given her much of that lately. He brushed an invisible speck of lint off his sleeve, eyes still locked on hers.

"I know you mad at the world. I know you been through stuff you don't talk about. And I know you need somebody who don't look at you like you already broken."

That last part — it landed so clean and cruel it made her breath stick in her throat. She turned her face away, hoping he wouldn't see the shine in her eyes. But he didn't reach for her. Didn't crowd her. He just *stood there,* holding space like maybe that was enough. And for a girl who had felt invisible for so long, *being seen* was almost too much to hold.

For the first time in weeks, the night didn't feel like claws waiting to tear her open. It felt almost soft — like maybe there were still corners where a girl like her could stand and not fall straight through.

Dante didn't say goodbye when he pushed off the pole and stepped back toward the crosswalk. He just tipped his chin, one last glance over his shoulder, and walked on.

And Frieda stood there — cold breath fogging the bus shelter glass — wondering if maybe, just maybe, being seen could be its own kind of armor. And if maybe, just maybe, *this* — this moment — was what love might feel like when you'd never really had it.

The Turning Veil

THE NEXT NIGHT, Frieda found herself standing in the hallway outside Dante's apartment — its paint chipped and door slightly warped from years of careless slams. The cracked peephole above the tarnished doorknob stared back at her like an eye that didn't blink. She hesitated just long enough for the cold draft from the stairwell to chill her ankles.

Then she knocked — soft at first, then harder. The door swung open, and there he was. Dante. Hoodie sleeves pushed up, cigarette tucked behind his ear, that easy smile he knew made her feel safe.

"Hey, Queen," he murmured, voice hushed as he stepped back to let her in.

Inside, the warmth was immediate — not from the rattling radiator that clicked like it might give out any moment, but from the small comforts scattered in the clutter. A candle burned low on the coffee table. A battered couch sagged under a mountain of mismatched blankets. The wallpaper peeled in curling edges by the ceiling, and the kitchen sink dripped into a pile of chipped mugs. It wasn't much — not by any measure Frieda had once known — but it was *his*. And somehow, that made it feel like hers too.

She sank onto the couch, letting the scent of old incense and fried chicken cling to her hoodie. Dante pulled the cigarette from behind his ear, tossed it on the table, and brushed a hand through her curls, thumb grazing her temple.

"You good?" he asked, voice like velvet scraped over gravel.

She nodded. It didn't matter if it was true. For a while, that small space felt like love. Or the closest thing she'd ever touched to it. She could stay late — sleep deep into the morning, his arm draped heavy across her waist. Sometimes she'd wake to his breath in her hair, the word *Queen* falling from his lips like a secret prayer.

In that cracked mirror above his bathroom sink, she saw a girl who wasn't invisible anymore. He said she was beautiful before she could argue with the reflection. He didn't flinch when her eyes were red from old grief. He didn't mind the way she shut down when the past rose up. In those nights, in that warmth, Frieda let herself believe she was more than the broken thing Lois prayed over every night. But the sweetness soured slowly — like milk turned in the fridge you forgot to check.

It began with a shrug that felt too cold when she asked where he'd been all night. A look that flicked past her like she was a window, not a girl. She laughed too loud once — he flinched, jaw tightening, eyes sliding toward the window instead of her. He came home smelling of cheap perfume and half-spilled liquor, cigarette smoke clinging to his collar. *"You worry too much,"* he'd mumble, brushing her aside with the same hand that once traced her jaw so soft.

Nights grew longer. So did the silences. Sometimes he wouldn't come back until dawn, the door creaking open on its rusty hinges, his boots tracking in the cold. Some mornings he'd slip beside her on the couch like nothing had changed, whispering sweet words into her hair that no longer stuck.

Other mornings, he'd stand by the cracked window, shoulders hunched, cigarette burning down to ash between his fingers. He'd say nothing. And she knew better than to ask. But she stayed. God help her, she stayed.

She snuck out of Lois's house more nights than she could count — toes cold on that same creaky floorboard, window easing open with a sigh she now knew by heart. She crawled through dark streets like a ghost looking for a grave that felt like a heartbeat instead. Because pain you know is easier than hope you don't trust.

ONE MORNING, THE WORLD SHIFTED. Not loudly. Just two pink lines — sharp, undeniable — staring back at her from the bathroom of a gas station that smelled like stale mop water and burnt coffee.

Frieda's fingers trembled around the plastic stick. Her reflection in the cracked mirror looked older — hollows under her eyes where sleep had run dry, lips cracked from too many cigarettes she'd never lit herself. She didn't look sixteen. She didn't look ready. But for a breath — for a heartbeat — she almost smiled. Because maybe this tiny thing, this flicker of life under her ribs, would be hers. Really hers.

Dante's reaction cut that thought clean. She stood in his apartment, stick clutched in her fist like proof she couldn't swallow. He leaned back in his chair, elbows on knees, eyes narrowed at the floor.

"You can't keep that," he said — flat, like asking her to toss out spoiled leftovers.

"But... It's mine," Frieda whispered. The word caught in her throat. *Mine.*

Dante didn't blink. Didn't flinch. His jaw worked once, grinding out whatever patience he'd scraped up. "You ain't ready. We ain't ready. Don't make this mess bigger than it gotta be."

He pulled his wallet from his pocket, flicked through bent cards until he found one — a business card, the corners soft from years in the fold. He tapped numbers into the rotary payphone down the block while she watched from the window — snow drifting past the cracked glass, soft as ash. He made the appointment like he ordered takeout. Gave her a look that said *Don't argue.* Paid in crumpled bills he never explained.

THE CLINIC SMELLED LIKE ANTISEPTIC and old flowers someone forgot to change. The nurse didn't meet her eyes. The chair was cold. The hum of the machines droned over prayers she didn't know how to say anymore.

When it was done, Frieda sat by the window, the foggy glass framing her reflection — split by tiny cracks she couldn't smooth with her thumb. Her palms rested on her empty lap. One tear slipped warm down her cheek, trailing salt over skin already raw. She didn't wipe it away. Just let it fall. And into that cold, sterile silence, she breathed a whisper so small it barely reached the glass:

"God, if You're still there… please don't let this be all I am."

Outside, the wind picked up. Somewhere down the street, a church bell rang six times. And somewhere inside Frieda Winslow — cracked wide and hollow — the echo of a prayer waited for an answer she wasn't sure would come.

Frieda didn't go back to Dante's that night. She didn't even decide not to — her feet just kept moving, street after street, until the city swallowed her up in its sleepless hum. She drifted past shuttered storefronts with metal grates pulled tight like tired eyelids. Past traffic lights blinking yellow into empty intersections. Past streetlamps that buzzed overhead — harsh, white, and constant, like flies circling wounds that wouldn't close. Her sneakers scraped against the wet grit of the pavement. Every step felt heavier than the last, her shoulders pulled forward by a gravity she couldn't name. Her breath made small clouds in the chill. Once she paused beneath a streetlight and tilted her face upward, half hoping rain would come — a cold baptism to hide the tears she was too tired to shed. But the sky held its breath, just like her.

By the time Frieda slipped through Lois's yard, the horizon was the color of ash — a pale bruise of dawn that made the whole block look worn thin. She pushed her bedroom window open with frozen fingers, careful not to wake the house with its soft sigh of old hinges.

She crawled through like a ghost that had forgotten how to haunt, her knees landing hard on the creaking floorboards. She didn't bother with her shoes. She didn't peel off her hoodie. She just folded into her bed like a question with no answer, blanket dragged over her like an apology. Sleep didn't come. Only the hush. The ache. The sound of her own heartbeat reminding her she was still here.

THE NEXT MORNING, Frieda drifted into the kitchen like a shadow. Lois was already at the stove, back turned, shoulders wrapped in that same faded housecoat that smelled faintly of starch and peppermint oil. The hiss of pancake batter hitting the griddle filled the air, soft and steady. She moved slowly — flipping each one with care, her lips moving in a silent prayer Frieda could almost catch if she tried. She didn't ask where Frieda had been. Didn't demand an explanation. Didn't reach for the rules they both knew by heart. She just set a plate on the table — pancakes stacked neatly, butter melting into syrup—a folded napkin. A small gesture that felt like more than forgiveness — it felt like armor she didn't deserve.

Frieda lowered herself into the chair. The wooden legs scraped the linoleum. She stared at the plate — the steam curling around her nose, the sweet warmth sinking into her hollow belly — and she felt nothing but the iron weight of shame. Her stomach cramped, but it wasn't hunger. Not anymore. She tore at the edge of one pancake with her fork — slow, quiet, shredding it into ragged strips she didn't eat.

"Thank you," she whispered, the words so faint they barely crossed the space between them.

Lois paused at the stove, spatula hovering in her hand. She turned — just enough to see Frieda's bent head — and in her eyes flickered something like surprise. She didn't say *You're welcome.*

Didn't preach. She just nodded once and turned back to her quiet work, letting the oil crackle fill the silence between them.

FOR THE NEXT THREE DAYS, Frieda moved through the world like she was underwater. Sounds reached her as if from the bottom of a pool — muffled, distant. Her feet found familiar paths — school, the sidewalk outside the corner store — but she didn't see them. Didn't feel the cold seeping into her bones or the wind that tugged at her hair like an old memory. Her phone stayed dark in her pocket. Dante didn't call. Didn't show up at the corner. Didn't ask.

On the third day, when the ache pressed so hard she thought it would split her ribs, she found the old landline in Lois's hallway — the one that still clung to the wall by a fraying cord. Her fingers shook so badly she misdialed twice, breath catching in her throat every time the rotary wheel spun back. When he finally answered, his voice was flat — thick with sleep or something else she didn't want to imagine.

"Yeah?"

She pressed her lips together, heartbeat hammering.

"It's done," she said. Her voice sounded small in her own ears.

A pause. A rustle. Then only one word — cold, final, like a door slamming shut.

"Good."

A click. A dead line. The dial tone buzzed in her palm — louder than his silence. Frieda stared at the receiver long after the dial tone faded. It felt heavier than the phone itself, like it carried all the weight he'd refused to hold.

THAT NIGHT, Frieda didn't lie in her bed. She sat cross-legged on the floor beside it, the old lamp turned off so the shadows could settle around her like a blanket. Her knees touched the cold floorboards. A Bible — pages uncreased, corners sharp from neglect — sat unopened by her hip. In her lap, a scrap of paper: her mother's note, its ink faded, the fold lines worn soft from years hidden in a drawer.

"You are more than the worst thing that ever happens to you."

She read the words over and over until they blurred. She pressed them flat against her thigh like maybe they'd soak through her skin and mend what she'd torn open. She rocked gently — forward, back — the silence pressing close enough to hear her breath catch at the edges. Then, when the hush felt too wide to hold alone, she did something she hadn't dared in weeks. She whispered His name.

"God..."

It fell out of her like a confession and a plea all at once — the word so small it made her ribs ache. And in that crack, the tears came — slow at first, then sharp and flooding, sobs punching out of her chest in jagged gasps that ripped through the room like a hymn no one taught her to sing. Not for Dante. Not for the baby. But for the girl she'd buried under every lie, every street corner, every *good* that was never real. She rocked forward until her forehead touched her knees, her mother's note crumpled in her fist like a lifeline.

As the first pale light of dawn cut through the blinds, soft and gold against her skin, Frieda's voice found shape again — raw and hushed but alive.

"I don't know how to start again..." she breathed, each word a splinter pried loose. "But I want to."

The hush held her. And somewhere in that fragile hush, something holy cracked open. And this time, she didn't close it back up.

Snapped

Days later, the living room felt too bright — the kind of bright that made Frieda's eyes sting. Late afternoon sun cut through the old lace curtains in hard slats, carving stripes of gold and shadow across the scuffed hardwood. Dust drifted lazily through the beams, tiny ghosts swirling with every shallow breath she took.

She stood stiff, rooted like something half-dead and stubborn about it. Her backpack hung off one shoulder — frayed strap digging into her collarbone, half-broken zipper, sagging under the weight of everything she didn't want to carry anymore. When she spoke, her voice came out flat — a stone dropped into a dry well.

"I had an abortion." The words cracked the air. Fell heavy. Sank.

Across the room, Lois sat in her old recliner by the window. A magnifying lamp hummed softly above her shoulder, its glow spilling over the gentle arc of her back as she stitched blue thread through linen cloth. The quiet hum of a hymn rose and fell in her throat — *"Nearer, my God, to Thee…"*

She didn't flinch. Didn't miss a stitch.

Frieda's arms twitched at her sides, fists clenched so tight her knuckles burned white. "Did you hear me?" she snapped, louder now, her voice splintering at the edges. "I said I had an abortion."

Slowly, Lois lifted her head. The lamp caught the silver in her lashes, the deep creases around her eyes — eyes that looked at

Frieda like they could see past bone and blood, all the way down to the ragged corners she'd tried to keep hidden.

"I heard you," she said. Calm. Steady. She laid the hoop of cloth carefully in her lap, removed her glasses with slow fingers, folded them once — click — and set them on the armrest. Her hands rested on her knees, palms up like a quiet surrender.

Frieda's breath caught. Her pulse thundered in her neck. The silence between them felt too wide, too raw.

"So… aren't you gonna yell? Huh?" She let out a bitter laugh, sharp as cut glass. "Kick me out? Tell me how I'm going to hell? Quote your precious Bible at me like it fixes what I did?"

Lois's chest rose and fell with a long, heavy exhale. She didn't blink.

"I knew," she said, her voice low — heavy as church bells.

Frieda's head jerked back. "What?"

"I knew," Lois repeated. She spoke like someone reading her own heartbreak off a page she'd worn thin with prayer. "Every night. I heard you slip that window open. I heard your shoes hit the grass. I prayed, Frieda. Lord knows I did. But you — you've been lockin' your heart up tight since the day you walked through this door. Tight against me, tight against Him. You think these walls are prison bars, but baby — they're the only thing holdin' you together."

The words cracked something deep in Frieda's chest. She stepped forward, shoulders bristling like a struck match.

"Stop it," she hissed. Her eyes shone, but she refused to let them spill. "Stop talking about Him. God. What has God ever done for me, huh? Where was He when my mom cried herself to sleep night after night? Where was He when my dad pointed that gun at her and— and—." Her voice broke, caught on the raw edge of memory.

Lois rose — slow, deliberate — and even standing, she felt taller than the room could hold. Her voice, when it came, was iron wrapped in velvet. Thunder that didn't need to shout.

"Don't you raise your voice in this house, Frieda Winslow. You may not believe in Him, but I do. And as long as I draw breath and you lay your head under my roof, you will show respect. For me. For this home. For the God who held you when you didn't know you were being held."

Frieda's mouth fell open — then snapped shut. Her chest rose and fell, jagged. Rage and grief tangled behind her ribs until she felt sick with it.

"I hate you," she spat. The words came out so small, so vicious. "You're just some old, bitter woman clingin' to fairy tales 'cause you're too scared to face the truth. I wish you'd—die!"

Her hands flew out — a shove, clumsy and mean. Lois stumbled back, landing hard on the edge of the couch. Her glasses tumbled from the armrest, clattering against the floorboards. A picture frame on the wall trembled, tipped, and crashed face-first. The glass fractured like ice under a boot heel — shards skittering across the rug. Silence swallowed the room.

Frieda's breath came fast — ragged, burning. She couldn't look at Lois — couldn't look at the broken glass or the hymn book half-buried under the couch. She turned — fists tight, shoulders coiled — and stormed through the front door so hard the screen slammed against the frame, rattling like the last word she had the guts to speak.

Outside, dusk draped the street in bruised purple. The air smelled like rain ready to break. Frieda's steps hit the sidewalk hard — boot soles slapping puddles, scattering grit. Streetlights flickered above her like indifferent stars, casting long shadows that twisted as she passed.

She didn't know where she was going, only that it was away. Away from that living room. Away from those prayers. Away from that suffocating, stubborn love she didn't think she deserved. Into a night that felt wide and reckless and hungry — waiting to swallow her whole.

The Night of Nowhere

IT WAS LATE AUTUMN in Frampton — the kind of night when the air bit at your cheeks and carried the faint, ghostly scent of burning leaves drifting from someone's backyard firepit down the block. But Frieda didn't smell it. Didn't feel the sting of cold on her face. Didn't hear the wind rattle the loose gutter spikes overhead or the far-off bark of a chained-up dog or the rising, falling wail of sirens across the rail yard. All she heard was her heartbeat — too fast, too loud — pounding out a rhythm to match the rage that burned behind her ribs like kindling.

You've been lockin' your heart up tight since the day you walked through this door.

Lois's voice pressed against the inside of her skull — soft as iron, stubborn as stone — and the echo of it made her jaw clench so tight it ached. She spat a curse under her breath, breath white in the chill, and turned the corner so fast her sneaker scraped an old pothole, nearly pitching her forward. She didn't stop. Couldn't. The cracked pavement under her feet changed with every block — smoother by the liquor store with the burnt-out sign, rougher by the old auto shop with its busted windows and fresh graffiti, someone's tag looping wild over the rusted door.

Outside the corner store, boys leaned against a wall, their laughter sharp and reckless in the dark. One of them glanced her way — eyes flicking from her face to her fists jammed in her hoodie pocket, then back again. He said something to his friend, and they laughed harder. But she didn't flinch. Didn't break stride. She kept walking. Past the alley where she'd once watched a girl trade fear for survival, a girl barely older than she'd been when her mother's screams still filled their house at night. Past the closed laundromat with its cracked windows, its half-torn posters fluttering like wounded flags. Everything looked the same. Everything looked wrong.

She didn't know where she was going. She just knew stopping was dangerous — because standing still meant remembering what she'd done, what she'd said.

"I wish you'd—die."

The words crawled up her throat again, raw and jagged, every repetition a fresh slice under her ribs. She hadn't meant it. Not really. But it had come out so fast, so ugly, like poison spit she couldn't swallow back down.

She slowed when the chain-link fence behind the old rec center came into view — sagging, half-bent where kids squeezed through to cut across the lot. She paused there, fingers hooking through cold steel, breath steaming in the dark. The lot was empty. Moonlight fell hard and cold on broken glass that glittered like ice across the cracked asphalt. The old basketball court sat silent, the hoops missing nets, backboards cracked down the middle like broken teeth.

She slipped through the fence, careful not to snag her hoodie, and crossed the court's flaking paint lines. Halfway across, her legs gave out. She fell to her knees. Hands curled tight in the fabric of her hoodie. Her shoulders heaved — up, down — but no tears came. Only her breath, fogging the night. Only the cold bleeding into her bones through the thin denim at her knees. The sky above her was a bruise — deep purple bleeding into black, stars scattered like salt flung across an empty plate.

"God," she rasped, voice raw, scratching her throat on the way out. "If You're up there... then say something."

Nothing. No whisper. No hush of wind through the bare trees. The clouds didn't part. The moon didn't shift.

"You let her die," Frieda spat, the words hitting the court hard enough to echo back at her. "You let me become this."

A sob cracked through her chest, sudden and sharp. She pressed her sleeve to her mouth and screamed into the fabric — a sound so low and guttural it scraped her insides raw but didn't empty the ache. It lingered — all that pain — thick as smoke.

She stayed there until her knees ached and her breath turned shallow from the cold. Until her spine curled and her body gave in. She lay down flat on the rough court, the grit biting her shoulder blades, the stars splintering overhead through her wet lashes. She remembered counting them once — little dots of promise. Her mother's voice beside her, pointing out constellations, whispering wishes for the girl she'd never get to see grow up safe. Now they felt too far away. All of it did.

When her legs finally carried her off the court, they led her nowhere — just miles of cracked sidewalks, dead lawns, streetlights humming their harsh white glow. She drifted until her feet blistered raw inside cheap sneakers, until her throat was sandpaper from sobs that wouldn't come again.

By dawn, she found herself curled beneath the splintered awning of a boarded-up church — its front doors locked, its windows nailed with weathered plywood, *GOD IS LOVE* spray-painted in faded white across the brick. She pulled her knees up, forehead pressed to them, the night's cold still trapped in her sleeves. Inside her pocket, her fingers found the edge of that note she always swore she'd burn — the one from her mother — the paper soft with wear, stubborn with memory. But she didn't pull it out. She wasn't ready to look at it. She wasn't ready to go back. And the worst part was — she wasn't sure she *wanted* to. Above her, the first gray streaks of dawn split the sky — thin as veins, pale as a promise she didn't know how to trust.

The Prayer Chair

THE FRONT DOOR CLUNG HALF-OPEN on its loose hinge, letting in a draft that carried the night's raw chill straight through the hall. It lifted the lace curtain by the window in slow, tremoring breaths — a ghost of motion that made the quiet feel alive.

Glass glittered across the hardwood where the picture frame had fallen — splinters of memory scattered like frozen tears. They caught the last slant of dusk coming in through the doorway, throwing tiny stars of light at Lois's feet. She hadn't moved much from where Frieda had left her — half-folded on the couch, one hand braced against the armrest for balance, the other limp in her lap where her sewing had fallen. The needle dangled from the loose blue thread, swaying slightly each time she breathed.

Her eyes were open — not red, not weeping, but bright and raw around the edges like a fresh wound. Her lips pressed together. She took in a long, quiet breath that shook the line of her shoulders, then let it out in a whisper that made no sound at all.

When her legs found their strength, Lois straightened her cardigan at the shoulders, smoothed the wrinkled fabric over her chest. She pushed herself to her feet slowly — joints creaking — and stooped to gather the sewing, careful not to tangle the thread. She laid it gently on the side table, as if still hoping she might pick it up again when the ache passed. She moved to the glass next. Each step made her knees ache, but she bent anyway — swept the broken shards into a metal dustpan with a soft rasp. The tiny shards clinked together like distant wind chimes as she tipped them into the trash. She set the empty frame, its edges sharp and pitiful, onto the kitchen counter — almost tenderly, like setting down an old photograph you weren't ready to look at again.

The house had gone completely still. The hum of the refrigerator seemed to hold its breath. No ticking clock from the hallway — just silence, thick and waiting.

Lois's hand drifted to the silver cross at her chest. She felt the chain cool against her skin, the metal small but so solid in her palm. She pressed it there until the shape etched itself into her skin. Then, with slow steps, she crossed the living room to her favorite chair — the old wingback tucked into the corner near the bookshelf. The cushion knew the shape of her knees, the dip of her shoulders, the press of prayers so many mornings and nights. The rug beneath it had grown pale where sunlight had knelt with her year after year. She lowered herself into it, joints protesting. Folded her hands together until her knuckles whitened. Bowed her head.

"Lord…"

The word slipped out like a sigh that cracked on the edges. Worn thin from so many nights like this one.

"She's so angry," Lois whispered, eyes shut tight. "So hurt. And I don't know what else to do for her."

She paused — listened for any creak, any stirring in the quiet. Nothing answered but the wind rattling the eaves. She opened her hands — palms lifted now, like an offering — and turned her eyes toward the ceiling, where shadows danced in the soft lamplight.

"I've said all I know to say," she breathed. "I've prayed every verse that's ever carried me through. I've tried to fight gentle. To love fierce. To stand in that hallway waiting for her to come home. But Lord — this battle… this one's Yours now."

Her voice cracked, and she rocked forward in her chair, leaning her elbows to her knees as if pushing the words up through the roof might carry them faster to the sky.

"She's not bad, Lord. She's just broken. Just a girl drowning in her own sorrow, looking for any place to set it down. You see her — even when she don't want You to. Even when she don't want me."

A tear slipped out then. It clung to her lashes before dropping, darkening a threadbare patch on her skirt. She didn't wipe it away.

"And if I'm the only one left standin' in the gap for her — then I'll stand, Lord. But I'm so tired. Tired in places I didn't know could grow weary. I need You to hold this ground with me — 'cause tonight, my knees feel too soft for this fight."

She drew in another long breath, the kind that scraped her ribs—reached for her Bible on the small table beside the chair. The cover fell open easily — worn leather, corners soft from years of turning. It found Psalm 91 on its own. Her eyes settled on the verse her fingers brushed — verse eleven — her lips shaping the words in a whisper that quivered but didn't break.

"'For He will command His angels concerning you... to guard you in all your ways.'"

She closed her eyes. Drew the cross to her chest. Rocked once more in that old chair that smelled of lemon oil and lavender sachets.

"Amen," she said softly — a word that settled the air around her like a quilt pulled up against the dark.

The phone on the hallway table rang. Once. Twice. Sharp in the hush, startling as a shout. Lois stiffened. Wiped her eyes with the back of her sleeve and forced her bones up out of the prayer chair. She shuffled to the receiver, lifting it with hands that trembled more than they used to.

"Hello?"

A pause. The familiar soft drawl of her cousin Irene, who also went by the name Lois, from Mississippi filled the line — gentle, but urgent.

"Lois? Honey, I hate to trouble you so sudden... but it's Clara. She's bad off, Lois. The doctor says if you want to see her again, you best come home now."

Lois's breath caught. Clara — her sister. Her oldest friend. The girl she'd shared Sunday dresses and secrets with. The woman who'd held her hand at the funeral. The last of her people down South.

"Oh, Irene..." Lois's voice quivered. "How bad?"

"Bad, Lo. She needs you. You know she won't rest if you don't come sit beside her. You know how she is."

Lois sank back into the hallway chair, the phone pressed hard to her ear, the cord tangling in her lap. Her eyes drifted to the open living room — the broken frame on the counter, the prayer chair waiting, the door half-open like it might catch Frieda drifting home on the wind. She swallowed the ache. Nodded, though Irene couldn't see it.

"All right," she whispered. "I'll come. Soon as I can."

When she hung up, she sat still for a long time, the phone cradle clicking quietly beside her. Her hand returned to the cross at her throat.

"Lord… how do I leave her now?"

The house answered with silence. She didn't know. But dawn would come — and with it, a choice. And for once in her life, Lois Winston didn't have an answer ready on her tongue.

Awakening

THE MORNING LIGHT BLED through the diner's greasy windows in slow, watery streaks — not gold, not warm, but the pale gray of a sky that didn't care if you made it home or didn't. It cast everything in a half-light: the chipped counter, the flickering neon sign that buzzed above the door, the rows of cracked vinyl booths that smelled like stale coffee and old stories nobody bothered to finish.

Frieda lay curled in the corner of one such booth — knees pulled tight, one sneaker hanging off her foot by the heel. Her coat, rolled into a makeshift pillow, smelled of sweat and cold night air. The tattered fleece blanket draped over her shoulders clung to her like damp paper, its faint mildew scent mixing with the sharp tang of burnt toast drifting from the kitchen.

Outside the window, her reflection hovered ghostlike on the glass — half-smeared by condensation that dripped down in thin trails, blurring her eyes, her hair, her mouth. She watched it with a kind of dull fascination. She looked hollow. She felt it too — the emptiness stretching from the hollow of her chest down to where her toes curled inside her fraying socks.

Behind the counter, the morning shift clinked and muttered — the metallic clatter of coffee pots, the scrape of butter across dry toast, the squeak of a spatula on a well-worn griddle. Somewhere near the kitchen door, a baby fussed against its mother's shoulder, the soft hiccup of a child trying not to cry.

Frieda didn't move. Didn't blink. Her eyes traced a droplet racing down the window, trailing through the steam marks where someone's breath had once lingered. Pieces of the night flickered through her mind like the broken frames of an old film — her fists tight at her sides, Lois's steady eyes gone wide, the shove that felt too big for her small hands, the picture frame that shattered like ice under boots.

And then — the silence.

The hush that had swallowed her up so thoroughly, she hadn't even realized she'd wandered for miles — past darkened storefronts and flickering streetlights, through alleys that smelled like sour garbage and old rain. Until her legs gave out and she'd stumbled inside this place — the diner that didn't ask questions, didn't close its doors, didn't look too hard at kids who looked like trouble.

She didn't mean to sleep. She didn't mean to stay. But here she was — half-waking in the scent of burnt coffee and cheap disinfectant.

A soft shape moved into her peripheral vision — the waitress, a woman in her fifties with tired shoulders and a kindness behind her eyes that made Frieda want to look away. She carried a chipped mug of coffee and a bowl that steamed like the promise of something warm.

"On the house," the woman said, her voice rough but gentle, as if it had been scraped clean by too many early mornings. "You look like you need it."

Frieda didn't answer — couldn't trust her throat to open. Her gaze stayed on the steam rising from the bowl, curling up in ghostly ribbons, like prayers that didn't quite reach heaven.

The waitress set the mug down carefully, sliding a paper napkin under it to catch the drip. She nudged the oatmeal closer.

"Bathroom's back there if you want to wash up, sugar," she added, her words brushing Frieda's raw edges like a warm cloth. "No rush. You just rest a minute."

Frieda nodded, barely. The motion felt huge. Her throat burned but her eyes stayed dry — a betrayal she didn't know how to fix. She wrapped both hands around the bowl. The warmth seeped into her palms, up her wrists, settling in her bones like an ache being soothed. She didn't lift the spoon. She just held the heat. Her mouth moved before she knew it.

"I'm sorry."

It came out cracked, so soft it barely reached the space between her and the window. Not loud enough for the waitress to hear, not pointed at anyone in particular — not Lois, not God, not even herself in the glass. But it was real. And it lingered in the steam, the booth, the hush of the all-night diner. Maybe it wasn't enough to fix anything. Maybe it never would be. But it was something.

She didn't know what to do next — where she'd go when the coffee went cold and the street swallowed her up again. But her hands were warm now. And for the first time in days, she let herself wonder if maybe — just maybe — she couldn't run forever. And maybe she wouldn't have to.

Lost in the Fire

Three months had passed — three months that felt like a single, endless night with no morning on the other side. Frieda sat hunched in the last row of a battered city bus, her spine pressed tight against the cold metal seat. Her hoodie was pulled so low over her brow it cast her eyes in shadow — not that she cared if anyone looked. Her eyes were raw, rimmed in red from too many nights staring at cracked ceilings, park benches, bus station walls. Sleep came in fits — scraps stolen between noise and fear and memories she couldn't outrun.

Her backpack, small and sagging, rested like dead weight in her lap. Inside: a pair of torn jeans, a faded T-shirt, a travel-size deodorant rolling loose in the seams. And deep in the side pocket, folded and re-folded until the corners had begun to split, was the photograph — her mother's smile caught in time. A smile Frieda gripped at night like a lifeline she kept losing hold of.

The bus jolted over a pothole, rattling her bones. The stale air smelled of wet coats, old metal, and something sour that reminded her how long it had been since she'd eaten — yesterday morning, maybe longer. Her stomach twisted around the memory but stayed quiet. Hunger had learned how to make itself small.

Outside the window, the city dragged by — rain sheeting down in streaks that turned headlights into smeared ghosts. Streetlights blinked dull yellow. Cars hissed through puddles.

Everything was blurred and too bright, like she was underwater and couldn't surface.

Then — brakes. A screech. A shudder that rattled her teeth. The bus lurched, and Frieda lifted her head, blinking as the world snapped back into focus. Two seats ahead, a man in a frayed windbreaker leaned into his phone, his voice low but sharp enough to cut through the hum of the bus.

"Yeah, Walker Street — burned all night. Lady didn't make it out. House gone, just gone. Whole block's talkin' about it. Tragic."

Walker Street.

Frieda's pulse slammed so hard it hurt her ribs. Her lips parted, but no sound came out. She didn't feel the cold metal seat anymore — just the roar in her ears.

No. Please, no.

She shoved herself up so fast her knee knocked the seat in front of her. Someone muttered an insult but it didn't land. She pushed past elbows, backpacks, stale breath, half-spoken curses — the bus driver shouting at her to watch herself as she stumbled down the rubber steps and into the rain. The city swallowed her whole. The downpour hit her skin like pinpricks, cold enough to steal her breath but not enough to numb the terror. She half-ran, half-slid across the slick street, traffic lights blurring red and green above her. Her feet pounded over the wet sidewalk, soaked sneakers slapping against puddles that splashed up her shins.

She ducked into the convenience store on the corner, door chime jingling sharp and shrill above her head. Fluorescent lights buzzed overhead, humming like a hive about to break. Frieda's fingers fumbled at the stack of newspapers by the door. She grabbed the top one — the ink already smudged where the rain dripped from her cuffs. Her hands trembled so badly she nearly tore the paper in half as she flipped through it. Page four. The headline waited like a knife.

LOCAL WOMAN DIES IN OVERNIGHT HOUSE FIRE
Electrical Fault Suspected. Home Completely Destroyed.
Remains Shipped to Mississippi for Burial
Name Released: Lois Winston

The paper slipped from her grip. It fell in slow motion — pages fluttering like wings that couldn't lift anything. Frieda sank with it. Her knees slammed the cold tile, a sharp pain shooting up her legs, but she didn't flinch. Her hands pressed against the newsprint as if she could smudge it into something else — another name, another house.

"No… please no…"

The words tangled with her breath, thin and ragged. A sob clawed its way up, tearing her throat raw. She covered her face with both palms — palms that still smelled faintly of rain and bus metal and cold, cheap coffee. All she could see was Lois's face — lined, soft, waiting at the window. The way she'd said *"I'll stand in the gap."* The way Frieda had spat poison in her face and slammed the door as if goodbye didn't matter.

"I hate you… I wish you'd die."

The hum of the store faded into a dull echo — the low beep of a register, a child whining for candy, a man muttering about lottery tickets. The cashier called out to her — something distant, something she couldn't gather into sense.

Slowly, on unsteady legs, Frieda gathered the crumpled paper, clutching it to her chest like it might forgive her if she held it tight enough. She pushed through the door into the wet dawn. The cold wind bit at her collar. The street smelled of soot and ash — a phantom echo of something precious gone to smoke. Somewhere, beyond the rooftops, she thought she saw a plume of dark haze still curling skyward where the house used to stand. She stopped on the corner. The rain stuck to her lashes. Her breath came in broken shivers.

"I'm sorry," she whispered into the gray morning. Her voice cracked like glass — too soft, too late.

The street didn't answer. And the dead — they stayed silent.

The Ashes of Mercy

THE NEXT DAY, Frieda came back to Walker Street — not because she wanted to, but because her feet carried her there like they knew she needed to stand in the ruin she'd made, whether she was ready or not. She needed to see the aftermath of her rage, her rebellion, and her callousness.

The sky above the neighborhood sagged low and bruised, swollen with clouds that threatened rain but refused to break open. Smoke still lingered in the air, mixing with the stale scent of wet ash that clung to the cracked sidewalks. Bits of charred insulation blew down the curb like blackened petals from a dead tree. Yellow caution tape fluttered around what was left of the house — bright against the soot, dancing lazily in the wind like a cruel party streamer left after the guests had fled.

Frieda stopped at the edge of the barrier. Her breath turned white in the chill, drifting upward and vanishing like all the words she'd never said. She should have turned away, gone back to the bus stop, to nowhere in particular. But her legs didn't listen. She stepped over the tape. Her boots sank into ash and shards of scorched glass crunched beneath her soles. The front yard — once neatly clipped, once dotted with Lois's potted lilies and thrift-store lawn statues — was a smear of gray mud and splintered wood. A cracked garden angel lay face down in the gutter, its wings chipped and charred.

Where the porch had been, there was only the skeletal frame of what once held a door. The front steps had caved in on themselves. Frieda found the old floral welcome mat, half-buried in soot and debris, its faded roses now black smears under her toe.

She stood there a long moment, chest heaving with something too tangled to name — regret, shame, hunger for a forgiveness she could never touch now. Rain threatened at the edge of the wind, cold pinpricks on her cheeks. She knelt anyway. Her hands dug through wet ash, fingernails scraping wood splinters, bits of scorched insulation clinging to her sleeves. Her fingers trembled as they closed around something cold and small — half-buried in the rubble where Lois's recliner must have been. A thin loop of silver — misshapen by fire but still whole enough to recognize. The little cross pendant Lois had worn every day, tucked under cardigans and pinned above her heart when she prayed over soup and Sunday devotions.

Frieda lifted it slowly. Ash streaked her palms. She pressed the warped cross to her chest, the chill of it sinking through her hoodie like a question she wasn't sure she deserved to ask. Her lips moved before her mind caught up.

"I didn't come back," she whispered — the words torn at the edges, softer than the hiss of the wind cutting through the beams overhead. "You prayed for me. And I never came back."

She sank lower, knees pressing into the cold, wet ruin. The cross dug into her collarbone. It hurt. It needed to.

"I wasn't ready to be loved like that," she confessed to the smoldering bones of what Lois had built for her — this home she'd spit on, run from, never said thank you for.

A gust of wind rattled through the collapsed rafters. Somewhere, a loose piece of gutter creaked like an old weathervane. The whole ruin seemed to breathe around her — a grave and an altar in one.

Frieda curled forward, pressing her forehead to her fists, to the ash, to the cold, melted silver in her palm.

"But I will be," she breathed. Her voice was raw. It didn't sound like hope yet — just a promise scraped from the bottom of a soul that had run out of places to hide.

"I will be."

The rain came then, soft but steady. It mingled with the soot on her sleeves, washed streaks down her cheeks she couldn't tell from tears. The cold soaked through her knees, her elbows, her hair. Among the ashes — where mercy had burned and grief had hollowed her out — Frieda let out the only prayer she had left.

"Help me rise."

The wind carried it up through the broken beams. The rain dripped into the ruin. And for a moment, the ruin felt almost holy — a grave where something old had died, but maybe — just maybe — something else could grow.

The Silent Room (Dream Sequence)

THAT NIGHT, Frieda found herself curled tight in the corner of an abandoned building — an old storefront stripped of its glass, its sign bleached blank by years of wind and rain. The floor was concrete and cold as stone. Her thin hoodie clung to her shoulders like damp paper, no match for the drafts that slipped through the cracks in the boarded-up windows. She pulled her knees to her chest and tucked her chin down, breath fogging the darkness in shallow bursts. Sleep took her like a tide — slow, then all at once — dragging her down past the ache in her bones and the rawness in her throat, past the bruised city outside and the ruin she'd left behind.

In the dream, she stood at the edge of Walker Street. But the house wasn't burned. It rose before her whole and unscarred, its porch light spilling soft yellow over the steps like a welcome she'd never earned. The screen door hung open, swinging gently on its old squeaky hinge. A hint of lemon polish and peppermint drifted out — the scent of Saturday mornings and quiet rules and a woman who had prayed over her when no one else would.

Frieda climbed the steps. Her feet made no sound on the worn wood boards. She pushed the door open with the lightest touch, as if afraid it might vanish if she forced it.

Inside, nothing was ruined. The air hummed with a hush that felt alive — not empty but full, like every memory she'd tried to outrun had gathered here, waiting. The recliner sat in its corner by the window, a crocheted blanket folded neatly across the back. The doily on the armrest hadn't shifted an inch. The little wooden cross still hung above the mantle, casting a shadow on the wall in the shape of hope she hadn't been ready to hold.

She drifted through the living room, fingertips brushing the smooth edge of the side table, the frayed arm of the couch. She moved toward the kitchen, where the table sat set for breakfast that would never come — an open Bible in the center, pages soft and wrinkled from years of turning. A pale blue ribbon marked Isaiah — the same book Lois read from when she thought Frieda wasn't listening.

The silence pressed close, but it didn't choke her. It felt like breathing in something she'd lost — the hush of being seen, even when she didn't want to be.

Her feet carried her down the narrow hall. Past the bathroom where Lois used to hum hymns while scrubbing the sink. Past the closet that always smelled like mothballs and cedar. To her old bedroom — the door slightly ajar, just as she'd left it the night she'd spit out her rage and run into the dark. She pushed the door open with her fingertips.

Inside — her bed, still unmade. The blanket a tangle of old patterns. The scent of peppermint oil drifted faintly from the dresser where Lois used to dab a drop on her pillow when she was sick. The cracked windowpane above her bed glowed softly with dream-light, making the shadows gentler than real life ever did. She stepped to the dresser, pulled open the top drawer with care. Inside, wrapped in an old handkerchief, lay the broken picture frame she'd thrown against the wall that last night. She lifted it carefully. The glass was cracked, but the photo inside was still clear: her eighth-grade graduation. Lois behind her, one hand resting proudly and quietly on Frieda's shoulder. Frieda's face caught in an almost-smile, the edges of her eyes questioning, hoping, afraid. She sat on the edge of the bed, the frame balanced in her lap like an heirloom too fragile to hold but too sacred to set down.

Then — footsteps. Soft, certain. She looked up. Lois stood in the doorway. Not the way Frieda imagined her on a gurney of fire and smoke — but whole. As she was. The same silver hair, pulled back in its simple twist. The same eyes that could see through any lie and loved her anyway. The same calm presence that felt like a house built of prayers.

Lois didn't speak. She stepped forward, each step slow and deliberate on the old wood floor. She reached for the frame, lifting it gently from Frieda's shaking hands. Then, her arms came around her granddaughter. Warm, steady. Unyielding as the prayers she'd once whispered into cold walls. Frieda collapsed into the hug. Her chest cracked open — the sobs that came were not polite or quiet, but ragged, fierce things that drenched Lois's shoulder.

Through the storm of her own breath, Frieda heard the whisper. *"Grace didn't leave you."*

It was all Lois said. And it was enough.

When Frieda woke, curled tight in her corner of cold concrete, her cheeks were wet — but her chest felt warm. Tiny, impossible warmth flickering inside her ribs like the pilot light of a stove that had been cold too long. Grace hadn't left. She hadn't risen yet. But somewhere, she felt the first spark that said maybe — maybe — she still could.

Brokenness

Frieda sat hunched beneath the half-collapsed archway behind the shuttered Southside Recreation Center. The old brick and concrete pressed cold against her back, rough and damp where the rain had seeped through the cracks. The rec center had once echoed with shouts and sneakers squeaking on polished gym floors. Now it was just an empty carcass—windows boarded, walls tagged in angry loops of graffiti, weeds clawing through what was left of the basketball court.

She was a ghost in its ribcage. Her hood was pulled low, shadowing her eyes. Her socks were damp, chilled through from nights spent curling up on gritty concrete. She kept her battered duffel bag wedged tight against her side like a shield—her whole life reduced to wrinkled shirts, a cracked bottle of dollar-store lotion, and one photograph: her mother's smile frozen in summer sun that felt centuries away.

Five weeks. Five weeks since the bus ride where she'd heard the word *fire* slip from a stranger's mouth like an accidental curse. Five weeks since she'd read *Lois Winston* on a crumpled newspaper in a corner store she would never go back to. Five weeks since she'd felt her heart give way under a grief too dry for tears. She hadn't cried. Couldn't. The sorrow inside her had turned to sediment— layered, unmovable, lodged deep behind her ribs.

Now the city's pulse drummed beyond the broken walls— horns wailing down State Street, a far-off stereo thumping bass through the night, wind curling under the smashed window like a thief searching for warmth to steal. She drew her knees tighter to her chest. Rocked slightly. Her voice cracked out of her like an echo through an abandoned sanctuary.

"You tried to help me," she murmured to the shadows. Her words vanished into the graffiti and peeling paint. "I wouldn't let you."

She sniffed hard, yanked her duffel open with stiff fingers, seeking her mother's picture the way a child reaches for a nightlight in the dark. Her hand sank through the thin fabric, brushing lint, frayed hems, the brittle corner of that photograph. But something else scraped against her palm. Rough leather. Cracked binding. A weight she recognized but hadn't touched in years.

Frieda's breath caught in her throat. She pulled it free, her pulse spiking. The book was small—brown, scarred by thumbprints and time. *Lois W.* glimmered in faint gold at the corner. Frieda knew every crease on that cover. The spine was soft from mornings Lois spent turning it page by page, reading aloud over stale coffee and cheap tea.

It felt wrong in her hands. Heavy with every prayer she'd mocked, every hymn she'd scoffed at, every time she'd called the house a prison when it was the only place that ever waited up for her.

She turned it over once, twice, as if it might vanish. Her voice cracked the silence. "How…?"

But she knew. Of course, she knew. Lois must have tucked it into the bag the night Frieda stormed out—while she'd raged, slammed doors, spilled cruel words across a living room that smelled like lemon polish and stubborn mercy. Lois, packing hope into pockets Frieda had already turned inside out.

A tremor ran up Frieda's arm. She hugged the book to her chest, pressed her lips tight to stop the sob rising like bile. Then the grief snapped—hard, sharp, bitter. With a strangled cry, she flung the Bible across the dark. It hit the far wall, bounced, and landed open—pages fluttering like wings half-broken. In the slice of moonlight, they shimmered silver, whispering words she couldn't bring herself to read.

"Where were You?" Frieda's voice tore through her throat raw. She pushed her knuckles against her eyes, digging out tears that refused to fall. "Where were You when she burned? When she prayed for me? When I left her alone—like trash?"

The wind answered with a hollow moan through the broken window. Somewhere down the block, a bottle shattered—someone else's anger echoing hers. Frieda's breath came in ragged pulls. Her vision blurred, but not with tears—just the sting of rage turned to ash.

She stared at the Bible where it lay sprawled on the filthy concrete. It didn't glow. It didn't hum. It didn't save. It just waited—like Lois had.

Frieda pulled her knees tighter, forehead pressed to them, heart pounding like a drum with no song to follow. Outside, the city kept moving—its cold, relentless promise: survive or disappear. But inside that ruin of brick and grief, Frieda wasn't sure which she was doing anymore. She only knew she was still breathing. And the Bible lay there in the dark—like a door she wasn't ready to open but couldn't quite leave behind.

The Quiet Spark

SHE HAD MASTERED THE ART OF VANISHING—of making herself smaller than the street noise, thinner than the shadows she slipped through. By day, Frieda drifted like vapor through the half-forgotten corners of the city library, her presence marked only by the faint scent of rain and old wool. She'd claim a seat near the far back, hidden behind towers of battered books with cracked spines and pages that smelled of mildew and neglect. A geometry textbook propped open, a dog-eared novel she never turned a page of. Her eyelids fluttered with exhaustion as she drifted in and out of a fragile sleep, the fluorescent lights overhead humming steadily and pale. Somewhere, a clock ticked. Somewhere, a janitor's cart squeaked past rows of encyclopedias no one touched anymore.

When dusk seeped through the dusty windows, she slipped back outside. No destination. Just movement—her only ritual. She pulled her hoodie tight around her face and walked until the edges of the city blurred, through alleys washed slick with old rain and gutters that swallowed the glow of passing headlights. She learned to watch, but not to make eye contact. To drift past shouting drunks, crouched figures under flickering streetlamps, corners where whispered deals changed trembling hands. She trailed the other girls from time to time—street-tough shadows in battered boots and layered jackets, hair pulled back in tight knots, eyes always scanning. They showed her, wordlessly, how to disappear without becoming prey.

No one asked her name. No one asked why a girl like her—so thin, so quiet—was out here in the cold. They all knew the city didn't ask. The city just took.

Some nights she slipped into the back of a church basement when the doors were unlocked, curling into herself on an old cot while hymnals and warm soup kept other souls from shivering too loud. Other nights, she made do with half-eaten pastries lifted from behind the bakery's dumpster—bitter with coffee grounds, soft enough to pretend they were a meal. But the worst nights—those were the nights she found herself in the abandoned building again. The place with broken windows and graffiti scrawled like secrets on every crumbling wall—the place where she'd screamed her grief at the dark. Where the wind whistled through the beams like an organ no one knew how to play anymore.

Tonight, she was back. Her footsteps brushed across the concrete floor, her breath curling white in the cold air as she reached the far corner where she usually curled up like a stray. The Bible was still there. The same small leather-bound shape she'd flung away nights ago—pages still open, spine bent in silent protest. It hadn't moved. Or maybe it had, in the way things move when no one is watching.

Frieda knelt slowly, knees pressed to the grit and dust. She stared at the open pages. Psalms. She didn't dare read the words. She wasn't ready to hear what they might say. But this time, she didn't shove it away. Didn't kick it under a broken chair or bury it behind the loose bricks. Her fingers hovered over the cover—fingers that had bruised knuckles, raw edges from cold nights and clumsy fights with hunger. She brushed the dust off. Smoothed the creased corner where Lois's thumb must have rested a hundred mornings in that kitchen that smelled of lemon oil and quiet mercy.

She closed the cover. Her hands shook as she tucked it back into her bag, slipping it beside the photo of her mother—two ghosts pressed together in the same dark pocket. The bag felt different on her shoulder now. Heavier. But not just with things. With something she couldn't name. A question. A spark.

Through the boarded window above her, a red neon sign from the liquor store across the alley flickered like a failing heartbeat—red on, red off, red on—painting stripes of bruised light across the wall like stained glass in an abandoned chapel. Frieda drew her knees to her chest. Rested her forehead there. Breathed in the cold and the dust and the faint echo of a hymn that once drifted through the crack under Lois's door when Frieda was still small enough to be found.

"I don't believe in You," she whispered into her sleeves. Her breath made her words warm, soft against her wrists. "But Lois did."

She closed her eyes. Outside, the city moaned and roared and forgot her. But inside this ruined room, she clung to the Bible she couldn't believe in yet—held close like an ember that might one day become a flame.

Cold Love, Colder Streets

FRIEDA WENT BACK TO DANTE like a stray returns to an open door — not because it's warm, but because it's familiar. The apartment hadn't changed. The front door still stuck at the hinges, the knob loose enough to jiggle with a push. Inside, the air hit her like a slap — stale sweat, greasy takeout, cigarettes smoked down to the nub and mashed into the same cracked ashtray by the window.

The mattress sagged low in the center of the room like it couldn't hold the weight of all they'd done on it — or all they hadn't said. A thin blanket twisted in a knot at the foot of it. Dante lay half-on, half-off the bed, one arm flung over his eyes, the tip of his cigarette flaring in the dark like a tiny lighthouse warning her she was about to wreck herself all over again.

When she stepped inside, he didn't move at first. Just cracked one eye, then flicked his hand lazily toward the corner where a greasy paper bag waited like a peace offering.

"You good?" he mumbled, voice rough from smoke and sleep.

Before she could answer, he flicked the butt into an empty soda can and rolled away, as if her presence was both expected and irrelevant.

She nodded anyway. "Yeah." A lie that tasted bitter as the fries she forced down cold later that night.

Days blurred. The place smelled worse each week — something rank settling into the sink, mold inching across old dishes, rotting sauce packets abandoned on the counter like forgotten promises. She picked up after him the way a ghost might rearrange furniture in a condemned house — folding shirts he'd toss aside, scrubbing stains from the carpet that never really came out, tossing laundry into a trash bag and dragging it to the gas station down the block with quarters she didn't have.

Dante drifted around her like smoke she couldn't breathe away. Some nights he'd pull her close, call her *Queen*, and press his lips to her forehead like he was blessing her. Other nights he'd slam the door, gone for hours, maybe days — and when he came back, he brought with him the scent of perfume that didn't belong to her.

Lying next to him on the old mattress, Frieda would stare at the ceiling, tracing the water stain that looked like a broken wing. Once, she turned to him in the dark. Her voice cracked the silence like glass.

"I still think about it."

He didn't even lift his head. Just flicked ash into the dark.

"What's done is done," he said. Flat. Final. A deadbolt on a door she wasn't allowed to open.

She turned her face into the pillow to catch the tears before they reached him. She didn't speak of it again — the tiny hope, the life she hadn't known how to keep, the decision that still haunted her heartbeat. In that room, her prayers dried up like water in a cracked dish. Her journal stayed shut, zipped in her duffel at the foot of the bed. She learned to live in small breaths. Small silences.

Then came Alyssa. It started as a name, murmured under his breath when he thought Frieda was sleeping — a laugh muffled in the bathroom while he texted, door half-cracked. Cousin, he said, when she asked. Cousins don't send hearts and hungry promises at midnight.

One night, when he was passed out, she picked up his phone — screen still glowing. A string of messages, pink emojis blooming like wounds across her vision. Her thumb trembled on the screen. She read every word. Each one scraped her ribs clean.

In the morning, she asked. She needed him to lie big enough to cover the hole in her chest.

"You're trippin', Frieda," he said instead, flicking a lighter at the stove for stale toast. "Always so emotional. Can't let nothing go."

And there it was. Dismissal. Erased like a smudge on a mirror. She didn't scream. Didn't beg. Didn't rage. She waited until he left for "a run" — which might have been anything. She packed in silence. Hoodie. Toothbrush. That same worn photo of her mother. No noise. No slamming drawers. No final word. She zipped her duffel tight. Tucked her regret deep in the side pocket where the photo lived. When she closed the door behind her, it didn't stick like it used to. She didn't look back to see if it stayed closed.

Outside, the city wind bit through her thin jacket, but it felt cleaner than the air she left behind. For the first time in weeks, Frieda exhaled all the poison she'd mistaken for love. And stepped into the street with nothing but empty pockets, a battered bag — and the raw, uncertain ache of freedom.

Back on the Streets

THE CITY TOOK HER BACK like a stray dog that never really left. No destination—just the comfort of motion under bruised streetlights that buzzed alive one by one as dusk slipped its fingers down Frampton's battered spine. Her boots struck the uneven sidewalk in slow, hollow thuds—like a clock ticking in a house no one lived in anymore. Each step felt borrowed. Each breath tasted like exhaust and old rain. She passed shuttered storefronts with security gates pulled down like sighs, windows smudged with city grime and promises of "COMING SOON" that never came.

A siren wailed somewhere behind her—one sharp note splitting the dusk, then fading into a hiss of traffic and bus brakes wheezing tired secrets at the curb. She moved without seeing. Just the gray blur of people brushing past, shoulders hunched against a cold that arrived too early this year. A cold that crawled under sleeves and behind ribs, making her bones remember every bad night at once.

When her legs couldn't carry her anymore, Frieda found a cracked bench at a bus stop beneath a flickering streetlamp. The wood groaned under her slight weight, damp from an earlier drizzle. She sat with her knees drawn tight, elbows propped on them, forehead pressed to her fists like a child pretending she could disappear if she just folded small enough.

Her phone buzzed in her pocket—one weak shiver of false hope. She dug it out, screen cracked at the corner. Three percent. No new messages. No missed calls. Nothing that would lead her home—if there even was a home left to find. She slipped it back into her pocket and fumbled through her bag. Wrinkled receipts. Loose coins. A balled-up sock. A half-crushed granola bar she couldn't remember pocketing. And then—her fingers brushed leather. Thin, worn, familiar. The Bible. Not for God. Not yet. For Lois. For the stubborn memory of a woman who fought for her soul when Frieda didn't even know she had one left to save.

She flipped it open on her lap, the streetlamp's sickly yellow glow pooling over thin pages. She didn't look for anything special. Just something—anything—to fill the black pit that yawned wider in her chest every night she didn't go back. Her eyes snagged on words she didn't remember marking:
"Though your sins are like scarlet, they shall be as white as snow..."
—Isaiah 1:18
She read it again. And again. Until the letters blurred and her reflection in the bus shelter glass behind the page looked like someone she might have known once.

"I don't believe You," she said into the cold air. Her voice cracked as it left her, part steam, part confession.

But she didn't close the book. Didn't shove it back into the bag like trash. She just held it open, letting the words sit there like an unanswered dare.

HOURS LATER, the last bus wheezed past and left her behind. She drifted down an alley behind a shuttered diner where the smell of rancid oil and stale bread clung to everything. She found her place between a rusted dumpster and a stack of cinder blocks—a pocket of shadows too small for anything but a girl trying not to be seen.

Rain found her there. Slow at first, then steady—dripping off the bent awning above and tapping out its cold rhythm on her shoulders, soaking her hoodie until it clung to her skin like regret. She didn't shiver. Didn't wipe the tears that mixed with the rain on her cheeks.   She just curled her knees tighter, the Bible pressed flat against her chest like a heartbeat she wasn't sure was hers anymore.

Her voice came out raw—scratched by cold, softened by something she wouldn't yet name.

"I don't believe in You…" she breathed to the dripping dark, "but Lois did."

Nothing answered. No wind shifted. No sudden warmth broke through the chill.

She lowered her head into the crook of her arm, her voice a thread:

"God… if You're still there… You have to find me. Because I don't know how to find You."

A whisper lost to the hiss of rain and the rumble of a city that didn't know she was there at all.

It wasn't a prayer. Not really. But for the first time in too long, it was something more than silence. A spark—tiny, stubborn—flickering in the cold.

Desperation

THE SUN CRAWLED UP over Frampton like it was ashamed of the work it had to do—casting pale bands of dull gold and watery gray across a city that hadn't slept but never really woke up either. The dawn was thin and bitter, more a warning than a promise.

Frieda sat slumped on a cracked curb outside an all-night laundromat that hummed behind her like a tired heart. She hugged her knees so tightly to her chest it looked as if she was trying to fold herself away, to shrink so small the world might step right over her and never know she'd been there at all. Her hoodie swallowed her frame, sleeves covering hands that hadn't felt warm in days. Damp socks pressed against the soles of worn-out sneakers. Each toe felt numb. Her stomach cramped with that sharp, hollow ache she knew too well now—hunger that twisted her insides and made her think of Lois's pancakes, of butter and syrup and grace she'd spat back like poison.

A low breeze stirred bits of trash along the fence behind her—plastic bags tangled like ghosts, flapping with a sound that mimicked whispers. Tires splashed through shallow puddles at the curb. Cars came and went, engines grumbling, windows rolled up tight to keep the morning's chill and the city's stories at bay.

Across the street, a broken shop window caught the sun in fractured streaks. Frieda could just see her reflection—bent, split, a girl hollowed out by too many nights and too few prayers. Her lips were cracked. Her cheeks sunken. Shadows lived under her eyes like bruises no fist had given but life had carved out anyway.

Her voice came small, raw, barely more than breath: "What am I doing?"

No answer. Just the groan of an early bus lumbering by, the hiss of brakes, the distant echo of a siren stitching itself through traffic.

She pushed herself upright. Her knees creaked. Her shoulders hunched as if she could carry her shame like an old coat pulled tighter against the wind. She drifted forward, one foot then the next, the city opening up before her like a mouth that didn't care whether it swallowed her or spit her out.

The gas station's neon sign flickered at the end of East Monroe—its buzz a tired greeting that said *come in, stay invisible.* The inside smelled of burnt coffee, stale air, something lemony and false from the mop bucket near the back. Behind bulletproof glass, the cashier—an old man with eyes sunk deep behind wire-rimmed glasses—didn't bother to look up. He swept dust behind his fortress, the rhythmic shush of bristles on tile the only sound that kept Frieda tethered to now.

She drifted down the snack aisle. Her fingers brushed foil wrappers—bright colors promising more than they ever gave. She hovered over granola bars. Simple. Small. Easy to hide. She told herself she'd pay if she could. She just needed something in her stomach to silence the gnawing ache for a few more hours. Her hand shook. She slipped one into her sleeve, tucking it into the fold at her wrist. Her heartbeat drummed against her ribs. She turned—head low, footsteps soft on the linoleum. She almost made it.

"Hey!"

The shout cracked the air open like thunder in a church. The old man's voice carried weight, the finality of someone who'd seen too much and decided kindness was a luxury he couldn't afford.

Frieda spun, a flight reflex sparking behind her ribs— *run*— but she collided with a shape she hadn't seen through the fog of fear. A firm hand clamped around her wrist. A uniform. A badge. Blue polyester that smelled faintly of cold coffee and tired authority. The off-duty cop stepped in front of her, blocking the door.

"Not so fast," he said, voice flat—neither cruel nor gentle, just… done. Done with her. Done with the day. Done with kids like her who slipped through every net. He twisted her arm behind her back. Her knees hit the sidewalk just outside the door. The rough concrete scraped her jeans and split the skin on her cheek when she fell forward. Her breath caught in her chest, an animal sound that never quite made it to a scream.

The granola bar tumbled from her sleeve—still sealed, still clean, its bright label smeared with grime. It landed in a shallow puddle, the reflection of the gas station's neon sign flickering across the plastic like a cheap promise. Cold metal closed around her wrists. The click of the cuffs was soft but final—like the sound of a door shutting behind her.

"You just bought yourself a night in holding," the officer muttered, tightening the second cuff. His tone was tired. Mechanical. He didn't curse her. He didn't comfort her. He didn't care who she was, only what she'd done.

Frieda didn't fight. Didn't beg. Didn't lift her eyes to meet his. She just stared at the granola bar lying in the gutter—unopened, uneaten—while rain from the awning dripped onto her sleeve.

Inside her, something whispered the words she could barely hold:

"This isn't who I was supposed to be."
But the city didn't hear her. The city just moved on.

A Second Chance

The holding cell was colder than the streets had ever been. Pale gray cinderblock walls pressed in on all sides, paint flaking like dry skin. A single metal bench jutted out from the wall—bolted down, unforgiving. No mattress. No blanket worth calling warm—just a scratchy square folded neatly on the floor like a dare to pretend it offered comfort.

Above her, a flickering fluorescent tube buzzed in and out of life. It made shadows jump at the corners of her vision, like ghosts testing the bars. Frieda sat curled in the corner, knees drawn up so tightly her ribs ached. Her cheek throbbed with a dull, raw sting where the sidewalk had kissed it hours ago. She didn't touch it. She didn't move. Her eyes—rimmed red, lids heavy—stared at the door that never opened except to remind her of who she wasn't anymore.

The girl who used to dance barefoot with her mother while gospel records spun soft in the living room—gone. The girl who once scribbled hearts in the corners of notebooks, dreamed about college, about maybe being a teacher—gone. The girl Lois fought for in whispered prayers at dawn—gone, too. All burned up. All buried.

A sharp knock cracked the silence. The metal bars rattled under it, a sound too big for such a small room. Frieda flinched, her chin jerking off her knees. Her vision struggled to catch up.

A woman stood there—tall, solid in a way that didn't feel like a threat but something steadier. Mid-fifties, deep brown skin soft with age and authority, her natural hair cropped short and flecked with silver. She wore plain clothes, sturdy shoes, and carried no badge—only a clipboard under one arm and a paper cup of cooling coffee in her hand.

"Frieda Winslow?" The woman's voice slipped through the bars, low and warm as a blanket on a cold night.

Frieda's throat worked before her head did. She managed a single, slow nod.

The woman's keys clinked softly as she unlocked the cell door. She didn't hesitate. She stepped in like she belonged there, like the cold concrete and stale air didn't touch her spirit at all.

"Name's Joyce Parker," she said, eyes kind but steady. "I'm a minister. But don't let that scare you. I'm not here to scold. Or fix. Or drag you somewhere you don't want to be." She held up the coffee with a small shrug. "Just thought maybe you could use a warm word."

Frieda's voice cracked from disuse. "I'm not... I'm not religious." The words scraped her throat like sandpaper.

Joyce just smiled—a soft, patient curve of the mouth that said *I know more than you think.* "Good," she said simply. "Religion never saved anybody. But grace does. Every single time."

The words didn't fit anywhere in Frieda's chest. But they didn't sting either. So she didn't flinch away. She didn't speak, but she didn't turn her face to the wall like she usually did.

Joyce sat—right there on the cold bench beside her, careful not to crowd her. She didn't preach. Didn't rattle off verses or tell Frieda how broken she looked. Instead, she asked her name again, just to hear Frieda say it. Asked if she'd eaten, asked if she wanted the coffee.

They talked—if you could call it talking. Frieda's voice was mostly silence, her answers clipped at the edges. But Joyce seemed to hear the whole story anyway, as if she could read the spaces between the words. She nodded when Frieda shook her head. She hummed softly when Frieda couldn't speak at all.

"I've sat with a hundred girls who thought they were too far gone," Joyce murmured, voice a hush that wrapped around

Frieda's bones like a blanket she didn't know she needed. "Haven't met one yet who really was."

When the guard outside cleared his throat, Joyce sighed and pushed herself up. She reached into her coat pocket and pulled out a small card, bent at the edges from being handed out too many times. She pressed it into Frieda's palm—held her fingers closed around it until Frieda had to look at her.

"New Morning House," Joyce said softly. "Shelter. Bed. Hot meal. No sermon if you don't want one. Just a door that stays unlocked and people who remember you're more than what brought you here."

The cell door groaned on its hinges as Joyce stepped back through it.

Frieda stayed frozen long after it clanged shut. She stared at the card in her hand—at the neat letters, the quiet promise tucked into its name: *New Morning*. She didn't trust grace. Didn't believe in second chances. But the card in her hand felt warm. And that warmth was enough to cling to—for now.

The Door of Dignity

THE NEXT MORNING ARRIVED pale and hollow, like the sun itself couldn't bear to look her in the eye. A guard's keys rattled outside the holding cell. The metal door groaned open with a tired sigh. "You're out," he said flatly, eyes already on the next clipboard. No warmth. No questions. Just another name off a shift report.

Frieda pushed herself upright, her back cracking from the concrete's cruelty. Her arms felt too heavy for her shoulders. The thin blanket slipped off her knees and crumpled to the floor. A plastic bag was pressed into her palm—clear and pitiful. Inside: a battered phone that barely powered on, a tangled hoodie, her limp duffel bag, and the small card Joyce had given her. The only thing that didn't feel like proof she'd failed.

She stepped through the station's front doors into Frampton's gray hush. The city greeted her exactly as it had left her—unimpressed. Indifferent. Car horns barked. A bus hissed to a stop down the block. Someone argued on the phone in front of the pawn shop, voice sharp and mean.

No one was waiting for her. No Lois leaning against a car. No mother's voice calling her name. Just her own feet on broken pavement. She paused on the sidewalk. The card felt warm in her palm despite the cold wind that cut through her cheap sweatshirt. *New Morning House—Safe Shelter for Young Women.* And underneath, in small, hopeful type: *A place to begin again.*

Five miles, she whispered to herself. Five miles might as well have been five hundred. Her shoes were cracked at the soles, the stitching frayed, the right heel loose enough that every step threatened to break her resolve. Her socks were damp. Her stomach knotted and growled. But her feet turned east, and east they stayed.

Block after block, she passed the city's tired witnesses: corner stores with bars over the glass, shuttered shops with faded *For Lease* signs, alleyways echoing with last night's sins. Graffiti marked the bricks—names of the dead, warnings for the living. At every street corner, a voice whispered inside her head: *You don't belong there. You'll ruin this too. They'll turn you out once they see what you are.* But her legs kept moving. Step. Drag. Step. Drag. She counted sidewalk cracks, lamp posts, boarded windows. Anything to drown out the noise in her skull.

When she turned the last corner, the sky had bruised into a darker gray. The clouds hung low, fat with unshed rain. Ahead, tucked between two leafless oaks, was the house: *New Morning House.* The sign was hand-painted—white letters on soft green wood. Nothing fancy. But the porch light glowed warm through the drizzle, and small hanging pots overflowed with stubborn winter pansies that refused to die.

The rain came steady now, cold rivulets trailing down her neck, soaking her hair. She climbed the steps, boots squelching on the wood. Her fist hovered over the door. She could almost hear Lois whispering through the crackling wind: *Grace doesn't leave you, child.*

But fear pushed back harder: *You don't deserve this.*

Her knuckles shook. Her shoulders trembled. *What if they say yes?* Acceptance was heavier than rejection. It asked for things she didn't know if she had left to give—trust, hope, a heart that might open again. Still, she knocked.

The door opened slower than she expected, its hinges creaking like an old church pew. A woman filled the doorway—

round-shouldered, soft-bellied, her curls pulled back under a colorful scarf. Her eyes were the warm brown of strong coffee, deep and steady.

"You here for a bed, baby?" she asked, voice as gentle as a lullaby.

Frieda swallowed rain and salt. She managed the smallest nod.

"Come on in, then. We got heat, food, and a place that don't judge what the street did to you."

Inside, warmth hit her like a soft wave. Cinnamon. Soap. Clean linen. Voices floated from a side room—low laughter, the shuffle of cards, a girl humming tunelessly. The floor creaked under her soaked shoes. A faded rug muffled the rest.

A young girl with a nose ring and candy-pink braids peeked from the common room, a grin half-hidden behind a deck of cards. "Fresh meat," she teased.

Frieda tensed.

But the older woman just chuckled. "Hush, Tasha. Mind your business."

Then, down the hallway, another shape emerged—rust-colored cardigan, keys at her hip. Joyce Parker. She smiled the moment she saw Frieda. Not wide. Not showy. Just real.

"You made it," Joyce said, like she'd known she would. Like hope had been waiting at this door the whole time.

She led Frieda down a hallway lined with framed prints—flowers, sunrises, scraps of scripture. None of it fancy. All of it felt chosen.

Joyce opened a door near the end. "This is yours," she said simply.

Inside: a bed with a faded patchwork quilt. A small dresser. A single lamp casting buttery light. On the nightstand, a folded note and a Bible—worn, familiar, lavender tucked between its pages.

Frieda stood there, dripping onto the threshold, too cold to shiver. Too tired to cry.

Joyce squeezed her shoulder. "Dinner's soon. You don't have to talk. Just sit. Tomorrow we'll worry about tomorrow. Tonight, you sleep."

When the door closed behind her, Frieda sank onto the bed's edge. Her wet shoes left dark prints on the quilt. She didn't care. For the first time in months, she didn't feel like she was about to run. The door stayed closed behind her. The storm stayed outside.

She peeled off her shoes. Pulled her legs under the covers. And lay back. Above her, the ceiling was plain. But it felt like a sky wide enough for second chances. And Frieda, girl who used to believe in nothing, closed her eyes and let herself drift. For once, she didn't fight the quiet. She let it hold her. And she slept.

The Circle

THE ROOM WAS SMALL, warm but worn—white walls yellowed at the edges, a humming heater rattling in the corner like an old breath. Ten metal chairs sat in a crooked ring around a battered box of tissues perched on a lopsided side table. A poster about *Hope* curled slightly at the edges behind the counselor's chair, the letters faded but stubborn.

Frieda sat hunched in her seat, knees angled inward, palms pressed tight to the frayed denim of her jeans. The air smelled faintly of lavender spray and old coffee. Around her, the other girls fidgeted—tapping shoes, picking at sleeves, pulling hoodies tighter as if they could hide inside the fabric.

When the counselor spoke, her voice was softer than the heater's groan. "Who wants to share today?"

Silence answered first. Heavy silence, like the thick air before a summer storm. Then, one by one, words broke it—fragile, halting, raw.

A girl with red streaks in her hair spoke of nights on train platforms, her mother's slurred voice echoing in the tunnels long after she was gone. Another, thin as winter branches, lifted her sleeves just enough to reveal bruises that bloomed like cruel flowers. Her words were a whisper. A story about fists and locked doors. A hollow-eyed girl didn't speak at all—her fingers just plucked threads from her knee, round and round until they frayed. Each confession cracked the circle open a little more.

When the counselor's eyes finally settled on Frieda, the silence turned inward. She felt it gather in her chest like a stone. She swallowed. Her voice, when it came, was rough—like pages torn too many times.

"I made bad choices," she said, staring at her knees. Her thumbs pressed into each other, digging for strength. "I ran from the only person who ever stayed. My grandmother. Lois."

She drew in a ragged breath. The room blurred at the edges.

"She prayed for me. Fought for me. And I left her. She died in a fire while I was out pretending I didn't care."

A cough caught in her throat. She forced it down.

"I got pregnant. Thought maybe that would fix the ache. It didn't. I... I ended it. I stayed with a man who made me feel like nothing. And I keep thinking—God can't want me back after that."

Her voice cracked on the last word—*that*—like the truth of it was too heavy for her ribs.

No one spoke. Not for a moment. A heater click echoed. A bus rumbled past outside the window. Frieda's head stayed down, eyes on the threadbare carpet.

Then the counselor's voice broke the hush, steady as a hand in the dark.

"He never stopped wanting you."

Frieda's breath hitched. She lifted her eyes—just enough to see the woman's kind, tired smile. Like she'd heard it all before, and still believed anyway.

Across the circle, a voice cracked—raw and hoarse.

"Same thing happened to me," whispered a girl with trembling fingers. Her eyes glistened like glass catching the dawn.

Another girl, knees pulled to her chest, nodded. A tear slid off her chin and vanished into her hoodie sleeve.

No one clapped. No one gasped. The heater hummed on. But for the first time, Frieda felt the hush shift—like something opening. Like a door she didn't know she'd been standing outside all along. She wasn't a ghost here. Not just a girl in the corner, bruised by her own silence. She was seen. She was heard. She was not alone. And in the circle of battered chairs and broken confessions, Frieda felt something almost like mercy settle on her shoulders—light as breath.

ONE EVENING, AFTER DINNER, a girl no older than twelve approached as Frieda sat quietly on the porch swing.

"Can I sit by you?" she asked, her voice small.

Frieda looked up, then nodded.

The girl sat close without a word. No questions. No expectations. Just presence. And something inside Frieda cracked—not shattered, not broken. Just… opened. Not healed. But open.

Beauty for Ashes

WEEKS UNFOLDED LIKE SHY PETALS. They didn't bloom all at once—they unfurled slowly, soft edges brushing against Frieda's bruised spirit until she could almost breathe again.

Joyce gave her chores—simple, steady work that tethered her to the present when her mind tried to drift backward. Mornings found Frieda folding towels still warm from the dryer, their clean cotton scent settling into her hoodie sleeves. Afternoons she wiped down the dining tables, tracing the grain of the wood with a rag, watching sunlight pool on the floorboards like mercy made visible. She lined canned beans and boxes of rice on pantry shelves with careful hands, each can clinking into place like a promise: *You still belong to something.* She liked it—this quiet tending to small, necessary things. Each task was a stitch, pulling her ragged heart back together.

Then there were the devotions. Most mornings, Frieda kept her hood up, earphones in but silent, pretending she wasn't listening while Joyce read aloud from her battered old Bible. The words drifted through the common room—soft, warm currents brushing past closed hearts. Frieda sat in the back, arms crossed tight, gaze locked on a chipped patch of linoleum. She didn't *believe*—not yet. But she didn't leave, either.

Then came that one morning. Joyce stood before them in her rust-colored cardigan, glasses perched low on her nose, Bible open in her strong hands. The heater hummed beside her. The girls around Frieda shifted in their chairs, some barely awake, some staring at the ceiling like they'd rather be anywhere else.

Joyce's voice, though—low, tender—commanded the room without demanding it.

"*…to give them beauty for ashes,*" she read, steady and sure, "*the oil of joy for mourning, the garment of praise for the spirit of heaviness…*"

She paused, closing the Bible softly, her thumb tracing the worn leather spine. Her eyes swept the room. They landed on Frieda for the briefest heartbeat—like a hand on her shoulder.

"Some of y'all," Joyce said, voice hushed but unflinching, "think God waits for you to clean yourself up before He'll bother with you. You think you gotta be polished, perfect, spotless—like ashes can't hold beauty."

She shook her head slowly. "But that's not His way. He meets you *in* the ashes. He *starts* there. That's where the good things grow."

The words cracked through Frieda's ribs like dawn breaking through a boarded window. Her chin dipped. Her fingers clenched her sleeves. And then—before she could help it—her shoulders trembled. Her eyes burned. Warm tears slid down her cheeks, dripping onto the folded hem of her hoodie. She bowed her head lower so no one would see. But Joyce saw. And she didn't say a word.

Later that week, as the morning bus idled outside the shelter's gate, Joyce found her folding donated coats in the laundry room. She pressed a small paper flyer into Frieda's palm—her touch warm, grounding.

GED Classes – Tuesday & Thursday – St. Matthew's Fellowship Hall

"You don't have to go back to who you were," Joyce murmured, her voice close. "You get to choose who you're becoming."

Frieda stared at the words on the flyer, her throat tight. The paper trembled in her hands. She didn't feel smart enough. Didn't feel enough *anything*. But something flickered beneath her ribs—like an ember that refused to die out. Hope. Or grace. Or maybe they were the same thing.

That night, long after the shelter had settled into sleep, Frieda sat alone at the worn kitchen table. The overhead light buzzed softly. A blank journal lay open before her—Joyce had left it on her pillow like an invitation. She held the pen for a long time, tapping it lightly on the table. Then, slowly, she wrote.

I used to believe I was cursed. That nothing good could grow in me. But Joyce says grace isn't earned. It's received.

She paused. Her breath shivered in her chest.

So… okay, God. I'm not saying I trust You yet. But I'm still here. I didn't run. That's something, right?

She signed nothing. Just closed the journal softly and pressed her palm to its cover.

In the hush of that dim kitchen, Frieda tilted her head back, eyes closed against tears that felt warm this time. And for the first time in years, her lips parted with a word she thought she'd forgotten.

"Thank You."

Soft. Unsteady. But true. A prayer in the ashes. A spark in the dark.

CHAPTER 10

What Healing Feels Like

The sharp scent of bleach drifted down the hallway like a ghost from another life—familiar yet jagged. To most, it was just a sign of clean floors and disinfected corners. But to Frieda, it was Lois's kitchen—sunlight pouring through thin curtains, gospel music humming from a battered radio, a pot of collard greens on the back burner, Lois gliding her mop in slow circles while humming softly under her breath. A memory now—warm but stinging at the edges. Here at New Morning House, the bleach didn't smell like home. It smelled like starting over.

Frieda stood still in the middle of the corridor, the mop handle pressed tight between her palms, sleeves rolled to her elbows. Her palms were raw from wringing the old wooden stick, nails bitten short. At her feet, the metal bucket steamed faintly, soapy water swirling like a mirror she didn't want to look into.

Joyce had given her this chore that morning with that small, knowing smile. The one that said *You can do this* without saying a single word. So, she did. Or tried.

She pressed the mop into the bucket, lifted it out, twisted the handle until water dripped steadily onto the floor. Then she pushed it forward—slow, even strokes. Back and forth. Again. Again. The tile beneath her shoes gleamed in wet ribbons of clean.

Each pull scraped something loose inside her—like she was trying to scrub her soul raw. Wipe away the nights she'd slept in alleys. The nights she'd curled her body around grief like armor. The nights she'd told herself she didn't want forgiveness because she didn't deserve it.

Halfway down the hall, the common room door gaped open. A song drifted out—low, sweet, carried by a scratchy speaker:

♫ *He looked beyond my fault… and saw my need…* ♫

Frieda froze.

The mop slipped from her fingers, landed with a quiet clatter that echoed down the corridor like a question no one wanted to answer. Her breath caught in her throat. That hymn. Lois's voice, fragile but so sure, floating through her memory—over clattering dishes, over morning toast, over whispered bedtime prayers Frieda pretended not to hear.

She pressed her knuckles to her mouth, felt the bite of her teeth against bone. Her eyes stung, but she blinked them dry. *"I don't deserve this,"* she told herself. *"This roof. This warmth. This hymn that finds me here, after everything."* But the clean floor shone anyway. The hymn kept drifting. And grace—unasked, unearned—stayed.

❖ ❖ ❖

THAT NIGHT, JOYCE GATHERED THEM in the back room. Ten girls, ten chairs, one circle. The heater clicked and sighed, throwing out a low hum that rattled the old vents. The overhead light flickered once, then held steady. The tissue box sat on the floor in the middle—white, square, unopened. Like a dare. Like a promise.

Joyce stood to the side, hands folded in front of her, eyes soft but sharp enough to see through all their armor.

"You share only when you're ready," she said. Her voice settled around the circle like a blanket.

One by one, the stories cracked the quiet. A girl with her hoodie pulled to her chin spoke of nights under bridges. Another, her hands shaking, told of a father's fists and a mother who never looked back. A third girl, eyes swollen, just whispered, *"I'm here. That's all."*

Then came Frieda's turn. She could feel it—every pair of eyes, gentle but waiting. Her tongue pressed against her teeth. Her hands knotted tight in her lap, nails digging half-moons into her skin. She took one breath. Then two. When the words came, they sounded small. Hollow.

"I killed my baby," she said. The syllables cracked open her chest. "Abortion."

Silence. A heater's sigh. The hum of pipes in the walls.

"I didn't want to." Her voice dropped to almost nothing. "But I was scared. He told me to. And I—" She swallowed, shoulders shaking. "I thought it would make it better. But it didn't. It buried me too. And now—" Her fingers twisted the hem of her sleeve. "Now I feel like there's nothing good left in me. Like all that's left is ashes."

No one spoke. The words lay heavy between them all.

Then, across the circle, Lena shifted. Sarcastic, sharp-tongued Lena—whose laugh usually cut like a blade. She leaned forward, pushed her braids behind her ear. Reached out. Took Frieda's cold hand in both of hers.

"I did the same thing," Lena said, her voice raw. "You're not alone, Frieda."

The words broke something open in the room.

A quiet girl with nail polish chipped to the quick nodded, tears tracking her cheeks. "Me too," she whispered. She didn't look up—just reached for the tissue box and nudged it forward.

Another hand. Another whisper. *Same.* The box made its way around—tissue after tissue pulled, tears wiped, silence held.

And Frieda sat there—heart pounding, vision blurry—and felt the circle close around her. Not like a trap. Not like judgment. But like arms. She didn't look at Joyce, but she could feel her presence, warm and unshakable at her back.

For the first time, Frieda didn't feel like a wound walking on two legs. She felt like something could still grow from the ashes. She felt—like mercy could make a bridge. And that maybe, just maybe, she could too.

The Kitchen Table

THE NEXT MORNING, dawn crept in like a soft breath—pale light sliding its way through the sheer curtains of New Morning House. It painted the scuffed linoleum floors in faint strokes of gold and pearl. Frieda lay awake on her small bed long before the alarm, eyes tracing the pattern of shadows on the ceiling. There was no reason to rise so early. But her body hummed with a restlessness she couldn't name.

She sat up, tugged her curls into a loose knot with an old hair tie, and slipped her feet into socks that didn't match. The floor greeted her with its usual chill as she padded out into the narrow hallway, quiet so as not to wake the girls still curled like secrets in their bunks.

In the kitchen, Frieda paused. For a moment, she just stood there—hand on the pantry door, breath steadying itself in the hush. The fridge buzzed in the corner. A single streetlamp outside flickered like an eyelid, blinking the neighborhood awake.

She opened the pantry. Her hands knew what they were looking for before her mind caught up: flour, sugar, eggs, a splash of milk still cold from the back shelf. She found cinnamon tucked in the spice rack, the tin dented but fragrant when she tapped it open. She whisked by hand. The spoon scraped the inside of the mixing bowl in a rhythm that calmed her—like Lois's old kitchen, like Saturday mornings before bitterness took root. She poured the batter onto the battered griddle, watched it sizzle and bubble up, releasing warm curls of vanilla and browned butter that wrapped around her like an old hymn.

Footsteps creaked on the stairs. A door clicked open. Then another. She didn't look up at first, but she heard them—bare feet on tile, slippers dragging, voices still heavy with sleep. Someone lingered at the doorway.

"You cook?" asked a girl—Jessie, maybe, her hair a wild halo around her face.

Frieda flipped a pancake and shrugged. "Used to. Haven't in a while."

Jessie drifted closer but didn't sit. Neither did the others at first—hovering like they were waiting for permission.

Then Lena—quick-tongued, half a smirk even at dawn—dropped into a chair, her palms drumming out a slow beat on the tabletop. "Smells like somebody's grandma's house," she muttered, but her eyes were soft.

The room shifted. Folding chairs scraped back. Mugs clinked. Someone found a jar of cheap syrup and passed it down. A phone played gospel under someone's elbow—soft chords weaving between forks and laughter like thread pulling frayed edges together. It wasn't Christmas. There was no special occasion. But it felt like something worth remembering.

Frieda stayed at the stove. She worked in gentle loops—flip, stack, pour more batter. The smell filled the room; the warmth clung to her arms. She didn't feel alone in her skin anymore.

When the last pancake browned and sizzled, she set down the spatula and leaned back against the counter, just watching. Watching the chatter spill and echo. Watching girls who flinched at touch reach for seconds. Watching hope flicker in small, reckless ways.

At the far end of the table, Alana sat hunched, a pancake picked apart in front of her. Her journal—battered, covered in stickers peeling at the corners—sat untouched by her plate. Her eyes flitted from her fork to her lap to Frieda.

Frieda wiped her palms on a dish towel and crossed the room. She pulled out the chair opposite Alana and sank into it, the kitchen clatter softening around them like a bubble.

"Don't like pancakes?" Frieda asked, voice gentle, coaxing.

Alana shrugged, her fingers pulling her sleeves over her knuckles. "They're good. Just... not used to waking up to warm things."

Frieda felt that. Deep. She leaned forward, elbows on the table, chin resting in her palm. "It's not just food. It's proof. You woke up. You came to the table. That's worth something."

Alana glanced up, lashes trembling. "It feels weird. Like I don't have to brace for... I don't know. Something bad."

Frieda smiled, soft and honest. "Safety feels fake at first. Like you're wearing someone else's coat. But keep wearing it. It'll fit."

Alana's eyes flicked to her journal. Then back to Frieda. Her fingers hovered over the cover, then pushed it forward an inch.

Frieda didn't push. Just waited.

Finally, Alana flipped it open. Pages curled. Pencil sketches bled across them—raw lines, shadows, tiny details: a hand curled into a fist, a girl curled in a corner, a window cracked open to a sky that promised more.

"These yours?" Frieda asked, awe threading her words.

Alana nodded, barely. "I don't show people. Ever."

Frieda traced a drawing with her eyes, careful not to touch the page. "These are brave. You know that?"

Alana scoffed, soft but not mean. "They're messy."

Frieda's voice dropped to a whisper. "So are we."

Alana's lips twitched. A ghost of a smile. She tugged her pancake closer and tore a piece free—slow, deliberate, like testing whether the world would let her.

From across the table, Lena's voice rose. "Yo, Miss Frieda! We got more batter?"

Frieda stood, tapping the journal once with her fingertip— a promise she'd come back. "Got you covered," she called, moving to the stove.

She poured the last of the batter onto the griddle. The kitchen hummed—cheap gospel through the phone speaker, forks tapping plates, chairs squeaking as someone shifted.

It wasn't a miracle. It wasn't a rescue. It was a morning. And for Frieda Winslow, who once believed nothing good could grow from her—this small table, this battered griddle, this circle of girls piecing themselves back together? It was holy ground. And she stood on it, spatula in hand, grateful for every unfinished thing about her life. Right there in the smell of cinnamon and warmth, she found something better than perfect. She found belonging.

The Calling

LATER THAT WEEK, after morning devotions, the chapel emptied in slow ripples—girls drifting out with sleepy chatter and soft murmurs, their laughter echoing off the faded walls. The last hymn still hung in the air like smoke that refused to drift away.

Frieda lingered on the second pew, her journal balanced on her knees, thumb brushing over a half-written line she couldn't quite finish. The wooden bench beneath her creaked as she shifted, her eyes tracing the simple cross above the pulpit—plain, worn, yet steady as ever.

Joyce stayed behind, too. She watched the girls leave—her eyes, calm and patient, following each one like a mother counting sheep back to the fold. When the door swung closed with a soft click, she turned and made her way down the aisle, her sensible shoes whispering against the old carpet.

She didn't speak right away. She sat beside Frieda instead—shoulder to shoulder on the narrow pew, hands folded neatly in her lap. The sunlight spilled through the stained-glass windows, brushing Joyce's profile in soft gold and blue.

Joyce exhaled, the sound warm and steady. She spoke like she was unwrapping a delicate truth.

"You ever think about working with girls like these?" Her voice was gentle—no push, no demand. Just an invitation that felt both weightless and impossibly heavy.

Frieda's eyes widened. Her fingers stilled on the page. She looked sideways at Joyce, searching her calm face for a catch. "You mean… staff? Like… here?"

Joyce's smile was small but full of knowing. "Or anywhere, Frieda. You're not just surviving anymore. You're leading, whether you see it or not. The others—" she gestured at the door the girls had just passed through, "—they watch you. They trust you. That's something holy in a place like this."

Frieda stared down at her hands. The skin was rough in places where bleach and soap had worn it raw. Small scars trailed her knuckles—old ghosts of nights and streets she barely spoke of now. She rubbed a thumb over one bruise that was fading to yellow. Her voice came out hoarse. "I don't think I'm ready. I still feel… unfinished."

Joyce didn't argue. She never did. Instead, she slipped a hand into the deep pocket of her cardigan and drew out a single folded flyer—creased and softened at the corners like it had lived a while in that coat, waiting for this moment.

She pressed it into Frieda's palm, her own hand warm and unhurried.

Frieda unfolded it carefully. The paper smelled faintly of lavender—Joyce's scent, the smell that always reminded her of something gentle and true.

Frampton High – Classroom Assistant Needed – GED In Progress Okay

The black letters wavered as Frieda read them twice. Then a third time. She felt something flutter in her chest—sharp and bright and terrifying all at once.

Joyce watched her, eyes soft as dusk. "You survived fires that should have taken you out. You learned how to breathe again when you didn't want to. Now maybe… just maybe… it's time to help another girl believe she can do the same."

Frieda's throat tightened. The pew felt suddenly too small for the hope that wanted to rise inside her. She wanted to protest. Wanted to say, *I'm not good enough. Not ready. Not whole.* But the words dissolved before they found her tongue. So instead, she just clutched the flyer like a fragile promise. She didn't fold it away. Didn't hide it in her pocket to forget later. She held it. Right there in the hush of the empty chapel.

And somewhere beneath the hum of the old heater, beneath the creaking pew and the dust that danced in the colored sunlight, a tiny piece of her whispered:

Maybe I can.

That Night's Mercy

THAT NIGHT, Frieda sat at the long, scarred kitchen table long after the last dish had been rinsed and stacked in neat, hopeful towers beside the sink. The overhead light hummed low above her—a warm pool of yellow that softened the edges of the chipped linoleum floor. Somewhere down the hall, muffled laughter flickered in and out—a girl telling another goodnight, the squeak of bedsprings, a door gently closing.

The old refrigerator kicked on, its motor thrumming steady and calm. Beneath her bare feet, the floorboards creaked and settled, carrying memories of every girl who'd paced this house at midnight—some restless, some afraid, some like her… simply awake because they'd survived too much silence to trust sleep easily.

In front of her sat her journal—its cracked spine spread wide like an open palm, waiting. Frieda's pen hovered above the paper, her fingers smudged faintly with ink from the words she'd scribbled over the weeks: prayers half-finished, lists of things she thought she might one day hope for, fragments of Lois's voice stitched between her own.

But tonight felt different. The page waited. So did she. Her shoulders dropped as she took a breath—slow and careful, like she might break the hush if she exhaled too fast. She thought of that girl earlier—tiny, fierce when she spoke but folded soft when the sobs broke through. How her tears had soaked Frieda's shirt. How her hands had clutched Frieda's sleeve like it was a lifeline. Frieda's chest tightened, then loosened. She lowered the pen.

Today I helped a girl believe she wasn't trash.

She paused. Let the words sit there, raw and plain, ink sinking into paper like a promise.

She cried in my lap like I was someone safe.
I don't know how that happened.
But maybe that's what healing feels like—
Not forgetting where you came from,
But finally believing it doesn't have to be your ending.

The pen stilled. She read the words twice. A small, sharp ache pressed at the corners of her eyes—tender but not unbearable. She set the pen down gently, careful not to smudge the wet ink. She lifted her eyes to the kitchen window. Outside, the night pressed its face to the glass—black and silent, speckled with the glow of a distant streetlamp. Her reflection hovered there too—soft edges, the faint halo of the overhead light circling her curls. She didn't look polished. She didn't look whole. But she looked… present. Not a ghost of who she'd been. Not a girl chained to the fire. Just Frieda. Tired. But softer.

She closed the journal with a quiet sigh, the sound small but sure. She didn't rush to bed. She didn't rush anywhere. She just stayed seated in that circle of warm light; hands wrapped around the mug Joyce had left behind—half cold coffee, but comforting in its weight. She let the quiet hold her. Let the old refrigerator hum its low hymn. Let her heartbeat slow enough to hear her own breathing. And for the first time in a long time, the silence wasn't punishment. It was peace. She let it be enough.

Return to Frampton High

FRIEDA STOOD JUST INSIDE THE GLASS DOORS of Frampton High, her breath misting faintly on the entryway's cold metal frame. In her hands, she clutched a manila folder so tight that the edges bent under her thumbs—inside were all the fragile proofs that she was someone new: reference letters, a half-finished GED transcript, and Joyce's steady handwriting looping a blessing in blue ink.

The front office smelled like old linoleum, pencil shavings, and the faint tang of burnt coffee from the machine by the nurse's desk. She could hear the hum of fluorescent lights overhead, the same droning hum that once filled the gaps between her skipped classes and the hallways she haunted with her headphones in.

Beyond the glass partition, rows of dull blue lockers still lined the corridor, chipped paint and dented doors like scars that hadn't healed. The same squeak of sneakers on tile. The same distant echo of a late bell—sharp and final, sending clusters of teenagers scrambling into classrooms.

A secretary with square glasses perched halfway down her nose barely glanced up as she stamped a paper and slid it across the counter. Her voice clipped, bored. "Room 203. Mr. Daniels. Tenth-grade science. You'll shadow today."

Frieda nodded, swallowing hard, her throat tight around words she didn't trust. She tucked the folder closer to her chest— like armor—and stepped into the hall. The corridor stretched ahead like a tunnel into the past. She half-expected to see her thirteen-year-old self slip around the corner—hood pulled low, eyes fixed on the floor, backpack hanging from one shoulder like dead weight. She could almost hear her old footsteps—fast and soft, always escaping something.

She walked on, each step echoing off tile and memory. The closer she got to Room 203, the steadier her pulse became—steady not because she felt brave, but because she couldn't afford to feel anything else.

The classroom door swung open with a quiet creak. Morning sun pushed through the half-closed blinds in stripes, casting bands of warm gold and gray across chipped desks and faded motivational posters. Dust motes floated lazily in the light, suspended like tiny prayers. Behind the whiteboard stood a man broad in the shoulders, his salt-and-pepper hair cropped close, a pair of reading glasses sliding halfway down his nose. He paused mid-sentence, chalk in hand, and looked over his shoulder.

"You're Frieda, right?" His voice was calm, cracked with age, but warm enough to smooth the edge of her nerves.

"Yes, sir," Frieda said, her own voice softer than she meant. She cleared her throat and forced the corners of her mouth to lift, just enough to meet him halfway.

He nodded once—approval brief but genuine. "Joyce says you've got heart. Heart's more than most come in with. The rest we can teach."

He gestured with the chalk towards the back corner of the room. "See that one? Hoodie pulled up like she's invisible? Tyesha. Sharp as they come. Quicker than the rest to slip through the cracks if you let her."

Frieda followed his eyes.

Tucked into the last row, half-swallowed by her oversized sweatshirt, sat a girl with hair pulled tight under her hood. Her arms were crossed so hard her knuckles blanched. One foot tapped an invisible rhythm against the leg of her chair—tap, tap, pause, tap. Her gaze slid from the clock to the whiteboard and back, restless and coiled, like she'd already memorized every possible escape route.

Frieda knew that look. She'd worn it herself once—sitting where the teacher couldn't see her flinch, braced for the world to prove it didn't care. She didn't approach. Not yet. Some storms you don't step into all at once. Instead, Frieda moved to the empty seat beside the desk at the front. She set her folder down, smoothed her palms over the cover, and drew a slow breath in through her nose. The smell of dry-erase markers. The quiet shuffle of papers. The muffled murmur of kids who didn't yet know how close the edge could feel.

She was here again—in the halls that had once swallowed her voice. Only this time, her silence wasn't fear. It was readiness. She didn't come back just to be counted present. She came back to stand guard for every girl counting down the minutes, tapping a secret song against a chair leg—waiting to see if anyone would notice she was worth saving.

Frieda's eyes flicked once more to Tyesha. *I see you,* she thought. *I know you. I won't leave you behind.* And when the bell rang again, it didn't sound like an ending. It sounded like a beginning.

The Lunchroom

LUNCH CAME SLOW AND SOFT at Frampton High—a lull in the middle of a day that carried too many ghosts.

Frieda sat in the far corner of the staff lounge, tucked into the sagging cushion of an old faux-leather couch that smelled faintly of dust and stale coffee. A peanut butter sandwich rested in her lap, the crusts carefully torn away like muscle memory from childhood lunches Lois used to make. A chipped mug, steam long gone cold, sat balanced on her knee—weak tea that tasted mostly of metal and tap water.

Around her, the room hummed with the muted noise of grown-up small talk. Teachers leaned against the counter by the microwave, swapping stories about missing homework, hallway scuffles, and the endless swirl of budget cuts and too-short lunch breaks. The hum of fluorescent bulbs overhead filled the spaces between their words. Somewhere near the mini-fridge, a bag of popcorn sputtered and popped.

Frieda kept her head down, shoulders curled slightly inward—not out of fear, but to savor this small, quiet moment. Just her, a sandwich, and the thought that she'd made it this far without disappearing again. Then she heard it—sharp at first, like a thorn catching the fabric of her peace.

"Frieda Winslow? Didn't she used to… disappear or something?"

The voice slipped through the soft drone of the lounge, too casual to be kind. Frieda lifted her eyes slowly. Jasmine Carter— sleek hair pinned smooth behind one ear, nails polished to a high-gloss pink. Her name tag swung gently from her tailored blouse like a medal. Once upon a time, Jasmine had ruled these halls with hallway whispers and well-placed smirks. She hadn't changed much—except now her gossip sat behind the mask of polite conversation. A few teachers paused their chatter, glancing sideways. The room seemed to lean in, curious.

Frieda didn't flinch. She let the silence linger, heavy as wet wool. Then, setting her sandwich down neatly on its napkin, she met Jasmine's eyes—steady, clear, unbothered.

"I did disappear," Frieda said. Her voice didn't tremble. It didn't rise. It just landed in the middle of the lounge like a stone in still water. "And now I'm back."

Jasmine's practiced smile faltered. She blinked once—twice—like she'd been expecting a smaller answer, something she could bat away with another careless comment. But Frieda didn't give her the chance. She turned back to her mug, lifting it with both hands, feeling its chipped lip warm against her fingertips.

Jasmine cleared her throat, gave a stiff half-laugh. "Oh. Well… good for you."

Frieda didn't bother nodding. She just let the moment close like a door. Around her, conversation resumed—a little softer, a little sharper at the edges. Jasmine busied herself with her phone, her eyes darting anywhere but back to Frieda.

The tea was lukewarm. The sandwich tasted plain. But Frieda sat taller, her shoulders no longer folded in. She didn't need to defend who she'd been. She didn't owe anyone an apology for surviving. She was here. That was proof enough.

THE FINAL BELL ECHOED down the corridors like a sigh of release. Classroom doors banged shut, sneakers squeaked across the faded tiles, and the murmur of laughter and slammed lockers drifted into silence, piece by piece. Frampton High exhaled its students into the afternoon light, leaving only scraps of noise behind—muffled giggles from the gym, a distant door slamming shut.

Frieda lingered in the hallway; her folder clutched under her arm like a fragile shield. She traced the cracked floor tiles with her eyes, the faded green lockers with their peeling stickers and scratched initials. The ghosts of her own past here seemed to flicker at the edge of her vision—thirteen-year-old Frieda, hoodie up, eyes down, headphones so loud she couldn't hear her own thoughts.

At the far end of the hall, she saw her—Tyesha. Alone, planted like a stone against a locker door plastered with peeling tape residue. One foot rested flat on the dented metal, her shoulder pressed firm into it as if to hold up the whole row. Earbuds in. Hood up. Head down. She didn't watch the world pass; she waited for it to empty out.

Frieda took a breath, steadying herself. Then she started forward. Her boots tapped a gentle rhythm on the tiles—loud enough to hear, quiet enough not to startle. She stopped a few feet away. Tyesha didn't look up.

"Mind if I sit?" Frieda asked, her voice soft, carrying just enough to bridge the empty space.

Tyesha didn't answer. Didn't nod. Didn't shake her head. She just kept her gaze locked on a crack in the floor, her jaw tight, her breath slow and deliberate.

Frieda took that as permission. She turned and slid her back down the lockers, the metal cool against her shoulders. She settled cross-legged on the grimy linoleum; her folder balanced on her knees. The hallway lights flickered overhead, humming their tired tune.

She didn't speak right away. She just let the silence settle, not forcing it to be anything other than what it was— uncomfortable but honest.

Finally, she let her eyes drift sideways to Tyesha's profile.

"You're not angry," Frieda said quietly, her words careful, as if they might slip and break if she spoke too loud. "You're just tired. Tired of folks pretending they see you when they don't."

Tyesha's head turned a fraction. Her brow twitched beneath the edge of her hood. She tugged one earbud out, the tiny pop of music leaking into the silence before she thumbed it off. Her eyes narrowed, sharp but curious.

"You don't know me," she said, voice flat as a locked door.

"No," Frieda agreed, her tone gentle but unyielding. "I don't. But I know that look. I wore it so long I thought it was my face."

The hallway stretched quiet again. A locker creaked somewhere far off—metal expanding in the cooling afternoon. Tyesha's foot dropped to the floor with a soft thud. She studied Frieda like she might disappear if she blinked too long.

"What do you want?" she asked finally. The question wasn't a threat. It was armor. The kind you build when you're used to everyone wanting something you can't give.

Frieda shifted, her folder sliding onto the floor beside her. She looked straight ahead, eyes on the faded mural of the school mascot at the end of the corridor.

"I just wanted to say..." Her voice caught for half a heartbeat. She swallowed it down. "I see you. Not here to fix you. Not here to preach. Just... I see you."

Tyesha's fingers toyed with the wire of her other earbud, twisting it around her thumb, then untwisting it. Her shoulders dropped—barely, but enough. The tight line of her jaw loosened. She didn't say anything. But she didn't put the earbud back in either.

They sat there in the hush of the emptied hallway—two girls years apart, wounds apart, yet stitched together for a moment by the simple, raw truth of being seen. It wasn't trust. But it was a crack in the wall. A breath of light. A beginning.

What Grace Looks Like

BY THE END OF THE WEEK, something subtle but unmistakable shifted around Frieda—like a ripple that spread out quietly and wide. It wasn't loud. It wasn't obvious. But in the drifting hush of Frampton High's halls, girls who used to keep their eyes down now paused—just long enough to stay near her orbit.

One Thursday afternoon, the final bell rang—a tiny, familiar clang that scattered the chatter of students down the corridors like startled birds. Desks scraped back. Backpacks zipped. Frieda lingered near the whiteboard, stacking papers into neat piles. Out of the corner of her eye, she saw her—a girl with a wild cloud of frizzy curls and too-large sleeves that swallowed her hands. She hovered a few feet away, bouncing on her toes like she might bolt if noticed.

Frieda turned. Softened her smile. Waited. The girl inched closer, eyes flicking up under her lashes before landing on the floor again. She held out a rumpled worksheet—corners bent, eraser marks smudged gray.

"Miss Frieda?" Her voice was small, sticky with nerves. "Um… could you… number seven? I don't get it."

Frieda didn't laugh. Didn't sigh. She just stepped closer, pulled a chair beside the girl's desk, and sat down so they were shoulder to shoulder.

"Show me what you tried," she said gently, tapping her pen against the margin. "We'll figure it out together."

They bent over the paper—two heads bowed under the humming classroom light. Outside the window, the late sun dipped behind a row of brick buildings, throwing long, golden shadows over cracked sidewalks.

THE NEXT DAY, Frieda was slipping through the hallway when she heard it—a shy voice behind her. She turned just as a girl with chipped nail polish and an oversized hoodie pointed down at Frieda's boots. Scuffed leather, blue ribbon laced through the eyelets—a piece of her story tied right into the knots.

"Those're cute," the girl said, words tumbling out too fast. She immediately looked away, like she'd said too much.

Frieda grinned—worn but warm. "Thanks. They've carried me through more than I thought I could walk."

The girl's shoulders relaxed just a touch. She nodded once, a shy flicker of a smile, then disappeared down the hall, her steps lighter than before.

FRIDAY. THE FINAL BELL. A hush after a long week's noise. Frieda returned to her desk to find something that made her breath catch in her throat. There, stuck crooked on the corner of her grade book, was a neon yellow sticky note—creased at one corner, the ink shaky but bold.

You make school feel less like prison.

No name. No frills. Just that.

She pressed her fingertips to the note as if the ink might vanish if she didn't hold it down. Her chest tightened in a way that felt nothing like fear and everything like grace. She peeled it off carefully—like it might tear if she rushed—and tucked it inside her journal, folding the page around it as if to say: *Stay. I need to remember this.*

THAT EVENING, as dusk folded the city into shadows, Frieda sat in her car in the quiet school lot. The streetlights blinked on overhead, one by one, humming like tired angels. Her hands rested on the wheel, but she didn't start the engine. She didn't cry because she was sad. She cried because, for the first time in so long, her tears were born from something soft—something so tender that it almost frightened her: purpose. The tears came steadily, and she let them fall.

Later that night, Frieda sat by her drafty window, steam rising from her chipped mug of tea. Beyond the glass, Frampton glowed in scattered dots—streetlamps, neon signs, distant headlights humming along cracked asphalt. Her phone rang in the hush. She answered without looking at the screen.

"Joyce."

"Hey, baby." Joyce's voice was a balm—worn, warm, carrying every answered prayer Frieda never knew she'd asked. "How'd the first week treat you?"

Frieda looked past her own reflection in the glass. A pigeon perched on the streetlight—its wings tucked in, its head tilted, watching the night. She swallowed. Her voice came out hushed, as if speaking too loud might break the fragile grace that had found her.

"I think…" She paused. Let the words settle on her tongue. "I think I'm starting to see it."

"See what, baby?"

Frieda closed her eyes, allowing the warmth to fill her chest where the old ache used to reside.

"What grace looks like… when it walks into a classroom."

Joyce didn't speak. She didn't have to. The silence on the other end was its own kind of *Amen.*

BEFORE BED, FRIEDA sat at her battered kitchen table, the overhead bulb flickering above her like a quiet promise that even broken things can shine. Her journal lay open under her palm. She lifted her pen—hesitated—then wrote:

Today, a girl said she wants to be like me when she grows up. She doesn't know the ruins I've walked through. Doesn't know what I buried to stand here. But she sees something worth becoming.

She paused, the pen trembling just a little. She let the soft hum around her resemble a heartbeat.

Maybe this is what redemption looks like. Not spotless. But blooming.

Her eyes drifted back to the window. And for the first time, the reflection that looked back didn't scare her. It looked tired. Yes. But rooted. And that was enough to begin again.

The Climb

The GED prep classroom smelled like dry-erase markers and stale coffee—like someone had tried to scrub out the past with ammonia but left the ghosts clinging to the corners. The floor tiles were scuffed to dull gray. The click-click-click of an old box fan in the corner punctuated the hum of the flickering overhead lights.

Frieda sat near the back, shoulders squared stiff against the plastic seat, arms folded tight like armor across her chest. A pencil—freshly sharpened to a needle—tapped lightly against her elbow. Her eyes drifted over the faded motivational posters taped crookedly to the beige walls.

Perseverance. You Can Do Hard Things. Never Give Up.

The words looked tired. Too bright against the gray of the room. But part of her wanted to believe them anyway.

Up front, the instructor—a woman with a frizz of wild hair and wide, determined eyes—moved like hope personified. Her glasses slipped down her nose every other breath. She kept pushing them up with an ink-stained finger, her other hand fluttering over a stack of handouts like they were holy writ.

"Alright, folks," she said, voice light but full of steel. "Let's start with something good today—Frederick Douglass. Page one. We highlight what jumps out. Circle words that catch your eye. He fought for his freedom—and his mind was his weapon. Let's see what yours can do." She clapped once, sharp as a spark.

Frieda looked around. A circle of strangers, each bearing their own quiet ruin. A young mother two rows ahead rocked her leg as she balanced a pacifier on her knee, her pencil wedged between chipped nails. An older man—deep lines etched around his eyes—pinched the bridge of his nose as if begging the words to stay this time. And the boy nearest the window, no older than fifteen, swallowed inside an oversized hoodie—his gaze fixed on the floor but his pen already moving.

The packet was open on Frieda's desk. It was a tidy stack of printed pages, with a bold heading: Narrative of the Life of Frederick Douglass. Her thumb brushed the paper's edge, feeling the rough tear where the printer hadn't cut it cleanly. She exhaled— a deep breath drawn from somewhere inside.

Five years ago, she'd run—slam door, break heart, burn bridge gone. She'd traded desks for cold nights, textbooks for streetlight shadows. She'd told herself she was done with trying. Done with hoping. And now—she was here. Back under fluorescent lights. Back on cracked linoleum floors. Back in a wobbly chair when she shifted. Her pencil trembled in her grip. She set the tip to paper. The graphite caught on the first word— freedom—and something sparked in her chest. Not loud. Not fierce. Just steady.

Outside the window, dawn spread wider, casting a pale light across the blinds. The fan whirred constantly, like a heartbeat she hadn't trusted in years. She traced a line. Then another. A small thing. But this was the climb. And this time—this time, Frieda didn't stand up and run. She stayed. She began.

The Long Nights

IT WASN'T EASY. Not even close. The math pages taunted her first—fractions and decimals smudged under the dim lamp in the corner of the New Morning House rec room. The numbers tangled together, dancing into meaningless little circles in the margins. Every wrong answer seeped into her like an old echo: You can't. You'll never catch up.

History wasn't any kinder. Each date, each chapter scraped raw from the time she would have rather forgotten—years that should've been spent in classrooms and chalk dust, not cold bus stops and broken streetlights. But Frieda stayed.

After her shift at Frampton High, she slipped through the shelter's side door just as the sky darkened into night. Her bag dragged on her shoulder, heavy with battered textbooks and a bundle of half-used pens. Some nights, she claimed the far corner of the rec room—legs folded in a thrift-store armchair that sagged just right. She spread flashcards over her knees like tarot cards, a mug of stale instant coffee cooling by her side. The room hummed softly around her—pipes rattling, floorboards sighing as others drifted to bed.

Other nights, when the hallway lights flickered out and the hum went quiet, Frieda stayed up under a pool of candlelight—half-melted candles squeezed into old mugs, their glow warm against the weary curve of her back. The scent of wax and burnt wicks curled around the pages as she scribbled answers, crossed them out, and wrote them again. Her eyes burned. Her wrist ached. But her pen kept moving.

Joyce's small reminders appeared in the oddest spots—yellow sticky notes stuck in textbooks, tucked under her coffee mug, and attached to the bathroom mirror.

You've already survived harder.
This test doesn't define you.
God's not finished.

Each note was a lifeline. A gentle tap on her shoulder when her head drooped, reminding her she wasn't alone with these numbers, these paragraphs, this climb. Sometimes the pages blurred so badly that the letters pulsed like fireflies. And on those nights, Frieda's cheek found the open workbook—her breath fogging the corner of the page, highlighters and hope mingling in the fabric of her hoodie. When she drifted off, it wasn't failure. It was proof she was trying. Proof she'd stayed. This wasn't homework. It wasn't just studying. This was resurrection—one stubborn equation at a time. One note of grace tucked like a seed into the folds of her tired heart.

The Certificate

THERE WERE NO BALLOONS. No confetti cannons. No clapping crowd waiting behind a squeaky gym door. Just a dull, flickering overhead light and the bored shuffle of paper on an administrator's cluttered desk. Frieda stood there—shoulders stiff, fingers twisting the hem of her thrifted coat—while the woman behind the counter thumbed through a stack of folders like they weighed nothing at all. A sigh, a rustle, a quick glance up that barely skimmed Frieda's face.

"Here you go," the woman said, voice flat. She slid the beige envelope across the scratched laminate. Her eyes had already dropped back to the next folder before Frieda's fingers touched the paper.

That was it. Frieda stepped back, the envelope light in her hand but heavy on her heart. She pushed through the double doors into the parking lot. The morning air bit at her cheeks—clean, cold, and edged with the hush that follows dawn rain. She crossed the cracked asphalt, feet crunching over scattered gravel, and sat on the concrete steps just outside the building. The cement was still damp, soaking into the seat of her jeans. She didn't care. With trembling fingers, she peeled the envelope flap open. The paper inside rasped softly as she pulled it free. Her name. Her score. Her certificate. Nothing fancy—just black ink on thin stock. But to Frieda, it might as well have been parchment sealed in gold.

A breeze lifted the paper's edge, threatening to carry it off. She pressed it flat against her chest; hands splayed over her heart like she was afraid it would dissolve if she didn't anchor it there. For a moment, she just sat, hunched over, forehead resting on the edge of the certificate. The world went soft around her—traffic murmuring a block away, birds busy in the tree above the shelter roof. She barely heard any of it over the rush in her ears.

A tear slipped free. Then another. Quiet. Slow. Not for the letters or the numbers or the signature in smudged blue ink. But for the girl she used to be—wild-eyed under broken ceilings, pulling her hoodie tight, telling herself she was born to fail. She wept for the nights she almost quit. For the excuses that didn't win. For the battered faith that refused to stay buried. She wept for Lois. For the prayer chair. For the pages of her old Bible that still smelled faintly of peppermint and lemon polish. She wept because it hadn't saved her overnight—but it had   steadied her long enough to stand up, to stay, to finish.

And when the tears slowed, Frieda lifted the certificate to the sky, as if Lois might see it from somewhere just beyond the morning clouds. "I did it," she whispered. Her voice cracked in the cold air. "I did it, Mama. I did it, Lois." She pressed her palm flat to her chest once more, sealing the paper there.

Then she sat on the rain-cold step a little longer, letting the morning wash over her, letting herself be proud—without shame, without fear, without running. For the first time, she didn't need a witness. Just the truth in her own bones: She hadn't given up.

The Diner

LATER THAT MORNING, the rumble of Joyce's old red sedan pulled up to the curb. The paint was faded in places, a scratch or two on the bumper—a car that had seen miles and mercy both. When Frieda climbed in, the faint hum of gospel music wrapped around her like a familiar blanket. Joyce tapped the steering wheel in sync with the choir's voices, glancing sideways with a smile that carried the warmth of a mother and the quiet strength of a soldier.

They didn't talk much on the drive—just let the city drift past in blurred murals of cracked sidewalks, corner stores, and half-awake traffic lights blinking yellow.

The diner was the kind of place that felt stitched together by time—red vinyl booths patched with duct tape, ceiling fans turning lazy circles overhead, and the smell of syrup and bacon grease baked into the walls. The bell above the door chimed as they stepped inside, a tiny brass note that sounded like old memories.

The waitress behind the counter gave Joyce a nod. "Morning, Ms. Parker. Usual spot?"

Joyce grinned. "Of course."

They settled into a booth by the window. The vinyl squeaked under Frieda as she sat, the seat warm from the sun slanting through the glass. She ran her fingertips over the seam of the cushion, grounding herself in the realness of it—like if she didn't, she might float away.

Joyce lifted her coffee, the steam curling up in soft gray ribbons. "To the graduate," she said, her voice rich with pride.

Frieda's cheeks flushed pink. She ducked her head, fiddling with the corner of her napkin. "You didn't have to do all this."

Joyce sipped her coffee, eyes twinkling over the rim. "I didn't," she said simply, setting the cup down with a soft clink. "But I wanted to."

Their food came on chipped plates—pancakes stacked high, edges crisp and golden, butter melting into warm pockets. The orange juice sweated on the sides of plastic cups, tiny droplets trailing down to form rings on the Formica table. Frieda cut her stack into careful squares, the syrup pooling in the shallow dents of her plate. She took small bites, tasting sweetness she hadn't let herself have in too long. Joyce dabbed her lips with her napkin, then reached into her big leather purse and pulled out a white envelope, the flap sealed tight. She slid it across the sticky table.

"What's this?" Frieda asked, her voice soft but wary.

"Open it," Joyce said, chin resting on her palm.

Frieda peeled the envelope open with careful fingers. Inside—paper crisp and fresh—a college application stared back at her. **Frampton Community College. Early Childhood Education**. She read the words twice before they settled into her bones.

"College?" she breathed. The word felt too big, too bright in her mouth.

Joyce nodded, eyes steady, a smile tugging at her lips. "Why not, Frieda?"

Frieda's fork hovered above her plate. "I'm not… I barely made it through this." She gestured at the envelope, at her own folded certificate tucked into her bag. Her voice cracked on the edge of old doubt.

Joyce leaned forward, both hands flat on the table now. Her tone dropped, gentle but fierce. "God doesn't rescue you just to keep you perched on the edge of the pit, baby girl. He pulls you out to see you run. To see you become."

The words settled into Frieda's ribs like a heartbeat. She traced the heading on the application with her thumb—*Early Childhood Education*. A seed of something new took root deep inside, fragile but alive. She didn't know how she felt about God yet—this invisible grace that chased her through ashes and night streets. But she believed in the woman across from her. And maybe, just maybe, she was starting to believe in the girl staring at the syrup-slick fork in her hand. The one who survived. The one who was sitting here now, not running. The one who might, for the first time, be learning how to live.

The Classroom of Becoming

THE SCENT OF FRESH INK mixed with the stale bitterness of burnt coffee drifted through the second-floor hallway of Frampton Community College, curling around old vending machines humming with half-empty soda rows. The overhead lights flickered faintly, buzzing in protest at the early hour. Students pressed past in loose knots—shoulder bumps, backpacks unzipped, earbuds tucked deep like secret doors to other worlds.

Frieda kept her steps slow, her notebook hugged tight to her chest, the strap of her worn bag digging a familiar groove into her shoulder. She moved like someone afraid to wake a sleeping ache—careful, deliberate, eyes scanning the bulletin boards layered with flyers for study groups, lost-and-found notes, and club meetings that felt like invitations written in another language.

She felt older here—not by years, but by miles. By the roads she'd crawled through just to stand under this flickering light. She didn't wear brand-new sneakers or laugh carelessly into the glow of a phone. She wore the hush of second chances, stitched carefully into the seams of her thrifted sweater.

At the end of the hallway, Room 214 waited—its door propped open, warm lamplight spilling across dull linoleum. A tattered poster beside the door read, "You Can Do Hard Things." The edges curled like a well-read page. Inside, Dr. Halbrook's voice moved through the air like steady water. She was tall and spare, her gray hair pulled back in a loose knot. Wire-rimmed glasses perched low on her nose, her eyes quick and sharp above them. The lecture drifted through the hum of scribbling pens and the faint squeak of sneakers on the floor under desks.

Frieda slipped into an empty chair near the back, careful not to scrape its metal legs too loudly. She laid her notebook flat and let her eyes settle on the board. *Why Students Act Out*—the words in blocky, sure handwriting.

Dr. Halbrook paused, glancing over the room. Her voice dipped lower, inviting, testing. "Why do you think some students misbehave—fight, skip, break rules—when they're obviously intelligent? What sits under that surface?"

The room went quiet, the kind of quiet that feels like a held breath. A boy two rows ahead clicked his pen twice but said nothing. A girl near the window flipped her braid over her shoulder, eyes down on her blank page.

Frieda's chest tightened. Her thumb traced the edge of her notebook. She could feel the answer inside her like an old bruise. She could hear Lois's voice in her memory: *Speak, baby. Even when it trembles.*

Slowly, she raised her hand.

Dr. Halbrook's head turned, the slight smile crinkling the corners of her eyes. "Yes, Frieda?"

The pen in Frieda's grip pressed a dent into the paper. She sat a little taller, shoulders pulled back, her voice soft but shaped by something sturdy.

"Sometimes it's not rebellion," she said, her words pacing themselves like careful steps across thin ice. "It's grief with no words. They don't know how to say they're hurting. So, they make noise instead."

A hush settled deeper over the room—not awkward, but alive. Pens hovered, frozen midair. Dr. Halbrook nodded, slow and deliberate. She stepped out from behind her lectern, her hand braced gently on its edge.

"That," she said, her voice lifting so the truth could reach every corner. "Write that down, please. All of you."

A flurry of pen scratches broke the quiet—ink spilling Frieda's truth across a dozen pages.

Frieda let her hand fall, her eyes finding the margin of her notebook. Her pulse slowed. The knot in her throat loosened just enough to let in a small breath of something warm. It wasn't applause. It wasn't a trophy. But it was a moment. A small, sacred victory. A sentence that proved she was here. A heartbeat that said she belonged.

WEEKS LATER, between lectures and half-finished notes, Frieda sat alone at her desk, the classroom emptied of chatter and chairs scraped across old tile. A hush settled in, the kind that feels almost holy when sunlight leans through tall windows in thin golden stripes. Dust drifted in the beams like soft confetti. Her pen hovered over the margin of her notebook—half a sentence left dangling. She looked up. Something pulled at her—a sense, like the shift of air before a door opens.

Through the narrow glass panel of the door, she saw her— Tyesha. Same hoodie pulled low, sleeves swallowing her wrists, backpack hanging off one shoulder like a weight she hadn't yet learned to put down. Her eyes locked onto Frieda's, steady and raw. She didn't look away.

Slowly, the door swung open on tired hinges. Tyesha stepped in. No slam. No shuffle of attitude or practiced armor. Just quiet steps that seemed to echo in the hush of the room.

Frieda sat up straighter, her breath caught in her throat. She opened her mouth to say *Hey*, but the word never landed. Tyesha crossed the floor with a softness that almost hurt to watch. No words yet. She came close—so close Frieda could see the chipped polish on her thumbnail, the shimmer of tears held too tightly behind steady eyes. Then, with a quiet exhale, Tyesha opened her arms. The gesture was small, but the meaning behind it could have split the walls wide open.

Frieda stood. She stepped in. And they folded into each other—an embrace that wasn't rushed or half-hearted. It was full. It was heavy with all the things they'd both carried alone.

Tyesha's voice came muffled against Frieda's shoulder. "You don't just teach." She paused, her breath trembling; her next words were a raw confession, cracked open. "You see."

Frieda's hands clenched the back of Tyesha's hoodie. Her eyes burned, the tears pressed stubbornly behind her lashes until they couldn't hold. She pulled back just enough to whisper, voice thick with the memory of who she'd been. "That's because no one saw me, Tye. And it almost killed me."

The truth laid bare between them. It didn't need fixing. Didn't need to be wrapped in pretty words. It just needed to breathe.

When they finally stepped apart, it wasn't awkward. It wasn't over. Tyesha's shoulders were looser, her eyes a little less guarded. And the classroom, with its cracked tile and fading posters, wasn't just a room anymore. It felt like a bridge. And for the first time, both of them were standing on it—together.

Becoming

THAT NIGHT, FRIEDA SAT CURLED UP in the narrow dormitory window seat, knees pulled tight to her chest, a thin blanket draped over her shoulders like a hush. The street below hummed with distant cars and the stray bark of a dog echoing through the rows of old brick apartments. A streetlamp flickered just outside, painting the edges of her journal in pools of warm gold.

Her pen hovered just above the page, its tip trembling slightly as if the words might slip away if she didn't hold them carefully. She drew in a breath, slow and steady, feeling the quiet rise and fall of her chest. The page smelled faintly of ink and the lavender hand lotion Joyce always pressed into her palm before lights-out. She lowered the pen; let it touch paper.

I don't want fame. I don't want money.

The scratch of ink against the lined page was soft—like a prayer whispered through a cracked door.

I just want to leave the door open for the next girl who thinks no one's coming for her.

Her lips parted, forming the words in silence as she wrote. The lamp outside hummed. A gust of cold air snuck through the old window frame, brushing her cheek like a reminder of all the nights she'd stared out at this same city, feeling invisible.

This climb is steep. But my hands are stronger now.

She paused, the pen's tip leaving a faint dot where she hesitated. She could feel it—how every bruise and every mile and every cracked piece of her had somehow fused into something solid. Something that didn't break so easily.

And every rung I grab—

She blinked, her eyes damp, but this time it didn't sting.

Grace is holding it steady.

She reread the lines—slowly, like turning over a piece of glass that used to be a shard but had softened its edges. With a soft sigh, she closed the journal, the cover warm from the heat of her hands. She set it gently on the windowsill beside her cooling mug of tea, the steam now just a ghost above the rim.

Outside, the streetlight flickered again. A bus rumbled past, taillights smearing red across the wet asphalt. Frieda pressed her forehead to the glass, the chill grounding her, a promise against her skin. She wasn't drifting anymore. She wasn't just surviving. She was becoming. And in that quiet space, wrapped in the hush of an old city still alive with possibility, she let herself believe it was true.

The New Morning

THE NEXT MORNING, Frieda woke before the sun found its way through the old dorm blinds—no alarm clock, no urgent tug of fear pulling her from sleep. Just the soft hush of dawn, the chill of early light brushing her face, and the faint scent of last night's rain drifting through the cracked window.

She sat up slowly, tugging an old sweatshirt over her shoulders, the fabric loose and comforting. Her feet touched the cold tile floor, grounding her in a way that felt earned. For a long moment, she just sat there on the edge of her narrow bed, palms resting flat against the blanket, breathing in a peace she hadn't known how to name before.

Outside, campus still belonged to shadows and hush—no chatter of passing students yet, no door slamming down the hall. The street beyond was almost empty, except for the occasional hum of an early bus or the soft patter of a jogger's shoes slapping wet pavement. Life was moving on out there. And for the first time, Frieda didn't feel like it was moving on without her.

She crossed the small room, barefoot, steps slow and careful, and filled the kettle in the corner sink. The water hissed and steamed, swirling into something warm and gentle. She stood by the window as the kettle clicked off, wrapping her hands around the mug, letting its heat sink into her cold fingertips.

Through the glass, the first thin pink threads of sunrise began to stitch their way across a bruised sky. Bare tree limbs stretched like fingers against the light. A delivery truck rumbled down the side street. Somewhere, a door slammed, a car engine turned over—ordinary sounds that felt, somehow, like promises.

Later, in her Child Psychology class, Frieda slipped into her usual seat near the window, journal wedged beside her open textbook. The professor spoke in a steady, even tone about resilience—definitions, theories, neat bullet points projected onto the wall. But Frieda's mind drifted past the bullet points and the printed lines.

She saw Joyce's steady eyes and sticky notes hidden on hallway mirrors. She saw Tyesha's arms wrapped tight around her shoulders in a hallway that used to echo her loneliness. She saw her own hands pouring pancake batter at dawn for girls who still flinched when the world got too loud.

Healing doesn't look like a finish line, she wrote in the margin of her notebook, the ink looping soft and careful. *It looks like choosing not to give up on yourself—again and again and again.*

At lunch, she carried her tray out to the quad, settling cross-legged beneath an old oak near the edge of campus. The bark pressed roughly against her spine. She watched two girls from her GED prep class drift by—one caught her eye and raised a shy hand. Frieda lifted hers too, a small wave that felt like sunlight breaking through. Once, she would have lowered her head and pretended not to see. She would have hidden behind her notebook, behind her scars. Now she stayed. Let herself be seen.

When the shadows stretched long across the grass and the breeze lifted her curls from her neck, Frieda opened her journal one more time. The pages were no longer filled with the heavy ache of old wounds, but with small, honest prayers—unfinished, unpolished, but real.

Thank You for letting me come this far, she wrote. *I don't know what's next. But I'm not walking alone anymore. And maybe that's enough.*

She closed the journal gently, pressing her palm flat against the cover as if to keep the words safe inside. Above her, the branches swayed, catching the last light. And Frieda stayed right there—unrushed, unworried—breathing in the quiet wonder of a life becoming new.

The Next Girl

The chance came without fanfare, quiet as a heartbeat in the rain. It was a Tuesday that couldn't decide if it wanted to be spring or winter—cold drizzle turning sidewalks into slick veins of reflected streetlight. By the time Frieda stepped inside the small brick community center, her shoes were soaked through, her socks clinging cold against her skin. She shrugged off her thrifted raincoat, the shoulders spattered with dark rain blooms, and shook droplets from her curls.

Inside, the smell of damp coats and instant cocoa mixed with the dry hum of the old space heater propped near the wall. A half-circle of girls clustered around its warmth, knees tucked to chests, chatter muffled under the low hiss of steam from the break room kettle. Frieda moved carefully, slipping her bag from her shoulder, nodding to a few familiar faces—girls she knew from spelling practice, from shared peanut butter sandwiches, from whispered confessions after dark.

A staff worker approached—Maribel, with a clipboard pressed tight to her chest and tired eyes that softened when she spoke. "There's one in the corner," Maribel murmured, voice low so the others wouldn't hear. "Name's Alana. Twelve. Been here three nights. Won't talk. Barely eats. Flinches when we get too close. Think maybe you could…?"

She didn't finish. She didn't have to. Frieda nodded once—no hero's nod, just a promise to stay. She found Alana tucked into the farthest corner of the rec room, knees folded so tight they looked stitched to her chest. The sleeves of an old gray hoodie swallowed her wrists, her small fists hidden inside the cotton caves. Wet hair clung to her forehead in limp strands. She didn't blink when Frieda sank to the floor—she just watched her, wary, her dark eyes shining like a stray dog's under a back porch light.

Frieda didn't speak at first. She knew better. She crossed her legs slowly, letting the cold of the linoleum seep through her jeans. She unzipped her canvas bag and pulled out her battered journal—frayed at the corners, its cover peppered with old ink smudges and bent Post-its that peeked like small secrets.

She opened to a blank page, thumb brushing across the faint lines, then lifted a pen from her bag and began to draw. Simple lines first—a house, a crooked tree, a window with light spilling out. She didn't look at Alana. Didn't force eye contact.

Minutes passed—slow and warm with nothing required of either of them but presence. Rain tapped gentle fingers on the old glass window behind them, the steady beat of something that stayed, even when everything else ran. When Frieda finished the little house, she slid the journal halfway across the cracked linoleum floor, the pen balanced on the open page.

"I draw," she said softly, her voice just above the hush of the heater. "When words feel too big. Or too small. Or both." She didn't push it closer. Just left it there—like a door cracked open in a dark room.

Alana's eyes flicked from Frieda's face to the page, then back again. Suspicion lingered, but curiosity was stronger. Slowly, so slowly it made Frieda's heart ache, the girl inched forward. One small hand emerged from the hoodie's sleeve. Her fingers were thin, nails bitten short. She picked up the pen like it might bite her back—then pressed its tip to the page. One line. Another. A circle that became a sun. A stick figure with spiky hair.

They passed the pen like that—back and forth. One drew a cloud, the other rain. A flower with too many petals. A girl on a swing. No words. Just ink and silence and the soft rhythm of rain. Time pooled around them until the heater clicked off and the other girls' laughter faded into another room. Frieda stayed. She breathed easy. She let the hush be enough.

When Alana finally spoke, her voice was a moth's wing against the dark. "You been through stuff too?"

Frieda's throat tightened, but she didn't let it show. She met Alana's eyes and nodded, voice low, steady.

"Yeah. A lot."

Alana didn't smile. But her shoulders dropped. The pen stayed in her hand. She tapped it once against the page. Her eyes didn't dart away this time.

"Okay then," she murmured.

Frieda didn't reach for her. Didn't say more. She didn't need to. She had already become what she once needed most— Not a fixer. Not a savior. Just a girl who stayed when staying was all that mattered.

THE DAYS STRETCHED soft and wet with spring rain. The center's front windows fogged with the breath of too many girls pressed inside, shedding soaked jackets and dripping umbrellas, leaving small puddles that caught the flicker of fluorescent lights overhead.

Alana came back every day after school—small, watchful, slipping in like a question nobody knew how to answer. She didn't make a noise. Didn't giggle with the others around the vending machine or fight for the first turn at the battered foosball table. She just drifted—hood up, sleeves swallowing her hands, eyes hidden under a fringe of hair she rarely brushed aside.

Frieda noticed her before Alana noticed herself. Some days, Alana sat cross-legged in the corner, scribbling jagged shapes and shadowed figures into the secondhand journal Frieda had slipped into her bag that first week. Other times, she hovered nearby while Frieda counted juice boxes, restocked granola bars, and folded blankets that smelled faintly of bleach and hope. She never asked for anything, not until that Tuesday afternoon.

The air inside the center buzzed thick with rainy-day energy—boredom bouncing off walls, the sharp slap of wet sneakers against linoleum, staff voices calling over the chaos to *share, sit down, wait your turn.* Frieda was kneeling by a low shelf, reorganizing board games that never stayed in their boxes. A slight tug at her sleeve made her pause. She turned.

Alana stood there, hoodie strings pulled tight around her face, eyes big and unblinking. Her voice came out small, like it had to fight through a cracked dam to reach daylight.

"Can I… can I sit by you?"

Frieda didn't smile widely or make a scene. She just nodded once and patted the space next to her on the sagging vinyl couch that faced the reading nook. Alana perched there carefully, knees up, arms wrapped tight around them. She leaned just close enough that their shoulders almost touched.

Another staffer read aloud to a circle of restless girls—*Because of Winn-Dixie,* soft voice winding around the hum of the broken heater. Rain tapped the windows in quiet applause. Halfway through the chapter, Alana's voice cracked the hush between them. She didn't look at Frieda—just stared straight ahead at a patch of peeling paint on the far wall.

"My mom's in jail."

Frieda's breath caught, but she didn't flinch. She didn't speak. She waited.

Alana's thumb picked at a loose thread in her sleeve. Her words came slowly, as if they were painful to force out.

"She said she'd come back for me. But she didn't. They put me at my aunt's. Her boyfriend…" A pause. Alana's shoulders twitched. "…he hit me."

Frieda turned then, slowly, careful not to break the small, fragile thing unfolding between them. "You don't have to—"

But Alana went on anyway. The dam cracked open. "So I ran. I kept running. Thought if I got far enough, maybe somebody'd see me. But nobody did. Not 'til…" Her voice faded into the sound of the heater kicking back to life with a metallic shudder.

Frieda reached over, her hand warm and sure, and slipped her fingers around Alana's small fist. She felt the girl's knuckles— cold, bone-thin, fierce.

"I see you now," Frieda said. The words weren't bright. They weren't magic. But they landed steady as an anchor thrown into deep water.

Alana didn't cry. But she held Frieda's hand like it was a rope in the dark. Like it might lead her out.

Later that night, long after the center had emptied and the mop buckets had been rolled back into the supply closet, Frieda sat at her small kitchen table. Steam curled from her chipped mug of tea. Her journal lay open beneath the cone of yellow lamplight.

She wrote, her pen scratching softly against the page:

She's not a project. Not a rescue mission.
She's a mirror.
A younger version of me—scraped, scared, half-believing.
She doesn't need answers.
She needs presence.

Frieda paused, listening to the silence breathe around her. She tapped the pen once, twice, then finished:

Maybe that's all healing really is—
Staying when someone else cracks open the door you once thought would never open for you.

The Color of Silence

THE BREAKTHROUGH ARRIVED hidden in crayon and silence. It had been a long, slow day. The community center's main room smelled faintly of drying glue and cheap fruit snacks. Outside, dusk pressed its cold palm against the windows, turning them into mirrors that reflected Frieda's own tired shape as she moved between chairs and half-open bins of art supplies.

She was gathering stray markers when she reached for her journal—worn leather corners soft from months of midnight scribbles. It fell open in her hands, and something unusual peeked out near the back pages. A single sheet of thin printer paper. Folded with careful edges, as if whoever placed it there had done so gently, with a secret in their palms. She sat down at the low craft table and unfolded it slowly, pressing the creases flat with her fingertips.

It was a drawing—simple, childlike strokes in waxy crayon. A little girl with stick-thin legs and heavy eyes stood alone under a sky of smudged gray. Rough clouds hovered above her like bruises. Blue lines—thick, uneven—poured down in streaks of rain that soaked her petite frame. The girl's shoulders were hunched as if the storm weighed her down. Her face was empty, just a pale oval with no mouth, no expression. The whole scene—clouds, rain, sky—was shaded in dull charcoal, navy, washed-out ash. Except for one thing.

In the girl's tiny hand, almost defiant against the gloom, was an umbrella. Bright orange—startlingly vivid against the gray. Its shape was clumsy but bold; the wax was pressed so hard that the strokes left tiny flecks on the back of the paper.

Frieda's breath caught in her throat. She leaned closer until her nose nearly brushed the page. She traced the orange curve with her finger, feeling the faint ridges of wax under her skin. A warmth stirred deep inside her chest—something tender and too big to name. The heavy silence of the room settled around her like a blanket. She sat there until the hum of the old furnace clicked on, breaking the hush with a low, steady sigh.

Later that afternoon, she was sorting coloring books onto a shelf when she heard the soft squeak of sneakers on linoleum. She turned. Alana had slipped inside—hood up as always, sleeves pulled low enough to hide her hands. She didn't say a word. Just lowered herself slowly into the empty chair beside Frieda, elbows resting on her knees, eyes fixed on the scuffed floor.

Frieda didn't force words either. She reached into her journal, lifted the folded paper, and smoothed it out on the table between them.

"You drew this?" she asked, her voice gentle, like it might spook the moment if it were too loud.

Alana nodded—just once, tiny. Her lashes flickered but didn't lift.

Frieda tapped her finger lightly against the bright umbrella. "Is this you?"

Alana's voice came after a pause, cracked and soft as moth wings. "No." Her eyes lifted just enough to find Frieda's. "It's you."

The words floated in the small gap between them—frail but weighty, like they held the entire air in the room.

Frieda's throat tightened around a sudden knot of tears. She wanted to say something—anything—but the right words refused to form. She didn't have to speak. Alana's drawing had spoken first, in a language that didn't need grammar. She pressed her palm flat over the umbrella, feeling the paper warm under her hand. "Thank you," she whispered.

Alana didn't answer. She just reached into her hoodie pocket, pulled out a stub of orange crayon, and rolled it across the table toward Frieda.

When the Center emptied for the night and the last sleepy girl was coaxed into a ride home, Frieda lingered in the soft hush of the dim-lit staff lounge. The smell of brewed coffee and lemon floor cleaner still lingered in the air. Above the corkboard—where bus schedules and stale flyers curled at the edges—she pinned the drawing with a single thumbtack. She stepped back.

There it was—gray clouds, blue rain, and that single bright flare of orange. A quiet promise. A shelter in a storm. Proof that sometimes the cracks let color in before they let the light.

Frieda stood there for a while, coat draped over her arm, keys cold in her hand. And when she turned off the light, the little umbrella glowed faintly in the hallway's spill of lamplight. Not loud. Not screaming. Just steady. A quiet reminder: You never know when your presence becomes someone's shelter. And healing doesn't always come in words. Sometimes… it comes in color.

Becoming the Bridge

Frieda never planned to start a movement. She just kept showing up. It began so quietly it could have been missed—just a gray Thursday afternoon, the kind that pressed heavy clouds against the windows of Room 213 until the world outside looked washed in pewter. Inside, the flickering classroom lights hummed overhead, the faint buzz weaving through the stale air like a restless thought.

Tyesha and Lena lingered after the final bell—two girls slouched low in their plastic chairs, sneakers braced against the scuffed linoleum, chip bags rustling between them. The smell of salt and vinegar mingled with the faint traces of dry-erase markers and old pencil shavings. Their laughter rose and fell in thin, uncertain strands—like it didn't quite believe in itself. If you listened closely, you could hear the ache beneath it: the sharp edge of jokes that hid old bruises, secrets folded tight in sarcasm.

Frieda knew how to hear it. She didn't force her way in. She didn't wedge herself between their words. She just pulled up a chair beside them, angled just so—close enough to hold space, far enough not to crowd it. She didn't offer lectures. Didn't slide in easy fixes. She let the hush linger between sentences until the silence softened and cracked open on its own. She listened.

The next week, there were five girls. They drifted in two at a time, heads down, shoulders tense. They took seats in a loose half-circle, fidgeting with their sleeves, snack wrappers, and hair ties snapped around their wrists. No one called it anything yet. It was just… a place. A pause. A breath.

The week after that, there were eight. Then twelve. No flyers taped to bathroom stalls. No announcements over the crackly PA. Just whispers passed from locker to locker, cafeteria table to bathroom stall— *Go talk to Miss Winslow. She gets it.* And she did. She stayed late every single day. Rearranged desks into ragged half-circles. Dug tissues from her purse when the box ran out. Handed out pencils that had seen better days.

She let them speak in jagged pieces—stories that spilled out like broken glass. Some girls sat wrapped in their silence like armor, flinching when words brushed too close. Frieda never tried to pull them out. She just sat in the mess with them, her own voice steady as an open door: *You don't have to hide it here.*

One afternoon, Tyesha stayed after the last girl had left, spinning an empty soda can in her palms, the silver catching the hallway's fading light.

"You know what this is, right?" she said, chin lifted, eyes sharp but tired. "This is like… a bridge. Like you're the space between where we're stuck and where we want to get."

Frieda laughed—soft, surprised. "Is that what you think?"

"Yeah," Tyesha smirked, flicking the can so it clattered against the desk. "Miss Winslow sounds like somebody who teaches geometry. You? You're Miss Bridge."

It stuck. It always does when a name is given by someone who needed you to be that thing first.

Lena started showing up with off-brand cookies in greasy corner-store bags. Jazmine—sharp-eyed, all attitude—made a flyer on the school's ancient library printer. The letters were crooked, the ink smudged, but it didn't matter. They taped it to the bulletin board by the water fountain:

THE BRIDGE. Thursdays. Room 213. Miss Bridge.

By month's end, even the assistant principal was saying it. *Miss Bridge can handle that. Go see Miss Bridge.*

One quiet afternoon, Frieda stayed behind after everyone had drifted out. She stacked stray chairs back into neat rows, wiped crumbs from desks, and settled at her own battered desk in the corner. Her grading pile waited—a soft leaning tower of essays and spelling tests. Halfway through the stack, she found it. A paper folded crisp, tucked into the back—*What I Learned from Miss Bridge.*

She unfolded it, read the scratchy lines pressed hard into wide-ruled paper. The words were plain. Unpolished. Honest in a way only teenagers can be when they don't know how to be anything else.

When she finished, her shoulders shook. A soft laugh cracked into a single tear that slipped down to the edge of her jaw. She wiped it away. She didn't feel embarrassed. Didn't feel small. Because this wasn't just survival anymore. It wasn't just healing. It was a bridge—plank by plank, voice by voice—stretching over every river she once thought would drown her. Built in folding chairs. Held up by bruised hands that kept reaching back. And maybe—just maybe—strong enough for the next girl to cross.

The Bridge Widens

THE BRIDGE OUTGREW ROOM 213 before Frieda even realized it. What began with two girls and a bag of vending machine chips turned into a low hum of thirty voices—thirty bruised truths stitched into a fragile tapestry that stretched from one cracked window to the next. The tidy rows of desks vanished long ago, pushed aside like relics from a life where silence ruled the room.

Now, every Thursday, then Tuesdays, then Thursdays again—those same rows were replaced with folding chairs borrowed from the janitor's closet. Chairs that squeaked on the linoleum when girls shifted restless feet, hugged knees to chests, or leaned into each other's laughter.

No one sat at the teacher's desk anymore. Frieda shoved it against the back wall so it wouldn't stand in the way—her old fortress of authority traded for a half-circle of faces willing to look each other in the eye, sometimes for the first time all week.

The whiteboard stayed blank, wiped clean of equations and grammar rules, repurposed now for doodles and scribbled song lyrics. Every week, someone left behind a message in loopy handwriting—*You are not your past. Miss Bridge was here.* There were no neat permission slips. No sign-in sheets. No spreadsheets to track who belonged. The door stayed propped open with a battered textbook, welcoming whoever drifted in—eyes lowered, hood pulled tight, secrets tucked in pockets.

They didn't need a budget. They didn't want one. But grace has a way of feeding hungry mouths. Word reached the little church two blocks down—a weathered brick building with a hand-painted sign that leaned left in the wind. The pastor's wife showed up one Tuesday carrying foil trays so hot they fogged the glass on the classroom door. Baked ziti that smelled like someone's grandma's kitchen. Chili thick with beans and quiet comfort. Sweet tea poured into cloudy plastic jugs. She never stayed long—just set the trays down on the scratched science table and pressed a warm hand to Frieda's shoulder. *"What y'all are doing here—it's holy,"* she'd say with a soft smile, the kind that didn't judge the chaos. Then she'd slip out before any of the girls could thank her.

They didn't serve up lessons with the plates of food. No PowerPoint slides. No bullet-point programs. Just that one sacred rule taped to the wall on scrap paper, written in Frieda's looping hand: *No Masks.* She reminded them every time: *"If you're mad, be mad. If you're broken, come broken. Don't bring your fake self here. Not with me. Not with each other."*

So, they came raw. They brought the things that made grown men flinch—stories about fists and bruises that bloomed purple behind sleeves. About pills hidden in socks, lighters tucked beneath mattresses, prayers whispered under blankets that smelled like stale fear.

No one asked Frieda to fix it.

They knew she wouldn't.

She didn't toss out neat solutions like candy. She just sat there, the Bluetooth speaker humming Lauryn Hill soft and steady behind their voices. Sometimes Maverick City, on nights when the air felt too heavy to hold alone. She passed out dollar-store journals. Plastic-wrapped granola bars. Packs of neon gel pens. Small things that said *I see you* without needing to say *I know how to fix you.*

When someone's voice broke under the weight of a confession—when the story cracked open like a rib cage and the tears wouldn't stop—Frieda didn't preach forgiveness or slap scripture on an open wound. She just scooted closer, placed her warm hand over cold knuckles, and said, *"I've been where you are. And I'm still here."* That was it. No sermon. No rescue mission. Just *still here*. And somehow, that was enough.

The Bridge was never about curing broken girls. It was about giving them a room where they could drag their ghosts into the light without fear. A place where rage wasn't shameful and silence wasn't failure. A place where ugly truths didn't mean ugly hearts.

No roster. No performance. No perfection. Just presence.

And Frieda—who once thought her life was too ruined to hold anything good—realized she had become the one thing she never found when she needed it most: An open door. A safe chair. A quiet place where breath could come easy.

Not a fixer. A bridge. And for these girls—these storm-eyed, soft-voiced, unbreakable girls—that was enough.

Warm With Stories

THE ROOM WAS ALREADY WARM with stories that Thursday—thick with the soft hum of whispered confessions and the low, steady beat of a playlist humming Lauryn Hill through a battered Bluetooth speaker. The folding chairs squeaked when the girls shifted. Plastic cups of sweet tea sweated onto napkins. A half-eaten tray of baked ziti sat on the table in the corner, its foil peeled back like an offering no one needed permission to take.

Alana sat where she always did—back against the cinderblock wall, hood pulled so far over her head that only the tip of her nose caught the low light. Her knees were drawn up tight, like she was holding herself inside her own ribs. Most days she didn't even pretend to join in—just watched, eyes sharp beneath her lashes, a silent question folded in her hunched shoulders.

Frieda moved slowly through the circle, passing out fresh notebooks and packs of cheap markers. She didn't hover too long by any chair—just a gentle pat on the shoulder here, a warm nod there. When she reached Alana, she paused, pressed the notebook into her palm, and didn't say a word. Then she kept moving.

The girls talked that day—some louder than usual. Lena cracked jokes about her ex, making Tyesha roll her eyes so hard the whole circle giggled. Someone new whispered about a fight she'd had with her mom that morning, her voice barely louder than the music.

No one pushed Alana. No one asked why her pen hadn't moved for weeks. Then, somewhere between the laughter and the hush that always follows when stories scrape too close to bone, Frieda glanced over. Alana wasn't standing this time. She was sitting. Shoulders still tense but grounded. In her lap, the notebook lay open, its cheap spine bent under her hand. And in it—lines. Careful. Small. Deliberate. She wasn't writing. She was drawing.

Frieda's breath caught, but she didn't rush her. She just held the space—let the moment breathe. The room sank into that quiet that only The Bridge could hold—soft, holy, wide enough for secrets and scars. Then Alana cleared her throat—a sound so small it might have slipped under the noise of the humming fan if Frieda hadn't been listening.

"I made this," Alana murmured, voice breaking on the edge of her words. She turned her notebook. Held it out for them all to see.

Drawn in thick, smudged marker was a girl—small, hunched, alone—standing on the raw edge of a canyon split wide like a wound. Across from her, sunlight spilled over rocks and tangled trees. Between the cliffs, a bridge stretched—crooked, patched with rope and vines, shaky but real. A path where there shouldn't be one. At the top, scrawled in blocky, half-shy letters: *Miss Bridge. You built this.*

For a moment, no one spoke. The circle stilled. Even the music seemed to soften, the bass a distant heartbeat. Frieda's throat burned. She blinked once. Then again, fighting the tide swelling behind her eyes.

"That's beautiful," someone whispered—Lena, voice hushed and reverent for once.

Alana shrugged like it was nothing, but her fingers trembled when she flipped the cover closed, thumb worrying the edge.

"It's not finished," she mumbled, words folding into the fabric of the room.

Frieda leaned forward, her smile soft but steady. Her voice low so Alana knew it was just for her—yet loud enough for every bruised heart to borrow.

"Neither are you."

No one clapped. No one cheered. They didn't need to. They just leaned in closer—chairs squeaking, shoulders brushing. No one offered advice. No one rushed to fill the silence. They left it open— wide and gentle—so Alana's words could echo in that safe, soft place where beginnings take root.

Not a testimony. Not a breakdown.

Something quieter.

Something braver.

A crack wide enough for light to slip through.

A bridge—still standing.

It was Alana's drawing that cracked something open—like a window eased just wide enough to let spring air slip in after too many cold seasons sealed tight.

THE NEXT WEEK, another girl stepped into that thin gap of courage. She came quietly, hair knotted under a beanie, shoulders hunched like she was waiting for the wrong word. She handed Frieda a single sheet of lined notebook paper—edges torn, the blue lines smudged with pencil marks that dug deep where her words had stumbled out. A poem. It didn't rhyme. It didn't dance. It just ached, raw and uneven, saying out loud what her voice still couldn't.

By the third week, the corner of Room 213 had bloomed into something no schedule could hold down. The back windowsill became a sanctuary of scraps—sketches curling at the corners, quotes scribbled on sticky notes, tiny origami stars folded with fumbling fingers when silence felt safer than speech. Each shape, a small testament that pain could be bent into something new.

Frieda started leaving colored pencils in a chipped tin next to the battered journals. She tucked packs of markers into old coffee mugs. She brought a roll of butcher paper when the lined pages began to feel too narrow for what the girls carried inside them.

Then, one slow Thursday, a stack of blank canvases showed up. Anonymous at first—until Joyce pulled Frieda aside, her eyes warm with a secret she couldn't quite hold in.

"Church youth group," she whispered, pressing a hand to Frieda's shoulder. "Said they heard what your girls are doing here. Said you're painting holy things, whether you know it or not."

So, they painted. They didn't sketch flowers or pretty sunsets just to cover the cracks. They painted storms—dark, churning blues and deep, bruised purples. They painted fists and broken glass and eyes swollen with truth. But on every canvas, somehow, the shadows gave way—smudged edges turning softer, dawn colors bleeding in around the wounds.

Then came the wall. It started with a single swipe of midnight blue on the cinderblock at the back of the room. Then storm clouds, layered with brushstrokes from hands that once shook too hard to hold a pen steady. In the middle, the girls painted a bridge—crooked and patchy, built from rope and planks that looked like they might snap but somehow never did.

On one cliff: a figure, small, curled in shadow, knees drawn to chest. On the other: the same girl, uncurled now, face lifted toward a rising sun that bled gold and rose and soft pink into the bruised night behind her. From her chest bloomed something bright—light painted with fingerprints pressed into the wet paint like prayers. They named it *Crossing*.

One Friday afternoon, with the paint still tacky in places, the girls stood shoulder to shoulder in front of the mural. Their chatter faded, laughter drifting into a hush that felt like a hymn.

Alana stepped forward. She didn't tug her hood up this time. She lifted her hand—scarred knuckles, bitten nails—and traced the painted bridge with the tip of her finger, slow, like she was remembering how to feel it sturdy under her feet.

"We built this," she whispered, her voice barely louder than the tick of the classroom clock.

A murmur of agreement moved through the girls. A rustle of soft sniffles, shoulders brushing, heads bowed together.

Frieda stood at the edge of them all, hands folded against her ribs like she was holding her own heartbeat still. She didn't say a word. She didn't need to. The bridge had spoken for her. And the room—bright with color, thick with breath and hope and things that wouldn't be silenced anymore—held every word they hadn't yet found the courage to paint. Together.

IT BEGAN LIKE ALL QUIET REVOLUTIONS DO—not with fanfare, but with small, steady ripples that slipped through the cracks of ordinary days. First, it was the whispers. Frieda caught them while she stood hallway duty outside Room 213—teachers leaning together at classroom doors, voices low but warm. A nod from Ms. Carter, the guidance counselor with the tired eyes and the rainbow pin on her lanyard. Then a sticky note, pressed into her mailbox between a stack of memos and cafeteria forms. In looping pen: *Thank you for catching what we keep dropping.*

She stood at her mailbox a full minute longer than she needed to, the note pressed between her fingers like a secret she didn't quite know how to hold. But it was Mr. Daniels who cracked the hush wide open.

A Tuesday afternoon. Faculty meeting in the library—fluorescent lights buzzing overhead, stale coffee in foam cups. They sat through budget cuts, test scores, and a PowerPoint that flickered so many times that Frieda's eyes watered.

Then Mr. Daniels cleared his throat. He was always gentle when he spoke—big hands folded on the table, voice rumbling low like distant thunder. "Miss Winslow's group," he said, pausing to let the words land, "is doing more for our girls than our entire counseling department."

Silence. Not awkward—honest. Someone at the back cleared their throat—a pencil tapped. But no one argued.

Three days later, the principal called Frieda into his office. She braced herself on the walk down—picturing a reprimand she'd already drafted apologies for. Overstepping. Liability. Too much heart, not enough policy. But when she stepped in, the principal leaned forward across his cluttered desk—photos of his kids behind him, trophies gathering dust on a shelf—and asked, "Would you consider expanding?"

Frieda stared. "Expanding?"

He nodded once, slow, like he'd been waiting to ask this for weeks. "You're doing something the rest of us can't get right. Let's make it official. Let's catch them sooner. The middle school girls, maybe even fifth grade."

And so, she found herself, days later, standing in front of the school board—hair pulled back tight, hands wrapped around the edges of her notebook. Her voice steady, but her palms damp. She spoke about The Bridge—how it wasn't therapy, but it was sanctuary. How it wasn't advice, but it was truth. How the magic wasn't in her, but in the circle. The courage. The hush that made room for the words too heavy to speak anywhere else.

After the school board came the city meetings—folding chairs in community centers, coffee going cold beside youth coordinators and church volunteers. Each session ended the same way: *How can we help?*

Help came like rain—one drop, then two, then a sudden, quiet downpour. Space donated in a church basement on the east side. An empty classroom near the westside projects turned into a second Bridge circle, then a third. All run by girls who had once sat cross-legged on Frieda's scuffed linoleum floor, juice cups in hand, stories spilling out in stuttered syllables like stormwater. They weren't therapists. They weren't counselors. They didn't need to be. They had lived it. And that was enough.

One evening, after the last meeting, Frieda locked Room 213 alone. She paused at the mural on the back wall—the bridge, the rising sun, the painted girl standing taller each week in someone's brushstroke. Her reflection caught in the dark window glass beside it—hair loose now, tired lines softened by the streetlight spilling in from the parking lot.

The Bridge wasn't a room anymore. It was a promise. It was the path. And Frieda—Miss Bridge—stood steady in the middle of it all, holding the line so the next girl, and the next, could cross.

Then the News Showed Up

IT HAPPENED ON A WEDNESDAY, the kind of wet, drizzling dusk that left the streets slick with reflections of brake lights and neon signs. Frieda sat curled in her corner of the staff room at New Morning House, a cup of chamomile cooling in her hands, when her phone chimed once. She almost ignored it—just another reminder, another appointment. But then it buzzed again. And again.

Earlier that week, a local news crew had visited The Bridge—one camera, one soft-spoken reporter, a few quiet questions asked in the hush between stories. Frieda hadn't thought much of it. She'd sat cross-legged as always, a ring of girls drawn close around her, a scatter of notebooks, folded tissues, markers uncapped and forgotten when words took over.

The segment aired just as the rain pressed harder against the dorm windows. *"From Runaway to Role Model,"* the anchor's voice intoned over a slow pan of Room 213. The footage caught the warmth in the small things: a girl reading from a wrinkled poem, her voice shaking but steady; another wiping her cheeks without shame while Frieda leaned in, listening, just listening—her arms draped loosely around her knees, her laughter like a soft light when someone cracked a joke through the tears.

Near the end, Frieda's voice filled the screen. Calm. Plain. True.

"Sometimes healing looks like sitting in a circle and refusing to let each other drown."

When the credits rolled, her phone hummed alive—one buzz, then three, then dozens. The messages poured in like the rain streaking down the window beside her. Old classmates she hadn't heard from since high school. Teachers from back when she used to slip through the halls like a ghost. A pastor's wife.

A mother from across town who wrote, *My daughter needs you.* A woman from Tennessee: *I wish I had this when I was sixteen.*

A girl from two cities over, her words raw and unvarnished: *Can I come? Please?*

Frieda read each one slowly. Some she answered right away—short, steady reassurances: *You're welcome here*—some she tucked into her heart like folded prayers.

She stayed rooted in the small things, even as her name flickered across the local station's replay loop. She still took the bus when she could, just to feel the hum of it beneath her, to remember the way a city looks when you're pressed hungry against a fogged window, wondering if anyone knows your name.

She still lingered after every circle ended, scraping plates clean in the church kitchen, humming gospel under her breath, the soapy water warm on her skin. Some nights, when the hush fell soft over the shelter, she'd sit cross-legged on her bed, a single candle burning beside her journal, the pen scratching out new prayers, new promises: *Keep me humble. Keep me close to where I came from.*

One gray afternoon, while folding fresh flyers for another meeting—new day, new corner of the city—Joyce watched her work from across the table. Her tea steamed quietly between her palms.

"You don't ever want to forget the street, do you?" Joyce asked, her voice gentle, eyes glinting with something like pride.

Frieda looked up, her fingers pressing the last crease into the stack of flyers. She shook her head once, a small smile ghosting her mouth.

"No," she said softly, almost to herself. *"It's where I found my calling."*

Joyce tilted her head, the corners of her mouth lifting as if she knew a secret Frieda had only begun to understand.

"No, baby," she murmured, voice warm as a blessing. *"It's where He found you."*

Outside, the rain kept falling. Inside, the flyer pile grew, each folded page a map for the next lost girl to find her way home.

THE GIRLS CHANGED. Not all at once. Not in some miraculous flash. But in the quiet, daily way that old wounds breathe when they finally taste air.

It started with small things—barely visible if you didn't know what to look for. They drifted in earlier now, jackets shrugged off before the bell, laughter slipping into the cracks between their guarded words. They lingered after the circle closed for the night, packing up markers, folding blankets, wiping down the chipped table they'd claimed as their own.

They traded secrets in the margins of their homework. Swapped phone numbers to study for GEDs together, to watch each other's babies when someone's shift ran late. They started saying, *"I got you"*—and meaning it. But healing doesn't shout. It whispers in the spaces where silence once dwelled.

One evening, the circle felt different. Softer somehow. The whiteboard was wiped clean, the folding chairs pulled tight in a lopsided ring. The air buzzed low with the aftertaste of a long week—exams, ex-boyfriends, jobs that didn't pay enough to cover bus fare home.

Alyssa sat in her usual spot, knees drawn up, hoodie strings tangled in her fingers. She'd been with The Bridge for months—months of avoiding eye contact, answering in nods and shrugs. But tonight, she kept glancing at Frieda. Her breath came in shallow pushes, like each inhale was a choice she hadn't always known she could make.

Then she stood. No one spoke. Lena shifted forward, elbows resting on her knees. Tyesha stilled her restless sneaker tapping. Even the old floor creaked quietly beneath them, as if the room itself was holding its breath. Alyssa's hands trembled where they clutched the hem of her shirt. But her voice—when it came— was steady as stone.

"I was gonna end it this summer," she said. Her eyes flitted to Frieda—*Miss Bridge*, the name they'd given her when she hadn't asked for one. "I even wrote the note. Folded it up under my pillow. I thought... I thought nobody would miss me long."

Silence. Heavy and alive. The kind that says *we're here. Keep going.*

Alyssa's fingers clenched tighter. She swallowed. "But then Miss Bridge looked at me one day—when I wouldn't even look up—and she said, 'You matter too much to disappear.'"

Her eyes flicked to the girls around her. To the mural behind them—storm colors bleeding into sunrise, a crooked bridge painted by their own hands.

"I didn't believe her then," Alyssa said, her voice breaking just enough to let the truth spill out. "But I do now."

No gasp. No applause. Just wet cheeks. Soft sniffles. Tyesha's hand brushing her own tears away with the back of her wrist.

Frieda didn't stand to answer. Didn't gather them up with some pretty speech about survival or second chances. She just opened her arms, palms up, wide enough to catch whatever Alyssa had left to give.

"Come sit by me," she murmured.

And Alyssa did—folding herself into Frieda's side, head pressed to her shoulder, the circle drawing a little tighter around them both.

Outside, the streetlights flickered on one by one. But inside Room 213, something warmer glowed—a small, defiant promise that none of them had to disappear alone again.

That Sunday

THE BREEZE CARRIED THE SCENT of honey butter biscuits from the church kitchen—warm, sweet, and so familiar it made Frieda's heart ache in a good way. She sat beneath the wide arms of an old sycamore tree that had stood watch over the churchyard for decades—branches stretching wide like a mother's arms, dappling the ground in shifting patches of soft shade.

Across from her, Minister Joyce poured tea from a chipped floral pot into mismatched cups. The café table between them was scarred with age—rings where mugs had once rested too long, scratches that told a hundred stories.

Frieda wrapped her hands around her cup, letting the steam brush her face. She breathed in the warmth, but her shoulders stayed tense. She told Joyce everything—words tumbling out in stops and starts. The new chapters sprouting in schools she'd never stepped inside before. The girls who trusted her with pieces of themselves they wouldn't give to anyone else. The news crew that had come and gone, leaving behind praise she wasn't sure she deserved. The weight pressing against her ribs every night when the lights went out and the silence asked if she was enough.

Joyce didn't interrupt. She never did. She just listened, nodding gently, the breeze fluttering the edge of her Sunday scarf. When Frieda's voice cracked on the last word— *"I'm trying, but I don't know if it's enough."*—Joyce set her teacup down with a soft clink. She reached across the small table, her hand warm and steady as it closed over Frieda's.

"Child," Joyce said, voice as smooth as riverbed stone, "you're not playing at this. You're walking in your call."

Frieda's eyes shimmered, blinking hard against the sudden sting. The church bell tolled once in the distance, low and gentle.

"But I still feel like I'm falling short," she whispered. Her thumb traced the edge of the cup, feeling the tiny chip near the rim. "There's always another girl. Another fire to put out. What if the bridge isn't strong enough to hold them all?"

Joyce squeezed her hand, her palm rough from years of work and worship. She leaned in just enough for Frieda to smell the faint trace of lavender that clung to her cardigan.

"Frieda Winslow," Joyce said, her tone slow, every word a promise, "God never asked you to carry the whole world. He asked you to stand where your feet are—*and stay*. You're building a bridge with your *life*. Not for you to cross alone, but so others can follow."

Frieda let out a breath she hadn't realized she'd been holding. Her shoulders dropped. The branches above them swayed, whispering secrets to the early afternoon light.

Joyce sat back, a small smile deepening the lines at the corners of her eyes. "A bridge doesn't ask who's crossing it, baby. It just holds steady."

And in that quiet patch of shade, with teacups clinking and honey butter biscuits cooling in the church kitchen, Frieda felt the weight in her chest loosen—just enough to remind her that even tired hands can build sacred things.

THAT NIGHT, FRIEDA STOOD in front of her mirror. Not the cracked shard of glass taped to a bathroom stall door on Monroe Street. Not the dull, warped reflection in a diner window she once avoided meeting. A real mirror. In a real room. Her room—walls soft with warm lamplight, a thrifted quilt folded neatly on the end of her bed, a Bible and a half-empty mug of tea resting on the nightstand.

She stared at herself, searching the reflection the way you search a familiar street for the first signs of spring. Her shoulders weren't hunched forward anymore like they were bracing for the next blow. Her eyes—still tired, still ringed with old shadows—held something new in their depths. A steadiness. A softness. A spark that hadn't come from her but refused to leave her.

Not a runaway. Not a dropout. A woman. A mentor. A living, breathing answer to prayers she once screamed into empty nights.

She pressed her fingertips lightly to the glass, tracing the faint line of her jaw, the curve of her hair curling loose around her face. Then she leaned in, breath fogging a small circle, and whispered into the hush, "Thank You… for not giving up on me." And this time, she didn't flinch from the echo. This time, she believed it.

She crossed the room and settled onto her bed, legs folded beneath her. She reached for her journal—its pages dog-eared and ink-blotted, the spine beginning to fray. She opened it slowly, let the pen hover for a heartbeat. Then, with hands steady, she wrote:

I used to wonder if anything good could come from me.
Now I know:
Goodness was never mine to generate—only to carry.
God gave me a story I wanted to bury deep.
Now it's planting gardens in places I never thought I'd stand.
We are building something sacred with our scars.
The Bridge is not made of programs or praise.
It's made of stories.
Of hands held in dark rooms.
Of pain spoken aloud.
Of girls daring to believe they are still worthy.
I was once one of them.
And now… I'm still one of them.
But I've learned to lead from the middle.
That's what a bridge does.

When the ink settled into the paper, Frieda closed her eyes and rested her palm over the words. Through the thin page, she felt her heartbeat—steady and real.

Outside her window, the city pulsed in gentle quiet, streetlights flickering like small watchfires keeping vigil for every girl still out there, waiting for a way across.

Frieda sat there a little longer, cradled in the soft hush of her room, letting the truth settle deep:

She was never meant to be the destination.
She was the crossing.
The proof that mercy, once given, can be carried
forward—one trembling step at a time.

CHAPTER 14

Fire Inside the Walls

The email came on an ordinary Wednesday, slipped between district bulletins and department memos about copier paper and new lunch protocols. It was so plain she almost missed it— subject line small and sharp: **URGENT**. No name. No logo. No breadcrumb trail back to whoever wrote it. She clicked.

Not everyone's safe at The Bridge

Six words.

No punctuation.

No explanation.

Frieda's eyes locked onto the screen, but the words blurred at the edges. She leaned closer, searching for something—anything—a signature, an IP, a stray clue that might anchor it to something real, something she could fight.

Nothing. Just that stripped-bare sentence, cold as an open window in December. She swallowed. Her throat felt raw, her chest tight under her ribs. The air in the tiny office turned heavy, pressing against her shoulders until they curled forward like they used to when she was seventeen, hiding from the world behind a locked bathroom door.

She pushed the chair back slowly. The legs scraped the floor, too loud in the hush. Her hands drifted to her chest, fingertips resting where the fear gathered, pulsing beneath her skin. She whispered into the small hush, voice trembling like the edge of a frayed page: *"Lord… what is this?"*

No answer. Just the low hum of the laptop fan, the soft tick of the clock above the door, the creak of old pipes behind the drywall. Her eyes drifted to the corkboard over her desk. Photos of the girls. Alana's drawing of the crooked bridge. Tyesha's sticky note with *You matter* scrawled in a slanted hand. Reminders of what this place had become—a crossing, a haven.

Not safe. The words pulsed again behind her eyes: *Not everyone's safe.* Her palms pressed flat to the desk. The wood felt solid beneath her skin, but her mind was already moving—names, faces, doors that might need new locks, secrets that could shatter if whispered in the wrong ear.

She closed the laptop with slow care, as if the weight of its hinge might muffle what had just begun to burn in her veins. She stood and moved to the window. Outside, the wind rattled the brittle branches of the courtyard tree. Kids laughed on the basketball court two blocks over. Life went on, loud and oblivious.

But inside the walls—inside her chest—a fire had sparked. Quiet. Small. But it would not stay contained. Frieda exhaled, the taste of old prayers on her tongue. *Stillness is over,* she thought. *Now I move.*

The Whispers

IT BEGAN LIKE A DRAFT UNDER A DOOR—something subtle, something you could almost pretend wasn't there. At first, Frieda didn't notice it outright. She just felt it. A faint ripple in the air when she stepped into Room 213—girls who once threw their arms around her neck now gave half-smiles, quick nods, then drifted away in pairs, leaving silence in their wake. A low hum of chatter would hush the second she passed, like a radio dialed down mid-song.

She told herself it was nothing. Maybe they were tired. Busy. Maybe they were growing up, drifting like they all did, like she once did herself. But in her chest, a small, sharp ache pressed against her ribs.

Then the tiny absences grew teeth. A plate of cookies, once dropped off by a local church volunteer every Tuesday, never came. A text to Lena—*You okay? Miss you.*—left unread for days. Tyesha's seat stayed empty, her notebook untouched on the shelf where she'd always left it behind by accident, pages filled with dreams and scraps of song lyrics.

At school, a teacher Frieda would usually swap lesson plans with, lowered her eyes and ducked into her classroom when they crossed paths in the hall. In the staff lounge, two aides went silent when she entered, their unfinished coffee cooling on the counter as they mumbled excuses and slipped out the door.

Frieda stood there sometimes, gripping a mug she no longer sipped, staring at the corkboard where announcements and PTA flyers blurred together. Her name—Miss Bridge—still there on a faded sticky note. But now, the title felt like a door that wouldn't open.

The circle shrank. The girls came, but they sat back, arms folded tighter than before. Their laughter was careful now. Their secrets, fewer. The warmth that once spilled between folding chairs like sunlight through blinds had cooled to a cautious hush.

One late Thursday, Frieda found herself wiping down tables alone after a meeting that had ended too early, the walls echoing with a quiet that hurt more than any slammed door. The cloth dragged across the laminate surface, her hand moving on autopilot as her mind churned.

Then came Joyce. Her footsteps soft as breath, her cardigan sleeves brushing the backs of the chairs. She didn't sit. Just stood there, hands folded, eyes as steady as they'd always been—but deeper somehow, as if they could see the storm under Frieda's skin.

"Is something going on, baby?" Joyce asked, voice like a porch light turned on in the dark.

Frieda paused, cloth limp in her hand. Her mouth opened, but no sound came. The truth swelled behind her teeth—heavy, sour, scared. She closed her lips around it and shook her head instead. Just once. Small.

Joyce didn't push. She laid her palm over Frieda's knuckles where they gripped the cloth, gave it the gentlest squeeze. But when she pulled away, the emptiness rushed back in.

Frieda watched the door long after Joyce left. She could feel it, deep in her bones. The warmth slipping through cracks she couldn't find. The walls she'd built with open hands starting to tremble at the seams.

And this time— This time, she feared her hands might not be enough to hold it all together.

The Break

IT CAME APART under harsh fluorescent lights that flickered like a warning no one could read in time. The multipurpose room— once alive with cut-out hearts and bright markers, crowded with whispered secrets and brave confessions—felt smaller now. Claustrophobic. Like the walls themselves leaned in to hear the fault lines crack.

Frieda stood near the whiteboard; her notebook clutched to her chest. Ink stains smudged her wrist, a faint trace of a day spent planning, scribbling, rewriting tomorrow. She watched the circle form—half full, half empty—volunteers murmuring over half-eaten cookies, a plastic pitcher of lemonade sweating on a folding table.

Maria rose slowly. Her chair scraped the linoleum in a sound that made everyone flinch. She didn't speak at first. Just stood there—arms wrapped tight across her chest as if they alone could hold back whatever was rising in her throat. Her eyes shone, but not with tears. They were hard. Wounded. Lit from somewhere Frieda couldn't reach.

When Maria spoke, her words came out flat at first, like an iron pressed too long on fabric: "We do everything." The chatter stilled. A paper cup crumpled in someone's hand. Maria's jaw flexed. She uncrossed her arms only to point them—sharp, accusing. "You just show up. Smile. Take the credit."

A silence spread like a spill. Even the old wall clock seemed to freeze—its second hand stuck between beats.

Frieda's throat worked around her breath. "Maria…" she said, softly, her voice searching for the warmth that used to live there. "What is this? Talk to me."

But Maria only stepped closer, her sneakers squeaking against the waxed floor. Her chin tipped up, eyes unblinking, voice slicing cleaner than any blade. "You stand up there with your journal and your nice words. And we—" she gestured wide, the circle shrinking back— "we clean the mess. We call the parents. We find the food. We sit with the girls at three a.m. when you're asleep in your safe little apartment."

A sharp inhale. Someone's pen rolled off a table—its plastic clatter cutting through the hush. No one reached for it.

Frieda felt her heartbeat at her temples, her palms damp around the soft spine of her notebook. "I've given everything," she whispered. The words cracked halfway out, thin as tissue. "I've given you my story. My time. My heart—"

Maria laughed—just once, humorless. Her eyes shone sharper now, brimming but unspilled. "*Your* story," she echoed, like the word tasted bitter. "It's always *your* story, Miss Bridge. Always *your* healing. *Your* redemption arc. But this—" she swept her hand toward the battered bulletin board, the half-done mural on the wall, the empty snack trays— "this is ours too. And maybe we're tired of standing behind you like your backdrop."

Frieda stepped back. The notebook slid against her palm, threatening to drop. She searched the circle—Lena, Tyesha, a handful of girls, and grown women who used to hold their scars out to her like offerings. Now their eyes slid away, fixed on the floor, the wall, anything but the rift splitting open in front of them.

A buzzing light above hummed. The clock ticked on, catching its second breath. In the stillness, Frieda felt it—her own voice folding inward. The warmth that had held them all together, seeping through a crack she couldn't find, couldn't mend.

The notebook trembled in her grip. She wanted to reach for Maria—call her back to that night in the hall when she'd called Frieda a lighthouse. A safe harbor. But the harbor had waves now. And the waves were breaking.

The Reckoning

THE BOARDROOM FELT TOO BRIGHT—fluorescent lights humming overhead like an interrogation lamp, pale walls so blank they seemed to echo every breath. The conference table stretched long and polished between them, the grain beneath Frieda's fingertips slick with condensation from the sweating pitcher of lukewarm water that no one had touched.

Frieda sat at the far end. Shoulders drawn tight, palms pressed together so firmly her knuckles whitened. Her notebook lay closed beside her—useless here. The pen she always carried sat untouched, its cap bitten from nights when she still believed words could hold everything steady.

Across from her, the board president sat rigid in a navy blazer that looked too stiff to breathe in. He cleared his throat once, then again, as if rehearsing how to wrap the next words in civility. His voice when it came was thin and practiced, shaped more by policy than by people.

"We've seen some concerning things," he began, each word carefully spaced, like stones laid across a river he wasn't sure how to cross.

Frieda lifted her eyes just enough to see the folder in front of him—edges sharp, a few loose papers clipped tight. Screenshots. Posts. Snippets of stories that had slipped into corners she couldn't control.

"Anonymous stories. Screenshots. Allegations." He didn't look at her when he said it. His eyes stayed fixed on the folder. His fingers drummed the table—steady, impersonal.

The words landed: *Favoritism. Emotional manipulation. Unqualified.*
Each syllable hit like pebbles dropping into water—tiny, relentless, leaving rings that spread outward until they touched every corner of her mind.

Frieda didn't interrupt. She didn't argue. She just stared at the faint swirl of wood grain beneath her trembling hands. The table felt cold, distant, a plane of polished judgment she couldn't cross. Her chest ached with something tight and familiar—shame, maybe. Or grief.

Across the table, the president leaned forward, voice lower now, almost gentle. "We need to consider a leave of absence," he said, like someone offering a blanket to a wounded dog. "Just until things are… sorted. While we investigate."

She almost laughed—soft, sharp. But her throat caught the sound before it could break free. Instead, her head dipped in a slow, reluctant nod. Her neck felt stiff, resisting the surrender that her heart already knew.

When her voice came, it cracked like an old door swinging open in the dark. "You don't know what it cost me to build this." The words fell into the silence like something sacred and spent.

No one answered. They didn't know. Couldn't.

She breathed out, long and thin, the ache loosening its teeth just enough to make room for the next word. "But…" She forced her eyes to rise—past the polished table, the untouched water, the folder that would decide if she still belonged here. "If stepping back keeps the work alive… then I'll do it."

To her left, Joyce sat steady. Always steady. She hadn't spoken once, but now her warm, calloused hand slipped across the cold veneer of the table, found Frieda's fingers, and wrapped them in a quiet promise: *I'm here.*

Frieda didn't pull away. But she didn't lean in either. Inside, something deeper than her role, deeper than her story, began to fray—like fabric pulled too tight at the seams. Not just the work. Not just the dream. But the core of who she was becoming.

Beneath the sharp hum of fluorescent lights and the polite hush of professional concern, Frieda sat very still. Her mind whispered what her mouth would not: *I am no longer the bridge. I am the question. And the ground beneath my feet was starting to crack.*

The Fire Within the Walls

THAT NIGHT, Frieda didn't bother with the lights. She slipped her key into the lock with trembling fingers, stepped into the hush of her tiny apartment, and let the darkness swallow her whole. The only glow came from a single candle she lit on the kitchen table—a stub of wax flickering inside a chipped mason jar. Its small flame quivered each time she breathed too close, throwing shadows against the peeling paint, the old bookshelf sagging with dog-eared devotionals, the frayed throw blanket tossed over her secondhand sofa.

The flyer for *The Bridge* lay on the table—creased, crumpled at the corners, like wings folded in on themselves. The bold letters that once made her proud now seemed to blur at the edges, shrinking beneath the weight of whispered betrayal and a boardroom's polite doubt. She didn't touch it. She only looked. Let the ache pulse behind her ribs, heavier with each silent minute.

The room smelled faintly of warm wax and the faint musk of old pages. Frieda reached for her Bible, the leather soft, the spine broken from nights spent leaning on words when there was nothing else to lean on. She flipped, not because she didn't know where to land but because her fingers needed the ritual—pages whispering like breath in a quiet chapel. *Isaiah 43.* She traced the words with her fingertip before her voice found them: *"When you pass through the waters, I will be with you..."*

Her voice cracked on *will.* She swallowed. Tried again.

"When you walk through the fire, you shall not be burned, and the flame shall not consume you."

The words trembled in the small room. The flame wavered—bent low, then righted itself again, stubborn and alive. She closed her eyes and let the weight of it break loose. The betrayal. The confusion. The question that scraped at her heart like a stone in her shoe: *Who am I if they don't trust me anymore?*

"Then *walk* with me now," she whispered, her hands pressed flat over the thin pages. "Because I feel like I'm burning."

The candle danced. Then steadied. And she stayed there—hands splayed, eyes shut, cheek damp where tears slipped and cooled. She didn't ask for an answer. Not tonight. Just presence. Just *stay with me.* Just *don't let me drown.*

She was still there when the knock came. A single, hesitant rap against the chipped wood of her door. She flinched, the echo snapping through her small space like an unwelcome gust. When she cracked the door open, the hallway light spilled in, haloing the girl on her threshold. Maria. Hoodie up. Eyes rimmed raw, shoulders hunched like the wind might blow her back down the stairs if Frieda didn't move aside fast enough.

Maria held out her phone. Her knuckles were white around it.

"It was me," she said—words thin, barely above a rasp. "The account. The posts. All of it."

The hallway was suddenly too bright. Frieda felt the words settle in her gut like cold iron. Her hand curled tighter around the edge of the door.

Maria's eyes flicked away. Her voice cracked. "I was jealous. I thought if I tore you down, I'd matter more. But I was wrong. I'm sorry."

The air between them filled with the noise Frieda's heart was making—thunder she didn't show on her face. She looked at Maria's small frame, the way her shoulders curled in on themselves, the way shame made her look twelve years old again.

Slowly, Frieda stepped back. Opened the door wider. Gestured inside. "Come in," she said, her voice softer than her pulse. "Sit down."

Maria moved like she wasn't sure the floor would hold her. She sank onto the small sofa, hands knotted in her lap, hoodie sleeves tugged down over shaking fingers. Frieda sat opposite her, the candle flickering between them on the table like a fragile witness.

Maria's voice was little more than a shiver. "I don't even know what to say."

"You already said it," Frieda murmured. Her chest ached with something that felt too big to be called forgiveness but too alive to be anger. "You told the truth. That matters."

Maria's tears spilled then—slow, salt lines down her cheeks. "You were everything I wanted to be. I hated that I couldn't be you. I thought… if I chipped away at your shine, mine might show. But all I did was ruin the light for everyone."

Frieda leaned forward. Her hands rested on her knees, steady now, her voice a thread of warmth in the hush. "I never wanted you to be me, Maria. The Bridge was never about *me*. It was about you. Becoming you. Fully. Freely. Unafraid."

Maria squeezed her eyes shut, shame pouring out in a single broken sentence: "I hurt you."

Frieda's throat burned. She didn't reach for a Bible verse or a sermon. She just reached for Maria's trembling hands, folding them in her own. "And yet you're here," she whispered. "Owning it. That's braver than pretending you didn't."

Maria's shoulders caved with a sob. "I don't deserve to be here."

Frieda's fingers tightened around hers. "Neither did I, once. Grace gave me another chance. And I think—" her voice cracked, then steadied, "—I think it's your turn now."

Maria broke then—broke like dawn breaks, tears washing through the ache, shoulders trembling. Frieda slid beside her on the small couch and gathered her in. No big promises. No magic fix. Just two girls in the flicker of candlelight—one who had built the bridge, the other who had tried to burn it down—and both, somehow, still standing on it together.

The room smelled of wax and salt and something warm that hadn't been there before. Forgiveness. Fire that didn't consume.

The Fire and The Quiet

LATER THAT NIGHT, with only the flickering candle for company, Frieda sat at her small kitchen table—elbows resting on the wood scarred by time and use. The apartment felt deeper in the dark, each corner hushed except for the quiet hum of the refrigerator and the faint creak of the old floorboards settling beneath her feet.

Her journal lay open in front of her, the soft leather worn to velvet where her thumbs had pressed it thin over countless nights like this one. She ran her palm across the blank page as if smoothing wrinkled linen, grounding herself in the slow weight of ritual.

She uncapped her pen, the click loud in the hush. For a moment, she just held it there—ink ready, thoughts waiting. Then, pressing down slowly, she wrote:

I used to think the fire was outside.

She stopped. Let the words settle. Outside, rain began to tap against the window—soft, searching. She listened to it. Let it echo in the hollow of her chest. Then she lowered her eyes and wrote again, slower this time:

Now I know—it gets in through cracks. Through pride. Through pain.

Through people we love who haven't healed yet.

The lines wavered for a moment, the ink smudged by the brush of her wrist as she lifted her hand to rub the tiredness from her eyes. A breath shuddered out of her—half sigh, half prayer. She leaned in, her pen hovering above the paper like a promise waiting to be spoken.

But I won't let bitterness win.

I've come too far.

I'll rebuild again.

The candle flame danced. Shadows on the wall moved with it—shifting, bending, refusing to be pinned down. Frieda's hand paused one last time. She breathed deep, deeper than she had all day, then let the ink spill the final thought:

Because grace doesn't quit when things fall apart.

It gets to work.

She set the pen down with care, its click against the table soft, final for now. She closed the journal gently, as though not to wake the words still warm on the page.

Outside the window, the rain whispered down the glass in silver ribbons. Inside, the candle had burned low, a single golden thread of flame stubbornly pulling light through the shadows that tried to swallow it. Frieda leaned back in her chair, her shoulders curling into the worn cushion. Her eyes were heavy. But her spirit— bruised, tired—held steady.

The fire was still there. But so was the grace. And maybe— maybe that was enough to begin again.

The Shutdown

THE LETTER ARRIVED on a Thursday morning, slipped beneath the door like an afterthought—just a plain white envelope stamped with the city's insignia, folded crisp as a final word. Frieda found it waiting on her desk among lesson plans, half-finished notes, and the battered mug she'd refilled three times that morning but never really tasted.

She sat down slowly, her heartbeat thudding in her throat as she broke the seal. The paper crackled—a sound too loud in the quiet room. She smoothed it open, her eyes tracing the neat, official lines:

Department of Zoning and Community Use.
Notice of noncompliance.
Unauthorized structural changes.
Unapproved occupancy.
Immediate action required.

Each phrase struck like a stone dropped in deep water—ripples spreading before she could catch her breath. She reached the last line and her eyes stopped moving, frozen on the words that seemed to echo in the hush:

Cease operations pending review.

The page trembled in her hands. For a moment, she didn't breathe. Behind her, life went on—laughter spilled down the hallway, the warm, ordinary chaos of The Bridge at work. Tyesha's laugh rose over Lena's groan—someone must've drawn a Wild Card. The Bluetooth speaker hummed with soft R&B, the scent of cheap pizza lingering in the air. The sound of safety. The sound of belonging.

Frieda folded the letter along its crease, sharp and neat, though her hands shook. She rose from her chair like her bones had doubled in weight, each step toward the main room heavy as a confession. They noticed her before she spoke. Tyesha's hand hovered over the pause button on her phone. Lena's smile faltered mid-sentence. A ripple of quiet fell over the room, their eyes following the envelope clutched in Frieda's hand.

She stopped in the center of the room—her circle—her sanctuary—and cleared her throat. The hush deepened.

"Can I get everyone's attention for a minute?" Her voice was low, but it carried. Tyesha muted the music. Bags of chips were set down, notebooks closed, knees pulled up to chests. The circle leaned in.

Frieda unfolded the letter with care. She lifted it, as if showing them the thing that dared to threaten what they'd built.

"This came today. From the city." She exhaled once, steadying her words on the edge of her breath. "They say… we're out of compliance. Permits. Zoning. Things we didn't know we needed. They want us to shut down."

A single gasp cracked the quiet—like a match struck in a dark room. A girl in the back whispered, "Wait—what?"

Frieda's eyes swept across their faces. Eyes wide. Some glistening already. Some hardened with disbelief. Every face she'd come to know—every story she'd held like a secret in her hands. She lowered the paper to her side. Took one step closer. Then another, until she was standing inside the circle.

"They can lock a door," she said softly, voice carrying on the hush. "But they don't get to close *us*."

She looked at Alana, who sat cross-legged near the window, journal hugged to her chest. The girl's voice was barely more than breath. "So… where do we go?"

Frieda crouched down until she was level with her—eye-to-eye with every girl who needed this to stay real.

"We go *wherever* we have to," she said, her words slow and certain. "Basements. Back porches. Church kitchens. Library corners. Living rooms. If there's breath in us, there's Bridge in us."

Lena wiped at her eyes with the back of her wrist, her mouth twisting into something that almost looked like a grin. "Miss Bridge," she said, her voice breaking and bold at once, "they really thought they could shut *us* down?"

A low laugh rippled through the circle—wet with tears but fierce. Tyesha slapped her knee. "Nah. They forgot who we are."

Frieda rose, standing taller now than the walls that thought they could hold them in. She lifted the letter once more, then let it drop to the floor at her feet—small, powerless against what hummed in that room.

"This is just paper," she said, her voice gathering every heartbeat in the circle. "We're the Bridge. We don't break. We *move*."

The hush cracked wide open—not with shouting, but with soft, steady nods, the kind of agreement that plants itself like a seed and knows how to rise through concrete. No walls. No permits. No verdict could undo what they'd built in each other.

The city might have slammed a door. But Frieda saw it now—clear as dawn breaking over the ruins: The Bridge was not a place. It was them. And they would carry it forward, wherever their feet found room to stand.

The Aftermath

AFTER SPEAKING TO THE GIRLS, Frieda returned to her office—closing the office door behind her with a soft click that felt louder than it should. The muffled hum of voices in the hallway faded as she pressed her back to the wood, her breath catching in her throat. She stood there for a moment, unmoving, the letter limp in her fingers like a flag of surrender.

Finally, she crossed the small room in slow, weighted steps and sank into her chair. The cushion squeaked under her, familiar but offering no comfort. She didn't take off her coat. She didn't bother to turn on the lamp. The late afternoon light, heavy with dusk, filtered in through the narrow window, washing everything in a bruised gray.

Her eyes drifted—over the shelf where her journals leaned in crooked rows, spines softened by nights of frantic scribbles. Over the frame on her desk: a photo from the first night The Bridge began—three girls in plastic chairs, heads bent close, eyes raw but bright. Over the bulletin board above it all, a chaos of flyers, sticky notes in messy handwriting—*Thank you, Miss Bridge, See you Thursday, You saved me.*

She stared at those scraps of ink and paper like they were proof that she hadn't dreamed this whole thing up. Then she looked down at the letter again. Its creases cut deep into her palm, the black ink cold and final. *Cease operations pending review.* She read it twice. It didn't change. A tremor climbed up her arm, tightening her chest. She dropped the letter on the desk and fumbled for her phone. The screen blurred for a heartbeat before she found Joyce's name. She didn't bother with a greeting when the line clicked open.

"Come by," she said, voice soft and frayed. "Please."

Twenty minutes later, the door creaked open. Joyce stepped inside without knocking—coat still buttoned, eyes sharp behind her glasses. She paused just inside the doorway, taking in the dim room, the hunched curve of Frieda's shoulders behind the desk, the letter half-buried under her shaking hand.

Joyce didn't say anything at first. She simply crossed the room and lowered herself into the chair across from Frieda's, the leather creaking beneath her weight. She placed her purse on the floor, folded her hands on her knees, and waited.

Frieda didn't look up. She just slid the letter across the desk with a motion that felt heavier than the paper itself. Joyce picked it up. The crinkle of the page seemed to echo in the hush. She read each line slowly, her brow creasing deeper with every word. Then she set it down with careful, deliberate quiet—like she was handling a live ember.

"This ain't about permits," Joyce said, her voice low, even—cutting through the room's hush like a warm blade.

Frieda lifted her head slowly. Her eyes were rimmed red, lashes damp. She looked younger in that half-light—like the girl who once curled up on a library floor and asked God if He was still listening.

"Then what is it about?" she rasped.

Joyce leaned forward, elbows on her knees, gaze steady and unflinching. "It's about fear," she said. "About people who've never had to sit in a circle and admit their own wounds. It's about control, baby. They see girls getting free—telling the truth nobody wants told—and they get scared."

Frieda let out a dry, cracked laugh. It stuck in her throat like splinters. "But I did it right, Joyce. I followed every rule. I filled out every form. I asked permission."

"And you built something sacred," Joyce said, her hand reaching across the desk, warm over Frieda's cold knuckles. "You didn't wait for their blessing. That's what scares them. You proved you don't need them to heal these girls."

Frieda's chin trembled. Her voice slipped out ragged. "It hurts, Joyce. God, it hurts. I'm so tired. Every time we get our feet under us, they push us back down."

Joyce's thumb brushed over her hand, gentle as a benediction. "It's always been this way. Liberation rattles cages. It shakes foundations built on silence. But remember—just because they shut the doors doesn't mean God closed the work."

The words settled in the dimness like soft embers, warm against the cold dread still gripping Frieda's chest. She lowered her eyes, staring at where their hands met—wrinkles and calluses, old scars and new, bound together on a desk littered with scribbled dreams. They sat there for a long while. No rush to fill the silence. No scramble for solutions. Just breath. Just presence.

Finally, Frieda's voice rose, barely louder than the hum of the heater behind her. "So, what do we do now?"

Joyce squeezed her hand, the corners of her mouth lifting into that calm, knowing smile Frieda had leaned on for so long. "We pivot," she said. "We pray. And we keep building, baby. Just like we always have."

Outside the window, dusk slipped deeper into night. But inside that little office—lined with paper hopes and flickering faith—a soft fire kindled in the quiet. And Frieda let it warm her enough to believe: the story wasn't done yet.

The Inspection

THE KNOCK CAME one mid-afternoon—sharp, precise, deliberate, like a gavel on wood. Frieda's breath caught. She rose from her desk, smoothing her shirt with damp palms as if she could press calm back into her bones. Through the small front window, she caught a glimpse of them: two men in crisp city shirts, clipboards hugged to their chests like shields.

When the door swung open, they stepped through without waiting for invitation. Both were trim and pressed, shirts pale as unbothered clouds, slacks so sharp they could have sliced the air. They didn't smile. Didn't offer a greeting.

Frieda mustered her best calm, her voice soft but steady. "Frieda Winslow," she said, extending her hand. "Director here."

One man flicked his eyes at her hand, then past her shoulder. He didn't take it. The other offered only the slightest nod before his pen was already out, tapping against his clipboard like a metronome.

They split—moving in opposite directions down the main hall with the cold efficiency of surgeons preparing for a cut. The shorter one snapped his measuring tape against doorframes; let it retract with a flick. The taller man pressed at the drywall with flat fingertips, listening for hidden faults only he could hear.

Every footstep echoed louder than it should in the hallway lined with affirmations—*You're not broken, just becoming*—one *step at a time*. Notes taped to the corkboard in soft loops of pink and purple ink, all but invisible to the men in pale shirts.

"Ventilation's noncompliant," one murmured, half to the wall.

The other tugged gently at a smoke detector, the plastic cover clicking loose. "Fire suppression is insufficient. And that egress is blocked."

Frieda stayed close, one step behind them like a shadow, trying to keep up with a moving storm. "We've run groups here for over a year," she said, her voice quieter than she wanted it to be. "Safe groups. No incidents. This place keeps girls off streets that would eat them alive."

Neither man looked at her. Their pens moved. Their clipboards thick with checkboxes no prayer jar could sway.

In the main room, a girl peeked out—a slip of a kid with too-big sleeves, licorice between her teeth, eyes wide at the sight of these strangers moving like they owned the air. Frieda caught her gaze, forced her lips into a calm curve, and motioned her gently back inside. The door clicked shut behind the girl, muffling a burst of laughter and the thump of Uno cards hitting the table. Ordinary, innocent sounds.

They reached the small galley kitchen—more hot plate than stove, counters lined with thrifted mugs and dented soup pots. The taller inspector crouched, eyeing the range hood like it had offended him.

"Improper clearance," he said flatly. "No fire suppression system. Unapproved appliances."

Frieda's voice cracked. "This kitchen feeds girls who haven't seen a meal all day. It's the first warm thing in their bellies all week."

This time, he did look at her—dark eyes unreadable behind square glasses. He didn't flinch. Didn't soften. "It's still a violation."

That was it. Twenty minutes. No questions about the prayer jar on the sill catching sunlight. No nod toward the mural blooming along the back wall—girls' hands painting hope where drywall once cracked. Just tape measures and cold verdicts.

Then the taller one peeled a red sticker from the clipboard—like peeling off a bandage—and pressed it flat against the inside of the glass front door. The adhesive hissed as he smoothed it down with two fingers.

TEMPORARILY CLOSED
BY ORDER OF THE CITY

They left as quickly as they'd arrived—doors swinging open, clipboards tight to chests. The car outside swallowed them up. The engine hummed. Windows rolled up. They were gone before Frieda even found her breath.

She stood there; fingers curled at her sides so tight they ached. Behind her, the soft thunder of laughter rolled on. Bags of chips rustled. Someone squealed at an Uno draw four. A world built from nothing but stubborn faith and second chances—still beating just inches behind that scarlet sticker.

Frieda turned from the door, laid her palm gently on the glass, and felt the cold edge of the sticker beneath her fingertips. She closed her eyes. Inhaled. The fire had come. Again. She could taste the old fear rising like smoke in her throat. But she knew this heat. Knew it didn't have to consume her. She'd been burned before—had walked out, not unscathed but still standing.

When she stepped back into the main room, the girls looked up—Tyesha, Lena, Alana—all eyes on her, waiting for the part that mattered. Frieda pressed a small smile through the crack in her ribs.

"This is not the end," she said, voice low but steady. "This is just the walls."

Outside, the city pressed its cold palm against their door. Inside, The Bridge still pulsed with warmth and life. And so did she.

The Backlash

The news spread before Frieda could catch her breath, faster than rumor, sharper than truth. By dawn, the red sticker—its bold letters shouting *TEMPORARILY CLOSED*—had been photographed from every angle, posted and reposted until it glowed on a hundred glowing screens. The words under each image swirled like windblown ash:

Why would they shut it down?

Another place trying to help, and they ruin it.

I've been there. That place saved my life.

Frieda arrived early the next morning, while the neighborhood still yawned awake under a thin veil of dawn mist. Her boots whispered through dew-slicked grass along the sidewalk. She paused at the front door, the cold air curling around her wrists where her sleeves had slipped. The sticker glared back—scarlet, defiant, unmoving. She traced the edge with a fingertip, half-expecting it to peel away like a bad dream. It didn't.

The key turned with its usual soft click. Inside, the hush pressed in—heavier than silence, thicker than dust. No laughter. No chip bags crinkling. No girls draped over bean bags or curled in corners with journals cracked open like tender ribs. But the warmth lingered—blankets still folded on chairs, crayons scattered across a low table, a prayer jar on the sill catching the weak morning light.

She dropped her bag by the door and just stood there, listening to the ghost of what they'd built. Listening for hope inside the hush. Then came the voices—rising first as digital echoes. Pings. Buzzes. Her phone blinked and breathed under her palm like a living thing: emails, missed calls, texts stacking on top of each other like bricks.

Parents wrote raw paragraphs in all caps, in trembling lowercase:

"My daughter spoke for the first time here."
"This is her safe place—how dare they take it?"
"We stand with you."

Social media unfurled banners of rage and loyalty:

#SaveTheBridge
#OurGirlsMatter
#GraceOverRedTape

Each post another pulse beneath her ribs.

A pastor's voice memo broke through, gentle but thunderous in her ear: *"Our basement is yours every Tuesday night until they come to their senses. Just say the word."*

A mother knocked softly an hour later, coat still damp from drizzle, balancing a foil tray of lasagna and a folded check with her other hand. "It's not much," she whispered, eyes brimming. "But I'll fight for what saved my child."

Some donors vanished, afraid of the mess. But others doubled down, messages crisp with promise: *"Tell us what you need. We won't let this die."*

When Joyce arrived, she didn't knock—she never did. She nudged the door wider with her hip, arms full of folding chairs. The scent of her vanilla lotion curled around the stale hallway air like comfort. She dropped the chairs with a soft clatter and crossed the room to Frieda, cupping her face in both palms. Her voice fell warm as candlelight.

"You lit a fire, baby," she said, forehead resting against Frieda's. "And no red tape in the world can put it out."

By noon, they came. The girls. Not for flyers. Not for programming. Not for credit. Just because the spark inside them wouldn't stay quiet. They drifted in—hoodies pulled tight, eyes sharp, laughter cautious but alive. They circled up in the alley behind the shuttered door. Tyesha brought her Bluetooth speaker, thumping soft gospel into the cold brick air. Lena led a circle prayer, voice breaking but strong. Alana passed out bracelets—thread and beads spelling out *STILL STANDING*—each one a tiny promise on a wrist.

Frieda stepped outside and saw them there: gathered like warmth on cracked concrete, notebooks propped on knees, snack bags torn open on the ground, laughter flickering through the ache. The sticker clung to the glass behind her. But it was just a sticker now. A threat that didn't understand what it was trying to cage.

The Bridge wasn't a room. It was a people. A pulse. A promise. And together, they refused to let it die.

So, Frieda breathed in that holy chaos—the soft music, the prayers, the bracelets clutched like armor—and she knew:

The doors might close.

But the Bridge would stand.

And she would stand with it—fire and all.

Wherever We Gather

THEY GATHERED WHERE THEY COULD—any space that would hold them, cradle them, keep the chill of the world at bay for a few hours at a time. This night it was an old bungalow on the east side, someone's aunt's living room with floral wallpaper faded from years of sun. Twenty girls sat scattered on thrifted cushions and couch arms, fleece blankets draped across knees, candles guttering low on the coffee table, painting everyone's shadows on the walls in soft, trembling gold.

The room smelled faintly of vanilla wax and borrowed safety—like a secret kept warm in the chest. Somewhere behind the hum of whispered laughter, a radiator hissed its low, steady lullaby. Frieda stood by the mantle, her notebook hugged tight to her chest like a shield and a lifeline all at once. The candlelight caught the curve of her jaw; the edges of her braids tucked behind one ear. She looked at them—these girls who once would not meet her eyes, whose voices used to break on the word *hope*. Now they leaned forward, knees touching, shoulders pressed close, hearts wide open in the hush.

She swallowed the knot lodged in her throat. Her voice came out low, careful, but steady as she stepped closer.

"They tried to close our doors," she said. The words brushed the room like a warm draft through cold spaces. "They think if they shut this place, they can shut us down."

A quiet ripple moved through the circle—someone sniffled, someone's shoe scuffed the rug.

"But this," Frieda continued, her voice growing steadier, "was never just about the walls. The Bridge was never brick and drywall and keys in a lock. It was you. It is you."

She scanned their faces—Tyesha biting her lip, fighting tears she'd never admit she felt; Alana with her hood half up, bracelet glinting under the flicker of candlelight; Lena with her knees pulled to her chest, a grin trembling just beneath the sadness.

"You're not your worst day," Frieda said, her throat tightening around the memory of her own worst days. "You're not too far gone to be brought home. You're not invisible. You're builders—carrying light in the same hands that once carried so much hurt."

A girl on the arm of the couch wiped her nose with her sleeve. Another shifted closer to her friend, their shoulders pressed tighter.

Frieda's fingers fidgeted around the notebook's spine. She stepped closer, so near now they could see the glisten in her eyes. The candles sputtered a little, shadows stretching wide on the ceiling like witnesses. "I was you," she said, voice hushed, raw. "I was the girl who ran and didn't believe there'd be a bridge back. But there was. Because someone stayed. Someone waited in the dark. And now, it's my turn to wait for you. To fight for you. Even if the city locks every door, we'll build circles wherever we stand—living rooms, church basements, parking lots, backyard porches. If there's breath, there's a bridge."

A murmur rose. Small nods. Soft sniffles.

She knelt then, the notebook slipping from her hands onto the blanket-covered floor. She reached eye level with them—one girl, then the next—looking right into the raw ache behind every guarded glance.

"One day," she whispered, "you'll look back and see this wasn't just somewhere to hide. It was where you learned to stand. To speak. To reach back for the next girl who thinks no one's coming for her." Her words lingered in the hush like smoke in lamplight.

From the far side of the room, Jada lifted her chin. Her voice was barely more than a breath. "I believe you."

Alana's bracelet clinked as she crawled forward first, palms flat on the rug. She took Frieda's hand—small, cold fingers wrapping tight around hers. Tyesha followed, leaning in, head bowed. Lena next. Then another. And another. Until the circle pressed in close—no applause, no shout—just arms and hands and closeness in the glow.

Frieda's eyes blurred, warm rivers catching the candlelight. She lifted her free hand and cupped Alana's cheek, just for a second.

"Then let's keep walking," she breathed.

They nodded. Some crying. Some smiling. Some doing both at once. They stayed there a long time, long after the wax burned low and shadows grew soft and kind on the wallpaper. When they rose, they rose together. They folded blankets. Blew out flames. Promised to meet again—wherever there was breath, and story, and a girl who still needed a bridge.

And in the months that followed, something new emerged: **The Bridge Network.** Not one location. Many. Not one leader. Dozens. Girls became mentors. Survivors became staff. Circles formed where buildings had fallen. Living rooms became circles. Church kitchens became meeting halls. Parks became open-air sanctuaries. One Bridge became many—woven together by scarred hands and stubborn hope. No official funding. No blueprints. Just fire that refused to flicker out.

The city thought they'd closed something down. But they didn't know. The Bridge was never brick and mortar. It was breath. It was story. It was girls who refused to drown. And women who chose to reach back.

A Bridge doesn't die when its walls fall. It multiplies—wherever broken girls gather and dare to believe there's still something worth crossing toward. And Frieda—Miss Bridge—stood in the middle of them all. Not saving. Just staying. And that was enough.

The Rally

THAT SUNDAY, the old rec center gym hummed like a heartbeat waking up from sleep. The place still smelled faintly of floor polish and old sweat—echoes of games long past, of sneakers squeaking on warped boards, of a scoreboard that hadn't lit up in years. Rows of mismatched folding chairs fanned out across the faded court. Some leaned to the side on uneven legs, squealing against the scuffed floor whenever someone shifted. The bleachers, chipped and sun-bleached near the windows, groaned under the weight of teens perched shoulder to shoulder—backs bent forward, knees bouncing with restless anticipation.

Above them, fluorescent lights flickered in and out of steadiness, buzzing softly like moths trapped in glass. A backboard hung crooked above the old free-throw line, its net long gone, dust tracing the rim like a thin gray crown. At the front, someone had dragged wooden crates together to make a stage. Plywood planks rested across the tops—uneven but enough. No banner. No microphone stand draped in silk. Just the raw, makeshift honesty of a space repurposed to hold what the city had tried to shut down.

Frieda stepped up slowly. Her flats whispered on the wood. She wore no robe, no title pinned to her chest—just worn jeans, a soft cardigan, and her old leather journal tucked beneath her arm like a promise she wasn't ready to let go of.

She paused at the edge, eyes drifting over the restless rows—girls with eyeliner like armor, sleeves pulled down over tattooed wrists; boys slouched into their hoods, jawlines tight, eyes darting sideways to see who else was listening. A youth leader with a clipboard mouthed a silent prayer near the wall.

Frieda breathed in the stale, hallowed air of that place. Let it fill her chest. Let it settle her shaking palms. She rested them flat on the crate.

"I'm not here to preach," she said. Her voice landed soft at first, but clear enough to hush the shifting feet. "I'm not here to fix you. Or fix myself." She paused. The hum of the overhead lights filled the silence. "I'm here to tell you a story."

It was enough—an exhale rippled through the bleachers. Shoulders relaxed. Someone near the back let out a soft, unexpected laugh, like relief cracking open in a chest too tight for too long.

"They tried to shut us down," Frieda said, her voice warming as she found its shape. "Tried to seal the doors and call it an ending. But what they didn't know—" she glanced toward a cluster of girls in the second row, one with a bright purple cast, another tracing circles on a battered notebook— "is that this movement was never about doors."

She stepped down from the crate then, her boots thumping softly on the warped court. She didn't need the height. She needed the closeness.

"It's always been about you," she said, walking past the edge of the stage. She caught the gaze of a boy near the side wall—knees bouncing, jaw set like concrete. She didn't flinch away. "You, with the scars under your sleeves. You, with the stories that taste like secrets on your tongue."

She kept walking, slow enough that they had to lean in to catch her next words.

"You girls who've been told you're too loud, too angry, too complicated to love. You boys who were forced to grow up in houses that never felt like homes. Who never learned how to cry because someone said it made you weak. You who learned to laugh with your fists and cry only when nobody's watching."

Her own throat tightened. She pressed her palm to her chest, grounding the ache. "I was you," she said, the words softer now. "I was the runaway. The girl who wrote her goodbye on crumpled paper and thought no one would care enough to find her."

Someone sniffled—a sharp sound in the hush. Frieda's eyes flicked to the bleachers. A girl ducked her head, wiping her cheek with her sleeve.

"I stand here because someone didn't give up on me," Frieda said, her voice trembling but refusing to break. "And now I get to tell you—no matter what they close, no matter who walks out, no matter how many times you fall—*you are still worth showing up for.*"

She stepped back toward the crates, back to the center, but she didn't climb them again. She stayed level with them—on the same cracked floor they all knew too well.

"You are not the worst thing you've done," she said. "You are not your father's fists or your mother's silence. You are not what they called you when they thought you weren't listening."

Her hands opened wide at her sides.

"You matter," Frieda said, her voice trembling but strong. "Not because of your grades. Not because of your social media. But because you are still here. You're still breathing. You're still trying. And that—" she smiled then, just a flicker through tears gathering in her eyes— "that's sacred."

No roar followed. Not at first. Just a ripple of breath. A tear slid down a boy's cheek; he didn't bother to hide. A girl clutched the sleeve of the friend beside her.

"And if no one ever told you—you are worth loving. You are worth healing. You are worth more than surviving." She stepped back behind the mic. Let her final words fall like stone in water:

"We're still standing. And we're not going anywhere."

Then someone clapped—a single smack of palms in the hush. Another joined. A third. Then the room cracked open—applause rolling out of bodies too tired to pretend they didn't need what she'd given them: permission.

Chairs scraped back as some stood. Others wept. One girl near the front clutched her heart, mouthing, "That's me."

Frieda smiled, but it wasn't pride. It was something quieter. Deeper—Presence. She stepped back, letting the sound wash over her like a river she'd nearly drowned in once. Frieda didn't smile for herself. She smiled for them, these kids whose names would never make the news, but whose lives were rewriting what survival could look like.

Under the hum of cheap gym lights, beneath a rusted backboard and splintered bleachers, a movement rose again. Not a revival. A reminder that broken girls still shine. That wounded boys still rise. That hope doesn't need a building. It just needs a voice willing to speak. And Frieda had found hers.

AFTER THE RALLY, the old gym didn't empty right away. It breathed—slow and pulsing with warmth like coals refusing to die in the ashes of a late fire. The folding chairs stayed scattered, half-tipped on scraped linoleum, as teens lingered in small knots. Voices dropped to hushed confessionals, sneakers shuffled against the floor. The echo of Frieda's last words still clung to the rafters, mixing with the faint hum of the exit lights overhead.

A line formed, unspoken. No sign, no usher. Just a ripple—one story at a time moving toward her like water to a shore. Jordan was first—lanky shoulders, rough palms shoved deep in his hoodie pocket, eyes darting everywhere but hers. He stopped a breath away, the distance between them trembling.

"My mom left two years ago." His voice broke before it found itself again. "I didn't tell anybody. But when you said numb… that's me. It's been me."

Frieda didn't rush in with pretty words. She didn't reach for a polished sermon. She just opened her palms, grounded him with a nod. "Thank you for trusting me with that," she said, voice low and warm as flannel. She watched his shoulders ease, just a fraction, as he turned away—lighter by an ounce, maybe two.

Near the corner where the stage crates still leaned against the wall, five girls from the back row huddled in a circle of whispers and shy glances. One stepped forward—tall, wire-frame glasses slipping down her nose, hands clasped tight in the hem of her jacket.

"I didn't come here to feel anything," she confessed, words stumbling out raw. "But I do. And it hurts. But it also feels like… maybe I'm not alone."

Frieda locked eyes with her and let the truth sink deep. "You're not," she promised, every word clear and sturdy. "Not ever again."

The girl's chin trembled. She ducked her head and moved back to the safety of her friends, but a quiet courage glowed where fear had lived before.

Next was Ayanna—fourteen maybe, purple braids brushing her shoulders, chipped nail polish catching the light when she held a battered notebook to her chest like a secret she was ready to risk.

Her sneakers scuffed the floor as she stepped close, eyes wide under lashes dark as dusk.

"Can I read you something I wrote?" Her voice was thinner than a whisper.

Frieda's answer was a step sideways, guiding her to a quiet corner near the trophy case still lined with dusty plaques. She tilted her head, inviting. "Whenever you're ready."

Ayanna cracked the notebook's spine with trembling fingers. She found the page—creased, corner dog-eared from too many read-throughs in the dark. Her voice trembled on the first line, but steadied when she felt Frieda's eyes steady her back.

I am the daughter of thunder,
Quiet in daylight, loud in the dark.
I have swallowed my screams
Until my ribs turned hollow.
I've worn silence like perfume,
But the rage still stains my sleeves.
And yet—I dream.
Of stars that don't fall,
Of a sky that doesn't close.
Of a girl who still dances,
Even barefoot on broken glass.

By the final word, both of them were blinking tears that refused to be hidden. Frieda reached out and laid her hand on the page, like sealing a promise.

"That's not just a poem, Ayanna," she said, her voice thick but steady. "That's a roar. A map. A mirror for someone else who thinks they're alone."

Ayanna's mouth twitched—something like a smile but braver, heavier, more sacred. She hugged the notebook to her chest and drifted back into the group waiting by the bleachers. She didn't look smaller when she walked away. She looked taller. Like her spine remembered it could hold weight.

Frieda watched her go, the memory of those lines tattooed somewhere in her ribs now. Around the gym, teens lingered—no rush to scatter, no hurry to lose what they'd just been given: proof their stories mattered.

Later that night, Ayanna's poem found its way onto the corkboard of the borrowed church basement where The Bridge now met by flickering basement lights. Tacked up with a bent thumbtack—careful, like an offering.

By Friday, five other pieces joined it. Lyrics scribbled on torn notebook paper. A sketch of a girl with wings stitched to her scars. A note that read, *To the girl I used to be: You are not dead yet.* And Lena, bold as ever, was the first to stand in front of the circle and say, "We should make a night for this. Speak our hurt. Sing it out. Call it *Louder Than Silence.*"

Someone's cousin offered a guitar. Another girl promised homemade cookies. Frieda just watched them—watched them build something new from splinters.

When she got home that night—feet tired, shoulders heavy but her chest alive—she poured a cup of tea that went cold by the time she picked up her journal. She cracked it open like a ribcage and wrote:

> *They lined up like offerings. Not to me—to hope. Each story a flicker. Each confession a flame. The gym wasn't a church because we preached. It was holy ground because we listened. Maybe that's what real love is—a listening that doesn't flinch.*

She paused, the ink pooling at the edge of her pen.

> *Systems may try to silence us,*
> *But I've seen something louder than corruption—*
> *Redemption.*
> *It doesn't wait for permission.*
> *It only asks for a yes.*
> *And I'm still saying yes.*

The tea stayed cold. The room stayed quiet. But in that quiet, Frieda could hear it—dozens of young voices daring to believe they deserved to speak. And that sound was worth every door that might slam shut tomorrow.

Wolves in the Fold

The multipurpose room of the East Frampton Library carried the stale hush of old pages and burnt coffee left too long on a hot plate. The hum of fluorescent lights overhead flickered like an anxious heartbeat, making the dusty floor tiles look colder than they were. Folding chairs, borrowed from a local church basement, formed an awkward, loose circle—each seat a patch of restless energy.

Plastic name tags clung crookedly to jackets. Styrofoam cups sat half-forgotten on the scuffed laminate tables, their rims stained with rings of lukewarm brew. The air tasted faintly of paper, nerves, and polite ambition.

Around that circle, a dozen voices braided together—nonprofit leads, youth advocates, city workers with frayed cuffs and forced smiles, neighborhood elders who'd lived here long enough to see hope arrive and leave too many times to count. Ideas clashed gently, small visions traded in careful, cautious tones.

Then a man stood. Not abruptly. Not awkwardly. He rose as if the floor itself had asked him to.

"Caleb Rios," he said, his voice poured smooth like honey warmed just enough to drip slowly. Each syllable intentional, his tone tuned for comfort. His suit—a gray so clean it almost shimmered under the cheap lights—fit his broad shoulders too well for Frampton. A slim silver watch caught the flicker overhead and threw it like bait.

"Founder of RiseFram," he continued, pausing just long enough for the name to settle on tongues and notepads. "A youth empowerment initiative here in East Frampton. We focus on mobilizing resources, creating safe transitional housing, and nurturing mentorship pipelines that interrupt cycles before they root deep."

A few nods. A pen tapped the arm of a chair. Caleb's eyes shifted, gentle and probing, scanning the circle until they settled at the back.

Frieda.

She sat partly shadowed by a leaning bookshelf, fingers resting in her lap. She straightened slowly; shoulders tense beneath her worn blazer. His words found her like a spotlight—too direct to ignore.

Caleb's smile widened, teeth white, lips soft. "I've been following The Bridge for some time now. What you've done—it's raw. It's rare. It's the sort of light this city forgets how to keep burning. I think… together, we could build something lasting. Stronger. Unshakable."

A chair squeaked as someone leaned forward. Another voice murmured an approving "Mmm."

Frieda felt the knot form in her gut. He spoke the right words. The *needed* words. But the way he shaped them—too smooth, too frictionless—made her throat tighten. She rose. Slowly. Carefully.

Caleb stepped from the edge of the circle, crossing the stale carpet with the measured grace of a man who knew how to fill silence without crowding it. He extended his hand—firm, warm, just enough pressure to feel sincere but not controlling.

Up close, Frieda caught the subtle polish—his cologne faint but sharp, a glint of cufflink at his wrist, the stillness in his eyes that didn't quite match his easy smile.

"I admire what you've built," he said, voice dipping just for her. "Truly. The Bridge—it's what so many talk about but never have the grit to make real. But tell me, Frieda—aren't you tired?"

She felt the question slip under her ribs like a cold draft. She held his gaze. "We carry a lot," she said, each word steady, measured. "But the work is worth what it costs."

Caleb tilted his head, a flicker of practiced empathy softening his jaw. "Of course it is. But exhaustion... it hollows out the good ones first. Let me help. Let's pool our re ach—my housing network, your trust in the community. Counselors. Beds. Vans. Meals. Whatever it takes to keep your girls safe *and* your spirit intact."

A hush fell behind them. Pens stilled. Even the old wall clock seemed to click slower. Frieda hesitated. The word *together* sat sweet in her mouth—but behind it, a dull warning flared. They needed help. They needed kitchens that didn't run out of bread. Rooms that didn't leak when it rained. But they also needed to know whose hand was really on the lever.

"All right," she said finally, her fingers curling into his handshake. "We can talk."

His eyes lingered just a breath too long. His smile fixed but never reached the depths of his pupils.

Then—"Frieda."

The voice floated through the stale room like a thread pulling her back. She turned.

Joyce. Standing in the doorway, a folder tucked beneath her arm. Her scarf draped at her collarbone like armor. She swept the room with her eyes, the slow warmth in her gaze landing on Caleb last. She nodded—polite but not soft.

Caleb barely flicked his glance her way. If he saw the slight narrowing of Joyce's eyes, he didn't show it.

Frieda forced her shoulders to settle. She felt the knot loosen but didn't miss the flicker behind Joyce's steady calm—like a lantern held behind thick glass: *Watch your step, baby. Wolves don't always snarl.* She turned back to Caleb, whose grip lingered like a promise.

Outside, a cold wind rattled the library's old window frames. Inside, the circle closed back around their polite chatter. And beneath it all, Frieda's pulse drummed the oldest truth she knew: Sometimes, wolves don't wait at the door. Sometimes, they walk right in—smooth suit, soft words—teeth hidden behind a smile. And sometimes, you shake their hand anyway.

Quiet Undercurrents

THE LAST ECHOES OF CONVERSATION drifted down the hallway as the East Frampton Library emptied itself out—chairs scraping back in hesitant squeals, Styrofoam cups dropped into bins, polite laughter dissolving into the hush of after-hours. The overhead lights, dull and flickering, made the lingering dust motes dance in the stale air.

Frieda lingered near the back corner, where an old poster for a long-forgotten book drive curled at the edges behind her shoulder. She moved slowly, methodically tucking her pen and fraying notebook into her canvas tote, her hands steady only because she willed them to be. She felt it before she heard it— Caleb's presence, like a coat slipping back over her shoulders uninvited. His cologne reached her first, something crisp and expensive that didn't belong in this tired wing of the library.

"Frieda," he said smoothly, his voice curling around her name like a promise. He stood just inside her personal space, hands loose at his sides, posture relaxed in a way that made her tense. "I meant what I said in there. I see what you're building. Let's carve out real time to talk. Just us—no noise, no middlemen."

Frieda lifted her gaze slowly. His smile was all warmth and no edges—except in the eyes, where something watchful flickered. She nodded once, her face polite but unreadable.

"You have a card?" she asked, voice even.

Caleb's smile widened a millimeter. He slid a single card from a slim black case—matte, thick stock, edges so sharp they looked like they could cut if you weren't careful. The font was stark: **Caleb Rios, Executive Director, RiseFram.** The minimalist logo below caught the overhead light like a distant star.

Frieda took it without comment. Turned it once, twice, between her fingers, reading it like it might confess something if she handled it long enough. Caleb dipped his chin in a parting nod, then turned away, footsteps quiet and certain as they slipped into the hallway's dim hum.

She exhaled, just once, as if reminding herself she still could. Behind her came the soft, steady tap of Joyce's heels crossing the linoleum—less an approach than an anchor finding her side.

"You're thinking about it," Joyce murmured, folding her arms like a question she didn't need to ask.

Frieda didn't look at her yet. She kept her eyes on the business card, pinched lightly between thumb and forefinger, the matte paper soft at the edges but stiff at the fold. "I'm thinking about a lot of things."

Joyce stepped close enough for Frieda to feel the faint warmth radiating from her. Her voice, when it came, was low—worn smooth by too many nights spent sitting with the aftermath of good intentions.

"He knows exactly where you're thin," Joyce said. "He's handing you help like a warm blanket—right when you're too bone-tired to notice it might cost more than it gives."

Frieda turned then, her shoulders stiff beneath the canvas strap digging into her coat. Her tone was careful, clipped. "So what—he's polished, so I'm supposed to see a wolf? Just because he talks pretty and makes it sound easy?"

Joyce's eyes didn't flinch. The faint library light caught the silver in her hair. "No, baby. You see a wolf because you know how the hunger works. They don't come slobbering at your door. They come offering to guard it for you."

The words lodged like grit under Frieda's ribs. She looked down again at the card, as if it might change its mind in her hand. Her thumb pressed an invisible crease along the edge.

"I just want to protect what we've bled to build," she whispered. The confession felt too soft in this bright, brittle room.

Joyce's posture softened. Her arms fell to her sides as she reached out, placing a warm hand between Frieda's shoulder blades—a touch that steadied, not steered.

"Then protect it," Joyce said, voice gentler now. "By asking the questions no one wants to answer. By remembering you're not the tired girl in a shelter anymore—you're the keeper of all these girls' tomorrows. Don't let anyone hold that gate who hasn't earned the key."

Silence pressed around them, heavy with the weight of what they both knew and couldn't name yet. Frieda's breath trembled at the edges as she folded the card sharply in half—one clean break through the perfect font—and slipped it deep into her tote, not her pocket.

She met Joyce's eyes. "I hear you."

Joyce's hand lingered, steady on her back for just a moment longer. For that breath of time, the harsh overhead lights felt warmer. The circle of borrowed chairs, empty now, seemed to whisper the promise of why they stayed so long after everyone else went home.

Outside the library's glass doors, dusk was slipping into something deeper. Streetlights flickered to life against a restless sky. Somewhere, a bus hissed to a stop, carrying another burdened soul to another sleepless corner of East Frampton.

And behind the softness of that quiet room, something else drifted in too—something sharp, shifting, waiting. Because storms didn't always arrive roaring. Sometimes, they began with a single card. A single handshake. A single smile.

CALEB MOVED like a man born for bright rooms and careful shadows. He didn't just show up—he multiplied. Within fourteen days, his signature slipped onto documents Frieda hadn't even known were waiting. Board meetings swelled with new faces—men and women in tailored blazers and sharp shoes, nodding with polite smiles and questions that felt too polished to be real. Checks cleared like water through open floodgates—amounts Frieda could barely comprehend.

A local paper ran a headline before she even saw a draft: *"RiseFram and The Bridge: A Partnership for the Future."* Her name was bolded beside Caleb's in the opening line. Her face—cropped from a staff photo—floated under words she hadn't written.

She caught herself staring at it on her phone late at night, thumb hovering over the screen until the blue light burned her eyes.

At the main shelter, a new twelve-passenger van idled in the lot. Fresh white paint. RiseFram's sleek logo coiled along its side like a signature. When Frieda touched the handle, it felt cold. Almost too new.

Inside, the girls posed for photos staged in quick bursts—journals open, arms looped around each other's shoulders, smiles caught mid-laughter. The photographer moved them like props: *Face the window—light's better. Hold the notebook higher.* Captions later bloomed on social feeds like carefully tended flowers: *Hope in action. When young women rise, communities follow. #TogetherWeRise.*

It looked—God, it looked—like everything she had begged for in prayer circles and tear-soaked nights. Food. Space. Staff. Beds. Counselors. A second shelter out on the edge of East Frampton, its hallway walls still smelling of fresh paint and promise.

And yet—

Behind the bright flyers stacked on the new welcome desk, something shifted under her ribs like a splinter she couldn't shake free.

Joyce watched from the corner of rooms she used to stand in the center of. Her arms folded more often now. Her voice soft but edged when she spoke. Questions slipped from her lips like slow drips of water carving stone:

Who signed this?

Did you read this line here?

Did you ask him how these donors found us so fast?

Sometimes, Frieda just nodded. Other times, she bristled—like a child called out in church. She told herself it was growth. *Finally,* she whispered late at night while scrolling grant proposals thick with new language—funding clauses, pilot initiatives, scaling strategies.

Finally, we're catching up to the vision.

Finally, I'm not carrying it alone.

But when she turned the pages under her desk lamp—RiseFram's clean black font stamped in the margins, Caleb's name in the CC line, words like *merger* and *integration* tucked inside footnotes—her chest stayed tight.

Sometimes she laid her palm there, over her heartbeat, and felt it drum like it knew something she wouldn't say aloud:

This blessing is growing teeth.

And if it bites, it won't come from outside the gate.

It'll come from inside her own walls.

Later That Evening — The Quiet Warnings

BY THE TIME the last giggle and shuffle of teenage footsteps faded down the hallway, the building seemed to exhale—its hum settling into the hush of tired walls and lingering warmth. The multipurpose room glowed softly under a single floor lamp. The space heater hummed in the corner, rattling gently, pushing back the edge of a winter chill seeping through the old window frames.

Joyce was there—kneeling by the supply shelf, folding donated blankets into neat squares and tucking them into clear plastic bins labeled *Extra Bedding* in black marker. Her movements were unhurried, almost tender, as if she were tucking in sleeping children instead of fleece throws.

Frieda hovered in the doorway for a moment; her shoulder pressed to the frame. She watched Joyce's hands—brown, worn, gentle—smooth each blanket flat before laying it down. Each fold seemed like a prayer.

"Can we talk?" Frieda's voice slipped into the room like a thread of smoke—fragile, curling at the edges.

Joyce didn't flinch. She looked up and met Frieda's eyes, a tired smile breaking across her face. "Always."

They drifted to the old couch in the corner—gray, sunken, the arms smudged by years of elbows and whispered secrets. Frieda sat first, her knees pressed together, hands twisting at the hem of her sleeve. Joyce settled beside her, close but not crowding, her presence warm as a blanket itself.

"It's about Caleb," Frieda breathed. The words caught in her throat like grit.

Joyce's nod was slow, patient. "I figured."

Frieda's eyes dropped to the scuffed tile under her boots, tracing a chipped patch where the polish had long worn away. "He's… efficient. Strategic. Doors open when he knocks. He says all the right things. It's like… every desperate prayer I whispered when this place was falling apart—he's answering them."

Joyce didn't rush to speak. She just let the weight of that truth hang in the warm hush. The space heater clicked and rattled. Somewhere down the hall, a loose vent cover rattled in the draft.

"And yet," Joyce said finally, her voice soft but edged like a blade hidden in velvet, "you're sitting here looking like you can't breathe under all that answered prayer."

Frieda's throat bobbed. Her eyes flickered up, then down. Guilt pulsed through her fingers as she knotted them tighter. "I keep asking myself if I'm just tired and suspicious... or if I'm not suspicious enough."

Joyce angled her body, folding one leg beneath her. She tilted her head slightly, studying Frieda like she was reading a familiar scripture that still found ways to surprise her.

"Tell me what your gut says," Joyce murmured. "Not the voice in your head that's grateful for help. Not the voice that's scared to lose it. The quiet one. Down deep."

Frieda drew in a breath so slowly it trembled at the end. Her voice cracked open like old paint. "He's too polished. Too perfect. Like he rehearses sincerity. And the girls..." She paused, a flicker of pain in her eyes. "They go quiet when he's in the room. They look at me like they're waiting for me to say it's okay."

Joyce's mouth pressed into a thin line. She didn't blink. "And did you vet him yourself? Or just the papers he handed you?"

"I called. Ran his name through every file I could afford. Everything came back clean." Frieda's laugh was hollow. "So clean it squeaks."

Joyce's hand lifted and rested warm and solid on Frieda's knee. "Baby, clean ain't always truthful. Wolves wear wool better than sheep some days. And they know how to iron it, starch it, and preach in it too."

Frieda's eyes burned. The words carved through her exhaustion, leaving behind something rawer than fear—something that felt like an old ache she thought she'd outgrown.

"What if I'm wrong?" Her voice was a whisper, a confession.

Joyce's gaze didn't waver. It stayed steady and kind—like iron under velvet. "Then you stand up straighter for being careful. But what if you're right... and you hush your gut because you're too tired to listen? What happens then?"

The heater hummed its low lullaby. For a moment, that was the only sound in the room—two women breathing under the hush of a question that didn't need an answer right now.

Frieda leaned forward, her elbows on her knees, palms pressed together like prayer. She let out the breath she'd been holding for weeks. "I'll watch him closer. Ask more questions. Keep the door propped open—but not wide."

Joyce's hand squeezed her knee once, strong and sure. "Good. And if he flinches when you do, there's your truth."

They sat there, quiet but not alone. The folded blankets waited in their bins like small promises—warmth for the cold nights ahead. And Frieda, sitting on that old couch, felt it deep in her ribs: Sometimes wisdom doesn't arrive loud and triumphant. Sometimes it kneels beside you with tired hands and tells you what you already know—*Be careful, baby. Be slow. Even holy places draw hungry wolves.*

Missing

IT STARTED LIKE A RUMOR drifting through the hallway—a whisper too faint to catch but too heavy to ignore.

Monique.

The name alone made Frieda's chest tighten. Small, sharp-shouldered Monique—always curled in on herself like an apology. She would slip in late, linger near the exit door, her eyes flicking to shadows more than people. But slowly—just barely—she'd begun to lean in. She'd stayed after meetings, folding chairs with trembling hands. She'd lingered at the snack table, picking at stale cookies while asking tiny, brave questions. On good days, she'd smiled. Not wide, but enough to glimpse the girl she might have been before the world turned cruel. Then she vanished.

One night, her chair sat empty—no backpack slung on the back, no journal balanced on her knees like armor. The second night, Frieda noticed the untouched coffee cup near the door. By the third, her chest buzzed with a restless dread she couldn't push down.

Frieda called her number first—an old prepaid phone that usually went straight to voicemail. This time, it didn't even ring. Dead line. Dead air. She paced the office long after the others had left, flipping through sign-in sheets and intake notes. Nothing. She opened the locked file cabinet, her breath shallow. Monique's folder wasn't there.

She checked again—one by one, finger trailing the edges of manila tabs as if she might have missed it. But it was gone—vanished like a ghost. So was the emergency contact card. And the battered journal Monique guarded like it was the only piece of herself she could still claim. Gone.

The pit in Frieda's stomach turned cold. Without knocking, she strode down the hallway—past the prayer board and the bulletin covered in scribbled affirmations—toward the corner office that hadn't existed before Caleb arrived.

His door was half-closed, light spilling through the cracked blinds. Inside, Caleb lounged behind the polished desk they hadn't even needed six months ago, phone in hand, scrolling like this was any other Wednesday night. Frieda pushed the door open fully. Her voice carried a rough edge she didn't bother to hide.

"Where's Monique?"

Caleb's head lifted slowly. A flicker of surprise—or was it annoyance?—crossed his polished grin before it smoothed into that effortless calm.

"Monique?" He repeated her name like he'd misplaced a receipt. He set his phone down, folding his hands together. "Oh—right. Family emergency. Her mom came to get her. Needed to pull her out. I handled the paperwork."

Frieda stepped closer, the stale office air pressing around her ribs. "You handled it?" Her voice cracked at the edges. "When? How? Without telling me? There's no file. There's no form. Her name is gone."

Caleb leaned back in his chair, spinning it slightly so the dull light glinted off his watch. His smile was casual, lips tugging just enough to feel friendly but not enough to touch his eyes. "Standard stuff," he said, tone airy, patronizing. "These girls disappear, Frieda. Runaways run. That's what they do."

Her hands curled into fists at her sides. "She was just starting to stay. Starting to trust. You don't just erase her."

He gave a low laugh, brushing invisible lint from his cuff. "Don't get so worked up. We can't chain them here. If they want out, they go. It's sad—sure—but you can't save everyone. You know that."

Something hot flickered in Frieda's gut. Anger. Grief. Fear. It all twisted together into a single sharp note: *This isn't right.* She stepped closer, her shadow crossing his desk. "Don't stand there and tell me who I can't save."

Caleb's eyes lifted—sharp now. The pleasant mask flickered, just for a heartbeat. Then it was back, his teeth showing in a cold grin. "Let it go, Frieda. This is the cost of the work. One falls through the cracks—another ten show up tomorrow. It's the math of what we do."

But Frieda didn't hear him anymore. All she felt was the cold certainty blooming in her bones—an echo of every gut instinct Joyce had taught her to trust. Not this girl. Not this time. Something was wrong. *Deeply* wrong.

She turned without another word, the click of her boots on the cheap carpet louder than Caleb's shallow reassurances behind her. Monique was gone. But Frieda had built her life on not walking away from lost girls. And she would not start now.

Meeting Miguel

THE GYM SMELLED like old sweat and yesterday's mop water—linoleum floors echoing the shuffle of tired shoes. Folding chairs were arranged in a loose, uneven circle, and at the edges, battered tables sagged under stacks of pamphlets that curled at the corners. A carafe of coffee sat half-empty beside paper cups that leaked at the seams. The air hummed with the low murmur of bureaucrats and advocates comparing crisis notes under flickering fluorescent lights.

Frieda sat two seats from the drafty door, coat shrugged tight around her shoulders even though she hadn't unbuttoned it yet. Her bag rested at her boots, bulging with scribbled notes and grant proposals that always seemed to need more signatures than she had time to collect. Her pen hovered above her knee, restless. The buzz of the overhead lights filled the hollow behind her eyes where sleep should have lived.

Someone sat beside her—she barely noticed at first. Another exhausted adult in a circle of exhausted adults. Then came the voice.

"You okay?" Warm. Gentle. Not the sterile concern of a social worker asking for a line on a report. This was a question that asked nothing in return.

She turned her head. The man next to her leaned back in his chair, elbows resting on spread thighs. Mid-thirties, maybe. Olive skin, a neat beard, black curls pulled into a low bun at the base of his neck. The sleeves of his checkered shirt were rolled up to the forearms—ink peeked out where a tattoo dipped beneath fabric. His ID badge, clipped to a navy lanyard, read: **Miguel Ramirez**.

Frieda lifted a shoulder, the ghost of a laugh caught in her chest.

"Just trying to keep kids alive," she said, her voice softer than she meant it to be.

Miguel's mouth curved, easy but not dismissive. "Same," he said. "Mine just happen to be dodging potholes instead of foster homes."

She caught the badge again. The city logo. Transit Division.

"Transit?" she asked, genuinely surprised.

"Transit planner," he confirmed with a nod. "Bus routes, safe stops, sidewalks that don't kill kids on the way to school. By night—youth mentorship. My side hustle for the soul."

He offered his hand, warm and work-worn. "Miguel."

"Frieda." She took it, let her palm rest in his a little longer than a handshake demanded.

After the panel—after the committee notes blurred into jargon and the last polite applause died off—Frieda lingered by the chairs, organizing her pages into neat stacks she wouldn't read again tonight. Miguel stayed too, leaning against the wall just far enough to give her space, but near enough that she could feel the way he paid attention.

They talked. Not the frantic, fix-it chatter that usually came after these things. No bullet points. No quick solutions. Just stories. Wounds shaped like bus routes and shelters. How a pothole and a prayer sometimes saved the same child in the same week. Frieda spoke of the girls—how they showed up shattered, how they left with tiny seeds of hope planted under their ribs.

Miguel listened. Not nodding just to agree, but nodding to say, *I'm here. I hear it all.*

"What keeps you from walking away?" he asked, voice low, almost lost in the hollow gym.

She looked at her hands. The ink smudge on her thumb. The ragged edge of a notebook page she'd torn too fast. "Faith," she said. "Some days, that's all that holds. And the girls. I see them stand when every lie says stay down. That's holy ground to me."

His mouth pulled into a soft grin that crinkled the corners of his eyes. "That's not a paycheck. That's a calling."

Frieda let a small smile slip, honest and tired. "It was never a job."

The gym slowly emptied—people filing out in pairs, pulling on coats, wrapping scarves tight against the sharp Frampton wind. Miguel reached into his pocket and drew out a business card. But when he turned it over, there was more than print—neat handwriting curved across the blank side:

If you ever need a safe place to think. Or just breathe.

He handed it to her without ceremony. No pitch. No angle.

Frieda turned the card over once, twice, feeling its weight press against her palm like a quiet promise. "Thank you," she said, her voice low, the words warm in her throat.

Miguel didn't push for her number. Didn't make it a thing it wasn't. He just smiled, dipped his head, and slipped through the doors into the cold.

Alone again, Frieda tucked the card into her notebook—slid it between pages filled with prayers and plans and pieces of herself she rarely showed. A pressed flower. A door, half-cracked open. Maybe, she thought, watching the empty gym settle into silence, not everything had to break to make room for something good.

Building Connection

THE DAYS BLURRED—first one, then another. Then a week, folded into late nights and heavy mornings. Frieda tucked the card into her journal every evening, telling herself she would do it *tomorrow*. She didn't dial. Not yet.

Then came the day that cracked her. A girl she'd coaxed back from the brink for months slipped out of reach again— relapsed, vanished into Frampton's labyrinth of shadows. That same afternoon, another girl ran. Left a note on a cot still warm with her absence. *I can't do this anymore.* Frieda read it three times before folding it into her pocket like a splinter she couldn't pull out.

She didn't go home. Instead, she stood on the cracked sidewalk outside The Bridge, dusk bleeding the sky a bruised purple. Her fingers found the card tucked deep in her bag—edges soft now, like it had been waiting for this moment.

She dialed.

Two rings. A click. Then his voice—steady, warm, surprised but calm. "Hey. You all right?"

Frieda's breath fogged the night air. She turned away from the traffic to hide the way her shoulders sagged.

"I… don't know," she said, voice raw. "I remembered your offer. I just… I needed somewhere that doesn't need me to fix it."

Ten minutes later, she found herself standing at the rusted gate of a tiny community garden wedged tight between two brick apartment buildings—like a secret pocket of green holding its ground against the city's concrete sprawl.

Miguel was already there. He lifted a hand in greeting, a thermos tucked under one arm, a paper bag under the other.

"C'mere," he called softly.

They sat on a battered wooden bench, the paint peeling away in soft curls under their elbows. Miguel poured tea from the thermos—steam rising, scented faintly with cinnamon and clove. He handed her a chipped blue mug, and when her fingers brushed his, she felt her pulse slow.

Around them, the garden hummed with small life—wind in the dry branches, a low whistle of sparrows settling for the night. Somewhere past the fence, kids' laughter lifted and fell like birdsong—feet thumping the sidewalk, someone's mother calling them in for dinner.

Miguel didn't ask questions. He didn't poke at the wound she carried, raw and wordless. He just sat beside her, their shoulders almost touching, the bench creaking when they shifted to sip.

"Sometimes it's just about not being alone," he said after a while, voice low, words drifting into the hush between passing cars.

Frieda turned the mug in her hands, feeling the warmth seep into her palms. Her eyes stung. She didn't brush it away.

"I forgot what that felt like," she whispered, so soft she wasn't sure if he'd hear.

But he did.

Miguel shifted, just enough so when he spoke, she felt the steadiness of him beside her. "Then let's not forget again."

Their eyes met—city shadows and garden lights catching in the dark pools of his gaze. No rescue in it. No false promise to make it easy. Just the quiet offer to share the weight. Frieda held his gaze a moment longer than she meant to, then exhaled—a tremor in her shoulders easing, as if the night itself gave her permission to rest.

Something rooted there on that splintered bench. Small. Steady. Not the wild bloom of rescue. But maybe—just maybe—the start of something built to hold. A partnership. A soft place to think. A promise: *You don't have to carry it alone.*

The Unraveling Begins

FRIEDA SAT CROSS-LEGGED on the thin rug in her cramped living room, the soft hum of the radiator mixing with the faint tick of the wall clock. Around her, papers sprawled like a tide—intake forms, receipts, case notes, donation slips, all of them creased and smudged from her shaking hands.

A single lamp threw a cone of yellow light over the mess, leaving the corners of the room in soft shadows. She shifted another stack closer, lips moving silently as she read each line, her pen tapping out a nervous rhythm on her knee. Every few seconds, she would pause—eyes closed, breath caught in her throat—then keep going. The forms all bore Caleb's tidy, looping initials. Neat boxes ticked. Addresses typed cleanly in rows.

But some details snagged. A middle name spelled differently here than there. A phone number that rang once before disconnecting. An address she knew for a fact was a crumbling foundation overgrown with weeds—nothing but gravel and rust. Her stomach twisted. She reached for the next file, her fingers brushing the paper like it might burn her. Monique R. Her eyes snagged on the name, her pulse thudding dully in her ears. She remembered the girl—those wide eyes that never landed on anyone for too long, the way her small hands clutched her journal like armor.

The form listed an emergency contact. *Aunt Regina.* Frieda's mouth went dry. She fumbled for her phone, the screen slick beneath her fingertips. She dialed. One ring. Two. Three.

"Hello?" A woman's voice—older, wary.

"Hi—hi, this is Frieda Winslow. I run The Bridge— Monique listed you as her emergency contact. I just needed to—"

A sharp inhale on the other end. "Monique? My niece?"

"Yes, ma'am. She was with us—"

"No," the woman cut in. Her tone hardened like a door slamming shut. "She *never* stayed at The Bridge. She told me about some man—Caleb something. Said he had a safe house. She left with him."

Silence clawed the line.

Frieda's voice stuck in her throat. "Do you… do you know where she is now?"

A brittle laugh—bitter, cracked. "No one does."

Then the click of the line going dead.

The phone slipped from Frieda's hand, thudding onto the carpet. She stared at the ceiling, her breath shallow, ribs tight. The shadows in the corners of the room seemed to shift, pressing closer. Slowly, she gathered the other forms again. Names she'd trusted. Signatures she'd skimmed too fast in her exhaustion, her hope. Caleb's neat notes, his polished promises—now bleeding through every page like poison.

A tear landed on an intake sheet. She brushed it away, but another came. Her voice cracked the silence. Small. Ragged.

"God… what have I done?"

The candle flickered beside her—its tiny flame bending wildly as if to protest the darkness gathering inside her chest. She pressed her palm over her mouth, holding in the sob that threatened to tear her open. The carpet's fibers prickled against her knees. The lamp buzzed. The city outside carried on, oblivious.

Inside her living room, Frieda felt the cost settle in her bones. Not a slip. Not an oversight. A breach. And the girls—*her* girls—were the ones paying the price.

She stayed there until the shadows blurred, until the papers blurred, until her tears soaked through ink and paper alike. Then she whispered it again—more plea than prayer:

"God... please... help me make this right."

And in the flicker of the flame, something inside her—hope, rage, resolve—began to gather, coil tight, ready for the fight that would come next.

A Midnight Call

THE SKY OVER EAST FRAMPTON pressed low and heavy, an iron lid smothering the city's edge in darkness. No stars. No moon—just the faint glint of distant streetlights catching on broken glass and slick oil patches along the cracked road.

Frieda stood motionless behind a tangle of chain-link fence, its rusted links biting cold against her gloved hands. The warehouse in front of her loomed like an unspoken threat—cinderblock walls tagged with half-faded graffiti, a single flickering floodlight casting a weak halo onto the gravel lot.

She checked the scrap of paper in her pocket again. The address Caleb had once handed her with a smile, calling it a "new sanctuary" for the girls slipping through the cracks. *A safe reintegration site. A healing hub.* But nothing about this place felt like healing.

A soft growl of an engine stirred her from her thoughts. Frieda stepped back, pressing herself into the shadows cast by a half-collapsed dumpster. She drew her coat tighter around her, breath clouding out in slow, shallow bursts as headlights cut across the yard.

A black van rolled out from behind the side loading bay—slow, deliberate, tires chewing the gravel in a hush that somehow felt more dangerous than a roar.

She froze. Peered through the chain-link gaps. Inside the van—shapes. She squinted, leaning closer. A flash of a girl's profile caught in the dashboard glow—too young. Shoulders curled in. Next to her, another shape—smaller, head pressed to the window. She could see the glint of cloth tied around an eye. Blindfolds.

Her pulse slammed against her ribs. They weren't leaving. They were *being moved.* A hand rose from the passenger seat—a driver's casual gesture—and the van turned, creeping toward the road that ran back toward the interstate. Delivered. Like cargo.

A bitter taste burned the back of Frieda's throat. She fumbled her phone from her pocket, her fingers raw and numb in the wind. The lens focused, blurred, focused again. She pressed the shutter—once, twice. The flash of captured light stung her eyes. A face caught in the photo: a man behind the wheel, eyes downcast. A girl behind him, half-turned, her hair caught in the faint spill of dashboard light. Her expression empty. Waiting.

Her thumb trembled over the message box.

To Miguel: *I need help. Now.*

She attached the photo. Hit send.

The van's taillights bled red into the night, disappearing around the corner. Frieda exhaled sharply, pressing her back to the fence as a hot wave of nausea hit her. Her knees wanted to fold. She made herself stand.

Forty-seven minutes later, she heard tires roll over broken glass again. Miguel's old sedan pulled up without headlights, engine still ticking as he stepped out, a gray hoodie pulled over his hair, laptop wedged under his arm. He didn't waste breath on greetings. He found her where she stood by her car and squeezed her shoulder—steady, grounding—and then they sat together on the curb, concrete still warm from the day's leftover heat. Miguel balanced the laptop on his knees, keys clicking soft and relentless. The glow from the screen flickered against their faces—two figures in the dark, hunched over secrets.

"Tell me everything," he said, voice calm but sharp at the edges.

So, Frieda told him—her voice raw but steady as she laid it all out: Caleb's charm, the expansion, the shell shelters, the files that didn't add up, the names that disappeared when no one was looking. Each word made her hands shake harder.

Miguel's fingers moved faster, pulling up filings, nonprofit ledgers, and donation routes that looped and twisted like snakes. He muttered to himself—matching addresses, flagging shell entities, tracing checks that should never have cleared.

"Here—look at this," he said at last, voice low but fierce. He turned the laptop so she could see the map on the screen. Dots. Lines. Overlapping names.

"All these nonprofits. Same donor web. Same lawyer's name on the paperwork. See this PO box? Every tax return they've filed lists it as their headquarters. It's a ghost trail, Frieda."

Her throat closed. Her voice cracked. "Two of those shelters—Detroit. Memphis. They were raided. Trafficking rings."

Miguel met her eyes, his own dark and wide in the glow of the laptop light.

"He used The Bridge," she whispered. The words nearly broke her jaw to say them. "He used *my girls.*"

Her body shook so hard her teeth clicked. She pressed her hand over her mouth, but the sob slipped through anyway—ugly, raw. Miguel set the laptop down and reached for her free hand, grounding her back to the curb, the cracked asphalt, the cold wind threading through chain-link gaps.

"We're not letting this stand," he said, voice iron wrapped in quiet. "We bring him down. And we get them back."

Frieda lifted her eyes—wet, burning, but alive with something stronger than fear. Resolve. Her breath shuddered out in the dark.

"Okay," she said.

And there on the curb, under the hush of a city too asleep to care, two people stitched a plan back together—thread by thread, truth by truth. A fight was coming. And this time, Frieda was ready to burn down every lie to get her girls home.

The Next Phase

THEY DIDN'T SLEEP. Not when the truth was burning holes through their veins.

By dusk, Miguel's small apartment looked like a crime scene from an old detective movie—except this wasn't fiction. The living room was a hive of light and paper and tired breath. A folding card table groaned under laptops, half-eaten noodles, and mugs gone cold.

Miguel had pulled an old corkboard from his closet. Now it stood propped against the wall, covered in a patchwork of maps, sticky notes, and scrawled names. Red yarn snaked from city to city, pinning dots no one wanted to believe were connected.

Frieda sat cross-legged on the floor beside the couch, her sleeves pushed up, a pen tapping restlessly against her knee. Her eyes were raw from hours of screen glare, but they stayed sharp, tracing every dotted line, every alias, every dead-end address that wasn't dead after all. Around her were the files she'd carried in like precious cargo—Monique's intake forms, the ghost shelters, the emails that started out like promises and ended like traps.

Miguel crouched beside her; laptop balanced on his thigh. He typed with quick, hushed keystrokes, the glow painting tired shadows beneath his eyes. He'd long since kicked off his shoes—his socks were mismatched, toes tapping the floor in a rhythm that matched Frieda's pen.

By midnight, they'd unearthed three more shell organizations hidden under RiseFram's umbrella. By two o'clock in the morning, they'd traced donations offshore, tax IDs that recycled across fake programs. One address looped back to a downtown law firm—polished windows that, on paper, claimed to house "Youth Development Initiatives."

"It's all paper walls," Miguel said under his breath. His voice cracked with the grit of too much coffee, too little sleep. "And it's held up by people we know—look at this—" He pointed to a name pinned just above Caleb's on the board: a city councilman Frieda had once thanked publicly for his 'generous support.'

She stared at it, the lines between trust and betrayal shredding apart in her chest. Her whisper came out raw. "I brought him to the table, Miguel. I did this."

"No," Miguel said, not looking away from her. "He *used* the table. And he's counting on your guilt to keep it standing."

Frieda's shoulders shook once. Then stilled. She sat up straighter, pen clutched like a blade. "I'm not leaving one girl behind," she said. Her voice didn't rise—it burrowed deep, like steel sunk in stone. "If I don't drag every name into the light now—then I never deserved to hold theirs."

Miguel's eyes softened, but his reply was fire. "Then we do it. All of it. Files. Photos. Testimony. Whistleblower protection, backup copies off-site. We blow the whole rotten wall down."

Outside, dawn seeped in pale and quiet through the cracked blinds. The city beyond was still half-asleep—commuters just stirring, buses rumbling to life. But in this apartment, two people were wide awake, steady as a heartbeat.

Frieda pressed her palm flat to the corkboard—over Monique's name, over all the other threads tangled with hers. She closed her eyes and saw every story, every frightened face that trusted her not to look away. When she opened them, the sun was spilling a thin promise through the window.

"This is war," she whispered.

Miguel nodded, reaching for the next file. "And we're not losing it."

So, they kept digging—while the city turned its face toward another ordinary day, never knowing that somewhere in a cramped living room, two exhausted believers were about to flip the whole thing inside out.

The Confrontation

THE NEXT MORNING, the hall outside Caleb's office felt too bright—sunlight spilling through tall windows, gleaming off floors polished to a shine so clean it could swallow a reflection whole. Frieda's boots struck that floor like a warning—each step an echo of her heartbeat, hammering, unyielding. She didn't knock. She didn't pause. She pushed the door open with the flat of her palm, hard enough that it rattled on its hinges.

Inside, Caleb's office looked like a magazine spread: mahogany desk so spotless it reflected the ceiling lights, crisp white blinds drawn half-open to catch the city skyline beyond. Awards gleamed from glass shelves—leadership, impact, civic excellence. All of them lined up like a lie.

Behind the desk, Caleb sat reclined, phone to his ear, laughter dripping easily from his lips. The sound curdled in Frieda's ears. He wore a tailored jacket today, charcoal gray, sleeves rolled just enough to flash his expensive watch when he gestured mid-sentence.

When he noticed her, his grin didn't falter. He lowered the phone, finger pressing the screen to end the call with lazy arrogance.

"Frieda," he drawled, smooth as oil on water. "You're early. Or am I late?"

She didn't answer. Didn't sit. She just stood there in the doorway, her breath hot in her chest, her fists clenched so tight, her nails pressed crescents into her palms.

"Where are they?" she said, each word clipped like snapped branches.

Caleb's smile flickered. A microsecond. Then it returned, polite but colder. "I'm sorry, what?"

"Don't," she snapped, voice trembling with the force of staying steady. She stepped forward until she stood across his gleaming desk—close enough to see her own reflection in the polished wood. "Monique. Deja. The girls who disappeared after you signed them up for RiseFram's *programs.* Where are they, Caleb?"

He sat back slowly, folding his hands. The pose was calculated—measured calm, an attempt at control. His eyes narrowed a fraction.

"Frieda," he said, his tone was soft but lined with warning, "you need to be very careful about what you're suggesting. Rumors like that can bury an organization."

She let out a short, humorless laugh that caught in her throat. "An organization? You mean your pipeline? I saw the van. I saw the warehouse. I know what you're funneling out of this city under the word 'mentorship.' You used *us.* You used The Bridge. You used *me.*"

A muscle jumped in Caleb's jaw. The room felt tighter, the bright window suddenly too small for the shadows crawling out of his eyes. He rose from his chair—slow, deliberate, as if his height alone could smother her fury.

"You don't know what you're doing," he hissed. "You're in way over your head, Frieda. Do you have any idea who you're trying to fight?"

She stood her ground, chin lifted, and her pulse drumming in her ears. "You think your money, your charm, your *title*—makes you untouchable? Maybe before. Not now. I'm done carrying your poison in my house."

He leaned forward, voice dropping low, venomous. "Walk away. Now. Or you'll regret this."

She felt the threat like frost along her spine. But her eyes didn't flinch. They burned, steady, alive. "I've regretted a thousand things in my life, Caleb." Her voice cracked once, but she didn't let it break. "But not this. Not telling the truth. Not fighting for them. Never this."

She turned before he could reply, the legs of his leather chair creaking behind her as he stiffened like a serpent poised to strike. She didn't look back. Didn't close the door gently—she left it open, the slap of her boots echoing down the corridor like a hammer on a wall about to crumble.

Behind her, the office stayed too quiet—those gleaming awards, the city skyline, the silence of a man who had just realized the girl he'd underestimated was the one who'd set fire to his carefully built throne.

And Frieda, her shoulders squared, her hands unclenched at last, felt the storm inside her finally sharpen into something holy. The walls were about to shake. And this time, they wouldn't fall on her. They'd fall on him.

Broken and Burning

LATER THAT NIGHT, Frieda stood in the middle of her tiny apartment, her back pressed to the cold wall as if it could hold her up when her legs no longer would. The streetlamp outside cast stripes of bruised yellow light through the blinds, painting her bare floor in broken lines.

She felt it first in her chest—a pressure, sharp and crushing. Then her knees buckled. She slid down the wall, her palms scraping against peeling paint as she landed on the floor with a muffled thud. Her breath caught, shallow and ragged. Her shoulders shook as the sob rose—too big to hold back this time. It broke from her throat like a storm. She clutched at her curls, fingers tangling, pulling tight as if pain might anchor her to this moment and stop her from drifting away under the weight of it all.

She had survived so much—Grief that hollowed her out. Nights on cold city benches, praying the sun would rise before the danger found her. Shame that wrapped around her like chains. Betrayals that taught her how to fight. But this?

She had invited the wolf in. Had smiled while he sharpened his teeth on her trust. Had handed him girls who had trusted *her*. And now they were paying the price for her blind faith. The thought tore her open.

"God…" Her voice cracked against the silence, hoarse, wet with grief. "I let him in. I opened the gate. And they're paying for it. I did this. I did this—"

She rocked slowly, knees pulled tight to her chest, forehead pressed against her clasped hands. The city hummed beyond the window—cars passing, neon signs flickering, a world moving on while her own felt like it was crumbling from the inside out. Tears dripped from her chin, soaking into her sweater, her jeans. She didn't wipe them away. She let them come—this flood of shame and fury and ache.

No more speeches. No more mantras to steady herself. Just a promise whispered into the night, a raw vow cracked open like bone:

"I'm going to bring them home."

When her voice gave out, she crawled to the coffee table and dragged her journal into her lap. Her hand shook so hard the pen skittered across the page at first—stuttering lines before words found her.

I trusted the wrong man. I failed the right girls.

Ink smudged where her tears fell. She didn't stop.

But I will not run. Not now. Not when they need me to stand. Not when they need someone to come back for them.

She closed her eyes, the pen pausing mid-sentence. The city hummed its indifferent lullaby. But in her chest, beneath the fracture, something small and furious flickered to life again.

Lord, if You can still use me—use my shame to break their chains. Use my voice to rip the mask off every wolf hiding in Your house. I don't care what it costs.

The page filled—crooked lines, fierce words pressed deep into the paper. When she set the pen down, she rested her palm over the final vow, her breathing slowing.

I will not stop until they're found.

Outside, a siren wailed and faded. Inside, the last of her tears dried on her cheeks. She sat in the hush that followed, back against the wall again, eyes on the window. Not whole. Not fearless. But lit from the inside by something she could not—would not— let die.

If the wolf wanted a fight, she thought, her fingers tightening around the journal's frayed cover, *then the wolf had just found one.*

Rise and Rally

The next morning dawned bitter and gray, the sky was the color of ash. The wind cut through the streets of East Frampton like it had a score to settle. And there, on the corner of Park and Hill—just outside the darkened windows of the shuttered Bridge center—stood Frieda Winslow. Her breath rose in fragile clouds, fogging the air in front of her like ghosts escaping from her chest. She wore a heavy coat zipped to her chin, but still, the cold found its way in. Her gloved hands gripped a clipboard in one and a scuffed megaphone in the other. The red sticker still plastered across the glass door behind her bled like a wound: **TEMPORARILY CLOSED – BY ORDER OF THE CITY**.

But that wasn't the loudest message on that block. Not anymore. Scrawled across the clipboard in her hand were thirty names. Thirty girls who didn't walk away. Who had shown up—in texts, in whispered conversations, in presence. Girls who still *believed* in the refuge they had built together, brick by invisible brick.

Joyce stood at Frieda's side, layered in scarves and the kind of quiet resolve that made walls tremble. Her hand rested gently on Frieda's back. Miguel was just behind them, hood pulled low against the wind, a messenger bag slung over his shoulder. His jaw was tight; eyes locked on the street like he was bracing for a fight and a miracle at once.

Frieda's voice, when she finally spoke, was low and steady. "We're not going to whisper this," she said, lifting the megaphone to her lips, "We're going to *roar*."

And they did. That day blurred into motion—like stepping into a current too strong to resist. Frieda made phone calls with a voice that cracked but didn't quit. She knocked on weather-beaten doors with calloused knuckles and asked for help without shame. She sat in meetings, across from weary principals, exhausted parents, skeptical pastors—and told the truth anyway.

"We were infiltrated," she said again and again. "But we're not broken. And we're not done."

And the people listened. By Friday, word had spread like fire catching dry leaves. They gathered in a borrowed gymnasium on the south end of town—one of those old rec centers that still smelled faintly of rubber soles and wood polish. The lights flickered overhead, not bright enough to dazzle but steady enough to see. Folding chairs were arranged in uneven rows. No podium. No banners. Just scraped floors, tired walls, and souls ready to rise.

Frieda stood at the front, her back straight, her notes trembling slightly in her hand. She wore no microphone. The room didn't need one.

"You've heard the rumors," she began, her voice quiet but commanding. "But this isn't about whispers."

A hush fell.

"This is about girls who trusted us. Girls who asked for safety and found wolves instead."

Gasps slipped through the room like sudden drafts. Some people reached for the hands beside them. Others bowed their heads.

"We have names," Frieda continued. "We have documents. We have evidence. But more than that—we have a responsibility. To protect the next girl *before* she disappears."

She stepped back, and Miguel moved forward. He didn't perform. He presented—clearly, calmly. A slideshow projected onto a wrinkled white sheet: photos of shuttered shelters with no staff, shell corporations with no purpose, tax forms linking Caleb's network to out-of-state funding sources. No sensationalism. Just truth.

Then Joyce stepped to the front. She didn't preach. She didn't stir. She read. A single verse about shepherds and wolves, about the burden of watching the gate. Her voice cracked once, but she didn't falter. When she prayed, it wasn't for vengeance. It was for covering. For strength. For light.

When Frieda opened the floor, there were no accusations. No panic. No demands. Just promises.

"I can get printing donated," one woman said, her hand rising like a flag.

"My cousin's church has a building we're not using during the week."

"I'll walk kids from school to wherever you land next."

"I've got grant-writing experience. Let's write new ones."

"I'll build you a website. A real one."

It came like a tide—pledges. Offers. Support that didn't come from pity, but solidarity. From shared ache and rising purpose. And Frieda stood there, eyes rimmed with tears, heart swelling not with fear, not with fury—but with *movement*. The tide had shifted.

That night, long after the chairs had been stacked and the lights turned off, she returned to her apartment and opened her journal. The pages still smelled faintly of smoke from her candle. She wrote slowly, carefully:

The fire came.
The wolves came.
But the people rose.
We are The Bridge. And now, we build again.

She didn't close the journal when she finished. She left it open. Let the ink dry in the quiet.

Outside, the wind still howled. But inside, something sacred had begun again. Not a rescue. Not a rebuild.

A rally. And this time, they were ready.

The Search

MORNING BROKE GRAY AND HEAVY over Frampton, casting a pale hush across the windowpane of Frieda's apartment.

Inside, the light barely touched the room, as if even the sun hesitated to disturb what was unfolding at the kitchen table.

Frieda sat motionless, a chipped mug of black coffee cooling between her palms. Steam no longer rose from it. She hadn't taken a sip. Before her, a large, worn map of the city sprawled across the table—creased, frayed at the edges, ink bleeding into the fibers where too many notes had been added and erased. Colored push pins dotted neighborhoods like warning flares. Yellow circles for the girls she could still reach. Blue pins for those she was still hoping to find. Red Xs marked places where the trail had gone cold.

Her legal pad sat open beside the map, lines of handwriting tightening as they descended the page. Monique's name appeared at the top, circled twice. Beneath it, dates. Locations. Notes scribbled in a furious hand: *"Last seen—RiseFram van. No follow-up. Shelter staff unsure."*

Frieda stared at that name until her vision blurred. Her fingertips trembled as she picked up her phone. She pressed a familiar contact. Held her breath.

Joyce answered on the second ring.

"Hey, baby."

Frieda's voice was hoarse. "Are you sitting?"

A pause.

"I am now."

Frieda's throat constricted. She didn't ease into it. She couldn't.

"We've confirmed three girls. Monique. Tasha. Brina. All disappeared after RiseFram 'placements.' None made it to where they were supposed to go. All had contact with Caleb or one of his people in the weeks before they vanished."

Silence stretched for a moment. Then Joyce's voice dropped, deep and raw, like a prayer ripped straight from the soul.

"Lord... have mercy."

Frieda swallowed hard, gripping the edge of the table. "I'm not waiting around for the city to find their conscience. Or for the police to remember these girls matter. I'm organizing a canvass. Flyers, boots on the ground, door to door."

"You say the word," Joyce said without hesitation. "I'll bring ten from church. We'll meet wherever you say."

Frieda closed her eyes for a moment—just one breath. "Ok," she said. Then she hung up.

The knock came a few minutes later.

Miguel.

He stepped in quietly, his transit worker polo rumpled, sleeves already pushed to his forearms like he hadn't stopped moving all morning. He paused in the doorway, eyes taking in the war table—map, notes, lists, pins. He set down his messenger bag and moved toward the table, his voice low, steady. "Walk me through it."

Frieda stood, circling the map with a fingertip. Her voice was tight but controlled.

"Three girls. All from different neighborhoods. Sent to different shelters, supposedly. Each went through a RiseFram referral. All disappeared within days. No follow-up, no accountability. One of the shelters listed doesn't even exist anymore."

Miguel leaned in, eyes narrowing. "You think it's Caleb?"

"I know it is," she said. "But I can't prove it yet."

He sat beside her, close enough for her to feel the heat of his focus. "And the city?"

She shook her head. "Not fast enough. They keep passing it between departments. Youth Services. Missing Persons. Licensing. No one wants to touch it."

Miguel's jaw clenched. "Then let's move without them."

She nodded. "We grid the city. North, South, East. I've got shelter contacts. Old social workers. Teachers. You've got transit cameras and access to city routes. We start pulling every thread."

They got to work. Phones buzzed. Notes grew. Miguel tapped into his network of bus depot clerks, maintenance workers, and security staff. He requested stop footage, transit logs, and last-seen routes. Frieda rang old church partners, youth centers, halfway houses—anyone who might have seen one of the girls, even in passing.

By noon, the kitchen looked like something out of a detective drama—notes taped to cupboards, strings connecting timelines, printouts layered over city maps. But this wasn't fiction. This was flesh and blood—missing girls. Real lives.

At one point, as Frieda sorted through a stack of manila folders, Miguel's hand brushed hers. She looked up, startled by the stillness in his face.

"You don't have to carry this alone," he said softly. His hand didn't move. His eyes didn't blink.

Frieda didn't flinch. For once, she believed him. She gave a slow nod. Then slid another file across the table.

And just like that, the war room came alive. Not with chaos. Not with fear. But with *purpose*. With resolve so sharp it could cut through concrete. They weren't just chasing shadows anymore. They were bringing the light.

On The Ground

BY MID-AFTERNOON, the streets of East Frampton felt different. Not quieter—just heavier. As if the air itself had thickened with names no longer spoken aloud, stories buried beneath concrete and neon. But today, those stories had legs. Voices. Clipboards. Eyes that scanned every corner and face.

Volunteers moved in pairs, some slow-walking the crumbling sidewalks, while others paused to tape flyers to lamp posts already layered with notices for missing pets and torn concert ads. Winter coats flapped in the wind as they moved from storefront to stoop.

Each flyer bore the face of a missing girl. Each voice asked the same questions:

"Have you seen her?"

"She was at The Bridge last month."

"She didn't just leave. Somebody saw her—near Pulaski. Near that old rail line."

"I heard she got a job... but no one's heard from her since."

"Doesn't feel right."

The stories came in fragments, in side-eyes, in whispers. Hope clung to each sentence like breath on glass.

Frieda sat in the front passenger seat of Miguel's aging sedan; her eyes locked on the map wedged between her knee and the glovebox. The city grid was littered with scribbles and circles—new leads, crossed-out names, buildings marked with question marks that felt more like warnings than curiosity.

Miguel drove slowly, one hand on the wheel, the other resting loosely on the gearshift. The heater wheezed through the vents, struggling to cut through the cold. Joyce rode in the back, her scarf wound tightly around her neck, a stack of extra flyers gripped between her gloved hands. The car turned down a side street lined with abandoned factories, graffiti curling up the brick like ivy. One warehouse stood apart—chained gate, crooked signage, and the kind of silence that felt watched.

Miguel eased the car to a stop. Frieda's eyes locked on the building, her heart beginning to pound—not in fear, but recognition.

"This is it," she murmured. "One of the girls mentioned a warehouse off Pulaski. Said someone told her Monique might've been seen there."

They got out slowly, the wind slapping against them with icy teeth. Joyce clutched her coat tighter as they approached the building.

Frieda stepped forward and knocked on the metal side door—three times. Firm. Intentional. A beat. Then another.

Finally, the door cracked open with a grating creak. An older man appeared—gray stubble, oil-stained hoodie, bloodshot eyes that flicked over each of them with practiced calculation. His posture screamed, "Don't ask."

Frieda didn't flinch. She held out the flyer with Monique's picture, her voice steady. "We're looking for this girl. Her name's Monique. She stayed at The Bridge."

The man's eyes lingered on the photo longer than necessary. Then flicked to Miguel. To Joyce. Back to Frieda.

No words. Just a sharp slam as the door shut again. Metal on metal. The echo rang down the alley.

Miguel exhaled sharply, pulling a pen from his jacket and scribbling the address on the edge of the flyer. "That wasn't just rude," he muttered. "That was fear."

Joyce stared at the closed door like it had insulted her spirit. "Something's in that building," she said flatly.

Frieda's knuckles were white against her thigh. She didn't speak for a long moment. Just stared at the flyer in her hand, then up at the rusted facade of the warehouse.

"We're close," she finally said, her voice low and tight with something that wasn't quite rage—but close. "I can feel it."

No one replied. Miguel stepped back toward the car and turned the key. The engine groaned, then hummed to life. Frieda slid back into the passenger seat, her shoulders squared. Joyce sat behind her, whispering something that sounded like prayer. The tires rolled forward slowly, gravel crunching beneath them like bones.

They weren't just chasing leads anymore. They were walking into places no one wanted to name. They were digging through silence. And every step was for the girls the city had tried to forget. Frieda wouldn't let that happen. Not again. Not ever.

The Basement Gathering

THAT NIGHT, the basement of Emmanuel Fellowship held a weight that had nothing to do with the low ceilings or cinder block walls. The overhead lights buzzed softly, their glow casting pale shadows across the cold concrete floor. The room smelled of old hymnals and lemony floor wax—faint reminders of a gentler purpose. A chalkboard in the corner, still dusty with pastel smudges, bore the faint outline of a Bible verse: *"Let your light shine..."* The last words blurred by time and tiny hands.

Now, that same space held something electric. Dozens of folding chairs, some dented, others rusted at the hinges, formed uneven rows. They creaked under the weight of community— volunteers, mentors, teens, mothers, teachers—all drawn together by the same ache, the same fire.

Frieda stood at the front of the room, her arms wrapped loosely across her chest, the edges of her coat dusted with the night's cold. Her eyes scanned the faces before her—Joyce with her hands clasped tight in her lap; Tyesha, sitting cross-legged on the floor with a notebook and highlighter; Miguel beside her now, no longer an outsider, but a fixed point. His sleeves were rolled to the elbow, a clipboard in one hand, the other flipping through maps and printed reports. He looked up and gave a slight nod. Frieda stepped forward. The room hushed.

"I won't lie to you," she began, her voice low, steady. "The police? They're stalling. The system doesn't move fast for girls who look like ours."

A rustle of discomfort swept through the chairs. No surprise. Just confirmation. She let the silence stretch a bit longer, then continued.

"But we're not waiting. Not another day." She raised her chin slightly, her words gaining weight. "Tomorrow, we go. We document every building tied to Caleb's so-called shelters. We talk to store clerks, bus drivers, and neighbors. Anyone who might've seen something, heard something. Because someone always sees. And someone always talks—if you ask the right way."

Soft murmurs rose—agreement, tension, readiness.

Tyesha looked up from the floor, her brows drawn. "But what if they don't want to talk?" Her voice was clear, edged with both fear and fire.

Frieda didn't hesitate. She stepped closer, locking eyes with her. "Then we ask again. And again. And again. We show up with names. With questions. With presence." She pointed gently to her own chest. "Because these girls? They're not data points. They're not runaways. They are daughters. Sisters. Souls."

The room fell still. No coughs. No chair creaks. Just breath—and belief.

"We carry their names like prayers," Frieda said, her voice tightening with emotion. "And we don't stop until we find every last one."

Joyce bowed her head slightly, murmuring, "Amen," her voice low but rooted.

Across the room, a younger volunteer—barely sixteen, her hoodie sleeves covering nervous fingers—whispered, "We ride at dawn."

A soft ripple of laughter followed. Not loud. Not careless. Just enough to crack the tension. And beneath the laughter, there was steel. Resolve. They were tired—bone-deep tired. But they were ready.

Frieda glanced at Miguel, who was already marking routes on a map. Joyce leaned forward, handing out updated flyers. A girl near the back reached into her bag and pulled out a handful of granola bars— "for tomorrow," she said, "just in case."

And then, slowly, without instruction, the room began to shift. Heads bowed, not out of ritual, but out of need.

Frieda led the prayer, her words soft but burning: "Lord, let us find what others have chosen to overlook. Give us eyes to see. Feet to go. And hearts that won't grow cold. Protect our girls. And guide our steps."

When they looked up again, the room no longer felt like a basement. It felt like a battleground. The Bridge wasn't just a shelter anymore. It was a searchlight. And tomorrow, they would rise—not to retreat, but to reclaim, because the battle had changed. But so had they.

The Rescue Network

THE BRIDGE GIRLS DIDN'T JUST MOURN. They mobilized. By sunrise, the old office space—once used for homework help and counseling sessions—had transformed into a makeshift command center pulsing with quiet urgency. Clipboards leaned against coffee mugs. Power cords snaked across the floor. Voices murmured around whiteboards scrawled with names, cross streets, and last known locations.

Lena, usually soft-spoken, now moved like a general. She stood at the center table, dividing the city into zones with the edge of a ruler, her voice clipped and focused.

"Tyesha, you take Zone A—anything east of Franklin. Take Marla and June with you. Knock on every door. Ask the corner store clerks, the bus drivers, the mail carriers."

Tyesha nodded, tying her braids into a high knot and strapping on her coat like armor. "We don't come back without something," she said, voice low and sharp.

In the back corner, Maria hunched over her laptop. Her screen glowed with grids of color-coded cells—sightings in yellow, confirmed interviews in green, dead ends in gray. She barely spoke, fingers moving with quiet fury.

"I'll link this to the hotline," she murmured. "So, everything filters live."

Joyce paced near the back, organizing food drop-offs and phone coverage with the precision of a seasoned field nurse. She barked into her Bluetooth headset while balancing three bags of pre-packed sandwiches.

"Every team needs protein and charged phones. No excuses. Don't tell me you're hungry and empty-handed. I'll meet you at the corner of 63rd and Warren with granola bars and battery packs."

Miguel swept in just before nine. Still in his transit jacket, hair damp from the morning fog, he carried two bus route schedules and a phone charger looped around his wrist.

"I rerouted the number 6 and number 9 buses. Drivers know to make unofficial stops near canvassing zones. Nobody gets left on foot," he said, already pulling out highlighters.

Frieda stood near the front window, staring out at the street where volunteers—some teens, some elders—gathered with flyers and staplers, bundled in coats, their breath rising in soft clouds. Her hands were steady, but her heart hammered like a drum.

They didn't ask for this war. But they were in it now.

She turned back to the room. "We're not giving up on our girls," she said, her voice low but thick with conviction. "Not one." Her words landed like iron.

Later, heads nodded. A few hands tightened on flyers. Someone whispered, "Amen."

In the far corner, an old barber's chair—donated from the neighborhood shop—became the unofficial dispatch seat. On the counter behind it sat a borrowed coffee urn, still steaming, next to a box of dollar-store pastries. Hand-drawn maps were taped to the walls with painter's tape. Each pin was a name. Each name, a life.

The hotline came next. Frieda and Joyce organized it in an old Sunday school office, its bulletin board still cluttered with felt-cross cutouts and faded prayer requests. Miguel installed a call log system, linked it to Maria's spreadsheet, then added a "whisper line"—a silent option for anonymous tips, traceable only through a secure channel.

They answered every ring. Some calls were choked with fear—a girl seen climbing into a black van, a strange car idling too long near a shelter. Others offered slivers of hope— "She was here last week. I swear it was her." Some were heartbreak. Some were hoaxes. But still—they picked up. Because this wasn't a nonprofit. It was a lifeline.

They plastered flyers across corner stores, church bulletin boards, and laundromats. Slid photos under apartment doors. Whispered names into community group chats and porch conversations.

The circle widened. Parents showed up with tearful eyes and open arms. Store owners donated paper, ink, and time. Retired teachers returned to organize routes with school-day precision. And the local barber opened his shop—no questions asked. He swept the floor, brewed coffee, and set up folding tables beneath the glow of a cracked ceiling light. They pinned maps to his walls and marked the places where hope had last flickered. They weren't trained in recovery. They weren't funded by the city. But they showed up because girls had gone missing. And someone needed to come looking.

That day, as night pressed close around the city once more, Frieda stood in the middle of the command center. Her eyes scanned the room—Joyce on the phone, Miguel double-checking bus routes, Lena leading a prayer over her search team. And she knew: This wasn't a charity anymore. This wasn't even just a rescue. This was reclamation. This was war. And they were not backing down.

A Bruised Light

THE APARTMENT WAS CLOAKED IN A HUSH that felt almost sacred. The only illumination came from the soft, blue light of Miguel's laptop, open on Frieda's kitchen table. Its glow spilled out in uneven ripples, casting strange shadows across half-drunk mugs, highlighters, and a mess of papers that blanketed the surface like a battlefield strewn with fragments of a buried truth.

Spreadsheets blinked quietly. Maps pulsed with color-coded pins. Names and addresses floated on the screen like ghosts.

Miguel sat still, elbows resting on either side of the keyboard, his fingers tapping a slow, restless rhythm against the wood. His face was drawn—focused, yes—but there was a heaviness behind his eyes. The kind that came from witnessing too much and trying to hold it all together for someone else.

Across the room, Frieda stood like a statue at the window. The amber streetlamp outside lit her from behind, draping her figure in a burnished silhouette. She didn't move. Didn't blink. Her arms were folded tightly across her chest, hands gripping the opposite elbows like she was trying to hold herself inside her own skin. She stared through the glass as if expecting the night to answer her. But her eyes weren't really seeing the street below—the cracked sidewalk, the trash bin overturned, the long shadow of a passing car. Her vision was somewhere else. Deeper. Farther. Somewhere full of questions that had no easy answers.

Behind her, Miguel's voice rose, soft and even. A low murmur cutting through the silence like a thread through cloth.

"You sure you want to go through with this?"

It wasn't a challenge. It wasn't doubt. Just a question. Honest. Careful.

Frieda didn't respond right away. Her fingers clenched slightly. Then relaxed. The streetlight caught the glint of moisture at the corner of one eye, but no tears fell. Not yet. When she finally spoke, her voice was quiet. Rough. Like it had been dragged over gravel.

"I don't have a choice."

Miguel watched her—really watched her. His shoulders shifted. His hand moved to close the laptop, not abruptly but deliberately. The sound of it clicking shut echoed in the small kitchen, louder than expected—a punctuation mark.

"You do," he said gently. "But I know you'll make the hard one."

That made her turn. Slowly. Her eyes met his, glossy with pain but blazing with something deeper—resolve wrapped in sorrow. She stepped toward the table with deliberate grace, as if the weight on her back made every movement slower, heavier. The wooden floor creaked beneath her steps—soft, weary protests. She didn't sit. Instead, she placed both hands on the back of a worn dining chair—knuckles white from pressure—and leaned in, as if the furniture might steady her.

"I trusted him, Miguel." Her voice wavered. "I vouched for him. I opened doors he never should've walked through."

She swallowed hard, breath catching in her throat. Her gaze dropped to the edge of the table, where a flyer with Monique's face peeked out from beneath a stack of notes.

"These girls…" she said, barely above a whisper. "They followed me. They believed because I did."

Her hands trembled. "And now…"

Miguel didn't rush in with reassurances. He didn't offer platitudes. He rose slowly and walked around the table, his socked feet soundless on the floor. When he reached her side, he didn't touch her—not yet. He just stood beside her, shoulder to shoulder, the silence between them a kind of shelter. He spoke gently.

"You're not guilty for being hopeful." His words hung in the air like smoke. Soft. Steady. "That's not a crime, Frieda. It's the reason they followed you in the first place. You saw something better. And you made them believe it was possible."

She didn't answer. Her jaw tightened. Her eyes dropped again, this time to her own hands—open now, palms pressed flat against the chair's backrest, still shaking.

"But if that belief put them in danger…" she said, her voice breaking. "If I let the wolf into the fold?" A tear finally escaped, tracing a line down her cheek.

Miguel turned toward her, his presence grounding. His voice firmer now, but still low. "You're only guilty if you do nothing now."

Silence followed, but it was a silence filled with meaning. With weight. With decision. Frieda closed her eyes. Inhaled deep. The kind of breath that reaches the ribs. The kind that clears more than lungs. When she opened them, the fire had returned. Brighter than before. Bruised, but burning.

"Then let's expose him," she said.

Miguel nodded once. "Together."

And finally—finally—Frieda sat down. Not in defeat. But in defiance. Not in sorrow. But in decision.

The light from the laptop flickered across their faces like the first spark before a blaze. And somewhere, just beneath the surface of the night, something delicate began to rise.

What She Couldn't Unhear

THE WEEK UNFOLDED LIKE A FOG—dense, heavy, and without edges. Time slipped sideways. Mornings bled into nights, and nights into darker hours lit only by desk lamps with buzzing bulbs and the cold glow of laptop screens.

Miguel worked at the far end of the kitchen table, surrounded by a clutter of USB drives, manila folders, and open browser tabs. His fingers moved with quiet urgency, piecing together a digital trail of betrayal.

Frieda sat near the window, a worn notepad on her lap and bank statements spread around her like fallen leaves. Venmo logs. Donation receipts. Wire transfers with names she didn't recognize—some in neat columns, others in careless strings of numbers and aliases.

There was one spreadsheet they hadn't meant to keep. But now they couldn't look away. It was mid-afternoon when Frieda's phone buzzed against the table. A number she didn't recognize. The screen pulsed once, then again. She answered.

"Hello?"

Silence. Then a breath. Not a deep one. A small, uncertain one. Like someone trying to convince herself she was allowed to speak.

"I… I don't know if I should be talking to you."

The voice was young. Barely above a whisper. Each word seemed to tiptoe out of her mouth.

Frieda straightened. Her fingers tightened around the phone. "You're safe," she said softly. "It's okay. Just take your time."

A pause. Then the girl spoke again, her voice halting.

"He promised me things."

Frieda's heart clenched. "What kind of things?" she asked, her tone even, careful not to push.

The girl exhaled shakily. "Said he could get me out of Frampton. Said he had people... jobs. That I was perfect. That he could set me up in Florida."

Frieda's pen hovered over the notepad. The words etched in the silence between them.

"What kind of job?" she asked gently.

"Salon work," the girl said. "At least, that's what he told me. At first."

The shift in her voice was subtle—but devastating. A crack at the edge of something deeper. Beneath the words, Frieda heard it: shame. Grief. That terrible realization that comes just after trust has been shattered.

"I backed out," the girl continued. "Something felt off. Too fast. Too polished. But... there was this other girl. She went."

Frieda's hand moved slowly across the notepad. "What happened?"

"She's gone," the girl whispered. "No one's heard from her. Her mom's called everybody. Friends. Cousins. Nobody knows where she is."

The silence that followed was suffocating. Frieda pressed the phone tighter to her ear, her voice steady even though her stomach had begun to churn. "I'm so sorry," she murmured.

The girl let out a sound—not quite a sob, not quite a breath. Just the kind of sound pain makes when it doesn't know where to go.

"I thought... I really thought he was helping me."

Frieda closed her eyes. She wanted to cry, but her body didn't move that way anymore. Not tonight. Not after all she'd heard, all she'd seen.

"You were brave to call," she said softly. "You did the right thing. And none of this... none of this is your fault."

There was another pause, then a click. The line went dead. Frieda sat in the stillness. The hum of Miguel's laptop filled the space, but it sounded far away.

She didn't move. Didn't speak. She let the weight of the girl's voice settle on her shoulders like ash. Then, slowly, she lowered the phone onto the table, picked up her pen, and wrote. Word by word. Line by line. Not just notes. Not just evidence. A record of the betrayed. A ledger of the lured and lost. And underneath each word, beneath every name, was something sharper than grief. Resolve. A vow not to forget. A promise to make it right.

You're Still Breathing

THE HALLWAY OF Emmanuel Fellowship stretched quiet and long, its tiled floor bathed in the amber light of a setting sun. Dust motes floated lazily through the air, stirred by the faint breeze drifting in through the cracked stained-glass window near the stairwell. The scent of old hymnals, wood polish, and warm paper filled the space like a quiet memory.

Frieda moved quickly down the corridor, arms cradling a precarious stack of files—names, dates, missing reports, and legal forms pressing into her like weight she couldn't set down. Her footsteps echoed sharply, and her face—tight with resolve—betrayed the storm she'd been carrying for weeks.

Joyce was waiting just past the doorway of the storage room, arms crossed, eyes soft and knowing. She stepped out slowly, catching Frieda gently by the elbow.

"Hold on now," Joyce said, her voice low and sure, like a hymn sung just above a whisper.

Frieda stopped mid-step, blinking as if someone had turned on a light. Her breath hitched. "What is it?"

Joyce didn't answer right away. Instead, she studied her—not just her face, but the set of her shoulders, the tremor in her fingers, the fire burning low behind her eyes.

"You look like a storm wrapped in skin," Joyce said quietly.

Frieda let out a laugh, brittle and sharp. "That's how I feel."

Without a word, Joyce reached into the pocket of her cardigan and pulled out a small, worn note card. The corners were bent and soft, the ink faded but still legible. She pressed it into Frieda's hand like a balm.

Frieda looked down, her breath catching as she read the handwritten verse:

We are hard pressed on every side, but not crushed; perplexed, but not in despair; persecuted, but not abandoned; struck down, but not destroyed.'

The words trembled in her vision, blurred by the swell of tears she hadn't permitted herself to cry.

"You're still breathing," Joyce said softly, her hand resting over Frieda's. "So, you're still fighting."

Frieda nodded slowly, her throat thick. The files pressed against her chest like armor she didn't want to wear anymore. "I just feel so… outnumbered. Like every time I get back up, the hits come harder."

Joyce reached out, wrapping one arm around her, the other cradling the back of Frieda's head like a mother would. Her embrace was strong. Still. Holy.

"That's when you remember who goes before you," she murmured, her voice a steady heartbeat. "You ain't fighting alone, baby. Not now. Not ever."

Frieda folded into the hug, letting the moment hold her— her grief, her grit, her bone-deep fatigue. And for the first time in days, the ache in her chest loosened, if only by a thread.

When she stepped back, her eyes were red, but her spine had straightened. Her hand slid the note card gently into her pocket like a keepsake. Not just scripture. A lifeline. A reminder. She was still breathing. And as long as she had breath, she would keep going. The fight wasn't over. And neither was she.

Nightmare Light

THE CITY HUMMED OUTSIDE Frieda's Apartment, a low, distant murmur of tires on wet pavement and far-off sirens—life still moving, even while she lay motionless beneath a threadbare sheet. The room was dim, lit only by the fractured moonlight that slipped through the bent slats of her blinds. Stripes of pale silver fell across the wall in uneven patterns, like ghostly prison bars.

Her brows were damp. Her hands curled loosely atop the blanket, twitching now and then. A sheen of sweat clung to her collarbone. Sleep had found her, but rest hadn't.

And then… the dream came. It started quietly, too quiet. The kind of silence that carried tension in its lungs. Then came the smoke—thin and sweet at first, curling like incense through invisible cracks. It drifted through the air, soft as silk, until the scent thickened, acrid and sharp, clinging to her throat.

The flames followed. They didn't roar at first. They whispered. Licked at the edges of her vision with slow, greedy tongues. The wallpaper in her dream peeled like skin. The floor beneath her feet—so familiar, so safe—fractured. Black veins split through it like broken glass.

And then the faces came. Dozens of them. Girls. Some she recognized in flashes—Monique, Daniella, faces from The Bridge etched into memory. Others were more elusive, dream-made and blurred, but their expressions struck the same chord: wide eyes full of questions they didn't need to ask.

"Why didn't you see it?"

The voice came not from a mouth, but from everywhere— from the crackling fire, the shifting fog, the heat itself. A girl stepped forward. She wore a tattered hoodie two sizes too big. Her arms were wrapped in gauze; dirt smudged across her cheek.

"You said we were safe," she said. Her voice was barely more than a breath.

Behind her, another girl emerged, gripping a journal torn at the spine. The pages fluttered loose, drifting like ash as they fell.

Frieda tried to speak. Her mouth moved, but the words came sluggishly, like she was underwater. "I didn't know… I didn't know."

The fog closed in.

A third girl stepped through the smoke—her dress scorched at the hem, her eyes dull and too old for her years. She didn't speak. She only raised her hand, palm open, a silent indictment.

Then, from the darkness, came a chorus of eyes— hundreds, maybe thousands—blinking open one by one. They hovered in the smoke. Wide. Watching. Some pleading. Others filled with sorrow. A few with blame.

"Then why," the air whispered, "do we feel forgotten?"

Frieda backed away, but there was no space to run. The dream held her tight, like water holds a drowning woman. The fire grew higher, flashing orange and gold against the shifting fog. But there was no heat—only pressure, a heavy breath that wrapped around her chest and squeezed. The faces blurred, but the eyes remained. And then she fell. Not with impact, not with pain—but with the sickening lurch of helplessness, as if the floor itself had been taken from beneath her. She gasped. Her eyes snapped open.

The room was silent again. Still. A single bead of sweat trickled down her temple. Her breaths came in shallow bursts. Her chest rose and fell too quickly, her body rigid in the aftermath of sleep's cruel ambush. Tears clung to her lashes. She sat up slowly, the sheet tangling around her waist. The lamplight cast a soft glow across the nightstand, where her journal lay unopened. The cover looked darker in the quiet, heavy with unsaid things. With trembling hands, she reached for it. But she didn't open it. Not yet. There were no words. Only breath. And the echo of all she couldn't unsee. And all she hadn't yet forgiven herself for.

You're Not Alone

IT HIT HER WITHOUT WARNING. A wave. A collapse. Frieda sank slowly to the kitchen floor, her back pressed against the humming fridge, knees drawn in so tight they touched her chin. The tile beneath her was cold, biting even through the soft fabric of her sweats. Her fingers—numb and restless—fidgeted with the frayed hem of her hoodie, pulling it, twisting it, releasing it again.

The apartment around her felt hollow. Still. The kind of stillness that didn't comfort. It accused. Overhead, the single bulb in the kitchen fixture buzzed faintly, casting a sterile light that flattened everything it touched. The refrigerator purred behind her, the only constant in a world that felt like it had tipped off its axis. Her eyes stared straight ahead, unfocused. Dry, but swollen. The kind of stare that came not from crying—but from running out of strength to cry.

Then the door opened. Quietly. No knock. Just the soft click of the lock turning, the creak of hinges giving way. Miguel stepped inside slowly, careful not to startle her. He paused in the entryway, the keys still in his hand. She had given him the spare for emergencies, but this wasn't a fire or a break-in. It was something quieter. Something heavier.

He spotted her immediately, curled like a shadow against the fridge, a woman made small by something too large to name. He didn't rush. Didn't speak. He set his keys on the counter. Slid off his coat. Then crouched down a few feet away and waited— knees bent, hands resting loosely on his thighs. The distance between them hummed with emotion.

Minutes passed. Frieda didn't look at him. But her voice broke through the silence, low and cracked like a fraying thread. "I don't deserve to lead anything after this."

Miguel exhaled through his nose, slow and measured. He shifted slightly, lowering himself fully to the floor so they were eye-level, cross-legged. Their knees nearly touched now. His voice, when it came, was soft but rooted. "You know what makes you worthy?" he asked. "Not that you've never fallen. But that you don't stay down."

She blinked. Her lip trembled. Finally, she turned her head just enough to look at him. Her eyes were rimmed with red, the lashes stiff from earlier tears. The kind of exhaustion in her gaze couldn't be measured in hours—it was the weariness of carrying too much, too long.

"What if I fail again?" she whispered.

Miguel's expression didn't change. He leaned in just a little closer—not to fix, not to rescue, but to be near. "Then we get back up again," he said, his voice steady. "Together."

That word hung in the air like a hand reaching through darkness. Together. Frieda's chin quivered. Her breath caught in her throat. For a moment, her shoulders shook—but she didn't collapse. Not this time.

"I'm scared, Miguel."

He nodded once, slowly. "Me too."

There was no fix. No grand speech. No spiritual platitude to smooth the jagged edge of what she carried. Just presence. Two souls breathing in the same silence. Sitting on cold tile. Bound not by solutions, but by love that stayed. And somehow… somehow, in that broken stillness, it was enough. She wasn't alone. Not anymore.

The Evidence

THE ROOM WAS WRAPPED IN HUSH. Only the soft purr of the space heater broke the silence, casting a steady stream of warmth across the carpet. It clicked occasionally as it cycled, a small metronome against the quiet. Outside, the late-afternoon light faded behind pale curtains, turning everything amber-gray.

Frieda knelt beside the coffee table, sleeves pushed up, her movements slow and deliberate. She opened each manila folder like a sacred text, laying its contents in neat rows across the worn surface—photographs, intake forms, missing person flyers, receipts, records. Margins scribbled with dates. Names underlined. Notes circled in red ink. Every page was a breathless piece of a larger, agonizing truth.

Miguel sat at her side on the edge of the couch, his forearms resting on his knees, a yellow legal pad balanced across them. He flipped through sheets of timestamps, van registration logs, and surveillance stills—eyes sharp, scanning, drawing invisible threads between places and people. His jaw worked in silence, muscles tight. The weight of it pressed in—paper and proof and pain.

Frieda's fingers lingered on a photo of Monique, half-smiling, her journal clutched to her chest. She swallowed hard. The hum of the heater suddenly felt deafening. Then, her phone buzzed. The sound snapped them both upright. Frieda's hand moved quickly, picking it up from the table. One glance at the screen sent a new wave of electricity through her spine. **Detective Corinne Reyes.** She exhaled and answered, her voice low. "You ready?"

The woman on the other end said, "Be there in an hour."

BY THE TIME CORINNE ARRIVED, the folders had been re-stacked, the coffee table cleared except for the evidence. A second chair had been pulled out. No coffee. No hospitality. Just truth.

She stepped inside like she'd done this a thousand times. Tall. Lean. Her eyes alert beneath arched brows, her short, coiled hair pulled back tight. She wore a dark trench unbuttoned over her badge and plainclothes. A leather notebook and pen already in hand. No small talk. No delay. She nodded once to Miguel, once to Frieda, and then sat, setting her badge gently on the table—visible, deliberate.

"What have you got?"

Frieda slid the first folder toward her. Miguel passed another. They didn't speak, not yet.

Corinne flipped the top cover open. Pages turned with clean, practiced fingers. Her eyes scanned quickly but thoroughly, her pen moving in sharp strokes across the page of her notebook. A van plate. A location. A time. She made no sound as she moved from folder to folder—just breath and ink and the soft, slow accumulation of horror.

She paused on a transcript of a survivor's account. Her eyes narrowed. Then she looked up. "This is real," she said, more to herself than to them. "You've got enough here to start a task force."

She pulled another sheet closer, comparing it to the notes she'd already made. "Patterns," she murmured. "Movements. Connections. And all of it wrapped up in Caleb's signature outreach fronts." Her mouth tightened into a line. "If we go on this—if we push it into motion—there's no second chance. Once he feels us coming, he'll disappear. And he won't go alone."

Frieda leaned forward, her hands clasped, voice steady but hoarse. "Then we make every second count. No leaks. No hesitations. We do it clean. We do it right."

Corinne studied her. Not just her words—but her posture. The fire behind her eyes. The weight she carried and the resolve that somehow still stood beneath it.

Then she gave a slow, single nod. "We'll do it right."

Miguel remained silent, but under the table, his hand shifted. His fingers brushed lightly against Frieda's. She didn't look down. But she let her hand meet his. Gave one firm, anchoring squeeze. And then released it. No words left to say. Only the next step forward. They weren't standing at the edge anymore. They had jumped. And now… they would burn the whole lie to the ground.

A Light That Doesn't Quit

THAT NIGHT, AFTER MIGUEL HAD GONE and the hush of solitude returned, Frieda stepped out onto her narrow porch. The door clicked softly behind her, closing out the warm breath of her apartment. She stood barefoot on the worn wooden boards, the wood cool and weathered under her soles, grooved from time and memory. The faint scent of rain lingered in the air, though the skies had stayed dry.

All around her, the city breathed its restless rhythm. Sirens wailed faintly in the distance—sharp and mournful. A bassline thudded from a passing car, its rhythm vibrating low through the concrete. From a few blocks down, someone's voice rose in an argument, ragged and echoing, then faded like smoke. It was all so familiar—too familiar—the soundscape of survival.

She wrapped her arms around herself and looked up. The sky above Frampton was murky, veiled in layers of haze, sodium streetlight, and the faintest stretch of smog. But there—buried in the grit—tiny stars still blinked. Dim. Distant. But present.

Frieda's breath caught in her throat. She closed her eyes. The prayer came not as a speech, but as a release.

"Lord... I'm still here," she whispered. Her voice was rough, like it had to claw its way out. "Bruised. Ashamed. But still breathing."

A pause. Her lips trembled. "Use me anyway." The words hung in the night air like mist. Honest. Bare. Then, quietly, she turned and stepped back inside.

The apartment greeted her in silence. A lamp glowed dim in the corner, casting a soft halo across the walls. She walked into the living room, her movements slow, like every step had to push through the weight still hanging on her shoulders. She reached for the small candle on the mantle—short, plain, burned down from nights before. She struck a match, its sulfur snap loud in the quiet, and touched it to the wick. The flame sputtered, uncertain at first... then caught. A fragile fire. But fire nonetheless.

She sat at the kitchen table, the surface worn smooth by elbows and years. Her journal sat on the shelf nearby—the battered one, corners frayed, ink smudged where tears had fallen. She pulled it down gently, like it might shatter. Opening to a blank page, she let her fingers hover over it, the pen poised in her hand. The weight of it felt heavier tonight. She pressed the tip to paper, slow and steady.

"Sometimes the light doesn't come like lightning."
She paused, heart beating in her throat.
"Sometimes it flickers. Bruised but burning."
A shaky breath. One final line.
"That's the kind of light I am now."
She stared at the page. The candle's flame danced gently beside her, casting flickering shadows that curled around her fingers, her words, her pain. And still—she stayed.

She closed her eyes and rested her hand on the page, letting the warmth of the candle reach her skin. Her breath slowed. The fear didn't vanish. But it didn't win either. Not tonight.

And in that quiet, beneath a sky too bright to see the stars clearly, Frieda believed again—just enough. Just enough to keep the light alive.

CHAPTER 18

The Weight of Truth

The fluorescent lights buzzed overhead, casting a cold, sterile glow across the small interview room. The walls were painted a tired shade of gray, the kind that felt neither warm nor cruel—just empty. A metal table sat in the center, its surface scratched with old stories, its legs bolted to the floor like it had seen too much and couldn't be trusted to move.

Frieda sat rigid in one of the hard plastic chairs, her spine straight but her shoulders heavy with something unshakable. Her fingers were wrapped tightly around a blue government-issued pen—the kind that always seemed to run out of ink when it mattered most. She hadn't written a word yet.

Across from her, Detective Corinne Reyes sat with quiet poise. No posturing. No pressure. Just presence. A thick manila file lay open in front of her—its contents fanned out across the table like fragments of broken glass. Pages of testimony. Photographs. Names. Addresses. Timelines. Pain woven into evidence.

And beside Frieda, not saying a word, sat Miguel. His presence didn't speak, but it anchored her. He was still in his transit uniform—creased sleeves rolled just below the elbow, his badge clipped neatly to his belt—but there was something about him tonight that felt older, worn in. His knee rested near hers under the table, a quiet offering—a place to steady her breath.

Reyes's voice was gentle but firm. "Take your time," she said, tapping a single sheet of paper. "But we'll need your signature before this becomes official."

Frieda didn't answer right away. She looked down at the page. The black print swam slightly, words rising and falling like they were underwater. She blinked, her vision sharpening. A statement. A name. A line where hers was meant to go. So simple. So devastating.

This wasn't just ink.

It was indictment.

It was confession.

It was courage, or the lack of it.

She exhaled slowly. And in that moment, her mind filled—not with facts, but with faces. Girls in sweatshirts and borrowed shoes. Girls who danced to music too loud in the rec room. Girls who cried in corners and peeled back their stories one fragile word at a time. Girls who had looked at her with wide eyes and called her "Miss Bridge"—as if that name alone could hold back the dark.

But some had disappeared. Some she hadn't seen in time. The weight of that truth crushed her lungs until she had to reach up and press a hand to her sternum. Miguel moved slightly, as if to speak, but stopped. He didn't need to say anything. He was already holding her up.

Frieda's fingers loosened around the pen, then tightened again. And slowly—deliberately—she brought it down to the page. The tip hovered for a moment, as if waiting for permission from somewhere deeper than her thoughts. Then she signed. Each letter curved with weight. With fire. With mourning. With defiance.

When she finished, she didn't lift her head right away. She stared at the name she'd written. Her name. Still hers. Still standing.

Reyes slid the paper back toward the folder. Her expression didn't change, but something in her gaze softened. Frieda leaned back in the chair. Her breath came slowly. Steady. Sharper than before. This wasn't closure. It was ignition. This wasn't the end. It was declaration. It was war—and this time, she wasn't walking into battle alone.

The Gathering Place

THAT SUNDAY EVENING, the sky hung low over East Frampton, bruised purple with clouds, as if the city itself were holding its breath. Inside the old brick chapel on Langston and 4th, the lights were dimmed, but the space was alive with presence.

The sanctuary still smelled faintly of dust and wood polish, of old hymnals and whispered prayers. Mismatched pews lined the narrow aisle—some sturdy, others wobbled with memory. Heat creaked from rusted vents in the floor, hissing in slow exhale, trying its best to warm the chill that clung to tired shoulders. Tall windows caught the last of the daylight, and along each sill, candles flickered like little defiant hearts—watchfires against the dark.

Frieda stood at the front of the room. Not behind a pulpit. Not framed by stained glass. Just her. Plain sweater. Worn jeans. Bare face. No title tonight—no shield between her and the girls.

They filled the pews slowly. Girls of all kinds—teenagers with braids, with chipped nail polish, with eyes that had seen too much. Some slouched back with folded arms. Some clutched notebooks or paper cups of tea. Some sat cross-legged on the floor near the front, closer than they ever used to be.

Frieda's hands were open at her sides. Her voice, when it came, was steady—but quiet. The kind of quiet you listen hard to hear.

"I need to tell you something," she began. "And it's not easy."

A murmur passed through the room. Chairs shifted. A few girls sat up straighter. One girl—Sariah—bit at a thumbnail.

Frieda took a breath. Her fingers twitched at her sides, curling once, then relaxing again.

"There was a man. His name was Caleb Rios. He came into The Bridge saying all the right things. Said he believed in us. Said he wanted to help." She paused, the air catching thick in her throat. "But he was hiding something. Something terrible."

The hush deepened. You could almost hear the air stretch between heartbeats.

"I trusted him," she said, slower now. "I opened doors that let him in. And because of that... some of our girls are gone."

Gasps. Soft. Sharp.

A girl in the second row sat forward, eyes wide. "Gone?" she whispered.

Another—arms folded tightly—spoke louder. "Wait, what do you mean 'gone'? Like—gone where?"

Frieda's voice cracked slightly. "We think... we know... they were taken. Recruited into something that wasn't safe. That wasn't real."

The silence that followed wasn't just stillness. It was rupture.

"You knew?" a voice called out. Angry. Young. Scared.

"Not soon enough," Frieda said, voice trembling. "I didn't see it until too much damage had been done. And I'm not asking you to excuse that." She stepped forward. Just one small step. Her feet felt like stone. "I'm asking you... to help me stop it. To help bring them back if we can. To protect the next girl before it happens again."

The weight of those words settled like smoke in the rafters. Nobody moved. Then—from the far back pew—someone stood. A thin girl in an oversized hoodie, her voice soft but unshaking:

"What do you need from us?"

Frieda blinked. Swallowed. Her heart thudded against her ribs. "Courage," she said. "Truth. And your trust."

There was a pause. A long one. Then another girl, maybe thirteen, barely audible, whispered into the hush:

"You still got it."

The words cracked something open. A few heads nodded. One girl wiped her nose on her sleeve. Another leaned forward and said, "Then let's go find them."

The room didn't explode with applause. It didn't have to. This wasn't a rally. It was a resurrection. One by one, girls started moving. Some stayed in their seats, curled beside each other, whispering pieces of old stories. Some stood and came to Frieda, wrapping arms around her waist, holding her with the strength of survivors.

Miguel stood in the doorway at the back, half in shadow, his eyes shining. When Frieda looked his way, he gave a single nod. Nothing dramatic. Just a gesture that said: I see you. I'm still here.

In the hallway, Sariah tugged on Frieda's sleeve. She held out a spiral notebook, pages bent, corners frayed. "Can we write letters?" she asked. "To the ones who are missing?"

Frieda's throat closed around her next breath. "Yes," she managed. "Yes, we can."

That night, pens scribbled across blank pages. Flyers were sketched on the backs of church bulletins. Names were whispered and remembered. Volunteers offered rides. One girl mapped out known shelters on her phone. Another started a list of questions they'd ask on the next canvass.

No more waiting. The Bridge wasn't closed. It was rising. And this time, they weren't just recovering what had been lost. They were building something that could never be stolen again.

The Eve of the Takedown

THE NIGHT BEFORE EVERYTHING WAS SET to fall into place—or come undone—Frieda stood barefoot on the weathered porch of her apartment. The wood beneath her feet was worn smoothly in spots, cracked in others; the grain chilled by night air and memory. Each creak echoed softly as she shifted her weight, like the house itself was holding its breath with her.

Above her, the city exhaled in long, restless murmurs. A siren wailed somewhere far off, rising and falling like a warning not quite meant for her. The hum of tires on wet pavement pulsed in waves, punctuated by the distant metallic groan of a freight train dragging its burdens through the edge of town. The wind smelled of smoke and old rain, like something had recently burned and hadn't quite forgiven the earth for it.

Her phone vibrated against her palm. She looked down. A single message from Miguel lit the screen, its white letters glowing like a flare in the dark:

"They're planning the takedown. Wednesday night."

She didn't move. Just stood there, phone cradled in her hand, eyes locked on the message. The screen dimmed after a few seconds. She didn't wake it again. Instead, she lifted her gaze toward the sky. It was murky tonight, washed out by city haze and the sodium-orange glow of streetlamps. The stars barely peeked through, smudged at the edges like old fingerprints on glass. But she looked for them anyway, searching the dark for something permanent.

Her voice, when it came, was barely more than a breath. "Cover them, God," she whispered. "Every girl. Every officer. Every room they're hiding in. Let Your light find them. Even if it's just one."

The wind tugged gently at her sweatshirt. She didn't ask for her own safety. She didn't ask for escape. Only for justice. Only for light.

Turning back toward the apartment, she stepped inside slowly, like walking through a veil. The door clicked shut behind her, muffling the noise of the city, sealing her into the quiet she had both craved and feared. The kitchen was dim—just the faint halo of the porch light spilling in through the window, casting the countertop in a bruised amber. She moved to the drawer without hurrying, pulled out the box of matches, and struck one with care. The scent of sulfur bloomed sharp and fleeting in the air.

She lit a single candle. Its flame danced against the chipped tile backsplash, throwing shadows that wavered and stretched like memories. She carried it to the table, setting it beside her open journal. The pen trembled slightly in her hand as she lowered it to the page. She didn't rush. Let the silence settle first. Let the flickering flame become the heartbeat in the room. Then she wrote:

Sometimes the light doesn't come like lightning.
Sometimes it flickers, bruised but burning.
That's the kind of light I am now.

The candle crackled softly, as if in response. She read the words twice. Let them take root. And when she closed the journal, her fingers were steady. She wasn't afraid. She was ready. Ready to fight. Ready to finish what had begun in shadows. Tomorrow, the darkness would face the light. And she—worn, weathered, but still burning—would not flinch.

The Visitation

THE NEXT AFTERNOON UNFOLDED in hushed amber, the sun dipping low behind the old sycamore that leaned like an aging sentinel outside Frieda's apartment. Its branches cast tangled shadows through the sheer curtains, sketching restless patterns on the kitchen floor. The quiet felt heavy—like it was waiting for something.

Two soft knocks broke the stillness. Then the door creaked open, familiar hinges groaning. Joyce stepped inside without ceremony; her coat dusted with cold air and her hands cradling a small container of homemade soup. Her presence filled the room like a hymn—low, steady, and full of comfort that needed no translation.

Frieda was at the sink, her back turned, rinsing a chipped ceramic mug. The water ran in a thin, steady stream. Her shoulders were curved inward, spine heavy with days of exhaustion. Her hair was tied back in a quick, uneven knot, and beneath her eyes bloomed the kind of darkness that didn't come from lack of sleep alone. She turned at the sound of the door and caught her breath.

"Hey," she said, softly. Her voice was raw, stretched thin from silence and restraint. Her eyes shimmered, full and unshed.

Joyce didn't answer right away. She walked straight to her and set the soup down on the counter with a gentle clink—then opened her arms and folded Frieda into them. It wasn't quick. It wasn't polite. It was the kind of embrace that spoke in silence: *I see you. I know. I'm here.*

Frieda stiffened at first—then broke. Her arms slid around Joyce, her forehead resting against the older woman's shoulder. Her breath came out in a shudder, and for a few long seconds, she simply held on, as if the ground beneath her had just remembered how to sway.

When they finally pulled apart, Joyce studied her face the way only someone who knew her long before the fire could.

"You look like you've been wrestling shadows in your sleep," she said softly.

Frieda gave a breath of a laugh, dry and worn. "That's because I have."

Without a word, Joyce reached into the oversized bag slung over her shoulder and pulled out a folded index card—edges softened from being carried too long. She handed it over with quiet reverence.

Frieda opened it slowly. A single verse, scrawled in Joyce's unmistakable looping handwriting:

'We are struck down, but not destroyed.'

Her breath hitched. She pressed the card to her chest like it could hold her up.

Joyce walked over to the small kitchen table and pulled out a chair with a soft scrape across the floor. She patted the one beside her. "Come on. Sit down, baby. Your bones are talking loud today."

Frieda obeyed, her body moving like it was underwater. She sank into the chair, one elbow on the table, chin nearly resting in her palm.

"I feel like I'm standing on a cliff," she murmured. Her voice was so low, it nearly disappeared.

Joyce didn't blink. She reached across the table, her hand warm and worn, and clasped Frieda's.

"Then jump," she said gently. "The same arms that caught you before will catch you again."

Frieda looked down at their joined hands, her eyes glossy. "What if I fall too far this time?"

Joyce leaned forward, her tone like steel wrapped in velvet. "You won't. You've got roots now. And wings you didn't have before."

The quiet wrapped around them again, this time not with weight, but with warmth. Through the window, the last gold rays of sunlight slid away, leaving only the soft glow of the kitchen lamp and the faint smell of thyme and lemon rising from the still-warm soup.

Frieda's voice cracked on the way out. "I'm scared, Joyce."

Joyce's grip tightened, just enough to say *I've got you.* "I know. But faith doesn't wait for fear to leave," she whispered. "It moves anyway."

A tear rolled down Frieda's cheek. She didn't bother to wipe it. Didn't need to. Instead, she nodded—just once. And whispered, "Then I'll leap."

Joyce smiled, a slow and knowing thing, and finally peeled back the lid on the soup.

"Good. But first..." she chuckled, handing Frieda a spoon, "you eat. You can't save the world on an empty stomach."

The candle on the table flickered to life as Joyce lit it without fuss. And for the first time in days, Frieda let herself breathe deep. It tasted like soup, and scripture, and strength she hadn't known she still had.

THAT EVENING, Frieda sat at her small kitchen table, the world outside hushed and waiting. The overhead light was off. Only a single candle burned low beside her, its flame trembling as if caught between breath and silence. The wax had melted into a soft pool at the base, and the scent of lavender and old smoke mingled faintly in the air.

Her journal lay open before her—its spine cracked, its pages wrinkled and worn with memory. The ink on the current page glistened in the shifting light, the script uneven and slow. She wrote as though each word was being sifted from her marrow, drawn up from somewhere deep and sacred. Her hand moved carefully, reverently, across the paper.

Her handwriting, usually neat and purposeful, had softened—thick strokes where tears had dropped, pauses where her breath had caught. The words came slowly, like honey warmed too long:

Tomorrow, everything could change.
I could lose The Bridge.
I could be blamed.
But I'm not doing this to protect my name.
I'm doing it to rescue theirs.

She paused, the pen hovering, then pressed it gently to the page again.

Let the light break open the dark.
Let the truth weigh heavy—
because I'm finally strong enough to carry it.

Her fingers stilled. The pen slipped quietly from her grasp, rolling once before settling against the journal's edge. And then—

without drama, without warning—Frieda wept. The tears came silent and slow, sliding down her cheeks and catching in the creases of her mouth. Her shoulders trembled, not with fear, but with something deeper. Something older. The kind of ache that doesn't ask for relief, only release.

She wept, not because she was afraid of what came next. But because she was *ready*. Because she had loved deeply. Because something holy was burning in her—not destructive fire, but refining flame. It flickered in time with the candlelight, dancing in the stillness. Soft. Steady. Sacred.

Outside, the city kept moving—sirens wailing faintly in the distance, footsteps echoing off concrete. But inside that small apartment, a woman of faith sat weeping over truth she'd chosen to carry. And in the quiet—where no one saw, and no one clapped—deliverance began. Not with thunder. But with a whisper and a flame that refused to die.

The Takedown

Wednesday night came heavy, like a thunderstorm without the rain. The street outside the church-turned command center buzzed with quiet tension. Police vans lined the block in neat rows, their engines idling low. Officers moved in silence, adjusting comms, tapping earpieces, speaking into radios with clipped efficiency.

The sky hung low and bruised, a curtain of dark gray pressing down on the city. Frieda stood outside with Detective Reyes, Miguel, and Joyce. Her hands were cold despite the thick fabric of her coat. She clenched and unclenched her fists, the rough paper of the flyer for The Bridge still stuffed in her pocket like a talisman.

Reyes checked her comm one more time and turned to Miguel. "Team One is in position. Perimeter secured. Surveillance is live."

Joyce laid a gentle hand on Frieda's arm. "You don't need to be here, baby."

Frieda shook her head slowly, her breath forming clouds in the chill. "But I do."

Miguel stepped closer, his face drawn but steady. "This is it," he said. "Are you sure you're ready?"

Frieda met his eyes, and there was no tremor in her voice. "I don't need to be ready. I just need to be willing."

Reyes gave a short nod and stepped back to give the signal. From down the block, shadows moved. Officers emerged, flanking a warehouse that had masqueraded as a youth outreach center but now stood revealed for what it truly was. The red door creaked as it swung open. Frieda held her breath.

The warehouse stood quiet, shrouded in darkness, its front porch still dressed in innocence—flowerpots by the stairs, a rusted wind chime spinning in the faint breeze. From the outside, it looked like a home. Inside, it was anything but. Curtained cages. Locked doors. Girls curled up on mattresses with no sheets. A silence that screamed.

The task force surrounded the block in hushed synchronization. Tactical boots padded across pavement. Radios crackled in clipped whispers. Reyes held up her hand. A signal.

Go.

In a flash, steel and command collided. The battering ram struck the front door. A deafening crack. Splinters flew. Then chaos. Gunfire burst from the second floor. Two officers ducked and returned fire, yelling commands. Screams tore through the air—shouts of "Hands up!" mixed with cries of panic from the girls inside.

Smoke grenades hissed into hallways.

Flashlights cut through the haze.

Frieda was in the recovery van outside, heart slamming against her ribs. She watched the live feed on Miguel's tablet, fingers clenched white around the edge of her seat.

Reyes's voice barked through comms: "Target detained. First room secure."

Then another voice: "We've got minors—some injured, some unresponsive."

Frieda was already out the door. She ran past the threshold, past debris, past Caleb Rios being dragged in cuffs, blood trickling from a cut above his eyebrow. He looked at her as she passed. Smiled—crooked, venomous.

"Told you," he rasped. "They always turn on their saviors."

Frieda didn't slow. Didn't look back. She found the girl upstairs huddled in a closet, whispering, "Don't see me" like a prayer.

Frieda knelt. "I see you. I'm Frieda. I came for you."

Tears streaked the girl's cheeks. "No one ever does."

"I do," Frieda whispered. "You're safe now."

The girl collapsed into her arms.

All around them, girls were carried out. Limp. Shaking. Crying. Officers led them gently into vans.

One girl turned to Frieda and asked, voice small, "Is this real?"

Frieda brushed the girl's hair back. "Yes, baby. You're going to be okay."

She looked back only once—at the door they had broken down, and the shadow of Caleb in the backseat of a squad car.

The last of the captives were loaded into transport. Some silent. Some sobbing. All free.

Frieda climbed into the van last, holding the girl from the closet tight to her side.

"Where are we going?" the girl asked.

Frieda answered without hesitation. "Somewhere safe. Some-where with light."

The Morning After

THE SUN ROSE SLOWLY over Frampton, soft and golden, like it was trying not to wake the city too fast. Light spilled gently across the cracked sidewalks and quiet streets. The news vans were already parked in front of the precinct, cameras angled, reporters rehearsing their lines in hurried whispers.

But Frieda wasn't watching them. She was in the kitchen at New Morning House, sleeves rolled to her elbows, hair tied back in a messy knot. The scent of butter and warm syrup wrapped around her like a blanket. The stove hissed softly behind her, a skillet spitting as it browned the edges of a pancake. Nearby, Joyce stirred a pot of cocoa. Miguel was collecting used dishes, quiet and steady.

And the girls—The girls were eating. Some sat with knees tucked beneath them, swaddled in oversized hoodies and borrowed flannel blankets. Others leaned close together at the long table, elbows bumping, syrup sticking to their fingers. The air buzzed with something fragile and holy—like laughter tiptoeing back into a place it had long been afraid to enter.

Plates clinked. Forks scraped. Steam rose from chipped mugs. A girl with tangled braids and tired eyes—maybe thirteen, no older—paused with her fork halfway to her mouth. Her voice was soft, but it cut through the hum of the room.

"This is the first time I've eaten at a table in months."

No one spoke for a moment. Then another girl, curled like a comma in her chair, looked up from her plate. Her voice trembled beneath the question.

"Do we have to go back?"

Frieda moved toward her slowly. She knelt beside the chair, so they were eye to eye. Her hand reached out, gentle, resting on the girl's knee.

"No, baby," she said, her voice steady with all the certainty the girl needed. "No one's taking you back."

The girl didn't cry. She just nodded, once, and returned to her pancakes.

At the far end of the table, a quiet child in an oversized sweater was doodling on her napkin with a crayon pulled from the donation bin. She didn't speak until her drawing was done—a simple, radiant sun with rays spilling past the edges of the paper.

"I dreamed about light," she said without looking up. "Last night."

Frieda's breath caught. She knelt again, watching the child trace her fingertip along the curve of the drawn sun.

"You're in it now," Frieda whispered. "You're standing right in it."

Her eyes filled, but she didn't blink them away. She let the tears stay, hot and honest.

Around her, girls reached for seconds. Poured more syrup. Passed napkins and stories in hushed tones. The sound of healing wasn't always dramatic. Sometimes it was the squeak of a chair, the scratch of a crayon, the sigh of someone who finally slept through the night.

Frieda didn't need to check her phone. She didn't need to see the headlines scroll across the screen.

City Nonprofit Leader Behind Trafficking Ring Busted in Joint Sting

Caleb Rios in Custody—Investigation Ongoing
"The Bridge Was Used, But the Community Fought Back"

She didn't need any of it. She had this. The rustle of plates. The murmur of soft voices. The smell of cinnamon. And girls—Not just surviving anymore. But living. One breath, one bite, one beam of light at a time.

The Return

THAT NIGHT, the city seemed to hold its breath. Frieda walked slowly down the damp sidewalk toward The Bridge, her boots landing softly against the glistening pavement. The spring rain had come and gone, leaving behind the scent of jasmine and wet earth—fresh, alive, expectant. Streetlights shimmered off the puddles like halos fallen to the ground.

She stopped at the base of the steps. The porchlight above the entrance glowed like a beacon of hope—steady, golden, unwavering. The key rested in Frieda's palm, cool and familiar. She stared at it for a long moment. It felt heavier than metal—like it held prayers soaked in tears, the ache of absence, the echo of a fight that had almost broken her. She closed her eyes, the wind pressing gently against her back, nudging her forward.

"This is Yours, Lord," she whispered. "Always was. I just turned the lock."

Her fingers tightened around the key. She stepped forward. The door creaked as it opened, not with protest, but like a sigh of welcome. The warmth from within met her like an embrace—soft music playing from a Bluetooth speaker on the windowsill, the rustle of pages from open journals, the gentle clink of juice pitchers being filled in the kitchen.

The string lights overhead still glimmered—some flickering, some burned out—but their glow danced across the walls like stars refusing to quit. The prayer jar sat on the windowsill, now more than half full, each folded slip of paper a cry, a hope, a testimony.

Girls filled the space with quiet joy: some sketching, others reading, a few sprawled on beanbags, their socks mismatched and hearts wide open. From the kitchen, Tyesha turned at the sound of the door. Her eyes met Frieda's, and for a moment, neither spoke.

Then—soft, reverent, full of knowing—Tyesha smiled. "Look who's home."

Frieda stepped in. Slowly. Like someone testing the weight of resurrection. She crossed the threshold one foot at a time, her breath catching as her eyes swept across the room. Nothing was perfect. The walls still needed paint. The couches sagged. One of the ceiling tiles was water-stained. But everything was alive.

"Miss Bridge!" The cry rang out from somewhere near the back—and then the girls rushed her. A tide of arms and voices and laughter. Someone wrapped her in a full-body hug. Another clung to her waist. A third buried her face in Frieda's shoulder and whispered, "We knew you'd come back."

Frieda laughed, the sound breaking through her tears like sunlight through clouds. She hugged them back—tight, fierce, grateful. Her heartbeat was so loud it filled the room. Not with fear. Not with regret. But with promise. She was here. They were here. And The Bridge—the place that had been wounded, closed, silenced—was open again. Not just its doors, but its heart. Its purpose.

The girls didn't stop cheering. They didn't let go quickly. And Frieda didn't rush them. Because this wasn't just a return, it was revival. And the sound of many daughters coming home was the loudest kind of hallelujah.

THAT NIGHT, FRIEDA SAT ALONE in the quiet office, the soft echoes of laughter still drifting down the hallway like the last notes of a hymn. The room was dim, lit only by the golden glow of a desk lamp that cast a gentle pool of light across the scattered papers and her open journal. Dust motes floated lazily in the warmth, suspended in the stillness. The old chair creaked as she leaned forward, elbows on the desk, fingers curled around a familiar pen—its edges smoothed by time, its ink nearly gone.

She closed her eyes for a moment and breathed in. The scent of lavender cleaner, old wood, and something new—something hopeful—lingered in the air. Somewhere, a floorboard creaked. A girl's voice giggled and hushed itself in the distance. The sound made Frieda smile, slow and quiet. Then, with a steadying breath, she put pen to paper.

We walked them out today.

Not just from a building. From shame. From silence. From a story they didn't choose.

And I walked out too. From fear. From failure. From believing my mistakes disqualified me.

Her pen paused, suspended above the page, ink beading at the tip. Her throat tightened.

God… You really are who You say You are.

You don't just restore. You rescue.

She laid the pen down gently, watching as the words bled softly into the paper, still damp with fresh ink. Her hands remained resting there, fingertips touching the edge of the journal, as if to steady herself on truth.

Tears filled her eyes—not the sharp kind born of pain, but the full, silent kind that come from reverence. From wonder. From the staggering grace of a God who had met her in ashes and called it soil.

Her gaze drifted toward the window. Outside, the porch light glowed like a sentinel, steady and unwavering. It spilled golden across the front steps, reaching into the darkness like an invitation. A few moths fluttered in its glow, circling endlessly—drawn, as she had been, to light in a world too often dim.

Inside, the air was warm not just with heat, but with something deeper. A sense of safety, of purpose rebuilt. Of hope with feet on the ground. And Frieda sat there a while longer. Not needing to fix anything, not needing to rush. Just letting the silence settle around her like a shawl, heavy with peace. She closed the journal gently, her fingers resting atop it in a silent prayer of thanks. The bridge was still standing. And so was she.

The Weight of Return

THE HEADLINES HAD FADED. The lawsuits dulled into paperwork and distant echoes. The media moved on, hungry for newer flames. But inside Frieda, the storm still churned.

Each morning, as she pushed open the doors to The Bridge, the air changed. Not loudly—but like the hush that settles over a sanctuary just before prayer. The new security system gave a soft buzz as she stepped through, followed by the click of the lock behind her. The center looked different now—brighter, safer. The walls, once smudged with age and memory, had been washed in pale blues and gentle creams, hues meant to comfort. Plush seating filled the common areas, edges rounded like a mother's hands. Sunlight spilled across clean floors. But no paint could cover what lingered beneath.

The weight was in the invisible.
It lived in the breaths caught mid-laughter.
In the flicker of a girl's eyes when footsteps echoed too sharply in the hallway.
In the slight stiffening when someone stood too close.
It clung to the quiet places:
The stairwell that once led nowhere good.
The door that used to stay locked for all the wrong reasons.
The prayer jar on the sill—still there, still receiving—but haunted by the prayers never written, the pleas that came too late.
Sometimes, Frieda paused there. One hand resting lightly on the rim of the jar, her reflection mirrored faintly in the glass. And she'd wonder—
Who never made it back?
Who slipped through while she was looking the other way?
And was it her fault for blinking?
But grace had a way of breathing even in broken rooms.
It came quietly.
Not in revival choirs or fanfare.

But in Wednesday art sessions where laughter reemerged like shy sunlight.

In notebooks brimming with raw, scratched lines of poetry.

In whispered prayers said under breath, yet meant with everything.

And then one afternoon—it came in Kiera. She was new. Withdrawn. Always a few paces behind the others, as though bracing for disappointment. But that day, in English class, she stood. Voice shaking but standing. She read a poem titled *"I Didn't Die."*

Frieda heard about it from the teacher first, her voice tight with emotion. Then, hours later, Kiera found her in the hallway. Said nothing at first—just held out a folded sheet of notebook paper, torn from a spiral and still warm from her hands. Frieda took it gently.

Kiera's cheeks flushed pink. Her eyes darted to the floor. "I thought… maybe you'd want to read it," she mumbled.

Frieda unfolded the paper slowly, smoothing it with care. The poem wasn't long, but every line was a fight, every word a thread woven back into her own story.

It wasn't just a poem.

It was resurrection inked in trembling hands.

It was defiance wrapped in soft-spoken syllables.

It was a voice that had been silenced, finally daring to sing again.

Frieda wept that night. Not because of what was lost—but because of what had survived. Because in Kiera's voice, in her poem, she saw the whole journey. Not just theirs, but hers too. And in that sacred quiet, she finally understood:

She hadn't stayed because she was obligated.

She had stayed because she was *called.*

Not because her wounds had vanished,

but because grace had taught her how to walk with them.

And now, she carried the light through the dark—not alone, but with hands reaching back. Pulling others forward. One poem. One prayer. One girl at a time.

The Promise of Something More

MIGUEL DIDN'T DISAPPEAR after the raid. He didn't vanish into the swell of aftermath or shrink into the shadows of trauma. He leaned in—gently.

It began with little things. A bouquet of sun-colored tulips for Joyce, delivered without warning, with a sheepish shrug and a, *"Saw these and thought of you."* A Saturday afternoon spent quietly hammering and sanding the splintered front steps of The Bridge, sweat on his brow, determination in his hands—no one asked him to.

Hazelnut coffee—extra hot, oat milk, just the way Frieda liked it—left on her desk during long mornings when hope ran thin and paperwork piled high. He never demanded. Never pressed. He just… showed up.

Frieda, guarded as ever, kept him at a distance. Not because she didn't notice. But because she did. She wasn't ready—not for something that looked like gentleness, like steady hands and soft laughter. Not when the world had only just stopped burning.

Miguel understood. So, he waited. He walked her home from late-night community meetings, hands in his pockets, never asking to come inside. He volunteered for Saturday cleanup, cracking silly jokes that made the girls giggle and drew reluctant smiles from Frieda when she thought no one was watching. He listened more than he spoke, and when he did speak, his words landed like anchors in the storm.

One evening, after a tense strategy session with city officials, Frieda found herself in the back hallway of The Bridge, leaning against the cool wall, her body sagging with exhaustion. The dim light flickered above them. Miguel stood nearby, quiet. Present.

"I'm no good at this," she said, her voice frayed at the edges. "This… life stuff. The after-everything part."

Miguel took a small step closer, not crowding her. Just closer.

"You're better at it than you know," he said. "The 'after'— that's where healing starts. It's the choosing part. Choosing to stay. To keep showing up."

She studied him, tired eyes searching. "Don't you ever get tired of holding space for someone still figuring it out?"

His answer came without hesitation. "Never. Especially not for you."

And something shifted. From there, what they built wasn't sudden or cinematic. It was slow. Earned. Intentional. Dinners at no-frills diners where they shared fries and stories. Evening walks through quiet neighborhoods, leaves crunching beneath their feet, the moon a silent witness. Wednesday night movies—sometimes with the girls, sometimes just the two of them—blankets, popcorn, and old DVDs. On Sundays, they served together, shoulder to shoulder, handing out meals and folding bulletins.

Miguel told her about his childhood—about his mother who prayed at the sink, about his father's old bike shop, about the dream he held in his chest: a mentorship program teaching teens how to repair bikes and rebuild what's broken.

Frieda opened up in return—tentatively, then fully. She spoke of Lois, her iron grace and tender strength. She spoke of the grief that still lingered like morning fog. Of mistakes that still bruised her in quiet places.

One night, after a heavy mentoring session where one of the girls broke down in tears, Frieda stayed late to fold chairs in the sanctuary. Her hands trembled. Her breath hitched. Miguel didn't say a word. He just placed his hand lightly on her back. Not to fix. Just to stand with her. And waited until she could breathe again.

The laughter between them grew more frequent. So did the silences—comfortable ones, where presence meant more than conversation. Even the hard days didn't press as hard when shared.

Then, one night—after a community dinner where the girls had read letters of gratitude and volunteers passed around spaghetti on paper plates—Miguel lingered behind to help clean. Frieda wiped down folding tables in silence. Miguel stacked chairs slowly, methodically. As he folded the last one, he paused. His voice, when it came, was gentle. Measured.

"I'm not just here to help you fight," he said. "I'm here to stay. If you'll have me."

Frieda froze. The rag in her hand stilled. The fluorescent light above hummed like a held breath. She turned to him.

He didn't fill the silence. Didn't rush. Just stood there—steady, quiet, waiting. And in his eyes, there was no demand—only the promise of something that didn't need to be earned.

She looked at him for a long moment. At the man who never tried to rescue her—only to stand beside her while she rose. The ache inside her didn't vanish. The scars didn't fade. But somewhere deep, in the quiet center of her chest, a truth whispered:

You are allowed to love again.

Frieda nodded. Just once. Not a yes. Not yet. But a beginning. And sometimes, that's more than enough.

Out of the House of Shadows

It was a Thursday afternoon, and the sun had begun to lean westward, casting golden slants through the windows of The Bridge. The scent of pencil shavings and warm paper lingered in the air from the just-finished creative writing workshop. Laughter still echoed faintly from the art room, and Frieda, holding a stack of journals to return to her office, let herself exhale—just a little.

Then she heard it. A voice. Not loud at first, but sharp. Frantic. Fractured. It rose from the foyer like a storm wind slipping through a crack in the foundation. Frieda froze; journals pressed to her chest. The front door burst open with a violent clang.

A woman stood in the entryway—shoulders tense, hair wild from the wind, grief clinging to her like a second skin. Her eyes—bloodshot, brimming, blazing—swept the room until they landed on Frieda.

"You!" the woman cried out, her voice trembling but loud enough to still the air. "You let him take her!"

Every conversation in the building fell silent. The lobby stilled like a held breath. A volunteer—Maria—stepped forward tentatively. "Mrs. Jordan, please—"

But the woman surged past her, raw pain propelling her like a wave crashing over stone.

"My daughter," she sobbed, staggering forward. "Aniya. She trusted this place. She trusted you. And now she's gone!"

Frieda felt the weight of those words slam into her chest. The journals slid from her hands and hit the floor with a dull thud.

She stepped forward slowly, palms open, voice soft.

"Mrs. Jordan…" Her throat felt tight. "I remember Aniya. She was bright. Brave. Gentle. And we are still searching. I promise you—we haven't stopped."

But the mother didn't hear her words so much as feel the ache of them. Her hands balled into fists at her sides, trembling.

"She never would've gone near that man if it weren't for this place," she choked. "You made him look safe. You made *this* look safe."

Frieda's voice barely held steady. "I know."

The silence that followed was unbearable.

"I know," she said again, this time lower. "And I carry that every day. I carry her. But I swear to you—we will not stop until she's home."

Mrs. Jordan's face crumpled. Tears spilled freely now, hot and helpless.

"Words," she whispered bitterly. "Words won't bring her back."

She took one shaking step closer, her voice raw enough to cut through bone.

"So, you better pray your God is listening," she said, her voice shaking with fury. "Because if she doesn't come home, you'll answer to more than just Him."

Then, without waiting for a response, she turned—her heels echoing against the tile—and yanked the door open. It slammed behind her with a force that rattled the windows.

Frieda stood motionless. Her breath caught in her throat. The girls in the room watched in silence. No one moved. No one knew what to say. The grief in Frieda's chest felt like fire—burning slow, leaving ashes in its wake. Her knees buckled slightly, but she didn't fall. Her arms hung limp at her sides. Her heart cracked open in a way that felt final.

And then—A small hand slipped into hers. Frieda looked down. A girl stood beside her—no older than ten. Wide eyes. Braids loose at the ends. Her tiny fingers wrapped around Frieda's with surprising strength.

"We're still here," the girl said softly.

Frieda blinked, vision blurring.

"I know," she whispered. Her voice barely rose above a breath. "And I'll fight for every one of you."

She squeezed the girl's hand, grounding herself in that quiet, living truth. Because yes—Aniya was gone. And the weight of that loss would never lift. But the ones who were still here—breathing, hoping, healing—needed her strength. Needed her voice. Needed her to rise. Even in the long, echoing shadow of what was lost, Frieda could still be light. And she would be. With everything she had. And everything she was becoming.

Searching For Aniya

THE NEXT MORNING BROKE gray and still, the kind of sky that pressed low over the city like a lid on a boiling pot. Inside The Bridge, the fluorescent lights in the conference room hummed faintly, casting pale halos across the long table where Frieda sat with Miguel and two of the peer leaders—girls who had once survived the storm and now helped others do the same.

The door was shut. The air inside the room carried a weight—something heavier than worry. It was urgency wrapped in grief. A city map was stretched wide across the table, its edges curling from overuse. Red pins dotted intersections like small wounds. Some were circled, others connected by ink lines drawn in hurried hands. Coffee rings stained one corner. A sticky note clung stubbornly to the map's edge with a phone number scribbled in faded marker.

Miguel stood slightly hunched, palms braced on the table's edge, his eyes narrowed at a cluster of pins on the southeast side. He tapped one gently—twice.

"Here," he said. "East Frampton. She was last seen near the corner store on this block."

Frieda leaned in. Her breath caught in her chest. "You're sure?"

Miguel nodded, slow and grim. "We pulled partial footage from a city bus that passed the intersection. It's not crystal clear… but there's a girl—her build matches Aniya—getting into a silver sedan. Driver's face obscured. No license plate. Not yet, anyway."

The words landed like stones in Frieda's gut.

"What's the timestamp?" she asked, her voice a notch above a whisper.

Miguel didn't look away from the map. "Three days after she vanished."

Silence.

Then Frieda exhaled hard and straightened. "We need more than footage," she said, her voice sharpening like steel drawn from a sheath. "We need eyes. We need feet on the street. Girls who've lived this life. Folks who know where the shadows gather and how to move through them without being seen."

One of the peer leaders—Kamilah, a sharp-eyed young woman with tight braids and the air of someone who'd wrestled life and won—nodded instantly. "We'll hit every shelter. Food pantry. Drop-in center. We'll check the no-name motels and alley couches. Anywhere someone might vanish into."

"Flyers," said the other peer leader, already flipping through a clipboard. "We'll print and post by noon. We'll translate them too—Spanish, Creole, whatever it takes."

"And get the prayer team moving," Frieda added. Her tone dropped to something fierce. "This isn't just a search."

She looked at each of them in turn. "This is spiritual warfare."

The room paused—not with fear, but with reverence. The kind that came when people understood the gravity of the fight ahead.

Then it shifted. Kamilah pulled out her phone, fingers already flying. "I'll start a contact tree. Volunteers for rides. Coordinated shifts. We'll need snacks, water, first-aid kits."

The buzz of action rose like a tide. Clipboards flipped. Phones lit up. Feet shuffled.

Miguel lingered, his gaze steady on Frieda. "We'll find her," he said. His voice wasn't loud, but it anchored the room like bedrock. "However long it takes."

Frieda didn't respond right away. Her throat was tight, her body coiled with tension and fire.

When the meeting broke, she stepped quietly into the hallway. The buzz faded behind her. Her boots clicked softly on the tile as she moved toward the wall of photos near the entrance. There, in a mosaic of color and light, were the faces of Bridge girls—past and present. Snapshots of joy. Of rebirth. Of girls who had survived more than they should've had to. Frieda's eyes moved until they landed on Aniya's photo. A wide, radiant smile. Big gold hoops. Head tilted in mid-laugh. That kind of spirit you didn't forget, even if you tried.

Frieda reached out, her hand trembling, and touched the photo gently—just beneath the curve of Aniya's jaw. "Hold on, baby," she whispered, voice catching in the hush of the hallway. "We're coming."

The hum of the city stirred beyond the glass doors. And inside, the search had already begun.

Into The Gaps

THE EVENING PRESSED in like a whisper. Wind curled around the corners of the building, brushing against the windowpanes with a low, restless sigh. Inside Frieda's apartment, the lights were low— just one lamp in the far corner casting a warm, amber glow over the room. Shadows danced softly on the walls, long and tired.

Frieda sat on the edge of her couch, her spine curved forward, elbows on her knees. The coffee table before her was buried beneath a sea of papers—missing person flyers, blurry street cam screenshots, maps creased and ink-marked with red pen, timelines threaded in desperation. Most of them bore one face.

Aniya.

Her eyes. Her smile. The gap in her front teeth. Her name printed in bold black letters above the word *MISSING*, which screamed in crimson across each page.

Frieda's own eyes were raw—rimmed in red, lids heavy from sleepless hours and the kind of grief that didn't quite allow for tears. Her fingers trembled slightly as she lifted a printout from the pile, gaze fixed on the timestamp in the corner. She'd read it before. Dozens of times. But she stared anyway, as if something new might surface.

"She's out there," she murmured, her voice barely more than breath. A vow spoken to no one… and to God.

From the kitchen came a soft sound—the quiet clink of ceramic. Miguel appeared a moment later, moving slowly, gently, like someone approaching the edge of a brittle ledge. He carried two mugs of tea, steam curling in faint halos above them. He set hers—chamomile, always chamomile—on the table beside the files. His own black tea remained in his hands, the warmth grounding him. He didn't speak right away. Just sat beside her.

"I know she is," he said finally. "But we need more eyes. More traction. More truth. Not just what we know—what we don't."

Frieda didn't respond. Her gaze had drifted to the far wall, where a large corkboard stood like a silent sentinel. It was cluttered now—thread-tied pins connecting addresses and sightings, scribbled Post-its in four different handwritings, names written hastily across index cards. Some were crossed out. Others circled. A growing constellation of the missing. Girls whose names had never made the news. Girls no one was searching for but them.

"She's not the only one," Frieda whispered. Her voice cracked slightly on the last word. "What if this doesn't end with Caleb? What if someone else picked up the pieces and kept moving girls like… like freight?"

Miguel's hands tightened around his mug, knuckles pale. He leaned forward, elbows resting on his knees, eyes on the photo nearest him—Aniya, birthday crown tilted over her braids, cheeks full of cake and laughter.

"Then we keep digging," he said. "We follow every lead. We get louder. We make it impossible to look away."

Frieda's hand reached across the table, brushing the edge of a flyer—creased, weathered, nearly falling apart. She smoothed it with slow fingers, as if the touch could make time rewind.

"Every name on this board," she said, almost to herself. "They were all somebody's daughter. Somebody's hope."

She turned to Miguel, her eyes glistening now—not just with pain, but fire.

"We won't let this keep happening," she said. "We find her. And then we burn down every lie that let her disappear in the first place."

Miguel nodded, the words sinking between them like roots.

Outside, a siren wailed somewhere in the distance. A dog barked. The wind pressed against the window once more, persistent and cold. But inside, the room was still. They didn't speak again. There was no need. In the quiet, they sat shoulder to shoulder, surrounded by paper trails and holy rage, breathing in the weight of what still needed to be done. Because the gaps were where the danger lived. And this time, they would not let another girl fall.

Street-Level Mobilization

THE CHILL IN THE CHURCH BASEMENT clung to the walls, damp and stubborn, the kind that settled in the bones no matter how many layers you wore. A space heater hummed in the corner, fighting a losing battle against the stubborn cold. Still, no one complained. Not today.

Frieda stood at the front of the makeshift strategy room— once a fellowship hall, now a war room. The whiteboard behind her was crowded with arrows, maps, and names. Next to it, a larger city map had been taped to the wall, covered in color-coded pins, hand-drawn circles, and bits of twine stretching across neighborhoods like veins.

Folding chairs ringed the center table, some occupied, others piled with boxes—flyers, notebooks, case files, half-eaten granola bars. It smelled faintly of printer toner, coffee, and cold concrete. The air was taut with purpose.

Five of The Bridge's eldest girls sat before her. Peer leaders now. Fighters. Survivors who had become protectors. Each one wore that look—eyes sharpened by what they'd endured, hearts pulled taut but unbroken.

Lena sat closest, a notepad balanced on her knee, hoodie sleeves rolled up over forearms marked with quiet resolve. Tyesha stood near the wall, arms crossed, her jaw tight, gaze unflinching. The others mirrored their intensity—Jamila with her long braid wrapped once around her shoulder, Sarai hunched forward, knuckles pressed into her thigh, and Mika, who hadn't stopped bouncing her knee but hadn't looked away once.

Frieda took a slow breath, the mist of it visible in the air, then pointed to the map.

"We're dividing the city," she said, her voice low but clear. "You know these streets better than any uniform ever will. You know who listens. You know who lies. And you know the girls who won't speak unless someone like you is asking."

The girls nodded, solemn.

Lena raised her hand slightly. "Two of ours already volunteered for the East Loop. We'll sweep it block by block—corner to corner. We've got names to ask and places to check."

"Good," Frieda said, walking slowly in front of the map. Her boots echoed faintly on the tile. "Start with the shelters, the alleyways behind the liquor stores. The benches where the streetlights don't work. Don't just look—listen. Watch."

Jamila raised her voice, her tone curious yet blunt. "What if people lie to our faces?"

Frieda didn't hesitate. "They will. But lies leave cracks. Listen for the stutters. The stories that change mid-sentence. Watch their eyes. Watch what they don't say."

A beat of silence passed. Then Tyesha pushed off from the wall and stepped forward.

"Some of the older girls are scared," she said, her voice low. "They've been near people like Caleb. They don't know if they can trust us—or themselves."

Frieda met her gaze. "Start small. Don't ask for stories. Ask for whispers. A corner. A name. A car. That's all we need to start."

Mika raised her hand quietly. "And if we hit a wall?"

Frieda softened, stepping closer to them. "Then we find a window. You're not alone out there. Pair up. Take the hotline card. Stay visible. But stay alert."

Just then, the basement door creaked open, and the scent of warm bread and roasted coffee followed Miguel in. He balanced a cardboard tray in one hand, breakfast sandwiches and steaming cups in the other. His eyes scanned the room—sizing up the tension, the hunger, the purpose—and set the tray down without saying a word.

Nobody had asked. He just knew. He bent beside Frieda, voice barely above a whisper.

"West side shelter called. A girl showed up last night. No name. Scared. Fits Aniya's age and build. She won't talk yet."

Frieda's heart clenched. Her body jolted like a match had been struck. "Then I'll go," she said instantly.

But Lena stepped forward, firmly.

"No," she said, voice steady. "You need to hold this down. Be the anchor. We'll move. You stay."

Frieda blinked, startled for a moment. Then a small smile tugged at the corner of her mouth—equal parts pride and surrender.

"Then go," she said softly. "Go find her."

Outside the strategy room, the lobby had begun to fill. Joyce was already leading a quiet prayer circle—hands joined, heads bowed, voices lifted in murmur. Girls whispered names of the missing, names of those feared forgotten. Some whispered their own.

"Let every girl in hiding feel light on her face again," Joyce prayed, her voice like warm oil over an open wound. "Let them know—help is looking. Love is coming."

And then they moved. Not as victims. Not even as survivors. But as seekers. As street-level saints in hoodies and sneakers, armed with flyers, fire, and names that mattered. Because somewhere, Aniya was waiting. And this time, they weren't coming with fear. They were coming with light.

Cracks In the Silence

THE CALL CAME JUST AFTER 11:30 P.M.

Kendra's voice trembled through the static of Frieda's phone, breathless and shaken. "I—I got a tip. Just now. It was anonymous, but the caller said they saw a young girl, limping, at that old motel off Trenton, near the freight yard. Said she looked dazed. And... she was with a man. Big. Never let go of her arm."

Frieda froze midstep in her kitchen, her mug of tea forgotten on the counter. Her fingers tightened around a pen as she scrambled for a notepad.

"What's the address?" she asked, her voice taut.

Kendra rattled it off. "I don't know if it's her. But something felt... off."

Frieda's hand shook as she scribbled the words. "Meet me there. But don't go inside. Wait for me, Kendra. I mean it."

She hung up, barely breathing. Her thumbs moved fast, texting Miguel. Then Reyes. No hesitation. No second guesses.

By midnight, they were there. The motel sat at the edge of the city like a scar—forgotten, rotting at its seams. The neon sign once announcing "VACANCY" hung crooked and dead, its letters dark. A few stray bulbs buzzed dimly in the windows. The parking lot was cracked and littered with broken glass, used needles, and cigarette butts, all shining faintly under the half-moon glow. The air was thick with silence and something colder—something that slithered beneath the skin.

Frieda stood outside the unmarked car, coat wrapped tightly around her, arms folded against her chest. Miguel sat inside with a tablet balanced on his knees, monitoring footage from a nearby city cam mounted high on a streetlight. The feed was grainy, but clear enough to make out silhouettes moving behind the faded curtains.

Reyes was parked down the block, already coordinating with backup units. She'd insisted they be close but discreet—five minutes out, no sirens.

The motel loomed in front of them. Paint peeled in long strips from the walls. Doors with missing numbers stood slightly ajar or not at all. Curtains hung limp and stained. Somewhere deep within, a dog barked once. Then nothing.

They waited.

Frieda's breath fogged in the cold. Her heart thudded slow and loud in her chest.

And then—

The sound of a creaking hinge, low and brittle. One of the doors opened, casting a narrow slice of yellow light into the night. A girl stepped out. Barefoot. Limping. Her shoulders hunched as if the air itself hurt. Her arms crossed tightly, sleeves pulled over her fists. Her hair hung limp and oily around her face, and her skin was pale beneath the sodium lights. One of her eyes was swollen nearly shut.

She stepped onto the crumbling concrete and froze—caught in the wind, caught in the moment. Her gaze lifted. And found Frieda across the street. For a long second, neither moved.

Then the girl's lips parted, her voice rasping across the still night like the rustle of dry leaves.

"You're the woman from the flyers."

Frieda's heart clenched. She took a slow step forward, her palms raised, her voice barely more than a whisper.

"Yes," she said. "I'm Frieda. And I'm not leaving without you."

The girl's jaw trembled. Her arms loosened just slightly from their guard.

Then, with a sudden, shuddering sob, she ran. Not smoothly. Not fast. Her limp broke the rhythm of her steps, but her legs didn't stop. She came like a tide—wild and broken and unstoppable—and collapsed into Frieda's open arms.

Frieda caught her like something sacred. Like a mother cradling resurrection. The girl wept against her chest, fists clutching at Frieda's coat, shoulders wracked with soundless cries.

Miguel was already moving, Reyes a few steps behind. But Frieda didn't let go. She held her. She whispered promises into matted hair. And when Reyes asked if they were ready to move, Frieda nodded slowly.

They took the girl in. Wrapped her in warmth. In safety. In truth. She wasn't Aniya. But she mattered. And they didn't stop. Because cracks in the silence meant light was getting in. And light meant hope. And hope meant they weren't done searching yet.

Staking Out the Dark

THREE NIGHTS LATER, the sky hung heavy over South Hollow—low clouds soaking up what little starlight there was. Streetlamps cast a jaundiced glow over cracked sidewalks, their flicker too faint to chase away the shadows. A thin wind rustled dry leaves along the curb, brushing them against the tires of a nondescript black sedan parked beneath an overgrown tree.

Inside, the windows fogged slightly with breath. Frieda sat in the backseat, clipboard resting on her knees, the pen in her hand tapping absently—rhythmic, anxious. Her coat was zipped up to her chin, but the cold still found its way through, curling into her collarbones and settling like a weight in her chest.

Next to her, Miguel shifted, raising a pair of compact binoculars to his eyes. He scanned the house down the block—a hulking Victorian that had been gutted and rebuilt from the inside out. Its fresh paint couldn't hide the silence that clung to it like mildew.

"Same two men," he murmured. "Patrolling the porch and driveway. One with a limp. One with the same black puffer and baseball cap. They switch spots every hour, almost to the minute."

He lowered the binoculars slowly. "No one goes in after sundown. No one's come out since Tuesday."

Frieda's eyes didn't leave the clipboard. She was sketching the perimeter—loose lines, quick arrows, notes in shorthand. "That van came again this morning. Same as last week. No logos. Tinted windows. No plates. Just pulled up like it belonged there."

Miguel glanced at her. Her jaw was tight, eyes fixed, breath shallow. He could see her knuckles whitening as she clutched the clipboard.

"You okay?" he asked quietly.

She didn't answer at first. Just kept writing. Then slowly, she exhaled.

"No," she said, voice low. "But I'm focused."

Their eyes met in the reflection of the rearview mirror—two silhouettes caught between streetlight and shadow. Not just partners now. Not just fighters. Something deeper lived in the silence between them. Something anchored. Steady. Holy.

Miguel leaned in slightly; the space between them crackled with quiet solidarity. He reached out and let his hand rest lightly on her shoulder—just enough to ground, not to overwhelm.

"We'll bring them home," he said, his voice rough with quiet promise. "One by one, if we have to. Whatever it takes."

Frieda's throat tightened, the lump forming too fast to swallow. Her voice cracked as she answered, "Then we start now."

She pulled her hoodie tighter and turned her eyes back to the house.

Behind those blinds, girls waited. And somewhere in that silence, she knew one of them could be Aniya. She wouldn't blink. Not tonight. Because the dark didn't get the last word. Not this time.

The Sting to Rescue Aniya

IT CAME ON A MONDAY EVENING, when the sky over Frampton was already bruised with twilight—clouds thick and low, their underbellies streaked with burnt orange and hints of smoke. The city seemed to hold its breath, caught between day and night.

Frieda was halfway down the hallway at The Bridge, her arms full of supply forms and tomorrow's plans, when her phone buzzed sharply against her hip. She didn't recognize the number at first—but she knew the voice the second it spoke.

"Frieda," said Detective Reyes, her tone clipped, tight with urgency. "We found her. We found Aniya."

The hallway fell away. Frieda froze, the papers sliding from her grasp, forgotten. Her lungs seized up as if time itself had narrowed to a single breath.

"Where?" she managed, barely more than a whisper.

"Southside warehouse. Confirmed sighting. She's alive. We're prepping the raid now. I thought you should know."

Frieda didn't remember moving, only the sound of her heart, loud and insistent in her ears as she grabbed her coat and keys and ran.

BY NIGHTFALL, a storm brewed low in the sky. The clouds hovered like a warning. Around the block from the warehouse, a black tactical van sat parked in the shadows—quiet, waiting. Its walls seemed to pulse with nerves. Inside, officers adjusted radios, checked ammunition, and nodded in silent communication.

Reyes stood near the back, her earpiece in, her voice low and composed. "Team One in position. Perimeter secured. No movement on the west side. We go on my mark."

Frieda sat just behind her, shoulders drawn tight, eyes locked on the folded photo of Aniya in her hands. It was creased from how many times she'd held it, studied it, and prayed over it. Her lips moved without sound—prayers layered over prayers.

Miguel sat beside her, gazing steadily at her face.

"You don't have to go in," he murmured. "No one would blame you."

Frieda didn't look away from the photo. "I'm not here because I'm brave," she said softly. "I'm here because she matters."

Reyes turned toward them. Her hand lifted—signal given. The van door slid open with a rasp of steel. Cold air rushed in, slicing through the stale tension. One by one, the team spilled out, low and fast, shadows melting into the street.

The warehouse loomed up ahead—weather-worn and rusted, its windows blacked out, its frame sagging like a lie long told. A single security light blinked above the side entrance, casting a flickering glow like a failing heartbeat.

Reyes raised her hand. "Breach."

A boot struck the door.

CRACK.

It splintered inward.

"POLICE!" came the shout.

Officers surged inside, weapons drawn, flashlights slicing through clouds of dust. The air smelled like mildew and old oil. Rusted machinery and forgotten crates littered the space.

Frieda kept close to the rear, flanked by Miguel, every step deliberate, eyes searching the dark.

Then—something. A voice. Barely audible. Thin. Fragile.

"Help… me…"

Frieda spun, her heart leaping. Down a narrow corridor, a single door stood ajar, pale light spilling out like a ghost's breath.

"Aniya?" she called.

Silence.

Then soft, uneven breathing.

She stepped forward, slowly, her hand brushing the wall for balance. The light flickered overhead.

As she crossed the threshold—

She froze.

A man stood inside. Tall. Silent. A pistol already raised. His eyes didn't flinch. Neither did his hand. Time snapped in half.

BANG!

Miguel's body collided with hers—hard, sudden, all muscle and instinct. They crashed to the floor as the bullet whined overhead, splintering into the doorframe behind them.

"MOVE!" Reyes bellowed.

The team stormed in—boots on concrete, orders shouted, weapons drawn. Gunfire lit the room in sharp bursts. The man turned and bolted through the opposite door. Reyes gave chase, shouting commands into her radio.

Miguel rolled to his knees, checking Frieda with frantic hands. "Are you hit?"

She shook her head, dazed but whole.

"Aniya," she gasped.

A soft whimper echoed from behind a stack of pallets. Frieda scrambled forward, heart pounding. There—tucked into a corner, shivering, cheeks hollow and eyes too wide—was Aniya. Her hair was tangled. Her arms wrapped around herself like a shield. But her eyes met Frieda's, and they widened with a flicker of impossible recognition.

"Miss Bridge?" she whispered, her voice hoarse.

Frieda dropped to her knees. "I've got you now, baby," she choked. "You're safe. You're safe."

Aniya fell into her arms like a bird folding into shelter.

Frieda held her tight—tight enough to say *never again.*

Outside, sirens howled and squad cars flooded the block. Backup arrived. The warehouse was cleared. The captor cuffed. And for once, justice didn't feel theoretical.

Inside, under the dim pulse of industrial lights and the silence that follows violence, something sacred happened. A lost girl was found. And hope, bruised but burning, was reclaimed. Not just by Frieda. By all of them.

LATER THAT NIGHT, Frieda stood still at the edge of the sidewalk, staring up at the building that had once been sealed in silence—The Bridge.

The red sticker that had screamed *TEMPORARILY CLOSED* was gone now—peeled away, leaving only a faint shadow behind, like an old scar. The door, once bolted and padlocked by fear, hung open on smooth hinges. It breathed in the night air and exhaled light.

Laughter drifted from inside—soft, full-bodied, real. Someone was strumming a guitar in the common room, the notes sweet and slow like lullabies. A voice rose in prayer—quiet but firm, like a hand reaching into the dark. Somewhere deeper inside, a girl giggled, and the sound cracked something wide open in Frieda's chest.

She didn't move right away. Instead, she lifted her chin, her eyes searching the velvet sky above. The stars were faint tonight, blurred by city haze and the veil of tears she didn't bother to wipe away. Her voice trembled as it left her lips, carried on the hush of evening:

"Your house, Lord. Not mine. I'm just the keeper of the key."

A breeze stirred—Jasmine from the garden below. Concrete was still damp from a passing rain. Frieda stepped forward—one foot, then the other. Crossing the threshold, a hush settled around her—not silence, but welcome. Warmth met her like a hug that needed no arms. The hallway glowed with string lights, the scent of cocoa and candles curling into the air. Girls moved past her with ease and belonging—curling on couches, coloring flyers, pulling blankets across laps. Some looked up and smiled. Others just nodded, their presence enough.

Later, long after the lights dimmed and most had gone quiet, Frieda sat alone at her desk. The lamp cast a soft golden pool across the old wood. Her journal lay open; its pages smudged with ink and memory. She held her pen for a long time before letting the words come—slow, deliberate, reverent.

We didn't just break down a door.
We broke chains.

We walked them out of the dark—not just from a building, but from silence, from shame, from forgetting their names.
And grace…
Grace walked before us.

She set the pen down. Folded her hands. And breathed. Not because the battle was over. But because for the first time in a long time… She knew they were home.

Aniya's Recovery

THE HEADLINES WERE EVERYWHERE by morning.

FRAMPTON TRAFFICKING RING EXPOSED
KEY VICTIMS RESCUED

Bold black letters bled across TV screens and newspaper stands, but Frieda didn't read them. She didn't need the world's echo. She needed this moment—this room.

She sat at the small kitchen table in New Morning House, its walls warm with soft yellows and the scent of cinnamon and soap. Outside the window, the day had broken gently—light slipping across the lawn like a whispered promise.

Across from her, Aniya sat curled into herself, wrapped in a blanket two sizes too big. Her knees were pulled up, her frame too small beneath the fleece. A chipped white bowl rested in front of her. Inside, the oatmeal has gone cool. She stirred it slowly, the spoon clinking against the ceramic with a soft, steady rhythm—like the ticking of a fragile clock.

She hadn't said much. Her lips were chapped. Her hands, trembling. Every sound—a creaking floorboard, a door opening, a voice calling from the hall—made her flinch just slightly. Her eyes darted like they were still looking for exits, even in safety.

Frieda didn't speak. She didn't fill the space with questions or comfort too soon. She sat with a pile of laundry in her lap, folding clothes with quiet care. Every now and then, she hummed—low, tuneless, something close to a lullaby. Her presence said, *I'm here. You're not alone. Not now.*

The silence held long and heavy. Then—A small voice cracked through it like thin ice breaking.

"I thought you forgot me."

Frieda stilled. Her heart clenched, slow and deep, as she met Aniya's eyes—wide, ringed with shadows, but finally looking into hers.

"I never forgot," Frieda said softly. "Not for a second."

Aniya looked down quickly, lashes quivering. Her next words came brittle.

"My mom… she probably hates me. She's probably glad I'm gone."

Frieda reached across the table. She didn't grab. She just placed her hand gently over Aniya's.

"No," she said, her voice firmer now. "She's been calling every day. Praying every night. She's the reason I didn't stop searching."

Aniya blinked fast. Her spoon slipped back into the bowl with a soft plop.

"She'll hate me," she whispered. "When she sees me like this."

Frieda's hand tightened just slightly. Her voice dropped to a whisper.

"She will cry. She will shake. But she will not hate you."

She leaned forward, her gaze steady, her words wrapping around Aniya like a balm.

"She loves you more than her own breath."

Aniya didn't speak. But her chin wobbled. Her hands curled into fists in her lap. A single tear slid down her cheek.

That evening, after the dishes were washed and the hallway quieted and the last journal had been tucked away in the resource room, Frieda stepped out onto the back porch and pulled out her phone.

She dialed. The line picked up on the first ring.

"Mrs. Langston?" Frieda said, voice trembling with hope. "She's ready."

A sharp inhale. Then—A sound caught somewhere between a sob and a prayer.

Frieda closed her eyes and let it wash over her. Because sometimes the sound of love returning isn't loud. It's a gasp. It's a weep. It's the sound of a mother knowing her daughter is coming home.

The Reunion

THE NEXT MORNING CAME softly, light pouring like honey through the gray hush of dawn. The small chapel room inside New Morning House waited—quiet, unadorned, sacred in its simplicity. Wooden pews, scarred by years of prayer and grief, stood in still rows. Colored glass threw fractured rainbows across the floor, baptizing the silence with warmth.

Frieda's footsteps were slow as she led Aniya in. The girl moved like mist—barely there, shoulders hunched beneath the oversized sweater Joyce had given her. Her arms wrapped around her middle, not for comfort, but for protection. Her eyes flicked around the chapel, wide and uncertain. She paused near the stained-glass window, where amber and violet light painted her face. She said nothing. But her body shook.

Then—the door eased open. Frieda turned. Mrs. Langston stepped in, hesitantly at first, her heels making soft clicks against the old wooden floor. Her purse was clutched tight to her chest, fingers white at the knuckles. Her eyes found her daughter in an instant—drinking her in, like air after drowning. Time slowed. Aniya turned at the sound. For a heartbeat—just one—neither moved.

Then— "Mama?" Aniya's voice cracked, barely louder than breath. Fragile. Hopeful. Disbelieving.

The purse slipped from Mrs. Langston's fingers and hit the floor with a thud. She didn't walk—she rushed. Crossed the chapel in two desperate strides and threw herself into her daughter's arms. They collapsed together, sinking to the ground, knees hitting the hardwood, clinging like it was the only thing holding them both together.

"I'm so sorry, Mama—I'm so sorry—" Aniya sobbed, her words tumbling out in broken fragments, muffled by her mother's shoulder.

Mrs. Langston cupped the back of her daughter's head and rocked her gently. Her voice trembled but didn't break.

"Don't you dare apologize, baby. Don't you dare. I'm here. I'm here now. That's all that matters."

Their cries spilled through the chapel, raw and beautiful, echoing off stained glass and worn wood. They clung to each other, wrapped in the kind of love that bruises and bleeds but never breaks.

Frieda stood still, just inside the doorway, hand covering her mouth. Her chest rose and fell with quiet reverence. This was not her moment—but she was its witness. And that, she knew, was holy.

Eventually, Aniya pulled back just enough to look up at her mother. Her face was blotchy and tear-streaked, eyes red, but finally—finally—alive again.

She turned to Frieda then, eyes wide with wonder. "You said she'd come."

Frieda blinked, her throat thick. "She never stopped looking," she whispered.

Mrs. Langston reached out then, without hesitation, and pulled Frieda into the embrace. Their arms wove around each other in a knot of pain, promise, and unspoken prayers.

Three women. One story. A thousand wounds.

And still—they were here.

LATER THAT NIGHT, long after the chapel had emptied and the light outside faded into navy dusk, Aniya sat alone at Frieda's small desk. It was nestled near the corner window of New Morning House—scarred wood, scratched edges, a faint scent of lavender oil and old books still clinging to the air.

Her hands moved slowly. Deliberately. She pulled a lined page from a worn notebook, smoothing the crease with her fingers. Then, she picked up a pen. The ink flowed in unsteady strokes.

"You didn't just rescue me.

You reminded me I'm still worth rescuing."

She read it once. Then folded the page, creasing it clean, hands trembling slightly. She placed it carefully on Frieda's desk—just under the lamp, where it would be seen. The paper fluttered gently in the draft from the window.

Frieda found the note after everyone had gone to bed. She stood in the doorway, the soft lamp glow spilling across the desk, and read the words in stillness. Her breath caught. She pressed the paper against her chest for a moment—then opened her journal and slipped it between the pages like a sacred offering. A scar acknowledged. A resurrection witnessed. And another promise etched into her bones:

She would never stop showing up. Never.

Uncovering the Web

The work hadn't ended with Aniya. It had only unmasked a deeper rot. The Bridge—once a sanctuary—had transformed into something more: a command center of resistance, a beating heart for truth in a city lined with shadows. In the weeks following the raid and Caleb's arrest, Frieda and Miguel met with Detective Reyes almost daily. Each meeting unearthed more than the last. What had started as isolated pins on a Frampton map now stretched like arteries across cities, counties—even across state lines. The second binder was already thicker than the first.

Calls came in from survivors far beyond Illinois—girls from Denver, Atlanta, even Kansas City. Some had escaped from shelters bearing Caleb's signature. Others had been trafficked like freight: no voice, no record, just movement. Volunteers—some driven by guilt, others by fear—began stepping out of silence. One volunteer handed Frieda a thumb drive with video footage. Another spoke in hushed tones of "scholarship files" stored in a locked basement office—documents that had never seen a school. A third dropped off a battered ledger full of falsified expense reports. Each truth cracked something open.

And then came the night everything changed. It was past sundown. The Bridge stood quiet, wrapped in the dim gold of a dying sky. Streetlights flickered outside as Frieda moved through the empty center, locking doors, shutting down lights. Her keys jingled softly as she neared the lobby.

The front door creaked open. A figure stepped in—barely more than a girl. She couldn't have been older than eighteen. Her jeans were torn, mud-caked at the cuffs. A sagging hoodie slipped from one shoulder. Her duffel bag, heavy and sun-bleached, hung off her frame like a weight she had carried too long. Her hair clung to her face, damp with sweat or tears—Frieda couldn't tell which.

For a moment, they just stared at each other in the twilight hush. Then came the voice—frayed, dry, trembling.

"I was one of them."

Frieda froze mid-step. Her breath caught in her chest. She moved slowly forward, each footfall deliberate, her eyes never leaving the girl.

"I got out," the girl said. Her lips trembled. "And I brought these."

With shaking fingers, she dropped the duffel onto a nearby table. The zipper rasped open like a wound tearing wide. Inside—documents. Folders stained at the corners. Receipts curled with time. Notes scrawled in panic. Envelopes stuffed with names. Movement logs, times, dollar signs. Bank records. Schedules. Polaroids. And faces. So many faces.

"Kept 'em," the girl whispered. "Didn't know if anyone would believe me."

Frieda reached out, her hand trembling as she touched the top folder. The paper was soft, almost warm from being carried so close. She looked the girl in the eye—raw, broken, courageous.

"I believe you."

THAT NIGHT, THE BRIDGE DID NOT SLEEP. Frieda brewed a pot of coffee so strong it steamed into the hallway. Miguel arrived just past midnight, eyes dark and jaw set. Reyes was next, flipping on the meeting room lights like they were about to stage a trial. Maps unfurled across tables. Walls were overtaken with pushpins, string, scribbled Post-its, cross-referenced names, shelters, and bus stops. A copier groaned under the weight of replication. File boxes filled. Phones rang. The quiet hum of injustice had become a war drum. What emerged wasn't just a ring.

It was an engine—a machine of shame, secrecy, and carefully choreographed silence. But now, someone had cut the wires.

Hours in, Frieda moved through a stack of folders, flipping slowly, methodically—until her hand stilled. A spreadsheet. Aliases. Code names. Assigned territories. Phone numbers. Bank routes. Her finger trailed down the list. Then stopped. One name. **Lex.**

Her heart skipped. Just a beat. But it echoed in her ribs like thunder. She blinked. Read it again. **Lex.**

Miguel looked up from the far table. "You okay?"

Frieda didn't answer. Her eyes dropped lower. Another name. **Keisha.** She couldn't breathe. The room felt distant, muffled—as if the walls had leaned back to give her space for the weight that had just dropped on her. She swallowed. Her voice, when it came, was barely a breath.

"Lex… and Keisha."

Miguel crossed to her side, his brow furrowed. "You know them?"

Frieda nodded slowly. Her lips parted, but no words came for a moment—just memory.

"I met them… years ago," she said, finally. "Back when I was running wild. Sneaking out of Grandma Lois's house. Lex was smooth, slick-talking, always two steps ahead of everybody. Keisha—she was sharp. Taught me how to survive the streets. How to move. She protected me." Her voice cracked on the last word.

Miguel crouched beside her, his face tense.

"They're not just involved," Frieda whispered. "They're running one of the new operations."

The paper fluttered slightly in her hand, the ceiling fan barely spinning above. She sank into a chair. The spreadsheet remained open, damning and undeniable. She pressed one hand over her mouth, as if trying to trap the grief from spilling out. And for a moment, all the years she had fought, survived, built something beautiful—they collapsed inward like a lung losing air. The betrayal wasn't abstract anymore. It had a name—two of them.

The spreadsheet still lay open on the table, but Frieda couldn't look at it anymore. Her hand dropped to her lap, the other still pressed over her mouth as though trying to keep something from unraveling—grief, anger, disbelief. Her thoughts spun too fast for words. How could Lex and Keisha—**her Lex and Keisha**—be at the center of this?

They had taught her how to spot a lie, how to walk Frampton's streets without fear. They had once been her lifeline in the chaos. Back then, they seemed like survivors. Warriors. Not monsters.

Her chest ached, not from surprise, but from the betrayal she hadn't seen coming. She had fought so hard to build something better, and now she saw: some of the same hands that once lifted her up had never stopped pulling others down.

Miguel stood silently beside her, his eyes scanning her face. He didn't touch her, didn't speak. He just stayed near, steady as a wall. That unspoken presence was the only thing keeping her grounded.

Reyes approached slowly from the other end of the table, a folder still open in her hand. "These aliases are confirmed," she said quietly. "Lex is 'K-92' in the chain. He's been running a corridor through St. Louis and East Chicago. Keisha handles the grooming network. Recruitment. Intake. Discard."

Frieda flinched. That last word—*discard*—landed like a blade.

"They're not just in this," Reyes continued. "They helped design the system."

Frieda rose from her chair with effort, slow and unsteady. The room felt too tight, too filled with ghosts. She crossed to the window overlooking the alley behind The Bridge. Neon bled into the street below. Sirens wailed faintly in the distance. Her voice, when it came, was low. Raw.

"They were my friends."

No one said anything.

"I thought they'd changed… like I did."

Miguel stepped closer. "You changed because you let yourself be broken. They just learned how to hide behind masks."

Frieda nodded faintly, still staring out the window. She remembered a night long ago—sitting on a rooftop with Keisha, sharing a stolen sandwich, laughing at the stars. Lex telling her she was "too good for all this." Keisha handing her a switchblade like it was a key to survival. It wasn't a memory anymore. It was a scar reopening.

Behind her, Reyes cleared her throat. "We have enough evidence to issue warrants, but we'll need you to keep quiet—for now. We want to catch them in motion, not on alert."

Frieda turned back, eyes sharp now, despite the grief still in them. "I don't want them arrested because of me. I want them stopped because of what they've done."

Miguel nodded. "Then we set the trap."

Frieda glanced at the table one last time. At the names. The codes. The receipts soaked in silent screams. She squared her shoulders. Her voice steadied.

"Let's finish what we started."

The Strategy

THE MORNING SUN BLED softly through the high windows of The Bridge's main conference room. Light fell across the evidence table like a divine spotlight—God's eye watching, waiting.

Frieda sat at the head of the table, her palms flat against the worn wood. Her eyes were red but focused, trained not on what had been lost, but on what still could be saved.

Miguel leaned against the far wall, arms folded, watching her quietly. Detective Reyes stood near the whiteboard, dry-erase marker in hand, already sketching timelines, alias connections, and city networks. They had all met before dawn. There was no sleep after a night like that.

Frieda broke the silence. "We can't come at this like it's just a bust. If we grab them now, they'll disappear before we get the full scope. We don't need a headline. We need the root torn out."

Miguel nodded. "Agreed. Lex is smart. He's always had eyes in too many places. If he senses heat, he'll burn everything before we get close."

Reyes tapped the whiteboard. "So, we let them move—controlled exposure. We track who they contact. Who they protect. Who they're protecting *for*. We bait the trap wide enough that they don't even see the cage."

Frieda's eyes narrowed in thought. "We need someone they trust. Someone they won't question."

A moment of silence. Then Miguel's gaze met hers across the table.

"You mean you."

Frieda hesitated. "They already think I'm the soft one. The church girl. The one who left the streets behind. But they still see me as one of them. I can use that."

"No." Miguel pushed off the wall. "Too dangerous."

"Too necessary," she replied firmly.

Reyes lifted an eyebrow. "You're suggesting a reverse infiltration? You want to walk back into their world."

Frieda looked down for a moment, gathering her thoughts like threads, then lifted her head.

"I was part of that world once. I know the signals. I know the drop spots. I know the language. But more than that… I know *them*. They trained me in survival. I'll use what they gave me to end what they built."

Miguel exhaled sharply, pacing now. "We'll need backup. Hidden surveillance. Tapped lines. Controlled environments."

Reyes started scribbling logistics on the board. "I'll assign plainclothes officers and reroute a van for mobile surveillance. I'll need you to wear a mic anytime you're within range."

Frieda was already making a list in her mind—names she could call, people still walking the edge between legit and illegal—people who owed her. "I'll find a way in. Lex has always loved a stage. He won't be able to resist a reunion."

Miguel's jaw clenched. "If he so much as—"

"I won't go in blind," she interrupted. "But I *am* going in."

A beat of silence settled. Then Frieda reached into her pocket and pulled out her grandmother Lois's worn Bible. She laid it on the table, her fingers lingering on the cover. She didn't quote a verse. Didn't preach. She just bowed her head, the room falling quiet around her.

"I didn't come this far just to save myself," she whispered. "If this is what it takes… then I'll walk into the fire."

Miguel pulled a chair beside her and sat down slowly. "Then I'm walking in with you."

Reyes gave a nod; respect etched into her face. "Let's build this right. One wrong move, and they vanish. One right move, and we tear down the whole system."

Frieda opened her eyes. Fire in them now. Hope. Righteous anger. Purpose.

"Then let's set the trap."

The Return

FRIEDA SAT ON THE EDGE of her bed as dawn crept through the thin curtains of her small apartment above The Bridge. The city was waking up outside—sirens, engines, the low hum of life that never really slept. But inside, it was just her. And the past.

Spread out on the bed beside her lay two pieces of clothing she hadn't touched in years: a faded black hoodie with fraying cuffs, and a pair of dark jeans, knees patched over scars that matched her own. They still smelled faintly of sweat and rain—old nights spent slipping through alleys, catching bus rides, ducking under streetlights. They weren't just clothes. They were armor. A language. A signal to people like Lex and Keisha: *I'm still one of you.*

She pulled the hoodie into her lap, running her fingers over a tiny, stitched cross near the pocket—an old act of defiance from when she was fifteen, when she'd tried to remind herself that God could find her in places churches wouldn't go. She closed her eyes. Took a breath. And dressed.

IN THE BRIDGE'S BACK OFFICE, Miguel was already waiting, leaning over a cluttered desk covered in burner phones, folded maps, and scraps of handwritten notes. The hum of the copier droned on—more files being prepared, just in case.

He looked up, caught sight of the hoodie, the jeans. For a heartbeat, something flickered behind his eyes—protective anger, maybe sorrow. But he didn't speak it. He just nodded.

"You ready?" he asked.

Frieda pulled her hair back tight, no trace of her usual soft waves. No earrings. No cross around her neck. Nothing marked her as the restored, rebuilt Frieda Winslow. She tucked it all away.

"I need the streets to see who I *was*," she said. "So they'll tell me where Lex is."

Miguel handed her a small, cheap, and untraceable flip phone. A single number pre-programmed. His. "One word— 'Go'—and we pull you out."

She pocketed it without comment and stepped into the hallway where Reyes stood waiting. She handed Frieda a file. "Contacts?"

Frieda flipped it open. Faces stared back—old names that once meant survival. She tapped three of them with her nail. "Kilo, Shonda, Juice."

"They still run South Point?" Reyes asked.

"They run more than that," Frieda said quietly. "They're the eyes. They hear things Lex never thinks they hear."

She tucked the file under her arm and slipped a battered notebook into her back pocket—her old code ledger, scribbled with phrases she'd once used to mark drop sites, safe houses, dealers, runners. She grabbed a black Sharpie from Miguel's desk and scrawled three words on the back of her hand: **Trust No One.**

OUT FRONT, the day had fully broken open—early sun glinting off the cracked sidewalk. Frieda stepped outside, the city air sharp and cold in her lungs. She tugged the hoodie's hood low over her forehead, checked the flip phone one last time. She whispered a prayer, almost inaudible, tucked under her breath.

Keep me hidden in plain sight. Keep me sharp. Keep me Yours.

Then she slipped into the street—past The Bridge's mural that read *HOPE RESTORES*, past the bus stop where she once spent nights waiting for nowhere, past the corner store where Lex and his crew used to hold court. Her boots scuffed the concrete in rhythm with old memories. Every step back was a step toward the part of herself she'd buried—brought back now, not to survive, but to set others free.

The Code

THE AFTERNOON SUN HUNG HEAVY over South Point's west end—a strip of half-shuttered storefronts, cracked sidewalks, corner boys leaning against graffitied walls. This part of Frampton hadn't changed much since Frieda had run these blocks as a girl with nowhere to be but everywhere at once.

She kept her hood low, hands deep in her pockets. Her eyes flicked across faces—some too young to be here, others old enough to know better. She passed a man who nodded at her, recognition flickering and then dying behind wary eyes. "Good," she thought. The old version of her still lived in their heads.

At the edge of an abandoned strip mall, she spotted her: **Shonda**. Lean, coiled, early-thirties now but still wearing the same defiant swagger she'd had at eighteen. Shonda leaned against the rusted frame of a busted payphone, braiding thin gold strands into her hair. Two of her crew perched nearby on milk crates, eyes sharp as razors. Frieda paused in the middle of the cracked asphalt, letting Shonda see her first.

Shonda's head lifted, her braid half-done, fingers frozen mid-twist. "Well, look what the wind dragged back," she drawled. Her mouth curved into a smirk, but her eyes stayed cold. "Ain't you supposed to be all churchy now, Miss Winslow?"

Frieda stepped closer, slow, deliberate, like approaching a coiled snake you don't want to startle.

"Still am," Frieda said. "But sometimes the streets call your name."

Shonda snorted a dry laugh. "That so? Thought you was done with us."

Frieda shrugged, letting the lie taste bitter on her tongue. "I never really left. Just learned to move different."

She lifted her chin at the boys on the crates. "You good?"

"They ain't your worry," Shonda said, braid finished now, her hands dropping. "What you want, Frieda? You ain't here for nostalgia."

Frieda slipped her hands from her pockets. Her left palm turned up, showing the faint scar at the base of her thumb—a mark from years ago, a back-alley initiation with a razor blade that had sealed her into Shonda's circle once upon a time.

"I'm lookin' for Lex," she said softly, her voice pitched low, careful. "Need to settle something old. Need to do it face to face."

Shonda's mouth twitched—half grin, half warning. "Lex don't settle old. He buries it."

Frieda stepped closer, just within arm's reach. She could smell the faint sweetness of cheap perfume and cigarette smoke. "I got something he wants," Frieda said. "Something that could clean both our slates."

Shonda narrowed her eyes. "You talkin' too pretty, Frieda. Use the tongue we know."

Frieda leaned in, her words barely a breath: "I got *shine* he left behind—coin and memory. You tell him *Dove* come callin'. Dove wants wings back."

Shonda's eyes flickered—recognition, maybe even a flicker of old respect. *Dove* had been Frieda's street name back then, when Lex labeled her "the one too sweet for the block."

"You know what you sayin'?" Shonda asked. Her tone lost its edge for the first time. "You know if you show your face, he'll test if you still bleed?"

"I know," Frieda said. "But tell him. If he wants what's owed, he'll meet me."

"Where?"

"Under the East Viaduct," Frieda said. "Midnight. Alone."

Shonda barked a humorless laugh. "Lex? Alone? Girl, you dream too pretty."

Frieda smiled, a sharp, weary curve. "Then tell him to come hungry. I'll be waiting."

A silence stretched between them. Then Shonda snapped her fingers at her boys. They stood, wary but obedient, drifting a few steps back to give the women space.

"You sure about this, Dove?" Shonda asked, voice lower now, almost something like genuine.

"No," Frieda said truthfully. "But it's gotta be done."

Shonda reached into her back pocket, pulled out an old burner phone—screen cracked, keys greasy. She pressed it into Frieda's palm. "If he says yes, you'll know."

Frieda slipped it deep into her pocket. Their eyes locked—two survivors, two different roads carved out of the same dirt.

"You got ghosts, girl," Shonda murmured. "Don't let 'em drag you back down."

Frieda held her gaze, steady. "I'm not here to stay, Shonda. Just here to finish it."

She turned, hoodie brushing her shoulders like a cloak of dusk, and melted back into the street—heart pounding, mind racing, praying that by midnight, every piece would fall into place.

IN A DIMLY LIT BACKROOM behind a shuttered liquor store on Frampton's north side, **Lex** sat alone at a scarred poker table. A single bulb swung above him, catching the gold in his teeth when he grinned. The walls were papered with handbills for underground fights, old flyers curling at the corners.

Keisha perched on the windowsill behind him, one boot pressed against the cracked glass. She was scrolling through a battered phone, nails drumming against its plastic back.

Lex flicked an unlit cigarette between his fingers, watching its tip dance like a fuse waiting for flame. He wasn't smoking — just thinking. Calculating. He always looked half-asleep when he was planning something lethal.

"You believe it?" Keisha asked, voice edged with contempt. "Little Dove flappin' around, all big and holy, now she wanna come home?"

Lex's grin widened just enough to show the wolf underneath. "Ain't no home for Dove," he murmured. "She left her wings in the gutter long ago. Now she thinks she found 'em in that pretty building of hers?"

He leaned back, chair creaking. "Nah. She's sniffin'. Someone's talkin'. We got a leak."

Keisha hopped off the sill, crossing the room to him. Her fingers curled around his shoulder — not tender, but possessive. "We shut it down?"

Lex twirled the cigarette, his eyes distant. "We don't just shut it down. We remind Frampton what happens when ghosts come back thinkin' they saints."

He snapped the cigarette in half, let it fall to the floor. Stomped it under his boot.

"Midnight," he said. "Viaduct. Bring the boys. And a lesson."

Keisha's smile was all teeth. "Dove's gonna wish she stayed saved."

The Bridge

BACK AT THE BRIDGE, dusk slipped through the high windows, soaking the walls in bruised blue and soft gold. Frieda stood at the big table in the conference room, unzipping the battered duffel bag. The burner phone Shonda had pressed on her earlier and tucked in her pocket, vibrated once like a tiny pulse of danger.

Miguel and Reyes flanked her, studying the crude map she'd sketched on butcher paper — the East Viaduct, the shadows under the overpass, the service roads feeding into it like veins.

"He'll come armed," Reyes said flatly, circling a spot with her pen. "He's never anywhere without muscle."

"He'll bring Keisha too," Frieda said, her voice steady but low. "She's his shield and his blade. Always has been."

Miguel leaned in, tapping a dot on the paper. "Blind spots?"

Frieda traced an old memory with her fingertip — her voice softened by distance and grit. "Drainage tunnel. Chain-link fence by the south wall. Old tag still there — says *YOURS TRULY.* That's Lex's sign he owns the ground. But the fence cuts two ways. If we block it, we trap him."

Reyes crossed her arms. "We'll position unmarked units on the main and back roads. Plainclothes close enough to watch. When you give the signal, we move in."

Miguel's jaw tightened as he looked at Frieda — the street clothes, the scar on her hand, the flame in her eyes. "I don't like you being bait."

Frieda met his stare head-on. "This city didn't heal me so I could hide behind its walls. I built The Bridge to stand in the places no one else would."

The flip phone in her pocket buzzed once — the only answer she needed.

"He's coming," she whispered.

Reyes snapped her notebook shut. "Then we're ready."

Miguel laid a hand on hers — solid, grounding — then let's go. "Be careful, Dove."

She almost flinched at the old name, but she didn't. She just nodded.

The Prayer

ALONE, LATER — the meeting room empty, the map still spread like a battlefield — Frieda slipped into the small prayer corner behind her office. No one else knew she came here when she needed to bleed her fear where no eyes could see. She dropped to her knees on the cold concrete, the air heavy with the ghost-scent of old incense and fresh paint. A single candle flickered on the shelf, its flame dancing in the draft from a cracked window. She pressed her hands together, forehead to the rough wood of a cross her grandmother had carved decades ago. She could still see Lois's hands in the shape of it — steady, certain.

Her whisper cracked the silence.

"Lord… I'm walking into the dark tonight. I'm not who I was back then — but I know the girl I was is still part of the woman I am now. Keep me steady. Keep me wise. Let me see what I need to see. Let them see You in me — even here, especially here.

And if I don't come back… let them know the fight was worth it."

A tear slipped free — just one. She wiped it away with her thumb. Then she stood, shoulders square, boots echoing softly as she stepped back toward the light, toward the plan, toward the trap. Toward the fire.

The Call

FRIEDA SAT AT THE CHAPEL DESK, the old wood worn smooth by years of prayers. She was about to pull her hoodie up over her curls when her phone buzzed. The screen glowed—Minister Joyce.

She answered with a shaky breath. "Hey, Joyce."

"Child," Joyce's voice wrapped around her like a quilt. "I heard what you're about to do. Miguel told me."

Frieda stared at the flickering votive candle near her elbow. "I have to."

A pause. The faint sound of papers rustling. "God raised you on your knees, Frieda. Don't forget how to stand on 'em when you're surrounded."

Frieda's eyes blurred. "I'm trying."

"No," Joyce said gently. "You're doing. But remember—when the wolves circle, you don't need to roar louder than them. Let the Lion roar through you."

Frieda's shoulders loosened. "Thank you."

Joyce's voice dropped, warm and fierce. "Be wise as a serpent. Harmless as a dove. But if you strike, strike with a clean heart. Justice ain't vengeance."

A ghost of a smile found Frieda's lips. "Yes, ma'am."

"Bring yourself home, baby. Whole. Don't leave your spirit in the dark with them."

"I won't," Frieda whispered.

When the line clicked off, she laid her phone beside the candle. Then she bowed her head over the desk and whispered, "Walk with me. Through the fire. Through the wolves. Through the dark."

When she lifted her head, her eyes were dry. Ready. She pulled her hood up, turned, and stepped into the night.

The Viaduct Showdown

THE EAST VIADUCT was a concrete scar beneath the old rail line—a stretch of cracked pillars and dripping shadows that swallowed the streetlight like a grave. A fine rain fell in a lazy hush, draping the concrete in a cold sheen. Somewhere above, a train rumbled—an iron ghost echoing through steel ribs.

Frieda stepped under the arch alone. Her pulse thrummed in her fingertips. The hoodie hugged her shoulders, damp and heavy. Beneath her boots, broken glass cracked like old bones—bottles, needles, fragments of nights better left buried.

She paused where the pillars converged, hands deep in her pockets, feeling the flip phone like a heartbeat. Somewhere in the dark, hidden in unmarked vans and blind alleys, Miguel and Reyes and the others waited—breaths held, radios silent, coiled like storm clouds.

A shape moved between the graffiti-scarred pillars. **Lex.** He emerged first—black leather zipped tight, gold chain glinting like tarnished royalty at his throat. Behind him, Keisha stepped out of the wet gloom—coat long and dark, her hair damp against her jaw. Three shadows drifted at their backs; muscle draped in hoodies and empty promises. Lex's grin was oil in a puddle—thin, slick, catching every scrap of light.

"Well, well. Look what the gutter spit back up."
Frieda didn't flinch. She tipped her chin higher, eyes steady as a blade edge. "You got my message."

Keisha folded her arms across her chest, the rain freckling her shoulders. "We almost didn't. You forgot how this works, Dove? Ain't your street no more."

Lex lifted a gloved hand. The men behind him stilled. He stepped forward—boots splashing shallow puddles—until he was so close Frieda could taste the rot of old nicotine on his breath.

"Dove," he murmured, his grin curdling. "I missed you. Thought you got too clean for concrete. But here you are. You come to kneel? Or come to beg?"

Frieda's fingers curled tighter around the phone trigger in her pocket. "I came to end it," she said, her voice even, low. "I know about the girls. The houses. The routes. You're done tonight."

Lex's grin cracked. "Done? Nothing ends, Dove. You think you can fix Frampton with your little prayers and your pretty posters? We're ghosts. You know what happens to ghosts? We haunt."

He turned to Keisha, chuckling—a dry rattle under the viaduct's drip. "Tell her, baby. Tell her how it works."

Keisha's jaw tensed. She didn't answer. Her eyes flicked to Frieda's—something moving there, like a door opening an inch in a house on fire.

Lex didn't notice. He leaned closer, voice slick as oil. "You think you can shame me? You think you—"

Click.

Keisha's switchblade snapped open, silver flashing at Frieda's throat. But her hand trembled. Lex didn't see it. He nodded at one of the men. The brute stepped forward—broad shoulders, reaching for Frieda's arm. That's when her thumb pressed the phone's button.

Go.

Farther down the service road, an engine roared to life—tires shrieked, boots slammed asphalt. Flashlights knifed through the rain, slicing the gloom into bright shards.

Lex spun, snarl twisting his grin into something feral. Keisha jerked back—blade wavering between Frieda and Lex. Her eyes snapped wide, words torn loose through clenched teeth.

"Run, Dove!"

Lex turned to her, confusion flickering into rage. "What you doing?"

Keisha's voice broke, raw and low. "I'm done, Lex. I'm done watching you sell pieces of us to the night. I'm done bleeding for you."

"Put the blade back on her," he snarled, lunging for Frieda. Keisha moved faster—shoulder slamming into Lex's chest, driving him back with a grunt. The blade pressed to his side now, not Frieda's throat.

"You think you own me?" Keisha hissed. "You don't own *nothing*. Not my blood. Not my fear."

Lex's face twisted. He slammed an elbow back, catching her ribs. The blade clattered to the concrete.

Shouts roared through the pillars—Miguel's voice, Reyes yelling orders. Flashlights flared like lightning. Lex spun toward Frieda—one last, desperate lunge—just as Keisha grabbed him again, dragging him sideways.

A shot cracked the night open. Frieda flinched. Lex froze—shoulder jerking as Keisha sagged against him. For a heartbeat, they stood locked together—Keisha's mouth at his ear, whispering something Frieda couldn't hear. Then Keisha slid from Lex's grasp—knees buckling, dark hair plastered to her cheek.

Miguel tackled Lex from behind—his shout drowned by the thunder of boots and barked commands. Officers swarmed the muscle, slamming them down onto wet concrete. Cold cuffs bit flesh.

Frieda dropped to her knees beside Keisha, rain pooling around them. Keisha's eyes fluttered open—just for a moment—finding Frieda's through the haze.

"You were… always light," Keisha rasped. "Don't… don't forget that.

Frieda caught her hand, squeezed it tight. "Stay with me. Stay."

But Keisha's breath shuddered once. Twice. Her last words were only a whisper: "Forgive me, Dove. Now, you get 'em out. Get 'em all out." And then her eyes slipped to the pillars above—unseeing now—rain painting her lashes like a baptism she'd never gotten.

Above them, the train screamed by on rusted rails—iron on iron, ghosts on ghosts. Frieda knelt there in the ruin—Lex pinned face-down in the mud, Keisha's lifeline seeping into her palm, and every choice she'd ever made pulsing like thunder in her chest. Rain fell harder. Sirens roared. But Frieda knelt there, Keisha's blood on her hands—knowing some wolves die in the fold, trying to break free.

Aftermath And Ashes

THE VIADUCT CLEARED SLOWLY—sirens fading, uniforms disappearing behind caution tape and paperwork. The hum of the rail line above still vibrated like a ghost pulse.

Frieda stood alone beside the chalked outlines and crimson stains. Rain had soaked through her hoodie. Her hands trembled from more than the cold. She stared at the spot where Keisha had fallen—where trust had cracked open and spilled onto broken pavement. A warm hand touched her shoulder. Miguel. He didn't speak. Just stood beside her, steady and silent. His jacket was half unzipped, soaked on the sleeves, a halo of worry around his eyes.

"She was trying to make it right," Frieda said softly, voice scraped raw. "She was trying…"

Miguel nodded. "And she did."

Frieda turned to face him fully. Her eyes were rimmed in red, but clear. "We have to finish it. For her. For the others still locked in it."

"I know," he said. "I've already spoken to the lead detective. The task force is moving. Raids are coming—tonight, maybe tomorrow. But they'll need intel only the girls can give."

Frieda nodded slowly, gears turning behind her gaze. "Some of them will talk now. After this. After her."

They stood for another moment beneath the dripping viaduct, sharing silence that didn't need filling. Rain rolled down Frieda's jaw, mingling with the dried blood on her sleeve.

"You're not alone in this," Miguel said. His voice dropped lower, closer. "You never were. But I think I need to say it again— just so you hear it."

Frieda blinked.

He hesitated for half a breath. "I'm with you, Frieda. However this ends."

She didn't speak—but her eyes softened. Not with surrender. With resolve.

They left the viaduct together—shoulders brushing, hearts heavy but in sync. As they stepped into the waiting squad car, Frieda clutched a folded slip of paper—Keisha's list. Names. Places. Codes. Evidence. It was the beginning of the end. And maybe, something else beginning too.

DAWN FOUND HER WALKING. The sun hadn't fully broken yet—just a pale smear of light bruising the horizon, turning the rain-soaked streets of Frampton to dull silver. The city felt hushed, as if it too was holding its breath. Sirens had faded behind her. The taste of gunpowder still lingered at the back of her throat.

Her boots left wet prints on the cracked sidewalk—one after another, steady, silent. Her hoodie clung to her shoulders, soaked through, smelling of rain, sweat, grief. In one pocket, the busted flip phone buzzed with calls she didn't answer—Miguel checking in, Reyes needing statements, someone asking for a quote for the news.

Frieda kept walking. She passed the corner where, years ago, she'd hidden spare cigarettes in the gutter drain. The alley where Keisha once pressed a stolen sandwich into her hand, saying *Eat or die.* The broken streetlight under which Lex taught her how to read a lie in someone's eyes. All still there. But they weren't hers anymore.

When The Bridge rose into view, its mural glowed faintly in the dim dawn—**HOPE RESTORES**, splashed in bold strokes across cinder block. She paused at the curb. For a moment, she almost didn't go in. Nearly turned her back to the door, like the old Frieda might've done—when the shame felt too heavy to drag inside. But she did go in.

The lobby lights hummed low—soft pools of warmth on the scuffed linoleum. A volunteer sat slumped in a chair by the reception desk, half-asleep, startled awake when she pushed the door open.

"Miss Winslow—" he started.

She lifted a hand—a gentle hush. No words yet.

Past the lobby, she drifted down the hallway lined with flyers—community meals, GED tutoring, free counseling. Her palm brushed the wall, grounding herself. She moved through the empty rec room where battered folding chairs sat in a loose circle—still warm with the ghosts of last night's prayer meeting.

At the end of the hall, she paused at the door marked *Office.* She didn't open it. Instead, she turned left—into the little prayer corner behind the kitchen. Bare concrete, old rug, a wooden cross nailed crooked into the drywall—her secret sanctuary when the world got too loud.

She sank to her knees there, the damp of her jeans seeping into the floor. No dramatic words. No bright declarations. Just a heartbeat slowing in the hush. Her palm rested flat over her heart, the other cupped to her lips. *Keisha.* The name stayed in her mouth like a vow. A sister betrayed by the streets, who chose—too late but true—to pull one knife away from someone she once protected. *No one else. Not on my watch.*

Rain dripped from her hair to the rug. Her breath turned into a whisper—half-prayer, half-promise. *This Bridge stands for the ones nobody saves in time.*

She closed her eyes, let the dawn slip through the cracked window, washing her in a light no ghost could snuff out. And when she rose again, she left Keisha's name there—woven into the walls, into the mission—part of her, forever.

Seasons of Grace

TIME PASSED. Not in the sudden sweep of dramatic headlines, but in quiet revolutions—leaves turning, sidewalks thawing, soft rain giving way to new green pushing through cracked concrete. Seasons turned. And with each turning, The Bridge reshaped itself—growing not like a fortress, but like a living thing: roots deep, branches wide, leaves catching sunlight for those who had never stood in the warmth before.

What began as a flickering refuge—one warm room, one pot of coffee, one broken soul finding rest—stretched into a launchpad. Inside, walls once bare now carried murals painted by kids who had nowhere else to belong—bright sprays of color blooming over old cinder block. The old fold-out chairs were replaced by sturdy tables where interns pored over job applications, laptops humming beside half-empty coffee mugs.

A row of counseling rooms was added—doors with frosted glass and soft lamps inside, places where secrets could uncoil in safe hands. Licensed counselors—once just a hope in Frieda's battered prayer journal—now walked those halls with clipboards and gentle eyes, their pockets filled with tissues and peppermints and the holy patience to listen.

The scholarship fund came next—one hopeful folder tucked into a battered safe at first, then dozens, then a whole shelf lined with files: girls who dreamed of college, trade school, culinary certificates—places their mothers never stood, doors their fathers never knocked on.

CHAPTER 22

Love Again

Spring arrived soft and shy, draping the city in dogwood blossoms and fresh rain that smelled like second chances. That was the year The Bridge held its first benefit gala—paper lanterns strung from the rec room rafters, donated tablecloths draped over borrowed banquet tables. People came in borrowed suits, secondhand dresses, and pockets mostly empty, but hearts wide open. They gave what they had—stories, prayers, spare dollars folded into offering envelopes.

Late one golden September afternoon, Frieda stood in the community park where it all began. The sun hung low behind the trees, pouring honey-colored light through branches still thick with late summer leaves. Shadows stretched long across the grass, weaving dark and gold together like a promise.

There were no cameras. No reporters angling for a quote. No shiny flyers or borrowed podiums. Just a clearing under the oaks, a scattering of mismatched folding chairs, and the hush of cicadas warming their chorus in the fading light.

Frieda stood barefoot on the grass—she'd slipped off her shoes without even realizing it. The cool earth soothed the restless heat in her feet. Beside her, Miguel straightened the cuff of his shirt for the third time—his nerves showing only in the small, careful way he glanced at her hand, then back to her eyes, then back again as if to be sure this moment was real.

A handful of Bridge girls stood behind Frieda—young women in dresses borrowed from closets and cousins, skirts brushing knees, sleeves too long or too short, but all of them radiant in the evening glow. Some clutched small bouquets of wildflowers. They were once runaway girls and dropouts and whispered cautionary tales. Now they were sisters. Some mothers themselves. Some soon to be. Some still healing. All standing, all rooted.

And Joyce—steadfast, gold chain cross catching the sunlight at her throat—stood at the front with a weather-soft Bible pressed to her chest, one hand wrapped around the leather cover, the other dabbing at the corner of her eye with a handkerchief worn thin by years of prayers.

A breeze stirred the hem of Frieda's dress—white cotton, plain but soft, the kind her grandmother Lois would have approved of. It fluttered around her ankles as Joyce opened the Bible and found her place.

Frieda's eyes flicked to Miguel—steady, solid, eyes bright with something fierce and tender all at once. For a heartbeat, she saw everything they'd survived to stand here: the raids and the raids that never came, the sleepless nights, the betrayal and the healing, the cold viaduct and the candlelit kitchen table where they once sat in silence, planning how to save a city that didn't know it needed saving.

She felt something loosen in her chest. Not an absence of fear—she'd long given up the fantasy of a life without fear—but the presence of peace. A rootedness. A quiet surrender.

Joyce's voice was warm as bread fresh from the oven. "Repeat after me."

Frieda's lips parted. Her tongue touched her teeth. She felt the sun on her shoulders, the grass beneath her toes, the breath of the girls behind her—holding her up, tethering her to this vow.

"I do," she said.

Her voice didn't shake. Didn't tremble. Somewhere deep inside, behind her ribs, a quiet prayer unfurled like a banner:

Let me never forget the darkness You pulled me from. Let me always carry the light You gave me into the places that need it most.

And in that moment, she knew: She was not a victim. She was not a statistic scribbled in a folder to be filed away and forgotten. She was a woman of faith. A mother, in all the ways that mattered. A builder. A restorer. A bridge. And beneath the oaks, as the last gold spilled over the grass, Frieda Winslow stepped fully into the promise she'd been carrying all along.

Their Beginning

THEIR EARLY MARRIAGE was not painted in grand strokes but built in small, steady brush marks—tiny acts that stitched one day to the next like a quilt pulled warm over old wounds.

There were no champagne toasts or candlelit getaways—only morning coffee sipped in mismatched mugs at a scarred kitchen table, steam curling around the edges of their unspoken prayers. Some nights, Frieda would wake half-strangled by a dream—visions of fire and shadows and cold viaduct concrete. She'd lie there, staring at the ceiling, feeling the old ghosts creep through the cracks in her ribs.

Miguel never demanded the story behind her silence. He'd shift in the dark, turn toward her without a word, and wrap an arm across her waist—his hand spread flat over her heart like a quiet benediction. He'd pray then, voice hushed, lips brushing her hairline. She didn't always catch the words. Sometimes it was just the shape of them she felt—a shelter she hadn't known she could trust.

They learned to read each other's silences like scripture—knowing when to speak, when to hold, when to let space be holy. Miguel never tried to fix the parts of her that still stung raw when touched. He made space instead—big, quiet rooms in his presence where her grief could sit without shame. And Frieda, who had once learned that strength always turned to fists or threats, began—slowly, clumsily—to rest in his. To lean back without flinching. To be held without bracing for the bruise.

They planted a little herb garden in a chipped ceramic box on the apartment windowsill—basil, mint, a shy sprig of rosemary that leaned toward the light as if it trusted there was more warmth ahead. Miguel called it their *home roots*—something small that claimed the cracked brick and thin glass as a place to put down hope. Frieda called it *proof*—that something green could grow where she once only saw ruin.

Most evenings, Frieda still walked the hallways of The Bridge long after dark—checking the locks, gathering forgotten coffee cups, praying over the sleeping city. But now, when she came home, someone was waiting to remind her that a leader still needed dinner. That a rescuer needed rest, too.

Miguel made sure she ate—laughing when she forgot, warming leftovers, and sitting across from her until she finished every bite. He reminded her to breathe when the headlines got too loud, when the budget was tight, when betrayal still knocked sometimes on old doors.

They prayed before meals, fingers laced over chipped plates and cheap forks. They kissed in grocery store aisles and at street corners, drawing smiles from strangers who didn't know the history stitched into each gentle touch. They learned each other's favorite Scriptures—traded verses like love notes tucked under pillows.

They fought, too. Of course they did. About the bills, about Frieda staying out too late at the shelter, about Miguel's stubborn habit of carrying too much alone. But even their fights were honest—grounded, never cruel, built on the unspoken promise: *I'm not going anywhere.*

Love, for them, wasn't fireworks. It was firewood—stacked daily, piece by careful piece, so the flame stayed lit when winter pressed its cold face against the glass. And in quiet moments— when Frieda lay in the hush before dawn, Miguel's breath warm against her shoulder, the city still sleeping below—she'd slip the same prayer into the silence:

Let me never forget the darkness You pulled me from. Let me always carry the light You gave me into the places that need it most.

She was not a victim. Not a statistic scribbled on a dusty file. She was a woman of faith. A mother—of a house, a street, a city full of daughters she refused to lose. A builder. A bridge. And when she rose each morning to choose this life again, she knew the promise held: *Something could grow. Even here. Even now.*

What Remains

The hospital room breathed with a quiet all its own—low hums and beeps that marked the edge between fragile life and something holy. Morning light spilled through the half-open blinds in pale stripes, warming the pale walls, catching on the chrome rails of the bed.

Frieda lay propped against a stack of crisp pillows, her hair mussed and skin dewy with exhaustion that felt more sacred than spent. In the crook of her arm rested her daughter—tiny, swaddled tight in a blanket soft as moth wings. The baby's cheek pressed to Frieda's collarbone, her downy head tucked beneath the curve of Frieda's chin. Each breath that rose and fell against Frieda's chest felt like a promise whispered straight into her bones: *Stay. Breathe. Live.*

Outside the door, nurses murmured in the hush of the new day—rubber soles gliding on linoleum, the soft rattle of a cart. Machines near Frieda's bedside ticked out quiet rhythms, each gentle beep and blinking light reminding her how thin the thread was that held this moment together—and how strong it felt, all the same.

Miguel sat so close his knee brushed the edge of the mattress. One of his hands cradled Frieda's, his thumb stroking her knuckles in slow circles—small, steady, reverent. His other hand rested on the bed rail, fingers twitching now and then as if resisting the urge to reach for the baby, to cradle them both at once.

His eyes were rimmed in red—part sleeplessness, part awe. When Frieda turned her head to look at him, she caught the flicker of moisture he didn't bother to wipe away. He just smiled at her— wide, quiet, certain. The kind of smile that anchored her when her mind still drifted between what was and what had nearly been lost.

Between them, the baby stirred, a tiny fist pressing against Frieda's collarbone. She marveled at the impossible weight of her— barely seven pounds, yet heavy enough to pull every piece of Frieda back to earth, to this single breath, this single heartbeat, this room washed in dawn.

They named her **Krystal**. Not for prettiness. Not for trend. But because grace—unpredictable, shattering, mending—had cracked Frieda's life open so many times, broken her hard edges down to shards of humility and hope. And this child, this warm, breathing miracle tucked in her arms, was the clearest piece that survived every storm. The unbroken thing that remained.

Miguel leaned forward, pressing his lips to Frieda's temple, lingering there like a vow spoken in silence. When he pulled back, he rested his forehead against hers, both of them watching the baby between them—two scarred people, breathing as one, tethered by something impossibly whole.

Outside the window, the sun climbed higher, spilling soft gold across the blanket that wrapped their daughter—new light falling on new life. And in the quiet of that hospital room, Frieda understood again what she'd known in every alleyway, every church basement, every courtroom, every broken place that grace had carried her through:

What remains is enough.

What remains is holy.

What remains is hers to hold.

Time slowed in that small hospital room—minutes stretching long and soft as the sun climbed higher in the pale blue window. Nurses drifted in and out on padded soles, checking monitors, scribbling numbers on charts, whispering to each other like they feared waking a miracle.

Miguel stepped into the hallway for a moment—someone had called, a question about The Bridge, the kind of daily crisis that never really paused. He squeezed Frieda's hand before slipping out, his thumb brushing Krystal's tiny foot as if to anchor himself to something purer than the city's noise. When the door clicked shut behind him, the room fell perfectly still.

It was just Frieda and Krystal then—no machines humming, no beeping, no quiet words from a watchful nurse. Just the hush of new breath and old prayers settling into the corners of the sterile room like incense.

Krystal stirred—a soft sigh, a flutter of lashes against her mother's collarbone. Frieda shifted, careful, pulling the baby closer until her nose brushed the crown of that velvet-soft head. She breathed in deep—warm milk, clean cotton, a sweetness so gentle it made her eyes sting. She traced a fingertip along Krystal's cheek, the skin impossibly thin and warm. She could see the faint blue map of veins beneath it—proof of how fragile and unstoppable new life could be, all at once.

A tear slipped down her own cheek before she even felt it coming. It splashed on the baby's blanket, a single dark bloom on white. Frieda let her lips rest near Krystal's ear—close enough that every word landed where only her daughter's spirit could hold it.

"Little light… you are proof that what's broken can still bloom. That what was meant to be lost can live instead. That grace leaves pieces behind for us to build on."

She paused, pressing her eyes shut against the weight and the wonder of it.

"You are not my second chance. You are your own first promise. And I swear to you—whatever shadows find you, I'll stand where they break, so you can pass through untouched."

Krystal shifted again, a tiny yawn opening her mouth like a rosebud. Frieda watched her daughter's eyelids flutter, the small, determined rise and fall of her chest. A breath. Another. A whole new world, bundled in cotton and heartbeat.

Outside, a bird called—a single trill in the concrete morning. Somewhere on the street below, a car horn barked and faded. Life going on, unaware of what had just been woven into its beating heart.

Frieda lowered her head until her forehead touched Krystal's. For a moment, she just stayed there—anchored, unarmored, unfinished, and yet more whole than ever before. What remained was in her arms. And it was enough.

After

THE WEEKS THAT FOLLOWED blurred together—less like days crossed off a calendar, more like a gentle tide that rose and fell in the hush between dawn and dusk.

It was tenderness in motion. The soft click of a lamp at 3 a.m. The quiet rustle of a blanket smoothed over tiny feet. The warm weight of Krystal's small body curled into the crook of Frieda's elbow, her breath shallow and even, a rhythm Frieda measured her own heartbeat against.

Diapers piled up beside the crib in neat stacks, bottles lined the counter in a row like glass sentinels. Sometimes Frieda found herself staring at them—so ordinary, so necessary—realizing how much the holy could hide inside the mundane.

Time didn't come in hours anymore. Clocks meant little now. She counted her days in feedings and burping cloths, in the sleepy sigh of a rocking chair squeaking back and forth under the soft moan of the floorboards. She learned the shape of night by the hush of Krystal's tiny breaths and the way shadows moved across the nursery walls when the streetlight outside flickered.

SHE STEPPED BACK from The Bridge—not out of guilt, not even out of duty, but because somewhere deep inside she knew she had poured herself out for years, ladling out every piece of herself to patch cracks that weren't hers alone to fix.

This season asked something different:

Stay.

Be still.

Receive what you've fought to give everyone else.

It wasn't easy. The restlessness hummed in her blood some nights, itching at her ribs like an old bruise. But then Krystal's tiny hand would uncurl in her sleep, fingers brushing Frieda's wrist, and the ache would ease—replaced by something warm and bright and impossibly gentle.

Joy came softly, almost shy. In the tiny laundry basket where folded onesies—some new, some handed down—sat stacked like small declarations of hope. In the smell of fresh baby soap clinging to Krystal's hair when Frieda tucked her close and breathed her in. It came in the way Krystal's miniature fingers curled instinctively around Frieda's thumb—so trusting, so certain of this tether between them.

Some afternoons, Frieda sat cross-legged on the nursery rug, a speaker humming out old worship songs that once steadied her when she was alone on cold city streets. Now she sang them half under her breath—verses drifting into Krystal's dreams as the baby dozed in a warm pool of sunlight.

Outside the nursery window, the world kept moving—horns honked, buses rumbled by, The Bridge pulsed with its usual heartbeat of meetings and meals and desperate prayers. But here, in this small circle of soft light and quiet lullabies, Frieda learned to let peace hold her—rocking her as surely as she rocked the tiny miracle in her arms.

The Runner

KRYSTAL'S LAUGHTER SPILLED down the narrow hallway like sunlight through a cracked window—sudden, bright, impossible to bottle. It bounced off the faded paint, wrapped around the corners, and settled warm against Frieda's chest.

Krystal had just mastered her first steps—wobbly, brave, a tiny miracle balanced on two chubby legs that seemed almost too soft to hold such fierce joy. Her arms shot out from her sides like a tiny ballerina mid-flight, fingers spread wide as if she could hold up the air itself.

Each step was a daring adventure—a forward lurch, a squeal of triumph, a half-stumble caught by a giggle so pure it made Frieda's throat tighten with something too big for words.

When she fell—which she did, again and again—Krystal never cried. She sat down with a surprised little huff, blinked up at her mother like the floor was just another friend she'd met on the way, then pushed herself up with determined fists, legs quivering, ready to fly again.

From the old couch tucked under the living room window, Frieda watched it all—one arm curled around a warm mug of coffee, the other hand absently brushing the baby monitor that hummed on the side table, though she barely needed it anymore.

Steam curled from her mug in lazy spirals, mixing with the faint scent of baby lotion and the lavender oil she dabbed on Krystal's pillow each night. The morning light slipped through thin curtains and turned the steam into pale gold. Frieda's grin broke wide and easy as she called out, voice thick with a joy that filled every hollow place in her chest.

"You're gonna be a runner," she teased, her tone low and full as a hymn. "Just like your mama."

Krystal paused at the end of the hall—tiny feet planted like roots in the faded carpet—then squealed and toddled back toward her, arms outstretched. Her giggles rose and fell like music in a room that once knew more silence than song. But unlike her mother, Frieda thought—watching that brave wobble, that fearless grin—Krystal wouldn't be running *from* monsters in the night. She wouldn't be running from fists, from shadows, from hunger, or the shame that clung like a second skin. No—her daughter would run *toward* things. Toward life. Toward freedom. Toward every good, wide-open possibility Frieda once thought she'd never be able to place in her child's tiny hands.

THEIR APARTMENT WAS SMALL, but holy in its ordinariness. One bedroom big enough for a crib tucked in the corner near the window—sunlight catching on the mobile Frieda had made herself, stringing felt stars together late one night while Miguel dozed on the couch beside her.

Scriptures—handwritten on bright index cards—were taped in neat rows on the fridge door: *I will restore to you the years the locusts have eaten. The Lord is my light and my salvation.* Verses Frieda spoke out loud when the world got loud inside her mind.

The scent of toast lingered in the air, tangled with faint notes of baby shampoo and warm cotton. No slammed doors. No sirens. No muffled shouts through thin walls. Just the soft hum of grace—steady as a lullaby, quiet as a promise kept.

Frieda tipped her head back against the couch cushion, eyes closing for a breath. Once, this stillness would have terrified her—this calm with no footsteps creeping toward her door, no cold nights on someone's floor, no gnawing fear waiting in the dark.

Now, the silence healed her. She opened her eyes to Krystal's squeal as the little girl collapsed, giggling at her feet, arms lifted to be gathered up. Frieda set the mug aside, leaned forward, and scooped her daughter into her lap—breathing in that sweet, warm scent, the proof of freedom wrapped in tiny arms around her neck.

Dawn

EVERY MORNING, before the world was fully awake, Miguel rose in the hush before sunrise. The old apartment floor creaked beneath his socks as he moved from their small bedroom to the kitchen—feet finding the same spots on the wood planks, the kettle hissing its steam the way it always did.

He'd slip his keys into his pocket, shrug on his jacket, and pause by the door where the faint gray light from the hallway cut a sliver across the floor. The front door always creaked on its hinges—Frieda teased him every few weeks to oil it, but he never did. He liked the sound, he said—it reminded him he was leaving something worth coming home to. And every dawn, no matter how early, no matter if Frieda was dozing on the couch after a midnight feeding or curled on her side in their warm bed, he would find her.

He would lean close—breath still minty from the quick rinse in the bathroom sink—and brush a kiss across her forehead. Sometimes his hand would cup her cheek just for a second, thumb resting near her temple, a quiet anchor. And every morning, just before he let the door sigh shut behind him, he'd murmur the same thing—soft as a psalm meant only for her:

"Don't forget who you are today."

He never raised his voice. Never needed to. And Frieda never forgot. Not anymore. She was not a statistic scribbled in the margin of a police report. Not a cautionary tale whispered by church ladies over stale coffee. Not just a survivor clawing her way forward.

She was a mother now—Krystal's heartbeat pressed to hers in the dark. She was a light—steady enough to scatter the shadows she once called home. She was the kind of woman who had walked barefoot through fire and come out on the other side with ashes in her hair and lullabies in her mouth.

Saturday

ON SATURDAYS, THEY MOVED TOGETHER through the neighborhood like any small family—blending in and yet shining in small, ordinary ways. They'd leave the apartment with Krystal tucked snug against Frieda's chest in a soft cotton sling, her warm weight pressed close enough for Frieda to breathe in that sweet, clean baby smell with every step. Krystal's tiny fists wiggled free of the sling now and then, waving at strangers as if she were campaigning for every smile she could catch.

Miguel would walk beside them in his favorite battered sweatpants and a hoodie that smelled faintly of the morning's coffee. He always carried the canvas bag at first but ended up giving it to Frieda so he could pick through the produce himself—fingering tomatoes, tapping melons, sniffing herbs like a man convinced his perfect bunch of cilantro would decide the fate of the whole week.

Vendors knew him now—called him *boss man*, teased him when he haggled over pennies. He'd laugh and roll his eyes, pretending it was all a game, but Frieda could see the seriousness beneath it. For him, every fresh sprig of mint, every handful of green onions was proof they'd made a home big enough for small rituals to matter.

They were just another couple to most passersby. Another small circle of warmth and new life weaving through crates of apples and jars of honey and bouquets of sunflowers taller than Krystal's entire body. But sometimes, just sometimes, someone would pause by the fruit stand or the flower buckets—an older woman, a tired man, a young mother with haunted eyes. They'd squint at Frieda like they were sorting through old memories, then lean in closer, voice low and almost reverent.

"Aren't you… Miss Bridge?"

Frieda would smile then—never wide, never prideful, but soft and sure as the dawn Miguel kissed into her every morning.

"Not anymore," she'd say, shifting Krystal's weight on her hip, feeling her daughter's breath flutter warm through the sling. *"Just Frieda."*

But inside, behind her ribs where the old prayers still burned steady, she knew the quiet truth that no name could erase:

Once a bridge, always a bridge.

And beneath the canvas tent roofs and fluttering market flags, she carried that truth the way she carried Krystal—close to her heart, weighty, warm, and full of promise.

<u>A Quiet Place</u>

ONE BREEZY AFTERNOON, the kind that carried the scent of fresh-cut grass and faraway city exhaust all at once, Joyce showed up at Frieda's door balancing a foil-covered tray in one hand and a sweating bottle of peach tea in the other. She knocked with her knuckles, three gentle raps that always felt like coming home.

Inside, Krystal was just drifting off—soft snores and tiny sighs echoing from her crib in the bedroom. Frieda cracked the door open to peek before she let Joyce in. The baby's little fist rested against her cheek, her blanket rising and falling with each quiet breath.

On the porch, Frieda settled onto the faded wicker loveseat while Joyce carefully unwrapped the tray—warm cinnamon rolls, their sugary scent drifting into the breeze like a promise. She tore off a corner of foil to let the steam rise, her thick fingers brushing crumbs from her slacks.

Before she sat, Joyce leaned over to press exaggerated kisses to Krystal's cheeks where she lay in her crib—a blessing, a benediction, as if sealing the baby's dreams with sweetness. Then she joined Frieda, sinking onto the cushion with a soft grunt, knees creaking but spirit light.

They sat there side by side, the late sun stretching lazy shadows across the porch boards. Down on the street below, the city murmured—car engines rolling past, a dog barking half a block away, children's laughter drifting faintly from somewhere unseen. Life moving, as it always did.

For a while, they didn't speak. They just breathed the same air, watching the world soften into evening. Joyce broke off a piece of roll, handed it to Frieda, and they ate with their fingers—sticky sugar and warm dough dissolving on their tongues.

After a long, comfortable silence, Joyce turned to her, her voice a hush, warm and sure.

"You've built something here," she said, eyes tracing the front steps, the small flowerpot by the railing, the open window where a soft lullaby still played. *"A quiet life. A holy life."*

Frieda tipped her head back against the porch wall, eyes fluttering shut as the breeze tangled with the curls at her temple. *"I never thought I'd get to,"* she murmured, the words drifting out on an exhale that tasted like cinnamon and mercy.

Joyce looked out at the skyline where the sun slipped behind the rooftops—her eyes soft but lined with knowing. *"Peace isn't always permanent, Frieda. But it's always worth the fight."*

The words landed in Frieda's chest like stones settling in water—sinking slow, solid, true. She nodded, not speaking, letting the hush between them say the rest.

A Prayer in The Kitchen

THAT NIGHT, after the porch had gone dark and Krystal's bath had steamed the bathroom mirror soft and foggy, Frieda rocked her baby girl to sleep in the small nursery—slow circles, hums that melted into sighs. She laid Krystal down gently, tucked the corner of her blanket under her chin, and lingered a moment just to listen: the faint squeak of the crib as the baby shifted, the soft hush of breath that reminded her why she stayed.

In the kitchen, Frieda lit a single beeswax candle. The tiny flame flickered to life, warm gold dancing across the old white cabinets, catching the edge of the sink where a bottle waited to be rinsed. The window above the sink was cracked open just enough for the night air to slip through—cool and carrying the faint scent of lavender from the pot on the sill.

She pulled her journal from the drawer where she kept the good pen, the one that felt weighty and certain in her hand. She sat at the table, shoulders curled, eyes damp but steady. She touched the tip of the pen to paper. The words came slow, each stroke a heartbeat:

The world is still spinning.
Evil still moves in shadows.
But right now, in this little apartment, there is peace.
A husband who held me.
A daughter who knows nothing of the fire I walked through.
A home.

A tear slipped from her chin to the page—inking itself into the margin, another mark of truth.

This is what grace built.
A quiet place.
And from here, I'll rise again.

She capped the pen, let her hand rest on the open page—feeling the shape of the words beneath her palm, the echo of them already living in her bones. She blew out the candle, watched the smoke curl up into the soft dark of her quiet kitchen. And in the hush that remained, Frieda felt it settle all around her—an unspoken promise that she would never stand alone in the fight for the light she now called home.

The Break

MIGUEL WAS STEADY. Present. Or so it seemed at first, in all the ways that made a home hum gentle as a hymn. He cooked breakfast before Frieda could ask—eggs scrambled with diced tomatoes and green peppers the way she liked, coffee brewed so strong it left a warmth on her tongue long after the mug was empty. Some mornings, he'd hum soft corridos under his breath while he flipped tortillas on their battered skillet, the smell of toasting corn filling the apartment before the sun rose.

He folded laundry at the end of the couch, shirts turned inside out and towels not quite squared at the corners—but folded, warm from the dryer, his big hands careful in their clumsiness. On bleary dawns when Frieda's eyes were too tired to stay open, he'd scoop Krystal up from her crib and rock her back to sleep in the living room—shoulders hunched, voice low with old Spanish lullabies that tangled their way into Frieda's half-dreams and left tears drying on her pillow. In those moments, he was the prayer answered. The calm she had never known she deserved.

But Frieda felt the fracture before it broke. A hairline crack under the paint, a draft through a door that should have sealed tight. It was in the small things first—Miguel's phone always turned just so, screen angled away when he typed. The vague replies—*just a late meeting, a church thing, don't wait up*. The shift in his laugh—how it sounded full but never made it all the way to the soft corners of his eyes. Eyes that had once looked at her like a vow spoken in silence.

Some nights, when he thought she was asleep, she'd feel the mattress dip as he sat on the edge in the dark, elbows on knees, head in hands—breathing deep and quiet, like a man trying to swallow something he couldn't spit out.

ONE MORNING, Frieda stood in their narrow kitchen, the dawn still gray behind the curtains. Krystal babbled in her arm—tiny fists clutching the collar of Frieda's T-shirt, eyelids heavy from an interrupted dream.

With her free hand, Frieda poured coffee—dark and steaming into the chipped ceramic mug that still smelled faintly of last night's prayers. She could feel the shape of the question before she spoke it—like a stone turning in her chest. She turned, the floor cool under her bare feet. Miguel stood by the counter, half-leaning on it, phone in his palm.

"Miguel," she said. Just his name first—soft but weighted.

He looked up, startled at how small her voice was.

"Are you seeing someone else?"

The question didn't echo. It just landed—soft and heavy in the tight kitchen air. Silence stretched between them—thin, brittle, deafening. He didn't rush to answer. Didn't trip over a lie. Didn't reach for her hand or offer some half-stitched reassurance. He just stood there—shoulders rounded, phone still in his grip, thumb frozen above the screen. His stillness was answer enough—an admission in the shape of a man who knew he'd been found out.

Frieda closed her eyes, pressing her cheek to Krystal's hair. She smelled the warmth of milk and baby shampoo. She breathed it in deep—an anchor against the sting that spread through her ribs. She did not scream. Did not fling the mug. The rage was there, buried deep under the heavier thing—resignation. A cold grief that tasted like old memories she'd promised herself she'd never feel again. *Not here. Not with him.*

The woman's name was Elena—from Miguel's church. Sunday school teacher. Soloist. Big bright smile that made people trust her before she even said Amen.

Frieda had seen it once or twice—the way Elena's eyes lingered when Miguel strummed guitar chords in the church basement. How her hand brushed his shoulder, light as dust, when she laughed too long at something small. But Frieda had trusted him. She *had* trusted him.

When she asked him again—when the truth could no longer live in silence—Miguel didn't craft excuses. He didn't hide behind half-finished apologies. He broke before her eyes instead— words tumbling out between broken sobs, shoulders heaving as he clutched the edge of the kitchen counter for balance.

"I thought I was broken," he choked. "I didn't know how to be a husband. I didn't know how to carry peace. I didn't—"

Frieda's voice cut through his confession—low, calm, razor-sharp in its grief.

"You didn't carry it, Miguel." She held Krystal closer, the baby stirring against her collarbone, a tiny reminder of what was still pure. "You broke it."

And in the hush that followed, Frieda felt the fracture split open—her own heart trembling not with fear this time, but with the fragile, painful knowing that she would stand again. Even here. Even now.

What Remains

IN THE END, there was no screaming in the hallway. No plates smashed or accusations hurled across a courtroom. No bitter arguments over who got what, or who deserved to stay. Just a quiet, raw parting—two people who had survived fire and storms but couldn't survive this fracture that crept in like a slow leak in the roof they'd built together.

Miguel left his key on the kitchen table—just a small, ordinary shape of metal catching the afternoon light. Frieda stood by the window, arms folded tight around Krystal, watching him tuck his hands into his pockets as if they could hide the trembling.

No custody battle followed—no paperwork passed back and forth like a weapon. Krystal was still too young to bear the weight of this loss. Her world was still simple: her mother's heartbeat, the warm lullabies at night, the scent of clean sheets and lavender. She didn't know how the air had shifted—how rooms could echo differently when a promise left them.

THAT NIGHT, AFTER THE DOOR CLOSED for the last time, Frieda sat on the edge of her bed with Krystal curled against her chest—small weight, tiny breath, soft hair smelling faintly of baby soap and the faint sweetness of sleep.

Outside, the city moved on—cars passing on the street below, the hum of a distant siren rising and fading. The same noise as always, but inside her chest, everything was quiet and aching.

She pressed her lips to Krystal's crown and let her eyes slip shut. The baby shifted, a sleepy sigh. Frieda felt her own heartbeat steady under the warm curl of her daughter's body—a tiny anchor in the storm that still raged in the back of her mind.

"I won't let this break me," she breathed, her words sinking into the hush like a promise. She tucked the blanket tighter around Krystal's back, thumb brushing the soft fuzz of her daughter's hairline.

"You are what remains," she whispered. *"And I will not lose myself again."*

JOYCE CAME A FEW DAYS LATER. She didn't knock with her usual brisk tap—just slipped inside when Frieda cracked open the door, the older woman's arms already spreading wide before a single word was spoken.

She didn't bring a sermon. Didn't bring advice. Just sat beside Frieda on the old couch—her purse at her feet, her hand settling warm and steady on Frieda's spine. The living room hummed with the soft sound of Krystal's toys rattling in their basket, a half-empty cup of cold coffee on the side table. The afternoon light pooled around them like a soft cloak, gold where it caught on Joyce's gold cross and the silver streaks in her hair.

Joyce's palm made slow, gentle circles between Frieda's shoulder blades. She didn't rush. Didn't fill the air with words that couldn't hold the weight anyway. When she finally spoke, her voice was low, threaded with the same gentleness Frieda remembered from every church basement prayer circle, every whispered blessing over battered hearts.

"God is not ashamed of your sorrow," she murmured, her breath stirring the hair at Frieda's temple.

Frieda's shoulders trembled. Her answer came out in a voice so small she almost didn't recognize it.

"But I am," she said. The words tasted bitter, but true.

Joyce's hand paused, then pressed more firmly—an anchor against the swell of shame. She turned slightly, eyes finding Frieda's, her gaze soft but bright as the last light pooling through the blinds.

"Then He'll carry that too," Joyce said.

And in that hush—just the creak of the couch, the faint coo of Krystal shifting in her sleep—Frieda felt the truth of it settle deep in her ribs. Heavy, but not crushing. Something she didn't have to hold alone.

The Candle

AFTER JOYCE LEFT — her warm hand lingering on Frieda's shoulder, one last squeeze before she slipped through the door and into the dusk — the apartment felt bigger somehow. The silence stretched out into the corners, filling the small kitchen, the narrow hallway, the soft hum of Krystal's breathing from the nursery.

Frieda lingered on the couch for a while, palms pressed flat against her knees, the imprint of Joyce's touch still warm between her shoulder blades. She listened to the tick of the old clock on the wall, the faint sigh of the refrigerator motor, the distant thrum of traffic on the street below. Ordinary sounds that felt strangely sacred now — proof that life went on, even when promises cracked wide open.

Finally, she pushed herself up. Her feet were bare against the worn wood floor, each step echoing slightly as she moved to the small kitchen. She flicked on the single light over the sink — soft, yellow, catching the clean glass jars on the windowsill where a few sprigs of mint still clung to life in water.

On the counter sat her little beeswax candle, tucked in a chipped saucer. She picked it up, turning it over in her palm for a moment — thumb tracing the grooves where the wax had melted and hardened again, drip by drip, from nights she'd lit it before. Nights she'd whispered prayers for protection, for healing, for a future that felt possible.

Tonight, she needed it for herself. She struck a match from the box by the stove, the scratch and flare of it loud in the hush. She cupped her hand around the tiny flame, lowered it to the wick, watched it catch — a small golden flicker trembling once before standing steady.

The candle's light danced on the cabinets, on the tired linoleum, on the slip of paper taped by the window — *He will never leave you nor forsake you.* The verse looked faded now, the ink smudged at the edges from steam and time.

She set the candle down in the center of the table, pulled out her chair, and sat. For a long moment, she said nothing. Just watched the flame sway. Watched the soft glow breathe through the dark that pressed against the kitchen window.

Her hands came together slowly — palm against palm, fingertips trembling but sure. She closed her eyes, felt a tear slip warm across her cheek, caught in the corner of her mouth. Her voice came small at first, but true.

"God…" She paused, swallowed. The words wavered, then steadied again. "I don't know how to carry this alone. And maybe I don't have to. If You want it — take the shame, too. Take the pieces that keep cutting. Take the empty places. I'm tired of holding what breaks me."

She breathed out, a shuddering exhale, a release.

"I'm still here. Still Yours. Still willing."

In the nursery, Krystal stirred — a soft rustle, then the hush of sleep settling back down. Frieda pictured her daughter's small chest rising and falling in the glow of the nightlight, untouched by the storm that had passed through these walls.

She opened her eyes to the flicker of the flame. It burned steadily — not loud, not proud — just steady. And for the first time since the fracture split her chest wide open, Frieda felt something stronger than sorrow settle into the hollow space. A quiet promise that grace would keep coming. A quiet place, where she could rise again.

The Return

When Krystal turned eighteen months, spring had already crept back into Frampton — shy blossoms pushing through cracks in sidewalks, city buses rumbling down potholed streets painted in fresh graffiti no one bothered to scrub away anymore.

Frieda returned to Frampton High not as the wide-eyed girl who once skipped class to breathe on rooftops, not as the young girl slipping in to volunteer when she could. But as Mrs. Winslow, certified, salaried, keys jangling from her lanyard, lesson plans tucked in the crook of her arm, the smell of dry-erase markers clinging to her clothes by fifth period.

Her classroom sat on the second floor, windows cracked open to let in restless breezes that carried the city's heartbeat right through her walls — sirens in the distance, engines growling at the red light by the corner store, kids cussing and laughing under their breath as they slipped down the hallway in untied sneakers.

Her students didn't know the whole story — not really. They didn't know how Frieda once sat in a police cruiser, for petty theft. They didn't know how many nights she'd gone without shelter. But they felt pieces of it — like warm drafts sneaking through the cracks when winter wanted to stay.

They felt it when she paused before handing out a test, head bowed, lips moving silently as she prayed over every pencil scratching across paper. They felt it when she sat at her desk long after dismissal, coaxing a half-asleep girl awake with an extra snack tucked in her tote bag, telling her to try again tomorrow.

They felt it in the way she noticed the quiet ones — the boys who never raised their eyes, the girls who wore sleeves too long in August. *I see you* was in every nod, every gentle hand on a shoulder as they filed out into hallways where shadows waited.

Her strength didn't come wrapped in gold or stitched into fancy degrees. It came from cracked places, stitched back up by choice, by faith, by the resolve to stand like a wall no storm had managed to wash away yet. And under her breath — sometimes while grading papers at midnight, Krystal's soft breath steady in the next room — Frieda promised herself again: *No girl under this roof would ever believe she had to survive alone.*

BUT OUTSIDE THOSE STURDY BRICK WALLS, the city's teeth were growing sharper. Frampton was changing — too fast, too ugly. Fresh spray paint bloomed on every block overnight — neon warnings, tags like war drums. Gunshots popped at two, three in the morning — distant thunder that crawled through the cracks in bedroom walls and settled in children's dreams.

One Friday, they buried a boy. Fifteen. Wrong block, wrong time, caught between street corners that belonged to no one and everyone. Frieda's students slipped back into her classroom Monday morning with swollen eyes, heads ducked. They didn't say his name — didn't have to.

The whispers started crawling in then. *Warlords.* A name Frieda didn't remember from her old days in the alleys, tagging garages and skipping curfew. This was no ragtag corner crew with beat-up sneakers and dime bags tucked in sleeves.

The Warlords moved differently — organized, slick, more suits than hoodies when they wanted to be. They whispered protection like a promise. They spread rumors about initiations so sick that Frieda couldn't stand to picture them when she lay awake at three a.m.

They targeted the ones they knew wouldn't be missed quickly — girls she'd taught fractions to last year. Girls who used to scribble their dreams in the margins of their notebooks, now gone with no explanation but a fresh tag on the back door of a corner store.

ONE EVENING AFTER DISMISSAL, Frieda lingered by her classroom window — hands braced on the sill, forehead pressed to the cool glass. Across the street, yellow police tape danced in the wind — flapping like a tattered flag. Another shooting. Another candlelight vigil waiting to happen on the corner.

Behind her, Krystal babbled to herself, tiny fingers stacking soft foam blocks into a crooked tower. Two years old now — baby scent fading, replaced with the sticky sweetness of toddler hair and half-chewed crackers tucked in chubby cheeks.

Frieda watched her reflection in the window — the lines deeper under her eyes now. A tiredness that no sermon could chase off. But a steel, too. Unyielding.

She flicked the old TV bolted to the classroom wall on — just static at first, then a local anchor, voice hushed and clipped.

"Authorities confirm a rise in gang-related activity—"
"Rival factions vying for corners once thought safe—"
"Police admit they're overwhelmed—"
"Residents describe a neighborhood on edge—"
"Feels like we're being hunted," a woman's trembling voice said, hidden behind a blurred face.

Frieda turned the volume down, the hum sinking into the thick silence. She thought of the fire— of the cold cell— of the shelter cot with springs that dug into her shoulder blades—of the rescue that saved her but left scars— of the betrayal— of the rebuilding— of the promise.

"Not again," she whispered, but even as the words landed on her tongue, she knew better. It *was* happening again. The storm was here again. The fire was licking at the doors. And so was she.

SOME MORNINGS, BEFORE THE FIRST BELL RANG, Frieda still walked down to The Bridge. She'd stand alone at the top of the steps, Krystal's tiny hand gripping her fingers tight. She'd bow her head, whisper prayers into the soft dawn that smelled of diesel and blooming weeds.

Remind me this matters, she'd think, her breath a vow.

Remind me I still do.

And when she turned to face the street — cracked concrete, fresh graffiti, echoes of gunfire that couldn't keep her down — she knew exactly who she was. A mother. A teacher. A bridge. Still here. Still standing.

The Kitchen Table

THAT WEEKEND, the air outside the apartment held a restless chill — the kind that slipped under the doorframe and curled around the ankles, reminding Frieda that summer was gone for good. Inside, the kitchen was warm but dim, just a single overhead bulb humming softly above the small table that had seen more whispered prayers than shared meals these days.

When Joyce knocked, Frieda didn't jump. She just opened the door and stepped aside, letting the older woman's familiar warmth slip past her into the quiet kitchen. Joyce came carrying a brown paper bag that smelled faintly of butter and something sweet, the corners darkened with a bit of oil that had seeped through. In her other hand, a dented old thermos — the kind that had lived in church basements for years, pouring out sweet tea like a promise that some things didn't change.

Joyce didn't say much at first. She just set the bag down on the kitchen table with a soft rustle, unscrewed the thermos cap, and poured the amber tea into a chipped mug Frieda pushed toward her without a word.

The two of them sat there for a while, the hush between them broken only by the faint whir of the old fridge and the distant sound of Krystal's sleepy breathing through the baby monitor perched by the stove.

Joyce studied Frieda the way only Joyce could — no pity, no judgment, just that quiet, steady gaze that had once made Frieda break down on the back pew of a revival tent when she was seventeen and half-feral with grief. Finally, Joyce reached across the table, her palm warm and heavy over Frieda's cold knuckles.

"You've been quiet," Joyce said, voice low enough to keep from stirring the fragile hush of the apartment.

Frieda's shoulders sank as if the question loosened the strings holding her upright. She let out a slow breath that trembled on the way out.

"I've just been trying to hold everything together," she said, staring down at the small pale scar on her wrist — the place Krystal's tiny baby nails had scratched her once when she first learned to grasp. "For Krystal. For my students. For... myself."

Joyce's thumb brushed her hand in slow, patient circles. "You've been holding a whole city in your spirit for years, baby," she murmured, her eyes soft but bright with that knowing fire. "But even the strongest bridges need maintenance."

Frieda's mouth pulled tight, a tiny breath of laughter that came out more like a broken sigh. She dropped her gaze, blinking fast as tears pricked at the corners.

"I thought maybe..." Her voice cracked, catching on the truth she didn't want to say out loud. "With Miguel... I thought this time would be different."

The name hung in the air between them like dust motes drifting in a single beam of morning sun. Joyce's eyes shone wet as she squeezed Frieda's hand a little tighter.

"Oh, baby," Joyce breathed, her voice cracking too now. "Love doesn't always stay. But God does. And so do I."

The tears came then — hot, silent, too many to blink away. They slipped down Frieda's cheeks and fell onto the back of Joyce's hand, where she let them pool like small baptisms.

"I feel like I've lost again," Frieda whispered, each word pulling something raw out of her chest.

Joyce leaned forward, her forehead nearly touching Frieda's across the table, her voice a fierce hush.

"No," she said. "You've survived again. And don't you forget it. You gave that baby girl a name that holds what's inside you. Krystal — clear, strong, unbreakable under pressure. Just like her mama."

Frieda's shoulders shook with a sound that wasn't quite a sob — more like the shudder of old walls when the wind pushes too hard. She wiped her eyes with the back of her wrist, breath slowing as the weight of Joyce's words settled in like warm water soaking into dry earth.

Joyce leaned back, letting her fingers slip away at last. She tugged open the paper bag, the buttery scent of cornbread drifting out to fill the small kitchen. She pressed one into Frieda's palm — still warm, crumbs clinging to the wax paper.

"Now," Joyce said, her eyes gleaming with the soft command that had once raised a dozen young women like Frieda from ashes to altar rails. "Finish one of these muffins. You got a little girl in that room and a whole city out there counting on you. But first — you gotta feed what's left of you, too."

Frieda looked down at the muffin in her hand — golden, imperfect, edges crisp where Joyce's old oven had browned them too much on one side. She broke off a piece, small, trembling, and lifted it to her mouth. The taste hit her tongue warm, soft, a sweetness that spread like mercy. She closed her eyes, let it melt down slowly.

And for the first time in days, Frieda ate. Not just to survive. But to begin again — crumb by crumb, promise by promise — to heal.

New Steps, Old Ground

THE MONDAY AFTER JOYCE'S VISIT broke cold and bright — sun slicing through the brittle clouds like a promise. Frieda rose before dawn, her breath making small ghosts in the quiet kitchen while Krystal snored softly in her blanket fort on the couch. She brewed coffee she barely tasted, tied her hair back tight, and pulled on the coat she'd once worn the first day she'd opened The Bridge's doors to the cold.

By the time she stood at the threshold, the city was fully awake — horns echoing down cracked streets, the hiss of bus brakes, the soft sigh of her boots on the salted concrete steps.

She paused there, hand on the worn doorknob, palm pressed to the chipped wood like it might remember her touch. For a moment, she rested her forehead against it, eyes closed, one breath whispered into the splintered grain.

"Still here."

Then she pushed the door open. It groaned on its tired hinges — that familiar, stubborn sound — and swung wide to release a breath of lavender cleaner, stale coffee grounds from yesterday's pot, and the faint sweetness of old wood that had soaked up a thousand stories. Sunlight poured through the tall windows, pooling across the floorboards in gold rectangles that caught on the circle of folding chairs arranged just off-center, their legs scuffed from years of scraping across these same boards. The place felt both bigger and smaller than she remembered — walls that had once held the weight of so many secrets now felt ready to carry a new one.

She didn't come to lead that day. Not to stand at the front, not to hold the clipboard or nod at volunteers with checklists and cautious smiles. She came to listen.

One by one, the girls arrived — some hesitating at the door, some slipping in like they'd never left. Older now. Shoulders broader with burden, but eyes still bright in places. A few had toddlers tugging at coat sleeves. A couple wore college lanyards around their necks like fragile armor against the world that still wanted too much from them.

Tyesha arrived last — quiet, her old denim jacket wrapped tight around her narrow frame, hair pulled back in a no-nonsense knot. She found her seat near the window, arms folded at first but eyes alert, watchful. Lena drifted in behind her, leaning against the far wall — arms crossed, jaw set, but the edge in her eyes dulled by time, by truth, by hope that refused to stay buried.

When the murmurs settled, Frieda stood. The floor creaked under her boots — a sound that reminded her she was real, here, needed.

"I'm not here today with answers," she said, her voice echoing just enough to hush the restless shuffle of feet and paper cups.

She looked at their faces — all those lives stitched together by fear, by stubborn hope, by the scraps of faith they carried like hidden blades.

"I'm here with the same ache I had when I started," she continued, her voice tightening around the memory of every loss she'd learned to carry without letting it drown her. "I've lost some things. I've learned some things. But one truth hasn't changed: this city still needs more light. And we —"

She spread her hands, palms open — a gesture that invited, instead of demanded.

"We are that light."

A hush settled then — the kind that doesn't choke but frees. The kind that lets something broken mend in the quiet.

She let the silence hold a breath before stepping closer, eyes sweeping the circle — seeing every scar, every promise, every new beginning waiting to be claimed.

"I want to rebuild," she said, voice stronger now. "Not just The Bridge. But something bigger. Stronger. A coalition. A legacy. Something that outlives our names and outlasts every flame they try to set at our door."

Tyesha sat forward then — the metal chair legs squeaking on the old wood. Her voice slipped out, half-wonder, half-challenge.

"You mean… like a movement?"

Frieda felt the word settle in her bones like a seed that had waited too long for rain. She nodded. Slow. Certain. "Exactly like that."

The sunlight shifted. A draft rattled the old windows. And for the first time in a long time, The Bridge felt new again — not just a refuge, but a match struck against the gathering dark.

The Call for New Leaders

THE NEXT FEW WEEKS MOVED like a heartbeat — quick, insistent, pounding through every cracked sidewalk and worn community bulletin board in Frampton.

Frieda hardly remembered what a free evening felt like. Her days began with a soft kiss to Krystal's forehead as dawn painted the apartment walls pink, and they ended long after the streetlights flickered on and the city settled into its uneasy sleep.

Each night, she found herself standing in a new room — her boots echoing on scuffed library floors, the hum of a rec center's broken vending machine buzzing behind her words, the smell of stale coffee and old hymnals clinging to the fellowship hall of St. Mark's on Seventh.

This time, the folding chairs didn't just hold girls clutching notebooks and shaky hope. Now the circles grew wider. Fathers sat in the back, caps in their hands, eyes down but listening hard. Mothers leaned forward, nodding slowly when Frieda's voice cracked through the hush. A youth pastor scribbled notes on the back of a church program, his pen scratching fast when Frieda called out the places the darkness still hid.

Survivors — girls turned women, scars tucked under sleeves, strength braided into their spines — stood along the walls, arms crossed but eyes fierce with something like belief. A few men spoke too, rough hands wringing baseball caps, voices raw as they stumbled over. *I'm sorry,* and *I want to help fix what I once broke.*

She didn't preach. She didn't plead. She told the truth — plain, steady, her voice echoing against cinderblock walls and stained-glass windows alike.

"We're not waiting for systems to save us anymore."

She stood in the center of each room, hands moving like she was weaving something bigger than herself — thread by invisible thread.

"We are the system now. We are the net that catches what this world keeps throwing away."

In side rooms and borrowed classrooms, she started the mentorship training. Folding tables covered in cheap notebooks, secondhand pens, half-empty coffee cups. Tyesha sat up front with her old denim jacket draped over the back of her chair, taking notes like her life depended on it.

Lena leaned back near the door, arms crossed but nodding slow every time Frieda pointed at her and said, "Tell them how you survived. Tell them what you know. Don't let your scars rot — turn them into maps."

Girls who once came shy and silent now found their voices. They practiced standing at the front of the room, their feet planted wide, their shoulders back, trembling but refusing to sit down when the silence grew heavy. Frieda gave them space. Gave them names.

Mentor. Leader. Sister. Gave them permission to stand in places she once thought belonged to people with perfect lives and tidy pasts.

"We are not waiting anymore," Frieda told them one night in the basement of a neighborhood library where the heat rattled through old vents and the smell of dusty books mixed with the sharp tang of fresh resolve.

"We are not waiting for permission. We are not waiting for broken systems to heal us. We are the change we needed."

And in the hush that followed — the scrape of a chair leg, the quiet hum of the exit sign — Frieda felt it. A city stirring. A circle widening. A fire catching, one honest story at a time.

Facing the Warlords' Shadow

BUT NOT EVERYONE IN FRAMPTON welcomed the light Frieda poured back into the cracks. It showed up first like a bruise on the brick — a message sprayed in jagged black letters across the back wall of the old Bridge building. Block letters, sharp at the edges where the can rattled too long. ***YOU DON'T BELONG HERE***

The paint dripped under the security light, the words raw against the faded mural Frieda and the girls had painted years ago — the hands reaching across the bricks, bright sunflowers rising behind them now smeared by the threat.

When Frieda saw it, dawn hadn't broken yet. She traced the edge of the word ***BELONG*** with her eyes — felt the threat coil around her ribs but refused to let it nest there.

THAT NIGHT, instead of bolting the doors and turning off the lights, she propped them wide open. She called the girls — the ones who lingered after class with heavy bags under their eyes and secrets pressed tight under their sleeves. They came with hoodies zipped up and hair tied back; shoulders set like armor. Frieda ordered three extra-large pizzas, hot and greasy, cheese pulling long and messy when the boxes opened on the folding tables.

She connected her battered old Bluetooth speaker — the one that always crackled when the bass hit too deep — and let soft worship songs float up into the rafters that still smelled faintly of lavender cleaner and hope. They sat in a loose circle on the scuffed floor, paper plates balanced on knees, the smell of tomato sauce mixing with the faint tang of fresh paint still clinging to the mural's sunflowers.

Frieda leaned forward, elbows resting on her thighs, voice calm but bright as she spoke.

"If we're a threat," she said, her eyes catching Tyesha's first, then Lena's, then the newest girl who hadn't said a word all night, "it means we're doing something right."

A small laugh — quick and sharp — broke the hush. Lena, shaking her head, her mouth twisting into a grin that didn't reach her eyes.

"Yeah, well, let 'em be scared," she muttered, but she didn't look away when Frieda's eyes found hers again.

Still — Frieda knew. The sharp edge of the threat was real. She felt it in the way her stomach tightened when she crossed the parking lot alone at night. Joyce knew it too — the older woman's silence on the phone more telling than any sermon. So, Frieda did what she'd learned to do — what the old her would never have imagined she could. She called a meeting.

THE NEXT AFTERNOON found her sitting across from a Frampton city councilwoman in a too-cold conference room that smelled of stale coffee and civic exhaustion. Beside the councilwoman sat the police liaison, tie loosened, pen tapping at the edge of his cheap notepad.

Frieda opened her binder — the pages soft at the corners, edges lined with yellow sticky notes and underlines in blue ink. She laid out attendance charts — lines dipping low near certain schools. She slid photos of fresh gang tags into the harsh light — bold on playground walls, bathroom stalls, even the bus stop by Jefferson High.

"Look at the pattern," she said, her voice steady, each word landing like a nail driven straight. "These girls disappear one at a time. At first, no one notices. Then they disappear by the streetful."

She flipped the next page — highlighted lines, names coded for safety. "These are the places they circle — schools, rec centers, grocery store parking lots. And this —" she tapped the photo of the tag on her Bridge wall — "— is what they do when you dare to stand in the way."

Silence. The councilwoman's pen stilled. The liaison leaned forward, elbows on the cheap folding table that felt too small for the weight they were holding up tonight.

"If we don't get ahead of this now," Frieda said, softer now, but fierce in the marrow of it, "we'll wake up in five years wondering where they all went. We'll look around and realize a whole generation was swallowed before we even knew they were missing."

This time they didn't just nod because protocol said they had to. They didn't smile politely and shuffle her out with a polite thank you. They listened — heads bowed in thought, eyes flicking over her binder, really seeing the lines she drew between shadows. Because Frieda wasn't just Miss Bridge anymore — the girl with borrowed chairs and coffee-breath prayers. She was a force. A warning and a promise all at once. Proof that no threat on a wall could chase out the light she'd poured too deep to be painted over now

Krystal and the Future

BACK AT HOME, the nights felt longer now — the early dark pressing its palms against the apartment windows, wrapping the small rooms in a hush that made every soft sound echo.

Krystal was walking now — tiny feet padding across the worn rug in the living room, her steps unsteady but bold, each one a small act of defiance against gravity and the past that would never touch her the way it once touched her mother. She was talking too, though not in full words yet — mostly questions asked with her wide, curious eyes, her head tilting like a bird's when she wanted Frieda to explain how the world worked, one new wonder at a time.

One night, after another long day of phone calls and forums, Frieda sat cross-legged on Krystal's small bed, a faded quilt draped over her lap. The storybook in her hands was soft at the corners, the spine cracked from dozens of retellings. She read slowly, her voice dipping low and gentle, her fingers brushing back the dark curls that had slipped across Krystal's forehead.

Krystal's eyelids fluttered, her thumb tucked in her fist, breath warm and steady as she drifted into sleep. When the last page turned, Frieda didn't move right away. She lingered there at the edge of the bed, her shadow long against the nursery wall where soft nightlight shapes turned slow circles — stars, moons, tiny suns drifting across peeling paint.

She pressed her palm to Krystal's small back, felt the steady rise and fall beneath her fingers. Proof. A heartbeat she'd promised herself she'd protect no matter what came pounding at their door. Frieda rose, careful not to wake her, and stepped into the hallway. She paused in the doorway — one hand resting on the chipped frame — and looked back at her daughter, small and soft in a world that had once taught Frieda to flinch first and hope later.

"This world's still broken," she whispered into the hush, voice catching just enough to remind her she was still made of old wounds. "But I'm still here. And I'm still building."

In the quiet kitchen, Frieda pulled out a chair at the old dining table — the one Joyce had once leaned across to pass her truth like bread in hungry hands. She set her journal down, the leather cover cracked, its pages swollen with ink and tears and plans scribbled in the dark. She flipped to a fresh page, the lamp overhead humming soft and yellow. The pen felt warm in her hand, familiar now — an extension of the vow that never left her bones. The first lines came slow, each word carving out space for tomorrow.

"Grace didn't make me invincible.
It made me resilient.
It didn't shield me from pain.
It taught me how to feel it — and still go on.
I'm building again.
Not from scratch.
But from memory.
From scars.
From hope."

Outside, the city murmured its restless lullaby — car tires whispering on wet streets, a dog barking at nothing in the distance, the hum of something broken trying to hold itself together. And at the small dining table beneath a tired lamp, Frieda held her pen steady. A mother. A bridge. A woman still building. Piece by piece, word by word — leaving no doubt that when the light rose again, she'd be there to greet it.

The Rising

On Sundays, when the city's noise softened just enough for a birdsong to break through, Frieda and Krystal walked hand in hand through the chain-link gate of the small community garden tucked behind the old rec center. The path was cracked and uneven, lined with raised beds patched together with scrap wood and painted signs that had faded under too many seasons of sun.

Sometimes Joyce was already there, stooped over a row of tomato vines, her gloved hands brushing away weeds as she hummed low hymns that blended with the breeze. Other times, Frieda found her perched on the green bench beneath the lone oak tree, a thermos of sweet tea by her side, her eyes soft and knowing.

Krystal toddled ahead, curls bouncing, her small fingers forever reaching — to tug a leaf, to pluck at the purple bloom of a stubborn wildflower growing where it wasn't meant to.

Frieda leaned back on the bench beside Joyce, her hands resting open on her knees, palms up like she was offering something invisible to the sky overhead. She watched her daughter's chubby fingers press the soft petals flat and then spring free. For a long while, they just listened — to the hush of branches, the sleepy buzz of bees, the tiny warble of a sparrow perched on the chain-link fence. For a moment, the city didn't feel so heavy. It felt breakable

— in a good way, like it could crack open and let something new grow.

Then, softly, Frieda leaned toward Joyce, her voice a hush too sacred for the birds to steal.

"I'm not done," she said, like a vow blooming slow on her tongue.

Joyce turned, raising one eyebrow over her glasses, the ghost of a smile teasing her mouth. "Not done with what, baby?"

Frieda's gaze drifted to Krystal — tiny knees pressed into the dirt, her giggles rising like sunlight as she patted the ground with the flat of her palm.

"Fighting," Frieda whispered. "Building. Believing. There's more work to do."

Joyce let the silence sit between them for a breath, for a heartbeat. Then her mouth curled into that familiar, fierce smile that always made Frieda feel like she was twelve again, safe under someone's covering.

"Then let's get to it," Joyce said, her voice carrying just enough steel to remind the garden — and the city beyond its fence — that some women don't retire from the fight.

A Crack in the Peace

IT STARTED AS A TRICKLE — one email blinking into Frieda's inbox late at night. Then another. Then a slow, relentless flood that turned her phone into an altar for prayers too raw to say out loud. Girls she'd once cradled in folded chairs under The Bridge's leaky roof. Mothers whose eyes she knew by name. Teachers who had once brushed past her in the hall, now writing *Please. Help. I don't know what to do.*

The Warlords were back — but not the same ragtag ghosts of Frieda's teenage nights. This time they moved like a machine — sharp edges tucked behind school fences, corners claimed in plain daylight. They whispered protection and swallowed resistance whole.

One afternoon, Frieda sat alone in the dusty faculty lounge — the stale scent of old coffee clinging to the air, her untouched mug cooling at her elbow. She held her phone so tight her knuckles ached. One message glowed on the cracked screen:

"Miss Winslow… they're back. And they're coming after the ones who say no."

The words blurred as she blinked, her vision watery, her throat tight. She could have put the phone down. Could have silenced the ding of the next cry for help. She could have turned off the lamp that flickered in her tired living room and wrapped her arms around Krystal tighter, promising herself that this time she'd choose the quiet, the safe. But Frieda knew. She knew the shape of the fight. The cost of ignoring the shadows until they swallowed the girls no one else claimed.

THAT NIGHT, long after Krystal's soft snore settled under the hush of the baby monitor, Frieda knelt by her daughter's crib. One hand pressed against the blanket that rose and fell with each tiny breath, the other curled in a trembling fist against her ribs.

"God…" she breathed, the word trembling in the dark. "I can't do this alone. But I'm willing. If You call me again… I'll go."

The words sank into the hush like seeds pressed into soft earth — fragile, hidden, but already breaking open. She felt it then — not thunder, not lightning, not the roaring voice she'd once begged for in her lowest hours. Just a nudge. Gentle but immovable. A warmth that unfolded in the hollow of her chest where the old fears once nested. A rising.

Because some fires never really die. Some bridges burn and get rebuilt plank by plank, stronger for the flames that didn't finish the job. And Frieda Winslow — daughter, mother, teacher, bridge — pressed her palm to her heart and rose from the floor, her shadow falling soft across her daughter's dreams. She was ready. Again.

Fire in Her Footsteps

FRIEDA CAME BACK TO THE BRIDGE not with headlines or speeches or reporters snapping photos outside the battered old door — but with her sleeves rolled up to the elbows and a battered black notebook tucked under her arm, its cover soft and bent from years of silent plans. No grand announcement. No fanfare. Just the soft creak of the front door as she pushed it open one chilly dawn, the scent of disinfectant and old wood meeting her like a memory half-forgotten but never lost.

Inside, the center still pulsed with life, but it felt different — like a once-mighty heartbeat now fluttering too close to flatline. The folding chairs were arranged in their imperfect circle near the big bay window. The sign-in sheets still sat neatly stacked by the front desk, pens tied down with yarn. The coffee pot in the kitchenette gurgled its same tired song.

But outside these walls, the city's pulse was louder — heavier — pounding with new graffiti on back fences, fresh rumors slipping like oil through alleyways and bus stops. Frieda didn't rush to fix it. Not yet.

She spent her first week drifting from corner to corner like a ghost people couldn't help but see — notebook open, pen tapping softly as she listened. Really listened. To the new girls curled on beanbags by the bookshelf, to the old volunteers scrubbing down tables after snack time, to the trusted peer leaders who had carried this place forward while she let her wounds scab over in private. She listened to what was spoken out loud — and to the heavier truths braided into what no one could quite say.

The tagging out back wasn't just ink bleeding down old brick. It was a warning shot fired quietly in the dark. The Warlords were here. Different now — slicker, more patient, their lure hidden under promises that sounded too much like Frieda's own old words spoken years ago.

"They're offering what we used to," Ava said one night, her voice a hush as she wiped down the front counter, the rag in her hand slowing over a dried coffee ring that wouldn't come out.

"Protection. Food. Belonging." Ava's eyes flicked up, tired but fierce.

Frieda nodded once, jaw tight enough to make her molars ache. Her pen hovered over the half-filled page in her notebook.

"Then we remind these girls where true belonging lives," she said, voice soft as a prayer — but with steel wound through every syllable.

THAT NIGHT, the last overhead lights flickered low over the long conference table. The big binder of old program outlines sat cracked wide open, its corners worn thin like paper bones. Joyce perched across from Frieda, the sleeves of her cardigan pushed back, glasses slipping to the end of her nose as she scanned the scattered notes and reports littering the tabletop like breadcrumbs back to a fight neither of them had ever really left.

Joyce watched her for a while — just watched. The way a mother watches her child when they think they've hidden their fire too deep to see.

"You're not just back," Joyce murmured finally, her voice weaving through the hum of the old space heater in the corner. Her smile was soft but proud, like an ember glowing in the dark. "You're burning."

Frieda exhaled a breath she didn't know she'd been holding, the pen still tapping its quiet rhythm near the stack of attendance charts.

"This was never about me," she said. Her voice cracked just enough to show the scar underneath. "But I let my pain hush me. I can't afford that anymore. They don't just need shelter. They need a map. A mission. A shield strong enough to stand between them and every corner that promises protection and sells chains instead."

Joyce leaned back in her chair, the old wood creaking under her small frame. "So, what's your first move, then?"

Frieda's eyes flicked to the big whiteboard leaning against the far wall, its marker ghosts still faint from old dreams and half-finished plans.

She tapped her pen twice on the table — a sound that sounded like thunder in the hush.

"Bridge 2.0," she said, and the words landed heavy with hope. "Longer hours. More boots on the street. Restorative circles in the schools. Outreach right up to the corners they're standing on. We take it to the edge — exactly where they're trying to pull these girls."

Joyce's smile spread slow, sure — the same smile that once dared a broken teen to stand up and fight instead of folding in on herself.

"Now that," Joyce said, rising from her chair, pressing her palm to Frieda's shoulder like a benediction, "sounds like the woman I always knew you were becoming."

Frieda's gaze drifted down to the corner of the table, where Krystal's crayon drawing lay half-tucked under her planner — crooked hearts, stick figures with wild hair, a sun smiling wide in a corner smudged with tiny fingerprints. She slipped the drawing inside her notebook — her plan stitched together with the softest reason to never stop building.

"My daughter's gonna grow up here," she said, her voice low but unshakable. "I'm not handing her a city too tired to fight for her future."

Joyce's hand squeezed her shoulder once more before letting go.

"Then we start with the shadows," Joyce said, her words bright as sunrise breaking through boarded windows. "We bring the fight where they think they own the dark. But this time — we come with more light than they know what to do with."

The Return of Drea

THE KNOCK CAME JUST AFTER DUSK — three soft raps on the old side door of The Bridge, too hesitant to be trouble, too late to be routine. The hum of the heater overhead was the only sound in the empty hall as Frieda looked up from the stack of program notes she'd been marking through with a new volunteer.

The pen slipped from her hand. She rose slowly, her shoulders heavy, but her mind suddenly clear. When she turned the knob and eased the door open, the cold air pushed inside like a whisper of something unfinished.

Drea stood there on the cracked stoop — a silhouette half-swallowed by the streetlight flickering behind her. She looked older, the soft braid she once wore now gone, replaced by a jagged cut that framed her face like armor. There was a rawness to her eyes — the rims dark, the stare deeper, guarded. A fresh tattoo peeked out just above her collarbone — letters Frieda couldn't quite read but knew well enough to guess what they claimed.

"Drea?" The name slipped out of Frieda like a gasp she'd held in her chest for a year.

Drea's shoulders lifted then fell in a half-shrug that looked heavier than her frame. "Hey," she mumbled, eyes dropping to the cracked stoop beneath her battered sneakers — laces frayed, toes scuffed raw by streets that had taken more than they ever gave.

Frieda stepped outside, the cold biting at her arms where her sleeves were still rolled up. The air smelled of rain coming, of diesel fumes drifting up from the street.

"It's been over a year," Frieda said, the words careful, steady, as if a sudden sound might scare the girl off the steps. "We thought—"

Drea's mouth twitched in something that wasn't quite a smile. "You thought I was gone," she cut in, voice low but steady. "I almost was."

Frieda didn't reach for her. She'd learned better than that. She waited instead — arms at her sides, door open, no questions forced.

Drea scraped the toe of her shoe against the stoop, rainwater dripping from the edge of her sleeve. "I heard you were back," she said, eyes flicking to Frieda's for half a breath before dropping again. "I don't know why I came. I just—"

She swallowed, her jaw clenching tight. "I didn't know where else to go."

Frieda's breath rose in a soft cloud. "Then you came to the right place," she said, the words warm enough to chase some of the night off Drea's shoulders.

Inside, they didn't turn on all the lights. Just the warm lamp by the old couch that still smelled faintly of lavender cleaner and the worn-out dreams of a hundred late-night talks.

Drea curled herself into the corner chair, knees pulled to her chest, fingers tugging at the loose thread on her hoodie cuff. Frieda moved around the small kitchenette — kettle hissing, tea bags dropping into chipped mugs that had survived so many nights just like this.

Drea stared at the mural on the back wall — the painted faces of girls who had come through The Bridge's doors before her. Some gone. Some standing tall. All of them woven into something bigger than the storms they'd walked through. When her voice came, it was raspy — raw but braver than her trembling hands.

"I been with them," she murmured, eyes locked on the painted eyes staring back at her. "The Warlords."

Frieda set the mug down beside her, the steam curling softly between them. "Okay," she said — no judgment, just a place to stand.

"They got me right after I left my aunt's," Drea said, her thumb digging into her palm. "Said I'd be safe. That they'd look out for me. I was stupid. Thought power meant I wouldn't be scared no more. But all it meant was..." Her voice cracked, her gaze drifting to the floor. "It meant silence."

A tear slipped down her cheek — a single line cutting through dirt and old makeup. She blinked it back, jaw tight.

"I've done things," she whispered. "Things I can't take back."

Frieda lowered herself to the edge of the chair across from her, steady and close but not crowding. "But you came back," she said softly, each word a hand reaching through the dark. "That matters more than the rest."

Drea's eyes lifted then — fierce, wet, aching. "Can I still be part of this?" she asked, voice breaking around the question she'd carried like a stone in her chest. "Even after all that?"

Frieda reached for her hand, palm warm against the cold tremor of Drea's fingers. "You were always part of this," she said, her voice the same steady hush she'd used on so many broken nights before. "Even in the dark. Especially in the dark."

Drea's shoulders crumpled then — the armor slipped like a sigh. She fell forward into Frieda's arms, her sobs muffled against the shoulder that had carried a hundred girls' storms and still refused to break.

In the hush of that side room — old flyers pinned crooked on the corkboard, stacks of new sign-up forms half-filled — grace made room for one more runner. One more girl learning how to turn toward the light again.

As Drea's sobs softened into ragged breaths, Frieda lifted her eyes to the hallway — and there stood Miguel, frozen just inside the doorframe, a folder of donation receipts forgotten in his hands.

His eyes — old regrets flickering in their dark depths — stayed locked on Drea curled like a child in Frieda's arms.

LATER, WHEN DREA SLEPT UPSTAIRS in the quiet room under an old quilt that smelled of cedar and mothballs, Miguel found Frieda alone in her office, the lamplight washing her tired face in gold.

"She looked like someone I knew," he said, voice careful in the hush.

Frieda didn't turn. "Who?"

Miguel's answer came soft, like a confession laid gently on a grave. "You. Back when I first found you. Same eyes. Like she didn't know if she deserved to be found."

Frieda pressed her palms flat on the cluttered desk. "She doesn't believe she's worthy of being loved."

Miguel stepped closer, the old floor creaking under his boots. "But she came anyway. That takes courage. Somebody taught her that once."

He set the papers down, but his hand lingered a moment — not on her, but near enough to say what words couldn't heal. "I know I broke something sacred when I failed you. But I see you, Frieda. Still. And I see what you carry — and what it costs you."

Frieda's eyes stayed fixed on the desk, her voice a raw edge. "I don't need apologies, Miguel."

"I know," he said. "I just needed you to know I see it. All of it."

When he stepped out, the door hadn't fully shut before Joyce slipped through it — as if she'd been leaning against the wall waiting for the moment the air cracked.

She sank onto the old couch, arms folded tight under her shawl. The clock on the wall ticked too loud for the silence between them.

Joyce's voice broke it — soft, the edges gruff like gravel. "You love like it's a warzone."

Frieda laughed — a sound with no humor, just tired truth. "Because for some girls, it is."

Joyce nodded, her gaze soft but unyielding. "And you keep picking them up off the battlefield. Even when you're bleeding too."

Frieda pressed her hands to her face, the smell of old tears and peppermint tea clinging to her palms. "What if I'm not enough this time? What if I'm too tired?"

Joyce leaned in, her hand warm on Frieda's knee. "That girl found her way back to you because somewhere in her spirit, she still remembered what safe felt like. You gave her that. And you'll give it again. But you don't have to hold the walls up alone."

Tears welled, hot behind Frieda's lashes. "It just feels heavier now."

Joyce smiled — sad but certain. "Because the light's getting brighter, baby. And the dark hates that."

In the hush that followed, Frieda let the ache settle — not to drown her, but to remind her what was worth carrying. Something deeper than exhaustion flickered to life in her ribs. Resolve. The kind that survives betrayals and rebuilds bridges anyway.

She rose slowly, shoulders squared like armor remade in grace. "I'm gonna help Drea rebuild," she whispered, more to herself than Joyce. "Not because I'm strong enough. But because I remember what it's like to have nothing — and someone believing in me anyway."

Joyce's grin spread, small but fierce. "Then we'll believe for her too. Together."

And in that small office, under flickering lights and walls lined with old dreams, Frieda felt the holy fire in her footsteps again — a promise no shadow could swallow.

Turning Point

That night, the storm didn't come from the sky — it came from the streets. Gunfire cracked open the fragile hush of East Frampton just after sundown — a chorus of staccato echoes that bounced off boarded windows and rusted chain-link fences. It came in bursts, sharp and precise, like the city itself had been split open along old scars no one bothered to stitch closed.

Five spots hit at once — word spread fast, carried on trembling voices, through half-closed blinds and burner phones that glowed in shadows. Two community centers — the same ones where Frieda had once spoken hope to wide-eyed kids who'd never seen a safe corner. A rival trap house — their competition for corners and fear. And a church. A small redbrick sanctuary tucked between cracked sidewalks, where an afterschool program had been winding down for the night.

Joyce was there. Always there — her arms full of donated books, her soft voice drifting over children's chatter as they packed their bags. She never saw it coming.

THE CALL CAME AT 7:42 P.M. Inside Frieda's apartment, the only light was the warm spill from the kitchen lamp, its glow stretching across the living room where Krystal toddled barefoot over foam puzzle squares, chubby hands full of plastic blocks as Frieda lifted her off the floor. The smell of leftover mac and cheese still lingered in the air, mixing with the soft hum of the baby monitor on the counter.

Frieda had her phone tucked between her shoulder and ear, one arm wrapped around Krystal's waist, her cheek pressed to the crown of her daughter's hair — the smell of baby lotion and warm breath grounding her, tethering her to something real.

She almost didn't answer. The number flashed up unfamiliar. But something in her gut twisted — the same old warning that never left, no matter how many times she swore she'd live softer now.

"Hello?"

The voice on the other end was all static and urgency — a man she didn't know, reciting details like a list he hated to read.

"Joyce Parker. GSW. Abdominal. Critical. En route to St. Luke's. They need family—are you—?"

The world stopped. Just for a breath. A heartbeat frozen in her ribs.

Krystal wriggled in her arms, fussing against the tightness of Frieda's hold. Frieda loosened her grip automatically — too fast — and Krystal slid down her hip, landing soft on the playmat, blocks clattering under her tiny feet.

Frieda's phone slipped. Clattered to the floor. The man's voice, muffled now, kept going, tinny through the cracked speaker.

"Ma'am? Ma'am, are you still there?"

But Frieda didn't hear him. Couldn't. Her knees gave first — a soft thud against the laminate floor, hands braced on the puzzle mat where Krystal watched her now, wide-eyed, the baby's mouth parting in a small, confused *mama?*

The walls pressed in — the yellow kitchen lamp flickering. The hum of the refrigerator, the muted noise of cartoons still rolling on the small TV in the corner. Ordinary sounds that felt obscene against the roar in her skull. Joyce. Her anchor. Her witness. The one who'd shown her how to rise and keep rising when every bone begged her to stay down.

A gunshot to the stomach.

Critical.

St. Luke's.

Frieda's hands pressed flat to the floor, breath tearing out of her chest in short, sharp gasps. Somewhere through the fog she felt Krystal's small hand brush her forearm — a soft pat, a question her baby couldn't form yet. Frieda swallowed a sob that threatened to break her ribs wide open.

"God—" she rasped, her forehead dropping to the cold laminate. "Not her. Please—God—"

The phone buzzed against her knee. The man's voice, distant now, called her name like a rope she couldn't grab hold of yet.

Above it all, the city kept screaming — sirens bleeding through cracked windows, distant and rising. The fire had come again. And this time, it came for her foundation.

Frieda pressed her palm to her chest, feeling the echo of her own heartbeat — a drum calling her back to her feet. For Joyce. For every girl who would run through her doors tomorrow. For the daughter who sat wide-eyed at her knees, still holding onto her mama in a world gone to flame.

Waiting Room

THE HOSPITAL SMELLED LIKE BLEACH and burnt coffee — that sharp, sterile mix that clung to your clothes long after you'd left, like grief that wouldn't wash off.

Frieda didn't remember the drive to St. Luke's. She just remembered buckling Krystal into her car seat with trembling hands, whispering prayers she didn't even try to shape into sentences. She remembered the blur of streetlights smearing past the windshield like ghosts trailing her bumper. The red-and-blue strobes flickering across side streets — more sirens, more evidence that the city's veins were bleeding open all over again.

Now she sat in the corner of the waiting room, Krystal asleep against her chest, tiny fingers twisted tight into the collar of Frieda's coat. The baby's breath was warm and soft, the only thing that anchored Frieda to the cracked vinyl chair digging into her spine.

The overhead lights buzzed. A vending machine hummed in the corner, its coils full of stale chips and plastic-wrapped muffins no one wanted. Two nurses murmured behind the half-shuttered triage window, their voices low, eyes flicking up every few minutes to check on the woman in the corner with the thousand-yard stare.

On her knee, Frieda's phone vibrated for the tenth time — texts from staff, volunteers, kids she'd taught, neighbors she hadn't spoken to in months. *Heard about Joyce. Is she okay? Do you need anything?*

She didn't answer. She couldn't. Her thumb hovered over the screen, but her mind refused to shape the words. Somewhere behind the double doors, Joyce lay under harsh fluorescent lights — stomach torn open by a bullet meant for chaos more than for flesh. Frieda could see it in her mind: the frail cotton hospital gown, the skin so familiar now pale and taut under machines that hissed and beeped.

She swallowed back the wave of nausea rising in her throat. Joyce's voice filled her ears, unbidden — the same fierce softness Frieda had leaned on a thousand times.

"You're not alone in this, Frieda Winslow. Not ever."

The automatic doors at the far end of the waiting room shuddered open with a hydraulic sigh. Miguel's boots hit the tile before Frieda could lift her head. He didn't say anything right away — just crossed the floor in three strides and crouched in front of her chair.

Krystal stirred at the sudden shadow but settled again when Miguel laid a gentle hand on the small of her back.

"They won't let me see her yet," Frieda said, voice rough, cracked, dry as old wood. "They said the surgery's still—" She broke off, swallowing the words like shards.

Miguel nodded, his hand steady on her knee now. "I know. It's okay. You're not alone."

Frieda let out a sound — half sob, half breath. Her free hand clenched the hem of her coat like she could wring the fear out if she just squeezed hard enough.

"She was just... she was just dropping off books," she whispered. "Children's books. She—she loved them so much, Miguel. How can—" Her voice cracked again, words unraveling into silence.

Miguel's eyes shone — old regret there, yes, but also that quiet, immovable loyalty that had never really left. "She knew who she was," he said softly. "She knew exactly who she was fighting for. Same as you."

A nurse stepped out from behind the security door — young, too young, his scrubs loose at the shoulders. He scanned the quiet room, found Frieda's eyes. Something about his expression made her blood turn to ice.

He knelt next to Miguel. "She's out of surgery. Stable, but she's lost a lot of blood. She's asking for you."

Frieda's breath caught — Krystal shifting in her arms at the sudden rush of air.

"Me?" she rasped.

The nurse nodded. "You. She was clear. We can watch your little one here — there's a blanket. We'll keep her close."

Frieda hesitated, arms tightening around Krystal's small body. Miguel leaned forward, brushing his knuckles over the baby's soft curls.

"I've got her," he said, voice sure, the old promise flickering alive in his eyes. "Go. She needs you more right now."

Frieda pressed her lips to Krystal's warm forehead. For one heartbeat, she let herself breathe in her daughter's scent — clean shampoo and sleep and the soft promise of tomorrow. Then she stood — slow, legs trembling, spirit not.

The nurse waited at the door, hand resting on the badge clipped to his chest. "Come on, Miss Winslow. She's awake. She's waiting."

As she stepped through the double doors, the smell of antiseptic and something deeper — something metallic and raw — hit her like a slap. The hallway lights blurred at the edges of her vision. But her feet moved anyway—toward Joyce. Toward the beating heart that had refused to stop loving this broken city — and refused to let Frieda stop either.

The Hospital Room

THE HALLWAY STRETCHED ON FOREVER — pale floors that smelled of bleach and echoes, overhead lights buzzing like tired bees. Frieda's shoes squeaked against the linoleum as she followed the nurse through a maze of quiet corridors where families sat slumped in plastic chairs, their whispers stitched together with the steady beeping of unseen monitors.

Each step closer, Frieda's breath felt tighter — caught somewhere between her ribs and her throat. She pressed a hand to her chest as if she could calm the thunder inside her with the same palm she used to soothe Krystal's bad dreams.

Finally, the nurse paused at a door half-cracked open, its paint chipped near the handle, a small nameplate taped hastily beside it: **Joyce Parker—Room 214.**

He turned to her; his voice hushed in the hush. "She's awake but very weak. Keep it short, okay?"

Frieda nodded, her pulse a drumbeat. The nurse slipped away, leaving her alone with the faint hum of machines leaking through the door. She pushed it open with trembling fingers.

Inside, the room was too bright. Sterile light flooded every corner, bouncing off the metal rails of the bed where Joyce lay propped up — thin blankets tucked around her like a fortress that couldn't quite hold back the truth.

Joyce looked small in the bed, smaller than Frieda could stand to see. Tubes trailed from her arm; an oxygen cannula looped around her nose. Her gray hair was flattened on one side; her dark eyes were sunk deep, but still steady, still fierce under the pale hospital light.

She turned her head when the door clicked shut. And when she saw Frieda, her lips curved into the tiniest ghost of a smile.

"Well, look at you," Joyce rasped, her voice raw but warm. "Standing when you should be laid out on this bed instead of me."

A breath punched out of Frieda — half a laugh, half a sob. She crossed the room in two steps and dropped into the chair beside the bed, her fingers wrapping around Joyce's cold hand, careful not to disturb the IV line.

"You scared me half to death," Frieda whispered, tears slipping free before she could stop them. "You can't do that to me. Not you."

Joyce's thumb brushed weakly over the back of her hand, the motion fragile but sure. "If the good Lord's still waking me up, there's work left to do."

Frieda glanced at the bandages peeking from under the blanket, the machines blinking their cold truths in green and red lines.

"They came for all of us tonight," Frieda said, her voice low and tight. "The centers. The streets. The church. You."

Joyce's eyelids fluttered, a flicker of that old stubborn flame. "They think fear will do what bullets can't." Her breath hitched, and she winced, but her eyes never wavered from Frieda's. "They're wrong."

A silence stretched between them — thick with beeps and the faint hum of the hallway outside.

"I don't know if I'm enough to carry this again," Frieda admitted, the words slipping out like a wound reopening. "I'm tired, Joyce. The girls are scared. The city's worse than before. What if I can't—" Her voice cracked, too raw to finish.

Joyce squeezed her fingers; a faint echo of the strength she'd lent Frieda so many times before. "You can. Not because you're strong. But because you remember what it's like to need someone to stand in the gap. You've always stood in it, Frieda Winslow. Even when you were bleeding yourself."

Frieda pressed her forehead to the back of Joyce's hand, her tears pooling warm against Joyce's cool skin.

"I don't want to lose you," she breathed.

"You won't." Joyce's voice drifted soft but certain, like an old hymn whispered through a cracked door. "And even if you do — you'll keep going. Because that's who you are. A bridge that don't burn easy."

They stayed like that for a long moment — Frieda's breath steadying against the beeps, Joyce's eyes fluttering closed under the soft wash of fluorescent light.

When Joyce opened them again, they were glassy but alive.

"When you go back out there," she whispered, each word pulled up from somewhere deep, "don't just protect them. Show them how to build. So when we're gone, they stand on something that can't be torn down by gunfire or fear."

Frieda lifted her head. Her shoulders squared. In her chest, beneath the grief and the ache, something iron-willed sparked — something holy and old.

"I promise," she said, her voice clear now. "I'll build them a city that fights back. Brick by brick. Heart by heart."

Joyce's eyes softened into a smile. "Then go on, child. The dark don't stand a chance."

Outside the hospital window, dawn hadn't come yet — but Frieda could feel it rising all the same. And when she left Joyce's side, she carried that fragile promise out into the long, waiting night — a bridge, unbroken, burning steady in the dark.

The hallway outside Joyce's room felt wider on the way out — every echo of her footsteps hollow but ringing with a promise she couldn't put down now, even if she wanted to. Frieda paused at the nurses' station. The same young nurse who'd guided her in gave her a tired nod. She mumbled a thanks she didn't remember finishing, then drifted down the hall, her palm pressed to the cool painted wall like she was steadying herself against the weight of what waited outside.

In the waiting room, Krystal lay curled sideways across Miguel's lap, her small mouth open in a sleep too deep to be disturbed by the hush of worried families or the vending machine's soft hum. Miguel looked up when Frieda stepped through the double doors. He didn't ask; he could read it in her face — the mix of grief and steel, the fire in her shoulders pushing past the exhaustion clinging to her eyes.

He shifted Krystal gently, passing her back into Frieda's arms like a precious torch. The baby stirred, mumbled something half-dream, then settled her head against Frieda's shoulder, her small fingers tangled in Frieda's hair.

"She's stable," Frieda murmured, her voice hoarse but strong enough to carry the truth between them. "Alive. Fighting."

Miguel's relief slipped out in a slow exhale. He braced a hand on her arm — not claiming, not apologizing, just steadying. "You ready for what's next?"

Frieda nodded once. The city outside felt different now — sharper, more alive with threats that had to be met, not just endured.

"Call Tyesha," she said quietly. "Tell her to wake Lena and Ava. Everyone who's stayed close. We meet tomorrow — before the sun's up."

Miguel's eyebrows lifted just a fraction, an old glint of respect flickering through his guarded gaze. "The old crew? The new crew? Everyone?"

"Everyone," Frieda repeated. Her hand cupped Krystal's head as if shielding a candle from the wind. "This time we don't just react. We set the ground before they do."

Outside, the hospital's automatic doors opened with a soft whoosh — the cold night air slicing through her coat, waking up every nerve that had dulled in the fluorescent glow. She stepped into the dark, Krystal pressed warm against her heart. Overhead, the city's skyline glowed with its fractured halo of streetlights and distant police flashes — a city always on edge, always half-burning.

Frieda breathed it in — the diesel fumes, the stale cigarette smoke, the rumor of dawn hidden somewhere behind the bruised clouds. She looked at Miguel, who fell into step beside her. No words now, just a quiet promise in the way he matched her pace, the way he glanced once at the soft bundle of Krystal's curls, then back at the streets ahead.

They crossed the parking lot, cracked asphalt glittering with old salt from last week's snow. Every breath rose in a small, silvery cloud that disappeared just as quickly.

As she reached her car, Frieda paused — the city's pulse rattling in her ribs, all the old fears wanting to find their voice again. She shifted Krystal's warm weight in her arms, pressed her lips to her daughter's temple. Her whisper rose into the cold air like a vow that could not be stolen by any gang or gunfire or fresh graffiti on the wall of her safe haven.

"Not this time," she murmured. "We rise before the dark does."

Tomorrow, the circle would widen. Tomorrow, new hands would join old ones. And Frieda — the girl who once ran from every fire — would stand in the middle of this one, feet planted, sleeves rolled up, notebook open.

A bridge rebuilt.

A mother.

A match against the dark.

The Early Gathering

BEFORE DAWN, the city felt different — not softer, just waiting. A cold hush clung to Frampton's cracked sidewalks and boarded storefronts, a false stillness that made the empty streets hum like a held breath before thunder.

Inside The Bridge, the lights flickered to life room by room — a worn bulb above the entryway, the old kitchenette lamp humming against the whir of the coffee pot laboring to fill a chipped carafe. The scent of strong brew drifted through the big open hall where folding chairs scraped softly against scuffed hardwood.

Frieda moved between them, sleeves rolled to her elbows, Krystal's drawing tucked into the front of her worn notebook like a secret promise. She paused now and then, palms brushing each chair back into the circle's imperfect shape — a shape that had held so many girls, so many prayers, so many ragged vows that refused to die in the dark.

The front door opened with a shudder as Tyesha slipped in first, hoodie zipped to her chin, hair tucked under a fraying knit cap. She looked older in the half-light — edges sharpened by her own battles, but her eyes still found Frieda's like a compass snapping north.

Behind her came Lena, shoulders squared in her patched denim jacket, arms crossed over her chest like she might have to fight the shadows before the sun showed up to help. Ava arrived last, out of breath, clutching a notebook and two half-broken pencils she'd found on her way out the door.

A few others trickled in behind them — old faces, new ones. Girls who'd once come here looking for safety, now standing like quiet sentinels ready to give that same safety back.

They dropped bags at their feet, wrapped hands around paper coffee cups someone had lined up on the folding table. No one spoke yet — they didn't have to. The air said enough. The city's wounds spoke for them all.

Frieda stepped forward, her notebook open, thumb brushing Krystal's scribbled hearts through the thin page. She let her eyes circle the room, touching each face, each pair of wary, waking eyes.

"I know you're tired," she began, her voice a low hush but clear enough to cut through the hum of the old heater rattling behind her. "I know you're scared. So am I."

She waited. Let the truth settle — no fire, no polish, just raw.

"The Warlords want this neighborhood to believe they decide who's safe. Who belongs. They think we'll scatter when they mark our doors or take a shot at the ones who stand up."

A ripple of shifting feet, soft murmurs — anger under their breath, not fear.

"They're wrong."

Frieda's hand dropped to her notebook, fingers drumming out the heartbeat she carried in her chest.

"Bridge 2.0 isn't just this building anymore," she said, voice rising as the first thin rays of dawn snuck through the blinds, stripes of pale light painting tired cheeks and hunched shoulders. "It's us. It's every girl who came here hungry and left with a plan. Every mother who showed up asking for help. Every teacher who won't look away when they see a new bruise on a wrist. Every volunteer willing to hold the door open when the world tries to slam it shut."

She looked at Tyesha, who lifted her chin. Fierce. No nod needed. At Lena, whose folded arms loosened as her mouth curved into something like a dare. At Ava, who pulled her pencil free and flipped open her own battered notebook.

"We're taking this light where they think they own the dark. Street by street. School by school. We give these kids more than safety. We give them a reason to stand up and stay standing."

The radiator hissed. A truck rumbled past outside, headlights slicing through the boarded-up houses across the street.

"They came for us last night," Frieda said, her voice steady as stone. "So we go to them today — and every day after — until they learn the only thing that dies here is fear."

Silence fell again — but it wasn't empty. It was thick with the weight of people deciding, piece by piece, to stand. To stay. To be the net Frieda had promised they'd be, back when all she had was a battered folder and the sound of Joyce's voice praying over folding chairs.

Krystal's drawing peeked out from Frieda's notebook — bright scribbles, stick figures holding hands, a crooked sun beaming down like it didn't care what shadows waited underneath.

Frieda closed the notebook, spine creaking. "This is how we fight back. Not alone. Not afraid. And not just for us — but for the ones watching from the windows, wondering if it's still worth hoping for light."

She stepped back into the circle. Placed her palm flat on the nearest shoulder — Tyesha's — then Lena's — then Ava's — passing the spark, one touch at a time.

"Let's get to work."

And outside, the city shifted — not because the danger was gone, but because the people who would stand in the way of it were waking up, sleeves rolled high, ready to carry light into places it was never meant to leave.

Community Response and Bridge Action

THE NEWS OF JOYCE'S SHOOTING RIPPLED through Frampton like a stone breaking still water — waves of disbelief, grief, and something sharper that refused to die down.

By the next evening, a cluster of candles flickered at the curb outside St. Luke's ER bay — tiny flames trembling in the cold wind that swept wrappers and dead leaves down the sidewalk. Teen girls gathered shoulder to shoulder under streetlights, their breath turning to mist as they held up torn cardboard signs: *For Miss Joyce. We Are Not Afraid.* Some stood silent, tears drying cold on their cheeks. Others led soft, quivering prayers that slipped through the hum of passing traffic.

Word spread faster than any siren. By Sunday morning, local churches unlocked their front doors but didn't hold their usual sermons. Instead, whole congregations crossed streets in clusters, their hymnals left behind for blankets and coffee flasks as they circled the bullet-scarred church steps where Joyce had fallen. A choir member laid lilies on the concrete. An old deacon wept with his hand pressed flat to the brick wall, as if he could hold back the city's bleeding with sheer faith alone.

At town halls that once sat half-empty on a good night, parents filled every folding chair, the echo of their voices vibrating off the community center's drywall. Fathers who'd once dropped their daughters at The Bridge without a word now stood at microphones, voices shaking not with fear but with rage and resolve.

"You want numbers?" one mother demanded, her finger stabbing the air at a row of weary council members. "Count the candles. Count our girls. We're not burying another generation because you don't have a plan."

Council members — the same ones who once deflected with polite nods — bowed their heads in silence on record, the hush more honest than any prepared statement.

Inside The Bridge's old brick walls, Frieda and her people didn't wait for permission. Within days, a battered corkboard near the door filled up with new posters: *Neighborhood Watch Contacts. New After-Hours Check-Ins. Trauma Response Resources.* An entire citywide mentorship hotline hummed to life on borrowed cell phones — manned by volunteers who showed up with clipboards, snacks, and old griefs they were ready to turn into purpose.

Peer leaders who once slumped silently in the back rows stepped forward, sleeves rolled up, voices raised. They sat with counselors, learned the right words to say when a girl came through the door shaking from the inside out. They didn't just stand watch. They stood *with*.

Donations came in a trickle at first, then like rain bursting through a cracked roof — small bills folded into offering envelopes, local businesses tapping open their books for the first time. The coffee shop down the street started leaving a fresh urn by the front counter, labeled *"Bridge Fund."* No locks on it. Nobody needed them.

And the girls — the ones who had once slipped away without a word, and traded safety for the thrill of danger when the dark seemed more honest than hope — they came back. Not in shame. Not in rags. They came back with chin up, fists unclenched, sleeves rolled just like Frieda's.

They did not come back broken. They came back *ready*. To guard doors. To sweep floors. To hold each other when the street got too loud again. To rebuild what gunfire tried to erase.

Outside, the candles kept burning — short wicks replaced each night by new hands. Inside, the folding chairs sat in bigger circles now, the hush between prayers filled with plans, maps, hot coffee, tired laughter that felt like armor.

The fight wasn't over. Not by half. But The Bridge? Under the cracked windows, the flickering lights, the steady heartbeat of girls who knew the cost of survival and the promise of rebuilding. It had never stood stronger.

The Reckoning

THE WAR ROOM WASN'T REALLY A WAR ROOM — just a windowless storage closet with cracked linoleum floors and a door that didn't close all the way anymore. But in this city, in this moment, it was the pulse of something that refused to die quietly.

Maps papered the walls — overlapping, curling at the edges from the damp. Old city grids, bus routes, and hand-drawn street corners marked with red pushpins stabbed deep into neighborhoods that still bled when no one was looking. Each pin was a name. Each pin was a story Frieda refused to let the dark swallow without a fight.

She stood close to the biggest map, one palm braced on the cheap corkboard, the other tracing a line of pins that stretched from the abandoned warehouse near 9th and Garrett to the corner store off State — all the places where girls went missing or reappeared with new scars and new silences.

Behind her, the small room thrummed with restless energy. Tyesha paced from wall to wall, hoodie sleeves shoved to her elbows, her boots thudding softly against the floor. Lena sat hunched over an ancient laptop, the glow of the screen making her eyes look older, sharper, as she cross-checked names and coded addresses that meant nothing to outsiders but everything to the kids who lived in their shadows.

In the corner, half folded into herself, Drea sat on a milk crate they'd dragged in as an extra chair. Her fingers worried the hem of her sleeves, her jaw set so tight it looked like it hurt to breathe. The tattoo at her collarbone peeked above her sweatshirt — a ghost of the mark she was here to burn away.

"We can't wait for the city to step in," Frieda said, voice low but thick enough to drown out the hum of the old overhead light. She didn't turn from the map — she didn't need to. The room's hush told her they were listening. "They're too busy with press conferences and pretty promises. Task forces that won't touch a corner until they can stand in front of a camera for it."

Tyesha stopped pacing. "So, what do we do then?" Her voice was sharp, but there was no fear in it — only the same old defiance Frieda had seen when she'd found her curled up on The Bridge steps four winters ago.

Frieda's fingers tapped one of the pushpins — a mark for a girl named Destiny who hadn't come back yet. She turned then, slowly, eyes landing on each face in the cramped room.

"We confront them."

Silence. The old heater clicked to life in the hall, filling the pause with a ghost of warmth.

Drea's voice cracked the hush. "That's suicide." She didn't spit it out like a challenge — she said it like a prayer she was afraid wouldn't be answered.

Frieda looked at her — not with pity, not with judgment. With steel. With memory.

"Then let it be resurrection," she said, the words tasting like old sermons and new blood on her tongue. "If they want to bury us, they're gonna learn we don't stay dead."

The Streets Remember

WORD SPREAD BEFORE THE SUN COULD. A murmur at bus stops. A whisper in the halls of Frampton High. A cautious nod between teachers who saw too much and too often stayed quiet. The Bridge was building something bigger than prayer circles and handouts.

Mothers who'd once banged on Frieda's door begging for bus fare now stood beside her on street corners with flashlights and clipboards. Former crew kids, tattoos half-faded, arms crossed tight, kept watch under the flickering glow of corner store bulbs. Youth pastors came with battered bullhorns and a pocket full of gospel tracts, they slipped into trembling hands too young to be that hungry for safety.

No weapons. No fists thrown first. Just presence. Just eyes and cameras and the quiet roar of a people who refused to look away anymore. They stationed themselves where the dark liked to feed — bus stops by the old viaduct, playground fences that cracked under the weight of night, the back lot behind the fast-food joint where the Warlords liked to circle like crows picking a carcass clean.

They didn't shout. They didn't threaten. They just *stood*. Stood in the middle of a street that thought it owned every girl who ever dared to claim herself worth saving.

ONE NIGHT, NEAR 12TH AND CHAMBERLAIN, Frieda stood under the flicker of a half-dead streetlight. Her breath clouded in the cold, the plastic bullhorn heavy under her arm. Beside her, Tyesha handed out bottled water to passing kids. Lena filmed on an old phone — shaky, but enough to catch the faces that thought they could snatch lives unseen.

A girl — maybe fourteen, maybe younger — sat alone on the curb, arms wrapped tight around her knees. Her eyes darted to Frieda, then back to the pair of boys who circled her slowly, loose-limbed but watchful. Warlord scouts. Too young to know what ruin smelled like yet — but eager enough to learn.

Frieda stepped off the curb. Her boots sank into a crack in the asphalt, but she didn't flinch.

"You need to back off," the older scout said, his mouth twisting around the words like they tasted sour. He spat on the ground near her boots. "This ain't your corner."

Frieda met his eyes — that soft, flat black that never stayed soft long enough to remember it was once a child, too.

"You're right," she said, voice calm enough to cut glass. "It's hers. And I'm reclaiming it."

The younger boy's shoulders twitched. The older one scoffed, spat again. "You got guts, lady."

Frieda tilted her head, the streetlight catching the edges of her steady gaze.

"No," she said, voice rising just enough for the girl on the curb to hear every syllable like a promise. "I've got God."

And in that brittle stretch of midnight street — between the old pushpins and the new map lines they were carving with their feet — The Bridge didn't just stand. It declared itself unburied. Unbowed. And brighter than any dark dared to dream.

Standing Their Ground

THE COLD PRESSED IN HARDER as the street fell quiet again — that tense hush that always came after someone dared to say *no*, where *yes* had been the only safe word for too long.

The older scout sucked his teeth, eyes flicking between Frieda and the girl still crouched low on the curb. His hoodie sleeves were pushed back just enough to show the half-finished tattoos climbing up his wrist — cheap ink, half a crown, half a name he'd traded freedom for.

The younger one shifted from foot to foot, glancing behind him where Lena stood now — phone lifted, recording steady, even with her breath fogging up in the freezing air. The soft red glow of the recording light looked tiny in the night, but its promise was enormous: *We see you. We keep receipts.*

"Yo, let's bounce," the younger scout muttered, voice too loud in the hush. He flicked his chin at Frieda — a mix of nerves and anger. "Ain't worth the heat."

The older boy spat once more, but he stepped back — slowly, like he wanted her to know it wasn't surrender, just a pause. His eyes locked on Frieda's — dead flat and burning at the same time.

"Ain't over," he rasped, voice low as he jerked his head for the kid to follow.

"It never is," Frieda answered, her tone soft as a prayer and sharp as a blade.

When they were gone — boots scuffing into the darkness, curses thrown over shoulders to save face — Frieda let her shoulders sag just a fraction. Tyesha stepped closer, her hoodie half-unzipped now, breath visible in ragged clouds.

"You good?" she asked, her voice clipped but warm, eyes darting past Frieda to the girl on the curb.

Frieda nodded once, then crouched low, knees popping as she lowered herself to the girl's level. The kid's arms were locked tight around her knees, chin tucked to her chest so that all Frieda could see was a spill of braids and the soft curve of her cheek pressed to the tops of her shoes.

Frieda kept her voice low, careful — the same hush she used when Krystal woke crying in the dark.

"Hey, baby. You hungry? Cold? You want to come inside?"

The girl flinched when Frieda touched her shoulder — just a tap, enough to say *I'm here,* but not enough to force her up.

After a long heartbeat, the girl lifted her head. Hollow eyes rimmed with red, mouth set like stone but trembling at the corners. No words yet. Just a tiny nod — so small Frieda almost missed it.

Tyesha stepped in behind her, a blanket pulled from the trunk of her old Civic. She draped it over the girl's shoulders, tucking it close like a mother who knew what it felt like to be cold on a corner too long.

Lena lowered the phone, thumb hovering over the screen. "We keeping this?" she asked.

"We keep everything," Frieda said, eyes never leaving the girl's face. "If they think we'll bury proof, they're wrong."

A car slowed at the curb — one of the new volunteers behind the wheel, headlights sweeping over them like a promise of safe passage. Frieda offered her hand, palm up, nothing forced.

"Come on, sweetheart. We'll get you inside. Some food. Somewhere warm. Somewhere you can sleep without looking over your shoulder."

The girl's small hand slipped into hers — dry, ice-cold, fingers trembling but gripping tight. Frieda pulled her up slowly, carefully, like the city might shatter her if they moved too fast.

As they walked her to the car, Frieda felt the fire in her ribs hum again — not the old rage that used to burn her out, but a clean flame. The kind that spread when one girl found her footing again and stood on a corner the darkness thought it owned. Behind them, the street settled — not safe, not silent, but different. Watched. Claimed.

Tyesha clapped Frieda's shoulder as they closed the car door. "That's one corner tonight," she said, a quiet pride threading through her exhaustion.

"And tomorrow we take another," Frieda replied, her breath fogging as she turned to look back at the cracked asphalt, the half-burned streetlight, the ghosts that thought they still had the right to haunt this block.

"Street by street," she whispered, more to herself than anyone else.

Lena grinned, sharp and fierce in the dark. "They better run out of corners first."

Frieda didn't smile. She just nodded once, her palm pressed flat over her heart where Krystal's scribbled sun lived in her notebook pocket — proof that light could spread from the smallest spark.

The city didn't know it yet. But tonight, under cheap lamps and cold stars, it was losing its grip — because The Bridge was moving, not just standing, not just waiting. *Claiming. Lighting. Rising.*

The Night of the Threat

THEY CAME IN THE HUSH BEFORE DAWN — when the city's breath was heavy with frost and most good people were still dreaming. One brick through the front window. One hiss of glass splintering into the quiet, echoing down the block like a warning shot no gun had to fire.

By the time the cold wind slipped through the gaping hole, the vandals were long gone — their mark left behind in angry red slashes across the cracked wall just inside the lobby: **YOU'RE NEXT**

The paint dripped down the brick in fat, lazy rivulets, soaking into the pale grout like blood into linen.

<u>*The Standing*</u>

BY SUNRISE, FRIEDA WAS THERE — barefoot on the floor where the shards glittered like broken ice. Her boots sat untouched by the door. She hadn't bothered to lace them up yet. The cold from the open window licked at her ankles, but she barely noticed. She stepped carefully but sure, the sharp edges pressing against her heels. A tiny bead of blood welled near her arch, but she didn't flinch. Didn't lift her foot. Let it remind her: *Real ground is never soft.*

Behind her, the rising sun crawled across the front hall — a thin gold stripe catching every sharp edge, every broken piece.

Krystal wasn't here. Frieda had made sure of that — tucked safe with Joyce, her godmother, buried under blankets that smelled like lavender and old prayers. *No child needs to stand in glass when they're still dreaming.*

Joyce's voice — ragged and warm — filled the hush around her. *Not just with fists… with truth. With light.*

Frieda whispered it back, just once, like an echo sent up to the cracked ceiling beams.

"With light."

<u>*The Word Made Fire*</u>

BY NOON, WORD SPREAD. A local reporter caught sight of the window — snapped a picture, ran it with a headline dripping dread. *"Retaliation at The Bridge."*

By mid-afternoon, the front steps were a crush of cameras and hungry mics. News vans idled at the curb. Neighbors leaned out porches to watch. Some mothers who'd once crossed the street when The Bridge was just rumors and trouble now stood on the sidewalk, arms crossed, daring the world to see which side they were on.

Frieda stepped through the front door in a plain black coat, sleeves rolled just above her wrists. No podium. No official statement clutched in shaking hands. Just her — the same woman who'd once walked these streets trying to disappear, now standing here, daring the dark to look her in the eye. She paused at the top step, broken glass crunching under her boots — she'd finally put them on, laces pulled tight, soles steady.

The news crews angled forward. A few mics rose. They expected her voice to tremble. To plead. To promise fear would push her back behind thicker locks and security cameras.

But Frieda's voice came low at first — calm enough to hush the restless shifting. She let the silence stretch until even the camera shutters seemed to flinch.

"They think we'll hide now," she began, her breath ghosting in the cold. "That we'll shut our doors, board our windows, go quiet so the night can feed on our girls again."

She lifted her chin — eyes sweeping the cluster of mics, the half-circle of waiting faces. Mothers. Teachers. Old street kids who once called her Dove and watched her run.

"They are not a gang," she said, and her voice rose, catching on the sharp edge of every shard scattered at her feet. "They are a disease. Feeding on fear. Thriving on silence. And we — we are the cure."

A hush. Then a stir — people leaning forward, breaths caught between fear and something brighter.

"We are not just girls," Frieda called out, each word striking the crowd like a match. "We are daughters. Mothers. Fighters. Flames. And we are not backing down. Not today. Not ever."

Behind her, the broken window gaped wide — glass glittering in the sun like tiny mirrors, reflecting the faces of every girl who'd once walked through these doors with shaking knees and left stronger than the city knew what to do with.

Frieda stepped back, hands spread open at her sides. She wasn't covering the wound. She was letting the world see it. A threat might break glass. But it would never bury a bridge built on blood and grit and girls who knew how to rise.

The Sweeping and the Standing

WHEN THE CAMERAS DRIFTED OFF — when the last reporter had packed away their microphone and the curious neighbors had slipped back into their warm kitchens — The Bridge settled into the quiet that always came after a storm. But this hush wasn't defeat. It was resolve — a low hum of hands and brooms and voices carrying each other through the ruin.

Inside, the floor glowed with tiny shards catching the late afternoon sun. The broken window breathed cold into the main room, swirling the smell of old lavender cleaner with the sharp tang of fresh paint from the mural they'd finished last month — a burst of faces and bright colors right behind the front desk.

Tyesha dragged the old yellow mop bucket from the back closet, its wheels squealing on the floor. Lena grabbed the heavy push broom — the same one they'd used to sweep out so many other messes — and pressed it into Drea's hands.

Drea hesitated, staring down at the splintered glass, the red paint on the wall still tacky and glistening under the flickering ceiling light.

"Go on," Lena murmured, voice just rough enough to keep Drea's shoulders squared. "You help make this clean again. You help claim it."

So, Drea pushed the broom, slow at first — the bristles scraping glass into neat piles. She flinched when the shards shifted under the bristles, their sharp edges catching the light like tiny knives. But she didn't stop. She swept harder, gathering every piece like a confession she was ready to lay at Frieda's feet.

Frieda stood near the door; Krystal perched on her hip now — Joyce had dropped her off with a kiss and a whispered "She needs to see her mama stand tall."

Krystal's small fingers tangled in Frieda's collar, her warm breath soft against her neck as she blinked at the broken glass and the half-finished sweeping.

"Mama, what happened?" she asked, her voice soft as dust.

Frieda brushed a curl off her daughter's forehead, her thumb tracing the smooth warmth of her cheek.

"Some people tried to scare us, baby," she said, voice low but clear enough for Drea and Tyesha to hear, too. "They think if they break things, we'll stop building."

Krystal's brow furrowed, tiny lips pressing together like she was storing the question for later. She didn't understand yet — not the way Frieda did — but her small arms wrapped tighter around Frieda's neck, as if her hug could hold the walls up all by itself.

Near the mural, Tyesha laid a fresh sign on the floor. Hand-lettered in thick black marker, all caps: *WE STAY OPEN*. She taped it to the broken window frame — a bandage over a wound still raw but healing in the light.

"Should get a new glass pane in tomorrow," Lena said, brushing the last of the glass into a dustpan. Her voice was dry, but there was pride tucked under the grit. "Till then, let 'em see it open."

Drea dumped the dustpan into the trash barrel with a clatter that made them all pause. She looked at Frieda — eyes fierce, face flushed from bending and sweeping and claiming every broken shard like a piece of herself stitched back in place.

"We're not next," she said, breathless but certain. "They are."

Frieda didn't smile, not all the way. But she stepped forward, rested her free hand on Drea's shoulder — steady, warm, heavy enough to remind her this circle didn't break just because the window did.

"We are the cure," Frieda said, echoing her own words from the steps outside — but here in this room, with the glass swept, the cold wind blowing in, and her daughter safe in her arms, the words sounded more like a promise than a line for the cameras.

As night crept in and the last shards were carried out in plastic bags, The Bridge didn't feel fragile. It felt alive. Open. Daring the dark to try again. And deep in her bones — deeper than the cuts on her heels or the ache in her spine — Frieda felt something holy flicker like a stubborn flame.

They could smash the glass.
They could mark the walls.
But they could never shut these doors.

The Reckoning Weekend

BY FRIDAY NIGHT, the streets told a secret Frieda could feel before she saw it — the kind of hush that came before something mean and desperate clawed its way into the light.

It started with fresh paint. Red spray hissed across brick and concrete — half-formed threats, snarled names. Back walls behind corner stores. Bus stops where girls waited after late shifts. The Warlords' tag was there in dripping letters, a promise scrawled where the city's streetlights flickered out too early.

By Saturday, phones went missing. Quick snatches in broad daylight. Teen girls left holding empty bags and rattled nerves. The word spread in whispers — hallways at Frampton High buzzed with them. Boys in oversized hoodies leaning in too close, words pressed like poison into ears that still held algebra notes and tomorrow's test dates. *"Tell Miss Bridge she's next. Tell her to close her doors. Or we'll close them for her."*

BUT BY SUNDAY NIGHT, the night bit back. A kid — maybe seventeen, maybe younger, bones sharp under a borrowed hoodie — crouched behind a rusted fence behind an old tire shop. His phone, held tight in trembling hands, caught what no parent wanted to see but everyone needed to.

A circle of young bodies, shivering bare-chested under a yellow barrel flame. Laughter too loud. Orders barked by older boys whose tattoos looked half-finished and half-claimed. A branding iron — makeshift but hot enough to press a mark onto soft skin that hadn't finished growing.

The kid filmed every second. Even when they turned, eyes glinting in the dark. Even when the camera shook like his breath might give him away. He didn't run until it was done.

BY DAWN, THE FOOTAGE SLIPPED onto a half-forgotten community page — shaky and raw. It should have died there. But it didn't. It moved. Fast. From mother to mother. Teacher to teacher. Pastor to pastor. A spark that burned through screens, cracking the careful silence that had kept fear in charge for far too long.

By Sunday evening, the outrage wasn't just words anymore — it was porch lights left on. It was fathers standing at bus stops where girls once stood alone. It was old men with canes showing up at corners just to look a Warlord scout in the eye and remind him whose neighborhood this really was.

The Call

BY MONDAY MORNING, Frieda stood in her office, the video looping silently on Lena's laptop in the corner. She didn't watch it again — she didn't need to. Every frame was already burned behind her eyes.

The old landline phone rang sharp against the hush. Joyce lifted it halfway, but Frieda reached out, palm steady. She pressed the receiver to her ear, shoulder squared as if the voice on the other end could see her spine.

"Miss Winslow?" The mayor's voice was raw, a little too careful, like he hadn't found the right tone yet for a city that wouldn't let him hide behind policy lines anymore. "I've seen the footage. I— we— the city... we need to respond. But I won't pretend to know how to fix what's broken here overnight."

He paused — the hesitation loud in Frieda's ear. Then, softer:

"What do you need from us?"

Frieda's hand pressed flat to her chest — to the thin paper scrap of Krystal's crooked sun still tucked in her shirt pocket. Her voice didn't shake. Didn't soften.

"Protection," she said first, the word tasting like iron. "For our girls, our staff, our families. Not just tonight but for as long as it takes."

She breathed once. Let the next word come heavy.

"Prosecution. The ones at the top. The ones behind the doors. No more hand-slaps for foot soldiers while the architects sleep easy."

She drew in the cold air from the broken window still waiting on fresh glass. The wind felt clean in her lungs.

"And policy change. Not a statement for the press. Real laws. Real teeth. So the next generation doesn't inherit our silence."

On the other end, the mayor exhaled — a thin, tired sound.

"You'll have it," he said. "Whatever it takes."

The Shift

THE WARLORDS DIDN'T VANISH OVERNIGHT—they weren't ghosts that simple. Their whispers still lingered near bus stops, their marks still stained brick. But something had cracked.

They hadn't counted on a girl with a phone. They hadn't counted on a city with memory and backbone. They hadn't counted on Frieda — who wasn't just holding turf. She was reclaiming territory — the kind no spray can could stain, no threat could choke quiet.

One trembling girl at a time.
One block still worth fighting for.
With truth.
With light.
With a fire that didn't destroy the broken — but burned them clean.

And under that broken window, under her breath, Frieda whispered it like a vow stitched into every shadow that dared to listen:

"Not again. Not on my watch. Not ever."

The Final Betrayal

Frieda knew the signs of a cornered beast. She'd seen it too many times — a wild glint behind human eyes, a twitch in the hands, a sloppy arrogance that smelled more like fear than power. And the Warlords were stinking of it now.

In the Bridge's dim war room — still just that old storage closet with its maps and pins and tangled strings — the signs pulsed like a heartbeat under fluorescent light. Surveillance shots tacked to the corkboard in crooked rows. Grainy phone footage from volunteers who watched from busted cars and behind cracked blinds.

The abandoned textile mill — once just another rotting carcass of Frampton's old industries — now glowed at the center of the board like a fresh wound. Foot traffic at odd hours. Headlights flickering through back alleys, turning off, then on again. Girls slipping inside shadows — some alone, some with shoulders hunched like they were holding secrets tight against their ribs. Some of them came back out. Some didn't.

Frieda stood in front of the board that Friday night, arms folded so tight her knuckles burned white. The folding chairs scraped the floor behind her as the task team gathered — Tyesha perched on a stack of file boxes, Lena cross-legged on the scuffed linoleum, Drea leaning against the door frame, hood pulled low to hide the way her jaw clenched every time someone said *mill*.

The room smelled of stale coffee and tired prayers. Outside, the city hummed with its usual restless lies — sirens far off, wind rattling the old windows like ghost fingers. Frieda's voice cut through the hush, sharp and taut as wire.

"We're close. Too close," she said, thumb tapping the pushpin jammed through the photo of the mill's side door. "The textile mill's the hub. It's where they run it all — supply, money, flesh. We get inside, we pull the bones from the spine. We find records. Maybe girls. Maybe alive."

Her words left that last hope hanging like a weight. *Maybe alive.* Miguel leaned forward in his chair, elbows on his knees, eyes locked on the board's tangle of red string and shaky Polaroids.

"You're sure?" His voice was calm but carried an edge — the old cop in him tasting the trap.

Frieda didn't blink. "I'd stake my life on it."

From the doorway, Drea let out a soft, bitter laugh that snapped like a twig in the quiet. She crossed her arms tight over her chest.

"You might have to," she said, voice low. Not a threat. A truth. One that settled into the floorboards.

Frieda turned — not a flicker of fear in her eyes, just that steady flame that burned down buildings in silence and dared the wind to snuff it out.

"Then I will."

The Plan

IT CAME TOGETHER THE WAY IT ALWAYS DID when something holy pressed down on the backs of their necks — fast, desperate, stitched together with shaky hands but iron spines. Joyce's old contact in Vice — a man who owed her more than a few favors — signed off on a sweep. Nothing official. Just a whisper in the dark. Enough to keep uniforms out of the way while they gathered what they needed to crack the walls open.

The Bridge's digital crew set up in the back hallway, wires taped down like veins, eyes locked on flickering screens that pulsed with

Instagram posts and half-deleted videos. Every tagged photo, every coded caption, every blurred license plate run through the net.

Hours ticked past like slow-dripping IVs. The maps on the table bloomed with fresh ink — time stamps, loops, escape routes marked and crossed out.

By Sunday, the air in the war room felt like the breath held before a storm. Too much static. Too much waiting.

Frieda stood in the doorway, coat half-buttoned, flashlight clutched tight in her pocket like a last prayer.

"When that wall cracks," she said to no one and everyone, "we walk through it together."

The Mill

NIGHT FELL HARD—like a fist. Clouds sagged heavy enough to choke the moon, sealing off the sky. The air tasted of rust, oil, and rain that hadn't yet found the courage to fall.

The textile mill rose before them, a blackened relic from another century—four stories of rusted bones, windows gaping like eyeless sockets. The breeze slid through broken panes, carrying the mill's dead whispers into the cold.

Frieda sat in the back of the unmarked van, knees pressed tight together, hands twisting the edge of a worn flyer in her lap. Miguel sat beside her, radio scanner balanced between them, its low crackle filling the space.

Two detectives—Vice—moved in from the shadows, shoulders squared against the chill. They didn't speak much. They didn't need to. The clipped reports over the police band told the story:

"Team One breaching. Keep perimeter locked down."
"Copy."

Frieda closed her eyes for a moment, picturing what might be inside—locked rooms, frightened faces, the air heavy with fear. Her chest tightened. Through the van windshield, she watched the officers approach the corroded steel door. The hinges groaned when they pulled it open, the sound twisting up into the night like a warning. Their boots sank into the black belly of the mill. Flashlights cut the dark into ribbons, beams sweeping over crates, rusted barrels, and hanging tarps that swayed in the draft.

But the voices coming through the radio began to shift—less confident now.

"First floor clear."

"Nothing on second. Feels scrubbed."

"Negative on visual. No movement."

Frieda leaned toward the scanner. "Scrubbed?" she whispered.

Miguel shook his head, brow furrowed.

The next report came sharper, urgent.

"Hold up—what's this?"

Static.

"Wires. I've got wires—red and yellow—running into the main support beams. This—this is a—"

The transmission cut out.

Frieda's heart slammed. "Miguel…"

Then the voice roared back—screaming now:

"BOMB! GET OUT—"

The rest never finished.

Light swallowed the mill from the inside out with a loud, resounding boom. A roar like the sky itself tearing open split the night as the blast punched through brick and steel.

The van rocked violently, heat slamming into it like a wave. Miguel threw himself across Frieda, the windshield flaring white with the fireball. The sound was deafening—metal shrieking, glass shattering, the world reduced to flame and force.

When the shockwave passed, Frieda could only hear her own ragged breathing and the faint hiss of things still burning. The mill— what was left of it—was a jagged silhouette against an orange inferno.

The radio lay silent on the van floor.

Frieda's hands shook as she pressed them to her mouth. Her eyes burned—not from the smoke, but from the knowing. They'd been too late. But someone had made sure of it.

For a moment, Frieda couldn't move. Her body felt poured from lead, her heartbeat loud enough to drown out everything else. The smell came first—burnt oil, scorched metal, something darker that clung in the back of her throat. The glow from the blaze turned the air itself into a living thing, writhing in reds and oranges. Embers drifted upward like the dead lifting into the night.

Miguel's arm was still across her, holding her in place. "You okay?" he rasped, his voice hoarse from the shockwave.

She nodded before she realized she was lying.

Sirens tore toward them, climbing louder by the second. Squad cars skidded to the curb, red and blue lights strobing over the cracked gravel lot. Fire engines screamed in behind them, their floodlamps cutting through the thickening smoke.

Frieda shoved the van door open and stumbled out. Her boots crunched glass that hadn't been there a minute ago. The air bit her lungs—hot, chemical.

The mill was gone. Not fallen, not collapsing—*gone*. Its center gutted, walls warped outward as though the building had been forced to exhale its last breath.

She could hear the firefighters shouting orders, the crash of a water cannon opening up, steam hissing where it struck flame. Officers swarmed the perimeter, scanning the ground for movement, for bodies. But deep down, Frieda knew. She stepped closer, the heat singeing her cheeks even from twenty feet back. The twisted remains of the steel door lay half-buried under rubble. Beyond it—nothing. No corridors. No rooms. Just smoking ruins. Her eyes darted across the chaos, searching for the Vice detectives she'd watched walk inside. No sign.

Miguel caught up to her, gripping her elbow hard enough to keep her from moving closer. "Frieda—"

"They were just in there," she choked out. "They were just..."

"I know." His voice was low, steady in a way that told her he was holding himself together for her sake.

A captain approached, his face grim, radio still in his hand. "This wasn't a meth lab. This wasn't some gas leak. That was military-grade. Whoever wired it knew exactly what they were doing."

Frieda's breath faltered. "They didn't just destroy the evidence..."

"They sent a message," Miguel finished, jaw tight.

Through the smoke, a shard of metal caught the firelight. Frieda stepped toward it, crouching in the rubble until she could see it clearly. The edge was jagged, but the surface had been carved with two words—scorched, but still legible: **QUIT NOW.**

Her stomach twisted. Her fingers trembled as she reached out to touch the heat-warped metal, the sting making her flinch.

Somewhere behind her, another water cannon roared to life. The fire hissed in protest, but the night still burned.

Frieda straightened slowly, eyes fixed on the inferno. Her voice was quiet, but it cut through the noise when she spoke to Miguel.

"They're sending us a warning. They want us to stop looking."

Miguel met her gaze, eyes reflecting the flames. "But we won't stop."

And with the smoke curling up into the starless sky, Frieda knew she wasn't walking away from this. Not now. Not ever.

The Betrayal

THE BRIDGE FELT DIFFERENT when Frieda walked back in. Not safer. Not warmer. Different. The war room still hummed with the low buzz of fluorescent lights, but the air had turned thick, unmoving—like the city air right before a storm tears the sky open. Frieda didn't even take off her coat. The grit from the Mill still clung to her boots, leaving a dull trail of gray on the scuffed linoleum as she stepped inside. Smoke still clung to her hair, the faint metallic tang of burnt steel riding every breath.

Tyesha sat on the edge of the old metal table, arms wrapped tight around herself like she was holding something in. Lena was at the laptop, her fingers poised over the keys but unmoving, her eyes locked on the screen as though she couldn't bear to look up. In the corner, Drea paced—small, sharp steps, sneaker soles squeaking every third pass like a metronome no one wanted to hear.

Nobody spoke until Lena finally lifted her eyes. "They didn't make it out, did they?"

Frieda's chest tightened. She drew in a breath that scraped on the way out. "The Mill's gone," she said quietly. "It was wired. Vice went in first… they never had a chance. The whole place blew. We barely cleared the lot before it went up."

The room went still—silent except for the faint whine of the heater. Tyesha dropped her gaze to the floor; her lips pressed into a hard line. Lena swallowed and blinked twice, but her hands didn't move toward the keyboard.

Miguel, leaning against the wall near the map board, spoke into the quiet. "A setup. Clean floors. Empty rooms. And then a bomb?" He shook his head. "That's not running. That's erasing."

Frieda nodded once, but her eyes weren't on Miguel anymore. They'd found something else—someone else.

Drea's pacing had stopped.

"They didn't just clear out," Frieda said, her voice low but sharp as wire. "They knew exactly when we'd come, where we'd look. And how long they had to vanish before we got there."

Tyesha's head jerked up. Lena's hands stilled entirely.

"What are you saying?" Drea asked. But the crack in her voice wasn't fear. It was something else — something like a note gone flat.

Frieda took one step forward, the grit under her boots crunching in the quiet. "I'm saying you can only get a head start like that… if someone tips you off."

The words hung in the air like smoke that wouldn't clear. Drea's mouth twitched — an attempt at a scoff that died halfway. She crossed her arms so tight her knuckles whitened under old scars.

"You think it was me? After everything? After I came back?"

Lena's voice cracked just above a whisper. "Prove it wasn't you."

Tyesha slid off the table and stepped closer, her eyes narrowed. "You ghosted an hour before we rolled out. Said you were grabbing food. You never came back until we were loading the van."

"I *did*," Drea snapped, the sharpness too quick, too loud. She flinched at her own voice, her gaze darting to Frieda like she was hoping for cover.

But Frieda's eyes didn't move. She closed the distance until Drea had no choice but to tilt her chin up. "Where were you?" Frieda asked softly, but there was steel underneath.

For a long moment, nothing moved except the slow pulse in Drea's throat. The heater's hum grew louder. Somewhere beyond the walls, a siren wailed, distant but climbing.

Drea's mouth opened. Closed. She blinked hard, and when she spoke, the words scraped out like broken glass. "They have my brother. Said if I didn't feed them crumbs, they'd… they'd cut him up and drop him in the viaduct like trash."

Tyesha cursed under her breath, stepping back. Lena turned away from the table, jaw tight.

Frieda didn't yell. Didn't throw anything. She just stood there, looking into the eyes of the girl she'd once dragged out of the fire— only to realize she'd carried the spark back inside.

"And now?" Frieda asked quietly, almost like a prayer.

Drea's lip trembled. "Now they'll come for me too."

Frieda didn't look away. She couldn't. Because behind Drea's fear, she saw it—that shadow of the people they were really fighting. The ones who burned buildings to the ground and didn't care who was inside. The ones who made even loyalty a weapon.

And for the first time since the Mill exploded, Frieda felt the fire inside her shift from grief… to something ready to burn back.

The Cost of Light

THE COUCH SAGGED UNDER HER WEIGHT as she sat in the half-light of her apartment; the city stretched before her through the cracked blinds. Outside, Frampton pulsed in fragments—streetlamps blinking like tired eyes, neon signs sputtering in and out, the occasional flare of headlights sweeping across rain-slick streets.

Her journal lay open on her lap, a pen balanced loosely between her fingers, but no ink had touched the page. The only sounds inside were the slow, steady tick of the wall clock and the soft, even breath of Krystal asleep in the next room—innocent, untouched by the carnage her mother had walked through just hours earlier.

She could still smell the smoke from the Mill—sharp, chemical, clinging to her hair, her coat, her very skin. She could still hear it—the deep, gut-shaking roar of the blast, the shattering of glass, the scream of fire devouring air. She saw their faces—those officers, men and women who had walked into the dark believing they would bring light with them. They'd found only a fireball.

And she could still feel the sting of Drea's confession. *They have my brother.* Frieda had pulled her out of the street, clothed her, prayed over her, and trusted her. And yet, Drea had fed crumbs to the wolves until the wolves were too full to run.

The weight of it pressed against Frieda's chest. Betrayal wore the faces you loved most—that was the cruelest truth. She leaned back, eyes drifting toward the narrow alley below her window. Something moved down there—a shape slipping just out of the spill of the corner streetlight. Too slow to be a drunk. Too deliberate to be someone simply passing through. For half a second, a glint caught—metal, maybe. Or maybe her mind was stitching shadows together into a warning.

She rose, parting the curtain with two fingers. The alley looked empty again, but her bones told her differently. The dark wasn't gone. It had just learned how to wait. She sat back down, pen in hand at last. The words bled out slow, heavy:

> *The shadows didn't scatter because they lost. They scattered because they were seen. Light doesn't kill them. It makes them clever. Patient. It makes them change shape.*

She paused, listening to the city's low groan outside her thin walls.

> *Drea didn't fail me. She showed me how deep this thing runs. They don't just steal our girls. They dig into our families. Our blood. Our prayers. They turn the desperate into spies.*

She started to write more, but stopped, crossed it out. Began again.

> *If they think this will break the Bridge, they've forgotten one thing—we don't break. We burn. And when we burn, we rise.*

Frieda closed the journal and set the pen aside. She moved to the window, pressing her palm to the cold glass, feeling for the city's heartbeat beneath her own.

"This giant—the Warlords," she whispered, her breath fogging the glass, "has slipped into our streets and taken our daughters. Hidden among us. But with Your help, Lord, they will fall... like Goliath."

Somewhere in the alley, a motion light flicked on—catching the silhouette of a figure just before it slid back into the dark. A slow, familiar dread wound tight in her gut.

This wasn't over. Drea wasn't the only one. The shadows hadn't fled. They knew her name now. They were watching, waiting for her to stumble.

Outside, a bottle shattered against brick—sharp and sudden, like a warning shot. Far off, a siren began to wail, long and hollow, knifing through the air before disappearing west past 8th Street. Then... silence.

Not the kind of silence that soothes.

The kind that presses on your lungs.

The kind that makes the hairs on your arms stand on end.

Somewhere beneath the streets, something was rumbling—low, deep, patient. A storm, not from above but from below. Crawling through the bones of Frampton, seeping into cracked sidewalks, whispering in the names of the missing.

In her apartment, Frieda stood motionless at the window, the city's glow fractured into slivers of light across her face. Outwardly still, but inside—every nerve coiled, bracing for the storm she knew was already moving toward her.

One breath—to anchor herself in the woman she had become through fire and loss.

One prayer—not shouted, but whispered, sharp as steel in the dark: *Lord... here I am. Send me.* And one fire—unyielding, unquenchable, holy—burned in her eyes, through her chest, her hands, the very soles of her feet.

It was not rage. It was older than rage. Deeper than fear.

It was resolve, resilience, readiness.

She was no longer the broken girl who once hid in shadows. She was the bridge itself—a warrior standing in the light.

But outside, beyond the thin glass of her window, the silence was staring back at her. And in that silence lurked the war she hadn't chosen—yet would soon be forced to fight.

Because the wolves weren't finished.

The city wasn't safe.

And the night was just beginning.

End of Book One — To Be Continued...

• A C K N O W L E D G E M E N T S •

TO MY WIFE, TERRY, thank you for sharing this journey called life with me. You've been incredibly supportive, and I'll always love you. To my daughter, Kiersten—keep blossoming into the beautiful, intelligent woman you are. You make me a proud dad. Thanks to my siblings for always supporting me and cheering me on. And finally, to my reading fans, thank you for your continual support and for encouraging me to keep writing and sharing my gift with you.